PROLOGUE

Congresswoman Joan Kingsley moved quietly through the deep night-shadows of her home, not turning on any lights because darkness suited her these days. She resented the sun for shining, people for laughing, the days for passing. The anguish in her heart, her soul, was too all-encompassing for her to do anything more than function as she must.

She hated the house. It was big, much too big for just her, but even hating it now she couldn't bring herself to leave it. She and Dexter had fallen in love with this house as soon as they saw it; they'd strained every financial muscle they had to buy it, but from the first it had felt like home, like *them*. They had raised their son here. Here they had seen their dreams of power and riches come true; oh, they'd worked their asses off to make those dreams come true, but this was where so much of it all had been planned and seen to fruition.

It was just so empty now, without Dexter.

She had loved him so much—*still* loved him. Death didn't stop love, it just kept on, an ache now instead of a glow.

And it was her fault he was dead—hers, and Axel MacNamara's. She hated that son of a bitch with a fierceness that had only grown with time. He was still having her watched, followed, every communication intercepted and read. Well, he thought he was having every communication intercepted, but with luck, what he didn't know would definitely hurt him. She was planning on it.

MacNamara thought he had her pinned down. He'd forced her to resign from her position of power, her husband was dead, her cohort within the GO-Teams had fled the country.

She was content to let him think that, for now. Devan Hubbert was smarter than any of the other computer experts MacNamara had on staff, way smarter. Given the time and tools, there was no firewall he couldn't get through, no system he couldn't penetrate, no go-around he couldn't devise, and when the circumstances called for it, he was flexible enough to revert to low tech. He'd been in touch with her within a week of leaving the country.

She didn't know why; she had no power left to broker, thanks to MacNamara. She had no intel or influence to sell. Devan had been there for the money, the same as she had. Staying in power in D.C. was damned expensive, but that was where you had to be to make the real money. Dexter had been content, really, with what they already had, but he'd supported her all the way in her plan to sell relatively minor intel to the Russians and profit enormously. With enough money and power behind her, she could have gone all the way to the White House. How bitterly ironic that Dexter had been the one to lose his life because of the scheme, instead of her. He'd been doing what he'd done all along, backing her up.

For whatever reason, Devan had kept in touch. He had an idea for exacting revenge on MacNamara. Maybe he saw the possibility for making more money, though she couldn't see how; the knowledge of her involvement with the Russians might be contained, for now, but killing MacNamara wouldn't make it go away.

She didn't care. Money didn't matter, not now. All she wanted was to make Axel MacNamara pay for Dexter's death, and if she could take down his precious GO-Teams at the same time, all the better.

One way or another, he had to die.

THE WOMAN LEFT BEHIND

ALSO BY LINDA HOWARD

THE
WOMAN
LEFT BEHIND

A NOVEL

LINDA
HOWARD

wm

WILLIAM MORROW

An Imprint of HarperCollins*Publishers*

This book is a work of fiction. References to real people, events, establishments, organizations, or locales are intended only to provide a sense of authenticity, and are used fictitiously. All other characters, and all incidents and dialogue, are drawn from the author's imagination and are not to be construed as real.

HarperCollins books may be purchased for educational, business, or sales promotional use. For information please email the Special Markets Department at SPsales@harpercollins.com.

FIRST EDITION

Designed by Bonni Leon-Berman

Library of Congress Cataloging-in-Publication Data has been applied for.

ISBN 978-0-06-241901-9 (hardcover)
ISBN 978-0-06-274878-2 (international edition)
ISBN 978-0-06-285155-0 (BAM signed edition)

18 19 20 21 22   LSC   10 9 8 7 6 5 4 3 2 1

TO ALL THE AVON/HARPERCOLLINS editors and assistants and production staff who work tirelessly to make a book the best it can be, and to the art department for an awesome cover.

To my sweet girl Molly, who went to doggie heaven almost a year ago. I miss you every day, pretty girl.

To Tank, who climbs in my lap to cuddle and give comfort, and leaves behind enough white fur that I could knit another dog—if I knew how to knit, which I don't.

To the FBI, for not coming knocking on my door demanding to know why I was Googling such alarming things as mobile missile placement, Syria, night-vision devices, and such things as that. Thanks for not arresting me. I'm just a writer. Honest.

To my agent, Robin Rue, and my editor, May Chen, for the endless support this past year.

And last but definitely not least, to my beloved friends and family. I hesitate to start listing you, for fear of inadvertently leaving someone out, but if you count yourself as either, then know you're in my heart.

THE WOMAN LEFT BEHIND

ONE

"You're all being reassigned," Axel MacNamara said tersely.

Ten workers from various departments were crammed into Mac-Namara's office, which was surprisingly drab and small for the head of an organization. Jina Modell hadn't been lucky enough to be one of the first two to arrive, so they had gotten the two visitors' chairs and she and the other seven stood in various uncomfortable poses around the cramped room.

Her first reaction to MacNamara's announcement was one of relief; none of them had known the reason for the mass summons and she'd expected they were, at best, being laid off, though she'd been braced for the worst—being fired—because budget cuts happened, even to dark projects funded by money that was deeply buried and almost invisible.

She evidently wasn't the only one of her fellow workers to think that, because a low sigh, almost a hum, of relief went around the room.

Then she frowned. Yes, having a job was nice, and this one was very nice. She worked in Communications, and she really liked it. She liked the money, she liked the coolness factor—and it was way cool, even for D.C.—plus she liked the vicarious satisfaction of kicking terrorist butt through the actions of the GO-Teams, all without ever leaving the climate-controlled comfort of the Communications room. She liked climate-controlled comfort. Being reassigned might not be such a good thing.

"To where?" she asked, after a moment of silence with no one else voicing the question.

MacNamara didn't even glance at her. "The teams," he replied, picking up a sheet of paper and scowling down at it as if he didn't like what was written there, though as head of the agency he was almost certainly the one who had done the writing. "Donnelly, you go to Kodak's team. Ervin, you're on Snowman. Modell, Ace." He continued reading down the list, giving them their assigned teams, though none of them knew yet what the hell they were supposed to do.

"Ace" was the call sign for Levi Butcher. She knew the name but had never personally met any of the team operatives. Ace had the reputation for pulling some of the toughest jobs and now, oh hell, just what was she being reassigned to *do*?

Jina had trained herself to think before she spoke, because the cool job required it. No one could know what she really did, or where she really worked. She made herself pause and think now— for a whole second, because questions needed to be asked and no one else, evidently intimidated by MacNamara's nasty reputation, was making a move to ask those questions.

She raised her hand. MacNamara must have caught the motion, because he paused in his reading to lift his head and bark "What?" at her.

"What are we supposed to do on the teams?" she asked. She saw him register an instant of surprise at her voice, the realization that she was the one who had spoken before, instead of one of the guys. Her voice was what it was; she was used to the reaction. Of infinite more interest was the current situation. She didn't know about the others, but she was in Communications, and she had zero training for what the GO-Teams did, which was commit mayhem on a massive scale.

"I'll get to that part faster if you stop interrupting me," Mac-Namara snapped.

"I've only interrupted once." Was it her imagination, or did the coworkers standing around her all edge away, as if offering Mac-Namara a clear shot at her? Yeah, no, not her imagination.

"Twice, now."

He had a point. She sucked in her cheeks to keep her mouth shut, and after a second he resumed reading. When everyone had been given their assignment—or rather, their team, because they still didn't know what they'd be doing—MacNamara leaned back in his chair. "The ten of you tested highest on our spatial awareness and action tests—"

Jina bit her tongue, then sucked in her cheeks again. What spatial awareness and action tests? She hadn't taken any tests. As far as she knew none of the others had, either.

"What spatial awareness and action tests?"

Shit. Her neck just kept sticking itself out.

MacNamara turned his rabid-wolverine gaze on her, and once again silence filled the little room. He began tapping the end of his pen against the top of his desk in a rapid tattoo. His expression said he was thinking of places where he could dump her body. She imagined he knew plenty and might have used a few.

But then he said curtly, "The video games in the break room."

Ah. A low murmur circulated. Several months ago the video war games had been installed, and a bunch of them had immediately become immersed in playing all through their breaks, competing to see who could score the highest. Jina was an old hand at computer games and had really gotten into the friendly competition, consistently racking up the highest scores and pissing off the guys who had done a lot of big talking about girls not being any good at gaming. She'd shown them. The games were complicated and very lifelike, far more advanced than anything commercially available; the coolness factor had been off the charts. Evidently so had the sneaky factor.

She held up her hand again. Jeez, was she the only one with a mouth? Why didn't some of the others ask the questions and make the observations?

MacNamara pinched the bridge of his nose and muttered something under his breath.

"I'm not qualified to go out with one of the teams." She was a little embarrassed to be stating the obvious, but it was only God's truth. No matter how high she had scored in the computer games, the members of the GO-Teams were like supermen. They swam and ran for miles. They spent endless hours in training. They could shoot an acorn out of an oak tree at a gazillion yards. She knew sometimes they worked with women who had field skills, but she wasn't one of those women. She knew how to swim, she jogged around some, but Fanny Fitness she wasn't.

"None of you are," he snapped. "All of you will receive training. You won't be doing the physical part of the operations, anyway."

"Then what *will* we—" Jina began, to be cut off by a wearily upheld hand.

"Let me remind all of you that you're sworn to secrecy about any and everything connected with this job. The answer is, the team members are very good at situational awareness, but at a cost. Being aware of a goatherd coming toward them and how soon he'll get there distracts from mission focus. Not a lot, because we're talking about people good enough to be on a GO-Team, but still—seconds count. We've run thousands of analyses, and in every instance having an on-site operator dedicated to movement and timing and situational awareness has made a difference. The operator would be surveilling the surroundings via drone, controlled by a computer. With that extra eye, the chance of mission success increases by three percent; the chance of team member casualties decreases by two percent. The changes are small but critical."

Especially to the team members suffering the casualties, Jina thought wryly. Okay, she could see why this was important. What she couldn't see was herself in any field situation. She wasn't . . . well, she wasn't anything special. She wasn't particularly athletic, she wasn't intrepid, she wasn't psychic so how the heck would she know which direction the goatherd was going to take, and she'd never had any ambition to be good at those things. She was good at a particular war game, that was all.

This wasn't going to work.

"This won't work," she said.

MacNamara propped his head in his hands and gripped his hair with both hands, as if intending to pull it all out, though she had to admit he could be thinking about crushing her skull.

"Of course it won't," he snarled at his desktop. "It isn't as if we know anything about what we're doing, as if we haven't considered all the possibilities and potential roadblocks, as if we haven't analyzed all ten of you to the point we know more about you than you know about yourselves. We thought we'd just throw the ten of you out there for shits and giggles, to see how bad you can fuck things up."

She didn't like being analyzed without knowing she was being analyzed. It was kind of like some perv spying through a peephole in the women's bathroom. On the other hand, she knew the analysts were top-notch at their jobs, so that was reassuring even if it wasn't convincing.

"What if some of us aren't interested?" she asked, because no one else was uttering a word—*still*, the ball-less wonders. And she was the only one in the room who didn't have any, other than the ones in her mind. *Mind testicles.* Okay, gross.

"Then clean out your stuff and find another job." MacNamara gave her the evil eye. "I don't want quitters. People have already been hired to fill your previous positions."

Finally—*finally!*—someone else spoke up. "So if we can't handle the training, or get hurt on a mission, we're out of a job."

MacNamara's mouth thinned to a straight line, and his mad-dog eyes glinted, but thank God they were glinting at someone else. "I take care of my people," he growled. "If you get hurt, you'll be treated the same as any other team member. You'll get medical care, reassignment, a pension—whatever it takes. This is a hard job, people. Out of everyone who has played those games, just the ten of you scored high enough to be considered. I wouldn't be making this move if we didn't think the benefits were worth the risk. You won't be in direct action unless something goes wrong, but you have to be in good-enough shape, and have sharp-enough field skills, that you won't be a hindrance to the mission operators. Any more questions? Didn't think so. Clean out your old desks and report back at oh-seven-hundred tomorrow, to the basement. Wear shorts and tees, and athletic shoes. You'll be taken to another location and your PT will begin."

PT. *Oh, joy,* Jina thought. *Kill me now.*

THE DECREPIT, RUSTY, unremarkable fifteen-seat Ford Transit van came to a halt with a whine of brakes and groan of transmission. Its condition had passed "used" a long time ago and was now in the "could die at any time" category. The seats were worn and torn, and there was a hole in the floor through which Jina had watched the asphalt blurring beneath them. The motor coughed like a fifty-year smoker, the shocks were shot, and the steering groaned a protest at every move. She wouldn't have been surprised if they'd had to push it to their destination.

But the vehicle had made it, not without a lot of prayer and crossed fingers. The guy sitting next to the side door opened it, and the ten of them crawled out. The last one out closed the door, and the latch had barely caught before the driver stepped on the gas and the van wheezed and growled its way back to wherever it stayed when it wasn't needed.

They all looked around. "Where the hell are we?" one guy wondered aloud.

BFE, Jina thought, but kept her mouth shut. She'd kind of paid attention to direction and knew they were somewhere in Virginia. The van had deposited them at one end of a big open space scattered with piles of hay bales, wooden walls, giant knotted ropes, low tangles of barbwire, and other fixtures whose use wasn't immediately apparent but were probably meant for torture—hers. A dirt track encircled the entire thing, disappearing into the forest at the far end, and even the track wasn't a normal one. There were berms and hills and stretches of either sand or mud. What wasn't visible was any sign of civilization, such as a coffee shop.

No longer than they'd been standing there she could already feel the red dust beginning to coat her throat, her nasal passages. She'd seen plenty of red dust in Georgia; she wasn't afraid of it, but neither did she like it. She didn't like dirt, she didn't like sweating, she didn't like anything about this.

Suck it up, buttercup. Sweating was better than unemployment—for now, anyway. She wasn't making any promises about tomorrow.

People moved around them in a confusing tangle. She could see at least thirty men scattered around the training area, doing various things that looked impossible for normal humans. The sudden, rapid crack of full-auto weapons made her jump and look wildly around for where the shots came from, but there were no bull's-eye targets pinned up anywhere that she could see. The acrid smell of burnt gunpowder filled the dusty air, so the shots had to have been close by. Her small group stood knotted together, silently watching the men doing the life-endangering things they themselves were supposed to learn how to do. What was there to say? Their options were this, or go job hunting. She did the buttercup thought again, trying to buttress herself.

The sun beat down. Despite herself, she was sweating anyway. That infernal dust turned her throat into Death Valley. Finally someone noticed them—or, rather, decided they'd been made to wait long enough, because she doubted anything escaped notice by this bunch—and a burly guy with a shaved head, deep bronze tan, and short gray beard ambled toward them. He wore a sweat-soaked olive-green tee shirt, khaki shorts, and desert sand boots. A fine layer of dust coated every inch of him, except where sweat had turned it into streaks of mud. He looked like a moving wall of muscle. When he got closer, he said, "You the FNGs, right?"

Fucking New Guys. They couldn't work where they worked and not have picked up a lot of military slang, so none of them committed the embarrassment of asking what the initials meant. Instead there were some awkward head bobs.

"I'm Baxter." He didn't say if that was his first name or his last, not that it mattered. "Okay, we'll start out the same way as if you were entering the military. First you're going to run. We need to see who's in general good shape and who isn't. Follow me."

He took off at an easy lope, his bulk moving with surprising ease. The group of ten cast questioning looks around, then gamely set off after him. Jina settled herself firmly in the middle of the pack, trying to keep Baxter's shaven head in sight. She didn't want to come in last, but she had no desire to be first; either one would get her noticed, and she didn't want to be noticed. Pacing herself was the key; keep something in reserve, because she didn't know what would be thrown at them next.

That was a good theory, but in practice it meant the jostling bodies in front of her—and all of them taller than she was—sometimes blocked her view of the terrain. She stumbled when a berm rose sharply under her feet, barely caught herself when she topped it and the ground fell away, then stumbled again when abruptly they were running in sand so soft her feet sank into it and fine grains sifted over the tops of her sneakers. That explained why all the men she'd seen had been wearing lace-up boots instead of sneakers. Only she and the other nine FNGs were wearing sneakers, though Mac-Namara had specifically said athletic shoes.

Lesson learned. Ask the people who actually did this kind of stuff what type of footwear she'd need.

That was assuming she wasn't the first one to wash out of PT.

Damn if I am, she thought grimly. Not that she wanted to be assigned to an actual GO-Team, but neither did she want to fail. She'd grown up in the country, in southeast Georgia, running barefoot most of the year, so surely she could hang with at least some of the guys who likely had only done some jogging on a track or city street.

After about five minutes, her muscles were beginning to burn a little, her heart was pounding, and her breath was coming fast. Five minutes! She was in sorrier shape than she'd realized. About that time, the guys behind her evidently realized they were running behind a *girl*, and they all started pushing harder.

Jina dug deeper, ran harder, determined to stay in the middle of the pack. That was all she had to do. This wasn't a race she had to win, she just had to do what was necessary and not draw attention to herself.

Abruptly someone roughly brushed by her, jamming a shoulder into her and knocking her to the side. She lost her stride, and when she got back into gear, she was dragging at the end of the line. Panting, sucking air, she glared at the shoulder jammer. It was Donnelly; he'd been in her department, and she thought he'd been assigned to Kodak's team. Easygoing Kodak was the plum assignment, the one she'd have chosen for herself if she'd been given a choice.

Bastard. Donnelly, not Kodak. Jina sucked in deep breaths and pushed herself harder, driving her legs, passing a few guys and positioning herself just behind and to the side of Donnelly. The uneven terrain made it risky to take her attention away from her footing, but there were some things she just couldn't let go. Donnelly must have felt her presence behind him; he cast a quick glance over his shoulder, and she took advantage of his momentary lapse of attention to throw a quick kick into the middle of his stride. She didn't actually hook her foot into his because that would make her fall, too, but the kick was enough to make him stumble and windmill his arms in an effort to regain his balance. He failed and tumbled to the side, skidding face-first in the dirt.

Baxter must have had eyes in the back of his shaven head, because without turning around he barked, "Get up and run!"

Donnelly scrambled to his feet and lurched after them, now about five yards behind without much hope of catching up unless he had an untapped reservoir of strength, which she didn't think he did. She threw a quick glance over her shoulder; he was red in the face, his mouth open.

What the hell! Why had he jammed her? She'd never done anything to him, never had a cross word with him. Yeah, she'd beat him in the video games, but she'd beaten everyone, not just him. Guess he'd taken it personally.

Tough, she thought fiercely. It was a freaking game. She'd have never played the damn thing if she'd known it would lead to *this*. She'd much rather be sitting in an air-conditioned building instead of running in the heat, with sand scrubbing the skin off her feet and dust getting in her mouth and coating her lungs until she wanted to just *spit*—except her mouth was too dry and too full of dust. Her legs *hurt*. She thought she might throw up.

Some guy she didn't know peeled off and bent over with his hands braced on his knees while he lost breakfast. She sucked in air and willed herself not to do the same. She would not, she would not, she would *not*—

Just as she reached the point of being *sure* she was going to throw up, Baxter held up a fist. "Water break," he called.

Oh, God. She lurched to a stop and forced herself to stay upright as she desperately sucked in oxygen. Everyone around her was making the same harsh, gasping sounds. She wanted to bend over, but she was afraid she would collapse if she let her spine bend at all. Not only that, if she bent over, her stomach might take that as a sign to go ahead with its impending spasm. Instead she looked at the sky and concentrated on her wobbly knees, ordering them to not dump her on her butt in the dirt.

"Don't just stand there, you morons," Baxter barked. "Grab some bottles! Hydrate!"

Water. There was water. There was a big cooler sitting on a rough bench, lid open, revealing beautiful glistening ice and bottles of water nestled within. She stumbled over to the cooler, shoving her arm past the bigger bodies of her run buddies, and snagged a bottle. Every muscle in her body was trembling; she fumbled as she tried to twist the cap off, dropped the bottle, and watched it roll under their feet. *Shit!* Rather than chasing it down she went for another bottle, because she still wasn't certain she could bend over without barfing. Her clumsy fingers grabbed some ice along with the bottle and that struck her as a good thing; quickly she slapped the shards of ice on the back of her neck and sighed at the immediate relief. Maybe she wouldn't puke. Maybe she wouldn't pass out.

"Pitiful," Baxter said in disgust. Jina wondered if she should take offense, then realized he was talking to all of them. That was okay. She didn't mind being pitiful in a group of pitiful. "A herd of fucking turtles would be faster. Half of you are on the edge of passing out, and we've done a measly two miles. The other half of you aren't much better. Damn, son, are you *puking*?"

Huh. That couldn't be right. If the turtles were fucking, they wouldn't be covering any ground at all. She thought about pointing that out, but elected to keep her smart mouth shut in favor of guzzling water. *Discretion was the better part of valor.*

Wait. They'd run two miles? *Only* two miles? That was wrong on two counts. First, yay, because she'd run two miles! There was no "only" to it. But they'd been running for hours, it seemed, so shouldn't that have been something like twenty miles? Her lungs and heart thought it was twenty miles. Baxter's odometer was clearly wrong.

She wiped the sweat off her face and guzzled more water. When she lowered the bottle, her attention was caught by something . . . kind of threatening.

She squinted. Seven men were strolling toward the group, abreast like they were walking toward the showdown at the OK Corral. One and all, they were scary. And big. Big and scary. They were as dusty and streaked with sweat as everyone else, bare arms roped with muscles, not a smile anywhere in sight. The way they moved was fluid with power. Various weapons hung off their bodies, which was scary in itself, because this was a *training* ground, right? Those looked like real knives and guns and stuff.

Not guns, she reminded herself—weapons. They never said guns. She knew that much.

They were focused on the group of FNGs like lions on a herd of gnu, or whatever lions hunted. FNGs, evidently.

Jina could almost feel her skin twitching in alarm. She stared at the wall of man-flesh advancing toward them, uneasily wondering what was going on, if there was going to be some kind of God-awful hazing of the newcomers. "Hey, y'all," she said in warning, looking around at the others to give them a heads-up—only to find there *were* no others, that somehow Baxter had led them away without her having noticed, mainly because she'd been riveted by the man-wall.

Damn it! She took a hasty step after the group and that was as far as she got in all the time she had, because *it* was there, the man-wall, and it surrounded her. Seven men stared down at her, and there wasn't a smile in sight.

She felt as if the sun had been blotted out. She was a normal-sized woman, not a tiny one, but she suddenly felt insignificant and she didn't like it one bit.

Her heartbeat stuttered in alarm. Her head told her they wouldn't hurt her; too many repercussions. Her primitive instincts said she was at the mercy of a group of predators, and anything could happen. "Anything" had been happening to women since forever, since before caves and loincloths. Smart women never let down their guards.

She wanted a weapon, any weapon. Lacking that, she straightened her shoulders, narrowed her eyes, and glared belligerently around, waiting for them to speak. So far all they'd done was smother her with their closeness, choke her with the thick miasma of sweat and testosterone.

There were seven of them, one of her. She was already exhausted by Baxter's wretched running. Even if she could break free, any one of them could chase her down . . . *if* she ran.

She wasn't running. No way would they make her run.

The biggest one spoke, in a dark, rough voice that sounded as if he gargled with rocks.

"We hear you're our girl."

TWO

Jina's gaze darted around at all of them, though she was too on edge for her to really see their faces or focus on anything other than that they were big, and they had her surrounded. *Don't show fear,* she thought; they might attack. No, wait, that was dogs. Regardless, she knew she needed to be cool about this. Instinct also told her not to get pissy about being called a girl; a successful battle was about timing, and this wasn't the time, not on the first meeting and with them looming around her, probably a little hostile and already doubting she could do the job. Instead she said, "Then I guess you're my boys."

The big dude stared down at her. "Babe," he said, his tone faintly astonished. They all looked taken aback by her voice, which, yeah, was deep and smoky, a little raspy, and way sexier than her appearance. She'd dealt with that raspy voice her whole life; even when she'd been a little kid, people on the telephone had thought they were talking to an adult.

Another guy said, "I think you just named her."

What? No! Alarm shot through her. She knew what they meant. They all had nicknames, and she didn't want to be a "Babe," either human or pig. She wanted a cool nickname, a kick-ass nickname, something that would make people think twice about messing with her. "Babe" practically invited messing.

"Not Babe. I don't like Babe," she said. "I like Grenade, or Mankiller, something like that."

A round of snickers greeted that. "Sorry, you don't get to choose," the big dude said.

"No one will take me seriously."

"We don't anyway," he replied coolly.

How was that for smacking her in the face with the unvarnished truth? She couldn't even disagree with them, considering the circumstances. "Maybe you don't now, but you will," she said, and scowled at him to show she meant it.

They laughed, all of them except the big dude. He didn't look as if he had much of a sense of humor—not that she'd been joking, but still.

"We'd better, since our lives will depend on you being able to do your job." Big Dude looked impassively down at her. "That's why we're taking over your training. It's already set up."

Uh-uh. No. No way; they'd kill her. They were way out of her league. She wanted to run in the middle of the pack of FNGs, she didn't want to humiliate herself by demonstrating all that she couldn't do to a group as superbly trained as these guys were. Maybe in six months she'd be ready to join them for more training. She waved in the vague direction where she thought the others had gone. "No, I need to stay with my group. I'm not ready for your level, honest."

"We know that," the smallest guy said, small being a relative term because he was still a six-footer. His face was so dirty she likely wouldn't recognize him after he washed, but he had blue eyes and what looked like two small round scars in the middle of his forehead. "But we'll bring you up to speed faster than Baxter will, because he has to focus on everyone and we'll be focusing just on you."

A dread deeper than the Grand Canyon seized her. She swallowed hard, and said, "My cup runneth over."

"You have no idea," Big Dude said and crooked his finger at her. "C'mon, let's get started."

Oh. Hell.

SIX HOURS LATER, Jina lay flat on the ground staring up at the blue sky and thinking breaking a bone would be preferable to this. Maybe she could manage that, fall off or over something, break one or both her legs, get a concussion—anything to get her out of this hell. She didn't like being dirty and sweaty, but every inch of her was covered with grime. She didn't like physically pushing herself to the point of puking, but she'd done that twice already, puking in front of her new teammates. Unfortunately, puking hadn't earned her any sympathy from her tormentors; instead, the blue-eyed one—his nickname was Snake—had said, "We've all been there," and the big dude, who was Ace himself, had said, "Get up and get your ass in gear."

Asshole.

They *all* were assholes, but he was the biggest one, literally and figuratively. He was also the boss asshole, and something about the look in his eyes, as if he fully expected her to bail out and she'd have to scrape the bottom of the bucket to get as low as his opinion of her, kept her from bailing no matter how much she wanted to. She got her ass up and got it in gear. It was a gear that barely ground along, but she was moving, even when she'd have sworn she couldn't.

A bottle of water gripped in a big, grimy hand appeared in front of her eyes, and a drop of condensation dripped off the bottle onto her face. "Hydrate," Ace ordered, and she managed to move one aching arm enough to take the bottle from him, though how she was going to drink while lying flat on her back was another question entirely. Maybe just pouring it over her face would let her suck in an ounce or so.

No, not going to work. Puking in front of them was bad enough; she would damn well sit up and drink her water.

Groaning, she rolled to the side and got her left elbow braced under her, then heaved herself into a semierect position. More painful effort got her sitting up, though her body was unhappy about it. She twisted the cap off the water bottle and tilted it up to drink. She'd already learned not to guzzle, so after two sips she lowered the bottle and glared at Ace. "I hate you," she said grimly. "I hate all of you. You're bullies and sadists. You probably kick puppies for a hobby. You scare little kids at Christmas instead of Halloween. All of you," she said again, in case he thought she was railing against him in particular, though as team leader he was the worst of the bunch.

Snake dropped to the ground beside her. "Now, don't be like that," he said cheerfully. "We'll have you in the best shape of your life. You'll be able to run and swim for miles—"

"I don't want to run and swim," she interrupted. "I want to not hurt when I breathe. I don't like dirt under my fingernails, and look!" She held out her hand; all her nails were not only dirty, most of them were also broken and jagged. Not that she kept her nails fashion-model long, because long nails got in the way on the computer keyboard, so she could deal with the broken nails. Dirt—no. Just no.

One by one the team dropped to the ground until they were all in a rough circle. During the last six torturous hours, she'd learned their names. Ace was Levi Butcher, team leader, head badass. She had a tough time thinking of him as "Ace," which seemed kind of lighthearted for someone who wasn't. He was one scary dude, mostly because of the way his expressionless dark eyes drilled holes through her. He'd made it plain he didn't want her here, but because she was, he'd get her in shape if it killed her. She wasn't certain which he wanted to do most: kill her or get her in shape. She was betting on the first choice.

Snake was the team medic and he was generally the most cheerful, which at first had made her think kindly of him, but on second thought, what kind of sadist was put in such a good mood by making someone else suffer? She kind of wanted to smack him for making her distrust cheerfulness.

Crutch was blond, kind of quiet, which was misleading because from what she'd seen he was the most likely to pull a practical joke. His quietness was a dodge, and knowing he was deceitful that way made her give him a wide berth, lest she fall victim to one of his pranks. She couldn't handle pranks right now. She could barely handle walking.

Then there was Boom, who looked to be the oldest of the bunch, maybe late thirties. He was kind of bulky in build, but fast and agile anyway. She figured "fast and agile" was in the job description, so what the heck was *she* doing here?

Trapper seemed as easygoing as Snake, and again that was misleading, because she'd figured out that Trapper was the team sniper, which meant he was very good at killing people. Jina couldn't quite get her head around that. It wasn't that she didn't know what the GO-Teams did, but somehow she'd expected that they wouldn't seem so *normal*—excepting their superman physical conditioning, of course. Trapper was like one of the guys, kidding around, laughing at jokes, joining in the competitive nature with which they tackled everything.

Jelly, on the other hand, looked barely old enough to be shaving. He was also the most likely to instigate the others by ragging on them, sitting back with a smile of satisfaction if he could get something started between the others. He bore watching. What was it about these guys that made her suspicious of cheerfulness, smiling, and low-key geniality? That was just wrong. This whole situation was wrong.

Last was Voodoo, and he looked less pleased by her presence than even Levi. He'd had nothing to say to her, hadn't given her any tips or encouragement, hadn't interacted with her in any way. She might as well have been invisible to him. Too bad she hadn't been invisible to the rest of them.

"Drink all the water you can," Snake advised. "It'll keep you from getting so sore."

"Fat chance," she muttered. "I won't be able to move tomorrow."

"You will," Levi said. "One way or the other. When we're on a mission, we do whatever we have to do, no matter how it hurts or how we feel."

Great. She took that to mean she wouldn't get a day off to heal and work out some of the inevitable soreness.

"Soak in hot water," Snake continued. "Then cold water, ice if you can stand it."

Her horrified look told them how she felt about that, because most of them chuckled—not Levi or Voodoo; they both looked even more grim.

She drank more water, then capped the bottle and determinedly struggled to her feet. "It's been great, guys—" *Not.* "But unless you want to continue killing me after dark, I need to get back to my group and go home."

"Good luck with that," Levi said, tipping up his own water bottle. "They left over an hour ago."

What? Jina whirled—ouch—and in horror surveyed the empty training field. Even Baxter was gone. There were still some vehicles parked to the side, seven of them, which meant they belonged to the seven team members who had been getting their jollies by tormenting her.

"I'll take you home," Jelly offered.

"Don't trust him," Trapper promptly said. "He drives worse than a drunk eighty-year-old. I'll take you."

Snake snorted. "Forget that. You'd take her home via New York and think it was funny. I can drop her off."

"I'll do it," Levi said, getting to his feet. His deep voice cut through the chuckles, stopping the discussion in its tracks. "I need to brief her on some things anyway."

That was that. There were no more offers, no joking. The boss had spoken, and while they didn't hesitate to involve him in their rough joking around, when it came to GO-Team business, he was undisputed. "Let's go," he said, striding across the uneven ground to where the vehicles were parked. Resigned, Jina trudged in his wake.

There were two types of vehicles, she noticed: three sports cars, and four four-wheel drive pickup trucks. She was hoping for one of the sports cars, figuring she could simply drop into the seat, but of course her luck wasn't going to turn on a day that had been sucky from start to finish. He went straight to the truck that looked as if Darth Vader should be driving it. It was black, but not the shiny black of a normal paint. Instead it was matte, no shine to it. In fact, there was no shine anywhere on the truck, not an inch of chrome, not on the wheels, not on the rearview mirror or side mirrors, not even the door handles.

"How do you find it in the dark?" she asked. "Tie a balloon to it?"

"I'm good at finding things in the dark." He didn't crack a smile. "The doors are unlocked, get in."

Get in. Yeah, uh-huh. Already knowing what she would face, she opened the passenger door and stared inside. The floorboard was at least a foot higher than that of a normal truck, but on a normal day she'd have hoisted herself inside without much trouble. This, however, wasn't a normal day. Every muscle in her body was quivering with fatigue, to the point that walking was an effort. And he didn't even have running boards. The truck was as stripped down and no-frills as he was.

He slid behind the wheel and sat there, watching her expressionlessly.

Was this some kind of test? Was he expecting her to ask for help? Say she couldn't get in his freaking Vadermobile?

She started to do just that. Maybe she'd wash out; maybe all that was needed was for the team leader to nix her as an addition to his team. MacNamara had said that if any of them couldn't handle the physical demands, they wouldn't be fired. If not getting into Levi's truck would also get her out of this physical torture, wouldn't she be smart to jump at the chance?

Except she couldn't. Giving up wasn't in her. No matter how tempting it was to take the easy way out, she had to give her best effort or know she'd been a quitter.

Her best meant she mumbled a grumpy, "They must have been out of tanks when you went car shopping, so you settled for this," as she gripped the armrest with her right hand and stretched to grab the sissy handle. She strained, lifting one foot, her arms trembling as she tried to pull herself up far enough that she could get one foot on the edge of the floorboard. Didn't happen. Her biceps gave up the effort and with a grunt she dropped back to the ground.

Darth Vader didn't make a sound, just waited, his soulless dark gaze on her.

She glanced over her shoulder. All six of the others were standing shoulder to shoulder, watching. Even if they offered help, she couldn't accept, not that it mattered, because none of them looked as if they had any intention of offering. *They weren't her friends.* She had to remember that. She was here because she'd been more or less forced on them; she suspected straws had been drawn, and Levi had gotten the short one.

Short one. Hah! She cracked herself up.

By *God*, she'd get in that truck if she had to stick a knife in all the tires and bring it down to her level. She enjoyed that mental image enough that she managed to put some extra effort into her next lift and heave—for all the good it did, because she still couldn't manage to get her foot quite high enough.

One toe, she thought grimly; she needed just one toe. She didn't need her whole foot on the sill. She looked around, searching for a block, a bucket, a . . . *rock,* about as big as her fist, right beside the front tire as if God had placed it there to see if she'd yield to the temptation to throw it at her tormenters.

"Hold on," she said, stretching her leg under the door toward the tire and using her foot to drag the rock toward her.

"What're you doing?"

"There's a rock here. I need it."

"Don't throw—"

"I'm going to *stand* on it," she said tersely. "Don't be a moron." Oops. She probably shouldn't have called the boss a moron. "Sorry," she tacked on, while thinking, *Not sorry.*

He tapped his fingers against the steering wheel, waiting.

Okay, this was it. If the rock didn't work, she doubted he'd hang around while she scouted for something else to stand on. She could bum a ride with one of the others, but damn it, this was a *test.* She might fail, but it wouldn't be for lack of trying. She put her left foot on the rock and lifted herself a couple of precious inches. Gripping her handholds again, she mentally yelled at her quivering muscles to get their act together for *just a few freaking seconds,* bent her knee, and launched—well, kind of launched—herself upward at the same time as she pulled up for all she was worth.

Her left arm gave up the effort, the weakling, but her right arm hung in there. She twisted, swung her right leg, and by God got her foot high enough to hang her toes on the doorsill. Her leg muscles quivered, her arm shook, and the bastard sat there watching her with that inscrutable expression as if he didn't care whether she got in the truck or fell dead to the pavement, where he would undoubtedly run over her body as he left. She ground her teeth together, biting back her anger before she said something she might regret—though the "might" was just a faint possibility—and concentrated her puny store of remaining energy into boosting herself up using one arm and a tenuous connection with one foot.

Okay, maybe "boost" was optimistic. In reality, she hauled herself partway up, then her foot slipped out from under her but she landed on her knee, and that was better, more secure. She grabbed the far edge of the seat with her left hand, wedged more of herself into the floorboard, and from there laboriously crawled into the seat and sat down.

The six men watching from outside, lined up like cheerleaders, applauded and hooted. She shot them all a middle finger, then slammed the door, fastened her seat belt, and silently stared straight ahead. That was the only way she could resist shooting another finger toward the man behind the wheel.

He started the truck and put it in gear. The smooth, deep rumble of the engine caught her attention. No factory engine sounded like that, as if it had never had a catalytic converter anywhere near it. Considering the appearance of the truck and the sound of the engine, the modifications he'd done or had done had likely voided every warranty on the truck.

She wrinkled her nose. The truck stank. Or rather, Levi Butcher stank, fouling the air with his sweat and dirt and testosterone. After another sniff, she admitted that she herself was adding to the stench. Lord, she was rank! She needed a shower even more than she needed to lie down, which meant the situation was dire. Good thing the truck seats were leather, because cloth seats would be ruined.

"So you know where you stand," he said without preamble. "We don't want you here. None of us, and I'm talking about all the teams, like having to drag amateurs along with us. Untrained personnel can get us killed. Because you're a woman you're even more of a liability; I got saddled with you because Mac judged if anyone can deal with the handicap, we can."

"Wow," Jina said. "I'm honored."

The sarcasm in her tone wasn't subtle. He shot her a dark, level glance. "That isn't sexist. We work with female agents all the time. But they're trained, and they want to be there. You don't tick either one of those boxes."

She'd like to argue with that, but couldn't . . . damn it.

"If it comes to a choice between you and my men, I'm going to choose my men, every time. Don't think you being a woman means we'll jump in front of a bullet for you, because that won't happen."

Okaaay. That was plain. In case she ever mistakenly began thinking she might be of value to this bunch, all she had to do was remember this conversation. "Got it," she said. "I'm of no value."

Again the dark glance, but he didn't jump to reassure her. He let his statement stand. "You won't be going with us for a while. You have a lot of training to get through, not just physical training with us, but the tech stuff with the camera drone, plus enough weapons training that you aren't a complete burden in a tight spot, jump training—"

What?

"What?" she interjected. "Jump training?"

"Sometimes we have to insert by parachute. We can't run a special road delivery just for you."

"Uh-uh. No. I do *not* jump out of airplanes." She meant it. The very idea filled her with horror. She wasn't afraid of flying, or of heights, but her sense of survival was too fine-tuned for her to even try bungee jumping.

"You will," he said, his tone saying *Don't argue.*

She shut her mouth. She wouldn't argue now, but that didn't mean she was giving up. She'd find a way out of this, a suitable work-around—something, anything.

"Some of the places we go, you'll need to wear dark contacts. Your eye color is too light. Get some, and get used to them. Also, if you aren't already on long-term birth control, take care of that too."

She firmly kept her mouth closed. This was one of the times when no comment was the best response. Whether or not she was on birth control, and what type, was none of his business. Besides, she could see his point, and he didn't need to belabor it. They would be in some dangerous places; if she was captured, her treatment would be rough, rape a given. Her stomach knotted at the dangerous turn her life was taking, and whether or not she could go through with this. Maybe she should walk away now, given that her heart wasn't in this. She could walk into Axel MacNamara's office and tell him she couldn't do it, let him fire her, and collect unemployment while she looked for another job.

She didn't have to stay in the D.C. area. She could always go home, to south Georgia. Her family was there, she'd have support, and she could slip back into the lazy stream of life there as if she'd never hit the banks running in her haste to establish herself as an independent adult.

But she'd left because she wanted to test herself, and she'd stumbled into a damn interesting job. She was well paid, and even more, she looked forward to going in to work every day. That was worth a lot.

Quit?

How could she make herself quit? How could she stop trying?

A sane person would quit. A sane person wouldn't sit there listening to her boss telling her that everyone else on his team was worth more than she was.

This was proof positive that she wasn't sane, because instead of telling him she quit, she said, "Do you have a tracker on my car, or do you need to know where we met the van this morning?" Because he hadn't asked, and if he was taking her to the office building he was wrong; this morning they'd been directed to meet up at a different parking lot some distance away.

"I put the tracker on last night," he said tersely.

To her silent astonishment and fury, he wasn't lying.

THREE

She was the most stubborn little shit he'd ever seen, Levi thought dispassionately as he silently watched her almost fall out of his truck, then limp over to her car. He had to fight for the dispassion, which irritated him to hell and back. Everything about this situation irritated him to hell and back.

If it worked, Mac's idea was a damn good one—*if* it worked. Taking raw amateurs and training them to the point where they wouldn't be a liability was a tall order but not an impossible one. Taking a raw amateur woman who obviously didn't want to be there and bringing her up to snuff verged on the damn near impossible, so of course Mac had given her to *him*.

He and the guys had talked it over last night, decided then that if they were going to be saddled with her, they needed to be the ones overseeing her training and the sooner the better, and he'd cleared it with Mac. Then they'd watched her for a while, before approaching, to get an idea of what they were dealing with. Some guy had shoved her, causing her to lose ground in the run, but she'd caught up with him and tripped him. "Good," Boom had grunted. "Saves me from kicking his ass at the end of the day."

Levi grunted in return. He wouldn't have kicked the guy's ass, but he was glad she'd taken up for herself. The team couldn't function if they had to deal with a crybaby. But Boom was married and had a couple of kids, the youngest a three-year-old little girl. As the father of a daughter he'd since gone bat-shit crazy, swearing he was going to lock her in a convent when she was six, and he'd geld any dick swinger who got anywhere near her.

"We can't protect her," Levi said evenly. "She has to pull her own weight, or this won't work."

"I know, damn it, but—"

"No buts. No taking up for her. We have to see what she's made of."

And they had. What she was made of was bullheaded stubbornness, mixed with cussedness and a total inability to keep her mouth shut. She'd glared at them, cursed all their villages, called down the ten plagues of Egypt on them—and tried her damnedest to do everything they'd told her to do. She'd gone splat more times than he could count, eaten dirt, plowed headfirst into a mud puddle, blistered her hands and probably her feet, and not once had she asked for help.

Several times today he'd had to stop himself from catching her when he saw she was going to fall, even if "catching her" would have meant grabbing her by the ponytail. Instead he'd let her splat, hoping she'd say, "I quit," but she never had. She'd muttered, she'd cussed both under and over her breath, she'd called them sadists and told them numerous times how much she hated them all, but each and every time she'd gotten to her feet and kept at it.

How in hell was she still moving? She wasn't anywhere near being in shape. But she'd set her jaw in an obstinate look he and his guys had quickly become familiar with and kept on plugging. Jelly had made a comment about maybe trying his luck with her, and Levi had had to shut him down fast.

"You don't fuck with teammates," he'd said flatly. "That's the best way I know of to mess up the team. She's off-limits to all of us. If you're thinking about her that way, shut it down now."

Too damn bad he had to include himself in that order. But he, more than any of the others, had to stick to that rule. Doing anything else would tear the team apart and considering their lives all depended on teamwork, he'd do what he had to do.

All the single guys had looked disappointed, except for Voodoo, who hadn't warmed to her at all, but he was such a surly bastard he didn't like himself most of the time so he didn't count.

Levi felt surly about the situation himself, above and beyond having an amateur inserted into their tight-knit group. All of the GO-Teams were tight-knit; they had to be, to get the job done and survive. It was too damn bad she appealed to him, not so much in how she looked—though she was pretty enough, not flashy except for maybe her eyes, which were really blue but with a yellow ring around the pupil. She had boobs and a butt, but not much of them. She had a lot of dark brown hair, shiny like a little kid's until she got coated in dust. What appealed to him most was that attitude and mouthiness, when common sense should have told her to button her lip. She hadn't, and he liked that.

Didn't matter. She was off-limits. He'd cut her no more slack than he did the others, and if she couldn't do the job . . . well, then, that changed the rules of the game.

He knew where she'd left her car because the bus always picked up the newbies at the same place. He gave a quick grin at how she'd fallen for that bullshit about putting a GPS on her car; sooner or later she'd find out he'd lied, and the team would get a kick out of listening to her bitch at him. He had a thick skin; he could take it. In fact, he looked forward to it.

"SOAK IN A hot tub," was Levi's last bit of imparted wisdom just before he'd let her out beside her Corolla. "And drink a lot of water."

Jina had muttered a reply that was a sound, not a real word. She knew how to deal with sore muscles. Her only doubt was whether or not she'd be able to climb into the tub—and whether or not she'd drown once she was in there because she was too exhausted to sit upright.

Her muscles had stiffened enough during the drive that she didn't "get out" of the truck so much as she fell out and had to grab the door to keep from face-planting on the concrete parking lot. Without looking at him she closed the door—firmly, but not indulging herself by slamming it—and shuffled around to the driver's side of the Corolla. Because she wasn't stupid, she hadn't taken a purse that day; her remote was on a sturdy chain around her neck, and the remote itself tucked snugly into her sports bra. She clumsily fished it out and unlocked the door, opened it.

Levi was already rolling, not waiting for her to get in the car and start it; she, on the other hand, waited until he was completely out of sight before she clumsily dropped into the seat and used both hands to pick her legs up and swing them inside. Oh, God, she ached. Even the bottoms of her feet hurt.

By the time she dragged herself upstairs to her condo, cursing under her breath at every hellacious step, she was almost certain she was going to die. Her arms hadn't wanted to work enough to steer her Corolla, so she'd prayed her way through the D.C. traffic. The Corolla wasn't a rocket or a tank like the men all seemed to prefer, but damn it, she'd bought it new last year and she was proud of it and didn't want to wreck it. She'd taken such good care of it that it even still had that sumptuous new-car smell, though her sweat funk tonight might have killed it.

She headed straight to the bathroom, knowing she was so filthy she couldn't sit down anywhere without ruining her furniture. All she wanted was to lie back in a tub of hot water, and as soon as she saw her reflection in the mirror she knew that wasn't going to happen just yet. She was mostly monochromatic, caked from head to foot in red dust that had mixed with sweat and formed mud, which had then dried. In horror she stared at her hair. *Oh my God, my hair!* She'd never get it clean. Pulling it back in a long ponytail hadn't helped; it had merely caused her hair to be glued to her head with mud.

She turned on the shower and while the water was getting hot she painfully peeled off her filthy clothing. The worst was her socks, because the grit had worked its way through the fabric and rubbed her heels raw. Then the blisters had burst, sticking the fabric to her skin. Oh, crap, her feet were going to be sore tomorrow. *Get on the bandwagon*, she thought grimly; every inch of her body would likely be sore, hot tub and extra water notwithstanding.

She shampooed twice, the water sluicing muddy red down her body. The water burned her raw heels. It was the most unpleasant shower she'd ever taken, which really griped her because normally she loved her showers. When the water ran clean, she toed the stopper closed, turned off the shower, and let the tub begin filling.

She ran out of hot water before the tub was half full, courtesy of her extra-long, two-shampoo shower.

Swearing under her breath, she submerged as much of herself as possible in the too-shallow water. Maybe she'd manage a better soak before she went to bed . . . or maybe not.

Through sheer stubbornness, she made herself keep going, though she did pop a couple of ibuprofen to maybe help with the muscle soreness. She put antibiotic salve on her heels and covered them with extra-large Band-Aids. She drank a lot of water, more than she wanted. And she nuked a frozen dinner, ate it unenthusiastically, then chased it with a candy bar. There, that was better.

Just as she licked the last of the chocolate from her fingers, her phone rang, the special ring tone for her mother. "Hi, Mom, what's up?"

"Just checking in," her mother said lightly. Everything about her mother was light, from her slender build to her sunny hair to her voice. Jina's sisters, Ashley and Caleigh, had the same light, musical tone to their voices. Jina, on the other hand, sounded like their father and had his dark hair instead of her mother's blond. She was resigned to her fate now, but as a kid she'd been self-conscious and for a while tried not to talk much. That hadn't worked out well, because she wasn't great at keeping her mouth shut. "Anything new going on?"

That was mom-speak for asking if she was dating anyone significant. Jina made a face; it wasn't as if she hadn't had steady boyfriends over the years, or that there weren't already a couple of grandkids to spoil rotten: Ashley, the oldest, had two; and Jordan, Jina's second-oldest sibling, and his wife had one on the way. The only thing Jina could think was that her mom wanted her kids settled and producing in order of birth, which meant Jina was the next up.

There was something she needed to tell her mom, though, to head off future complications. "I got transferred at work," she said. "More pay"—a *lot* more—"and there'll be some travel involved."

"Wow, that sounds great!" Mom sounded genuinely pleased. "More money and travel isn't something I'd turn down. You'll still be able to come home for holidays, though, won't you?"

"At least some of the time. There's no way to predict the travel schedule."

"What will you be doing?"

"Computer stuff." None of what she was saying was a lie; whenever anyone was hired, they were coached in how to tell the truth, which was much easier to remember, while making it sound innocuous. If any family member searched for info on the company name, they'd be reassured by the commonplace details they found, none of which included "dispatched on a moment's notice to hot spots around the world, with a possibility of bullets and explosives."

"Do you start right away?"

"No, there's training involved." Every aching muscle in her body attested to that. "I'll be putting in twelve-hour days for a while."

"I hope you get overtime."

Nope, that wasn't going to happen. She caught up with the rest of the family—Dad was actually talking about the two of them taking a cruise, which Jina heartily endorsed; Taz, her youngest brother who was in the army, was being transferred to Texas, while Caleigh, the baby, was both having a blast in college *and* had made the dean's list. By the time her mother wound down, Jina was yawning and trying to prop up her heavy eyelids. "I gotta go, Mom," she muttered. "I'm so sleepy I can barely stand up, and I have to get up at five in the morning."

She had to get through commiseration at her early wake-up time, give a promise to call soon, and say "Love y'all" twice before she was cleared to end the call. She limped to the bathroom, brushed her teeth, and started toward bed before she remembered her hair was still wet. Swearing under her breath, she returned to the bathroom and leaned against the counter with her eyes closed while she blasted hot air at her head. She didn't care what it looked like tomorrow, because (a) it would be in a ponytail and (b) it would likely be caked in mud again by the end of the day anyway.

"Perfect end to a shitty day," she said to the night as she collapsed onto her bed. Even worse—tomorrow looked to be just as bad.

SHE WAS RIGHT. After slapping the vicious alarm clock across the room because it wouldn't shut up, trying twice to get out of bed the normal way—sitting up and swinging her legs over—which was too agonizing, she gave up and rolled out of bed onto her knees. The alarm clock was still bleating like an angry goat. Using the bed as support, she struggled to her feet and stiffly limped over to the clock; she eventually managed to bend over enough to pick it up, the effort accompanied by groans and curses.

She'd quit today. There was no way she could do this. Mac-

Namara's idea was idiotic, that he could take a bunch of computer-gaming couch potatoes and put them in the field. Why not just take some of the regular operatives and teach them how to operate the drone—oh, yeah, right, they were too valuable as operators to essentially take them off the mission. Well, that was his problem, because she was out, O-U-T, gone, adios.

And Levi, damn his devil eyes, would smirk as if he'd known from the beginning that she was a washout.

Damn it, she couldn't quit. She'd never forgive herself if she let him smirk. If she tried and he smirked, that was on him, but if she gave up . . . no, she couldn't stand that. She'd have to stick with it, somehow, until she either broke a bone or they threw her off the program.

She managed to get ready, eat, and drive herself to where they'd met the van the day before. If other arrangements had been made, she'd have been notified. Even though "her" team had cut her from the group yesterday, she was still part of it; nevertheless, when she parked she was glad to see some of the others already there, and best of all, they weren't moving any more easily than she was. Everyone was limping around hollow-eyed, as if no amount of sleep had been able to offset the unaccustomed physical exertion of the day before.

Yeah, no argument there.

The guys greeted her, but otherwise were a bit standoffish; she was annoyed, but understood. By singling her out yesterday, her team had sent a signal that her treatment would be different from what the others received. The others didn't know that meant she'd had a more difficult time than they had, they just thought of "different" as "special." She could do with a little less specialness.

The van rattled up, belching smoke, and they all stiffly climbed inside. Jina settled into a seat by herself, not surprised that the guys seemed to be avoiding her. Donnelly climbed in, glanced around, then sat down beside her.

A bit surprised, after what had happened yesterday, she looked at him with lifted brows.

He shifted uncomfortably, his sunburned cheeks turning a deeper shade of raw. "Uh—I'm sorry. About bumping you during the run." Once he got those words out without choking, he took a deep breath and continued. "It was just, I don't know, all of a sudden it felt like a race and—"

Enough said. Donnelly had always seemed nice enough, so she wasn't going to hold that one slip against him. "Yeah, I know. I have brothers," she explained. "One older and one younger. It's okay. I got you back, so we're even."

He shifted, winced, leaned down to rub his left shin. "Yeah. Anyway, the big dogs pulled you out of the group. Special training?"

She snorted. "You might say that. After telling me they'd leave me behind if I couldn't keep up, and that every other person on the team was way more valuable than I am, they tried to kill me and make it look like a training accident. None of them were thrilled at getting stuck with the only woman."

Donnelly frowned at her. "Don't they know you had the high score?"

"High score on a computer game doesn't mean much to them."

"But that's the whole point of us being here."

That's the way she saw it, but the "big dogs" saw it differently. "They're all worried untrained, unmotivated amateurs might get them killed."

"Hey, I'm motivated. I'm motivated to keep my job. Paychecks are nice things to have." He shifted again, winced again. "But I have my doubts about living through this. My feet have blisters on their blisters."

"We need boots," she said, "to keep the grit out. That's what the guys on the team were wearing. Baxter, too," she added thoughtfully.

"I couldn't get boots on my feet right now," he said glumly. "What doesn't kill us makes us stronger, right? We should be freakin' su-perheroes before this is finished."

After bouncing around on broken shocks, watching the pavement through the hole in the floorboard, and getting a headache from breathing exhaust, they arrived back at the training ground. Baxter met the van, grinned as he watched them all limp and stumble out of the vehicle. "What's the matter, everyone a little sore?"

Glowering silence met that gibe, and his grin grew until his eyes were wrinkled slits. "That's what I thought. I'm gonna take it easy on you today, because you didn't know you were going to get thrown into the shark pool, so to speak, and had no opportunity to get in better shape before training started."

Jina looked around, searching for her personal tormentors. She didn't recognize anyone, though again there seemed to be dozens of men moving around the area, heavily armed, blowing up stuff, kick-ing down doors. Baxter noticed her. "You're back with us, Modell. Ace's team got called out early this morning. He said to tell you to keep your ass in gear and be in better shape when they get back."

"Peachy," she muttered. "When are they due back—tonight?"

Baxter shrugged. "Could be a few days, could be a few weeks. You never know. Some situations blow up, nothing you can do."

Jina blew out a breath, caught in a jumble of relief and annoyance. She'd geared herself up to deal with Levi—not just with him, but all the others, too. She had a lot of animosity and grievance stored inside her, looking for a target, and now she had to bank it down. On the other hand, she wasn't going to die today. *Thank you, God,* she thought fervently. She'd take whatever reprieve she could get.

And she'd *show* him. She'd by God show him.

FOUR

The team's absence at least gave her time to get over her extreme muscle soreness. She and the others moved painfully through Baxter's routine, which he thankfully limited to stretching and some calisthenics that still hurt like heck. Then they were taken to a classroom where they began studying the leading-edge drone they'd be piloting in the field and probably in surveillance situations, though that wasn't spelled out. Jina was totally on board with sitting in a cool, dim room and moving not much more than her fingers.

The drone simulation program was awesome. The graphics were so lifelike there wasn't much difference between the program and reality. The drone's capabilities were way beyond what she'd thought drones could do, not that she'd ever paid a lot of attention to drones before other than knowing some of them were causing problems at airports. Now that she was seeing firsthand what their capabilities were . . . wow. This was serious stuff.

Donnelly took the station beside hers, but there was very little conversation between them; mostly they concentrated on their own screens. She was able to lose herself in the screen the way she did when she was gaming, grunting occasionally, muttering under her breath. This wasn't running up a score or winning points or gaining magic weapons; this was learning how the drone responded, how to zoom the camera in on tiny details, how to decipher what she was seeing. What amazed her the most was that she knew this was just the tip of the drone's capabilities, that she was taking baby steps; each new stage of training would reveal more.

She'd have loved this part of it even if she hadn't been able to sit down, rest her sore muscles, and not sweat herself half to death. For the first time she felt a frisson of enthusiasm for this new assignment. Yeah, it was geeky of her, but she was okay with that.

The following days settled into a pattern. On the third day, Baxter ran them through hard physical conditioning again, then on the fourth day their tired muscles were allowed some time to recover, and they spent more time on the drone program.

The fifth day, they had half a day off, and Jina forced herself to drive to the nearest mall and buy a couple of pairs of boots that were suitable for running, plus a multitude of thick socks. The boots that looked like the guys' boots were, unfortunately, made for men and slipped up and down on her heels, but she figured she could glue extra padding to the insides. If that didn't work, she'd see what she could order online, maybe from Army Surplus, but she needed something other than sneakers *now*.

By the tenth day, she was doing some extra running on her own time, and Levi's team still hadn't returned. She was fine with that. She could tell that her stamina had improved, and she'd dropped a few pounds, but she wanted to be in much better shape before she was subjected to the team's training again. The boots worked okay, after she beat them with a hammer to soften them up and added insoles to make them fit better. They were certainly more protective of her feet and supportive of her ankles. After she'd worn them a couple of days, the other guys began showing up in boots, too. They were all learning.

Donnelly asked her out, then they mutually decided they were too tired and maybe they'd have the energy for an actual date in another month or so. Then again, maybe not. Jina didn't feel any real attraction to Donnelly, though she liked him okay, and she didn't think he was wildly attracted to her, either. Besides, training took all her time and attention.

Seventeen days after they left, Levi and the guys were back. The first hint Jina had was when she got out of the van—for reasons known only to the PTB, the trainees still weren't allowed to drive their own vehicles to the training site, unless it was to prevent escape—and spotted a big, black pickup truck parked in the lot.

The bottom dropped out of her stomach, and every muscle in her body clenched. Oh, shit. Her "vacation" was over.

She thought about getting back in the van and hiding; she even half turned, but the driver had already put the van in gear and was pulling away. He never lingered, probably to prevent anyone from using the van as a getaway vehicle.

"Babe."

Levi. She didn't jump, but she felt as if every nerve in her body was electrified and made her hair stand on end. How did he *do* that? Where had he come from? She would have sworn he wasn't anywhere nearby, then abruptly he was right behind her.

Maybe facing a cobra would be worse than turning to meet those merciless dark eyes, but she doubted it. Still, she turned, and kept her expression blank. "Yeah?" she said, as if he were someone unknown interrupting her day.

His gaze raked down her and lingered momentarily on her boots. "The guys are this way. Let's get started."

Fine, no small talk. She was good with that. She didn't try to keep up with his long-legged stride, first because she wasn't in any hurry to get started, and second because she'd have to trot to keep up and damn if she would.

The others were jeering each other over a wall—*the* wall. All the trainees had seen team members scaling the wall as if they were monkeys, climbing the dangling ropes with legs and arms working in perfect coordination, kind of pinching the rope between their feet. Fearing the wall was in her future, Jina had begun doing some push-ups and chin-ups at home . . . okay, she was up to ten push-ups and two chin-ups, but both were now plural so she'd been happy with her progress, at least until this exact sickening moment when she realized she and the wall were going to meet much sooner than she'd hoped.

Snake waggled his eyebrows when he saw her. "Babe, you have a little muscle definition in those arms now. Good for you!"

Muscle definition? Her? Doubtfully she looked at her arms. All she could tell was that she had a tan, though she was diligent about putting on sunscreen every day. And, yeah, her sweatpants were a little loose now, but not much, because she was eating like a horse.

As far as the guys were concerned, she could definitely tell that they looked leaner and more tan. Wherever they'd been and whatever they'd been doing, they'd been in the sun and hadn't had enough food to maintain their weight. But they didn't look tired or lethargic; instead, they were like tightly wound springs, energy contained but ready to explode if needed, their reflexes on hair triggers, their alertness in the hyper zone. Jina had the feeling she shouldn't make any sudden moves, despite the joviality with which they tackled the wall.

Levi indicated the wall with a jerk of his head. "Let's see how far you are from getting up to speed."

Damn it, she'd *known* he was going to throw her at the wall. "A long way," she assured him. "Miles and miles. I'm nowhere near any speed."

He just gave her that implacable look, and she resigned herself to the inevitable. Grumbling under her breath—she hoped far enough under that he couldn't understand her, because she was calling him some really bad names—she wiped her palms on the seat of her sweatpants and approached one of the dangling ropes. The guys gathered in a loose circle, grinning, ready for some entertainment at her expense. Most of them grinned, anyway; Voodoo scowled, and Levi looked as if his face would crack if he smiled. Screw them, anyway.

She wasn't going to impress them, not when she could do a whole two chin-ups; the best she could do was get this out of the way, so she could suffer through something else. Glaring at the rope as if it were her mortal enemy, she picked out the spot as high as she thought she could jump, which wasn't as high as Levi was tall, but what the hell she had to start somewhere.

She jumped.

And missed. The damn rope was like a snake, coiling away from the impact of her hand, and she wasn't fast enough to catch it.

The guys were laughing as she got to her feet and brushed the dust off her ass.

She ignored them and studied the demon rope. Okay, she'd done that wrong. She shouldn't jump *at* the rope, she knew that, but she'd screwed up and jumped anyway. On the second try, she gripped the rope in her left hand, jumped, and caught the rope with her right hand while she groped with her feet, trying to imitate the pinching motion she'd seen the guys do.

She couldn't catch the wiggling length, her arms gave out, and she dropped to the ground. Thank God she didn't have far to fall, though she supposed she should feel humiliated that she wasn't quite a foot off the ground. She didn't, though, because what fool had thought being good at a computer game would equip her for climbing ropes?

Her boss, that's what fool.

"You have the right idea," Levi said, "but you're complicating things. You're right handed, so let the rope lie against the outside of your right leg, then catch it with your feet as if you're stepping in a loop."

That kind of made sense . . . kind of. And at least he was making the effort to be helpful, instead of just letting her lurch from one screwup to the next.

Boom moved to stand beside her. Sweat gleamed on his dark skin and stained the once-white bandanna he'd tied around his head as a sweatband. "Like this," he said, reaching up to grip the rope. He hauled himself off the ground, showing her how to hook the rope using his off-side foot, pulling it up under the instep of his rope-side foot and pinching the rope between them.

"The loop of rope, not your arms, will support your weight," Levi said. "Think of the loop as a step you're using to go higher."

"You still need arm strength to reach higher," Snake added, "but your legs will be holding your weight so this technique isn't as tiring as others."

She growled a little in her throat, annoyed they hadn't shown her this before she'd busted her ass, but she approached the rope with a determined air. She worked through the motions in her mind, then when she had it set what she needed to do, she gripped, hauled, hooked, pinched . . . and stood in the loop of rope. She was only inches off the ground, but she hadn't fallen again so that was a big plus.

"Up," Levi said.

Up. Okay. She reached higher, pulled herself up, caught and looped the rope with her feet, and damn if she wasn't a foot off the ground.

She did it again, her arms beginning to tremble a little, and this time she reached two feet off the ground. Again. Three feet now, and she repeated the process twice more and found herself a whole six feet off the ground because somehow she'd gained more each of the last two times, even though the rope had wiggled around like a snake and she'd had trouble snagging it. She didn't think her arms would hold out for another go, though. She was breathing hard and sweating like a pig. Why didn't they want her to run? She could run for a much longer distance than she'd been able to seventeen days ago. Running wasn't so bad, at least not as bad as rope climbing.

"Once more," Levi said, which she took to mean he'd noticed her arms shaking and while he didn't want her there, neither did he want her to fall and break her neck on his watch. Her feet were almost level with his head and she briefly fantasized about "accidentally" kicking him in the teeth, except he was smart enough to stand out of reach. Besides, if she freed either foot she'd have no anchor and she'd fall. Falling from six feet was way different from falling at ground level.

She stood in the loop for a few more seconds, letting her arms rest, then hauled herself up. Wow—seven feet. She was impressed with herself, though the sweat running down her face was stinging her eyes. She scrubbed her face against her shoulder and blew out a breath.

How in heck was she supposed to get down? The rough rope was already burning her hands, and she didn't want to slide down it. But she had to get down soon, because her arm muscles were quivering and could give out at any minute.

"Guys," she began in alarm, about to ask them how she was supposed to dismount or whatever one did to get off a rope, when her sweaty hands began to slip. She yelped, grabbed, and somehow lost the rope snagged between her feet. She had a split second to make a decision: burn her hands or let go and maybe break a leg, and she was about to opt for the burned hands when her sweaty palms decided for her and down she went—for about a foot, when Levi grabbed her with one steely arm wrapped around her thighs and hauled her away from the rope.

For one second, just one, he held her tight against him. Her senses spun; the bottom dropped out of her stomach again and every nerve went on danger alert. His body heat seared straight through her, all the way to the bone. Her entire body went rigid, as if she'd been electrified—and he let her drop with a thud, making no move to steady her.

Once more, she landed flat on her ass—thank God. Nothing was a better distraction than hard contact with Mother Earth.

Seven men stared silently down at her.

"My hands are sweaty," she muttered in excuse, looking up at them. They surrounded her like vultures, ready to pick her bones.

Voodoo wore an expression of intense disgust. He put his hands on his hips. "This is a stupid idea," he spat. "Shit like this can get us killed. She's worthless."

Jina's lip curled as she focused on the asshole, grateful he'd given her a target that took her attention away from Levi. She was a lot of things, but worthless wasn't one of them—and neither was timidity. She shot a rigid forefinger at him, glaring over it as if she were aiming a weapon. "Excuse the hell out of me, for not being as good as you after just seventeen days of PT. You know what? You can kiss my ass. And you better watch your manners, because if you make my inner redneck come out, you'll regret it!"

Jelly reached down and offered his hand to pull her up. She clasped his forearm and he lifted her with an effortless jerk that stood her on her feet. She didn't take her eyes off Voodoo the whole time. Being sandwiched between an older brother and a younger one had taught her to take up for herself, because they'd seen her as fair game—she was neither the big sister who had ruled the roost, or the baby sister who was, well, the baby—and she'd had to let them know she wouldn't take their crap.

"What does an inner redneck do?" Jelly asked, laughter quivering in his tone.

"It starts with a cutting," Jina replied without a hint of humor, "and escalates to a house burning. We don't want to go there."

"Voodoo's from the South, too."

"No, he's from Louisiana," Boom interjected. "That's different."

"Both of you cut this shit out," Levi ordered in a curt tone. "We don't have time for it. If you want to fight, do it on your own time, but if either of you gets hurt, I'll kick the other one's ass. Got that?"

"Got it," Voodoo said, because Levi's tone had said he damn well meant every word he said. Besides, they'd worked together a long time.

"Got it," Jina muttered. She hadn't worked with any of them long enough to either trust or like them, but she tagged along when they all headed off in another direction, as if they'd been doing something else and had just been fooling around with that damn wall, waiting for her to get there so they could have a laugh and see her get dirt all over her—again.

Mission accomplished.

"I HATE THEM. I hate them all."

That became her mantra over the following weeks. She was so tired the days bled together until sometimes she didn't know which day of the week it was, which was why she showed up to wait for the van on a Sunday, only to finally look at her phone and realize why she was the only one at the parking lot. She drove back home and fell facedown on the bed, slept until noon, and awakened only when her mom called to scold her for not calling.

"Mom," she said groggily. "I posted a private message on your Facebook page, letting you know I was okay."

"That was *two weeks* ago! And I posted one to you three days ago that you haven't replied to yet."

"Oh." She yawned, tried to sit up, and gave up the effort to flop back down. "Sorry. I've been too busy to even look at Facebook. I got up this morning and went to work, and when no one else showed up, I finally realized it's Sunday. I came home and went back to sleep."

Instantly her mom morphed into Mother Mode. "What on earth

kind of hours are you working? It isn't healthy to go without sleep. Are you eating?"

"I'm eating," she replied, though truthfully she couldn't remember what she'd had for supper last night, or *if* she'd had supper. She must have; she did so many routine things while on autopilot, these days, that she had to take it on faith that she was eating regular meals. She definitely remembered eating breakfast, though.

"*What* are you eating?"

"This morning for breakfast I nuked four miniature spinach and bacon quiches and ate them while I was driving to work. I'm ticked off I didn't realize it was Sunday, and I could have sat at the table and eaten like a human being, with a fork. I'm ticked off I didn't realize it was Sunday and could have slept through breakfast." She was more pissed about the sleep than she was the food. Food wasn't in short supply.

"You need a vacation."

That was the truth, but—"Can't happen until training is finished."

"We haven't seen you in over nine months. How long is this training supposed to last?"

Nine months? That couldn't be right. She'd gone home for Christmas, and now it was . . . she looked at her phone. *September.* Damn, how had that happened? She'd started training in June, and now three months were down the drain. "It's a six-month training program," she said, "but it can be extended if some new technology or programs come on board." All that was true, except for the six-month part. She lived for the time she spent on the computer learning more about the drone and honing her skills, not least because that got her out of the physical torture crap that they called PT. The truth was, though, the training period would last as long as it needed to last, because no way would any of them be allowed out in the field until they were ready.

"Can't you get some vacation time when Jordan and Emily's baby is due? We all want you here."

"It's doubtful," Jina replied, doing some quick math in her head. "It's due in November, right? I'll still be in training."

"But you're due some vacation time. Surely you can pick up with the training when you get back." That was her mom, family came first regardless, and as persistent as a snapping turtle.

"Surely I can lose my job," Jina said drily. "There's no vacation time during training, short of a death in the family, and let's not go there."

"That isn't right."

"I knew the terms when I signed up. Do you want me to be a quitter?" The whole family knew that calling her a quitter was the one thing that would make her dig her heels in deeper.

"No, but I do want to see you more than once a year. We might plan a trip up there, since you can't come down here."

"That'd be great," Jina said, though she fought back a surge of panic at the idea of her parents seeing the shape she was in when she dragged herself home at the end of the day. There was no way she could convince them that the sweat, dirt, and bruises were the result of any computer training. "Just remember I get only one day off, and I'm in training at least ten hours a day. You and Daddy would be on your own most of the time, though that would be a great time to explore all the museums and historical buildings." She'd love to see them, no matter what shape she was in. She'd have to ask some of the married team members how they handled family stuff. There couldn't be complete secrecy, that would never work, especially when the teams were out in the field for days, weeks at a time.

"I don't know," her mom said doubtfully, which likely meant they weren't going to show up on her doorstep any time soon. "Are you sure you'll be happy with a job that takes so much of your time?"

"It's really interesting," Jina said. "It's intense, but I'm learning a lot. And even if I don't stay in this job for longer than a few years, the training will stay with me forever." All that was true, and getting more true by the day. She loved working with the drone—or at least the drone simulator. None of them had seen the real deal yet, but maybe soon. She couldn't wait. Though she'd have sworn on the first day that being assigned to the GO-Teams was the last thing she wanted, and though she still hated every minute of the physical conditioning . . . she was beginning to feel at home with it all.

Damn it.

FIVE

They took a water break; chugging water was so important that they stopped even more than she would have thought necessary. Jina dropped to the grass, twisted the top off her water bottle, and chugged half of it at one go. Levi sat down beside her and said, "Hold out your hand."

She paused with the water bottle still to her mouth and gave him a narrow, sideways look. "Why?" she asked suspiciously, scowling at him. She'd been through this routine before. Two brothers had taught her to never trust that what they put in her hand would be anything she wanted; it had almost always been something gross, like a dead mouse or fake poop. One memorable time the poop hadn't been fake. Jordan and Taz had both got in trouble for that. Not only were those memories still sharp, but she figured any time Levi gave her his direct attention something was up, and she never liked it.

His gaze was cold and exasperated. "Are you going to question every order you're given?"

His tone was a warning, loud and clear; she had to trust them, and if she didn't, that was a big hurdle. Stopping to second-guess team members who actually knew what they were doing could get someone killed.

"Are you going to put a rat in my hand?" Around her, she heard the other guys start snickering, but she didn't look at them. Never take your gaze off the enemy, and maybe Levi wasn't exactly her enemy, but neither was he her friend. The philosophy held good for her.

Levi didn't think it was funny. "I don't waste my time with juvenile stunts."

Or anything resembling a sense of humor, either. Warily, ready to jerk her hand back at the least touch of anything furry or icky, she held out her hand. Palm down.

He made a frustrated growling sound deep in his throat, seized her hand, and turned it over. She had a sharp impression of heat, strength, a calloused palm, then he slapped something metal into her palm and dropped her hand. She blew out a mental sigh of relief. Thank God, it was metal, though she supposed he wasn't about to waste time with a dead mouse.

She looked down. The thing was about the size of an M67 grenade, and she was proud of herself for knowing that. She was also astonished at herself, for the same reason. What she was holding was army green and had a clam shell covering. It was a compass. "It's a compass," she said, then curled her lip at him. "What do I want with a compass? I have my phone. My phone even has someone inside it who talks to me and tells me when and in what direction to turn. I don't need no stinkin' compass." Computers. She was comfortable with computers. Compasses were . . . kind of rudimentary. Never mind that Columbus and thousands of others had sailed the ocean blue with nothing but a compass, and an astrolabe or two. Hey, she could put that to music:

> Columbus sailed the ocean blue,
> With nothing but a compass
> And an astrolabe or two.

She even sang it for them, though the tune wasn't noteworthy.

The other guys were outright laughing now, but Levi's expression said he didn't find either her song or her reasoning very funny. "You need a stinkin' compass when there's no cell service, or when you have to take the battery out of your phone so you can't be tracked."

"What will I be doing that I need a compass?" That was the main point, and one that alarmed her.

"Never can tell," Trapper put in. "We never know where we might get sent. We all have one."

Okay, there was that. It just felt discordant; what she would be doing with the team was high tech, so suddenly being forced to rely on a compass to get her to wherever she was supposed to be likely meant that everything had gone to hell in a handbasket—a situation she hoped never happened. She wasn't equipped to handle hell, whether it was in a handbasket or not.

"You're going to learn how to navigate by a compass," Levi said, telling her what she'd already surmised. "Then I go into the woods, call in the coordinates, and you have to find me."

She looked up at him, resigned. "Oh, freakin' joy," she muttered. "If I don't find you, do you stay lost?"

"No, but you crap out of training."

Well, losing him had been worth a shot.

She hadn't used a compass in years. She opened the case and examined the one in her hand. This was a serious piece of work, not something bought from Walmart. It had 360 degrees on the rotating bezel, a declination arrow, meridian lines—the whole deal.

"Have you ever used one before?" Levi asked, his tone resigned, as if he hoped for nothing more than total ignorance.

"Of course. I was in Girl Scouts." That was a lie. But her brothers had both been in Boy Scouts, and they had thought it was great fun to take her into the woods, give her the coordinates for home, then run off and leave her. At least they'd taken the time to teach her some about how to navigate by compass, though what had really saved her bacon a time or two was her own sense of direction, which was pretty damn great.

Another of those cool looks from him. "There wasn't anything about Girl Scouts in your file."

"Why would there be? I listed all my technological training, not my childhood extracurriculars."

"I wasn't talking about your application."

Oh. He meant *file*. Duh. Of course all the trainees had been investigated; she should have thought of that. Rather than trying to continue bullshitting her way through the conversation, she shrugged and got down to business. "You have a map?"

He pulled one out of the cargo pocket on his right thigh and handed it over. She examined the map; it was a detailed topographical map, with all the necessary declination and longitude/latitude markings. "Give me a refresher," she said. "It's been a while."

He got on one knee, to her right, and she did likewise, resting the map on her right thigh. A good compass did more than just point toward magnetic north, which wasn't true north anyway. With the compass and a good map, she should be able to find her way to any particular point.

Levi gave her terse directions, leaning closer and watching sharply as she followed his instructions. He was so close that her shoulder was pressed against his rib cage. She could actually feel his heartbeat, strong and slow and steady.

Just like that, an avalanche of information overwhelmed her senses: the smell of sweat and dirt and man; the musk of his skin mixed with gunpowder from the live-fire exercises they'd run through earlier; the heat of his body, scalding her skin more than the prickling heat of the sun. It was somehow too much, too intimate, that she could feel his heartbeat. For a second she felt dizzy from the overload, then she took a deep, quiet breath and pushed all that away so she could concentrate on what he was saying.

He had her plot a course to something she could actually see, which was the main training course, a good half mile away. Some of what her brothers had taught her came back, and that was an easy test anyway, so she nailed it.

"Maybe you were a Girl Scout," he commented, narrowing his eyes as he glanced up at the sun.

"I lied," she said nonchalantly. "My brothers were in the Scouts, and they taught me."

He rubbed between his eyebrows, pinched the bridge of his nose. "Plot another one."

He could have skimped on the instruction, made it more difficult for her to successfully do the task, but he didn't. Jina was still sharply aware of how much he didn't want her there—he made that plain every day, in a hundred ways both large and small—but she couldn't accuse him of undercutting her with inadequate training. Taking it easy on her would have been the fastest, easiest way to get rid of her, but he hadn't taken it. She had to admit to a grudging respect for the strength of character he revealed every time he barked at her to go faster, run longer, to dig for resolve and second wind. If she crapped out of training, as he put it, the fault wouldn't be his.

While she was working out a new course, he and Boom had a quiet side conference, maybe deciding whether or not they'd bother looking for her if she got lost.

He checked her results and nodded. "Okay, let's do this. You have a time limit," he added, glancing at the watch on his left wrist. "You have to find me in time for us to walk out before dark. If you're slow, we'll keep repeating the exercise until you get it right."

"Tonight?" she asked in horror, because the afternoon was already half over and she didn't like the idea of running around in the woods at night. That was a good way to break something, not to mention woods equaled snakes, and in the darkness she might step on one. No way would she ever admit it to them, but she was also a little night wary. She could sleep in the dark now, but growing up she'd needed a night-light, and she'd endured endless teasing about being a scaredy-cat. She knew she'd have a flashlight, but still.

He seemed to be reaching for patience. "No, not at night." Then he looked thoughtful. "Not now, anyway. We might do a night exercise later."

She should have kept her mouth shut.

One of the instructors drove up in a utility vehicle. Levi swung aboard, and she turned her back to him as they left. "Is there more water?" she asked the guys as she went over to the big cooler that was usually kept packed with water and ice. Normally the cooler was replenished about every hour, but according to the schedule they should be almost finished with all the PT so maybe it hadn't been.

There was still plenty, though; she drank another bottle while she was standing there, because the heat and humidity sucked the moisture right out of her. Some days she felt as if she couldn't physically drink enough water. She began scrounging around for something to put the extra bottles in, and Snake tossed her a small canvas bag that smelled like six-month sweat and man funk. It also looked as if it had never been washed. She didn't care. She'd gotten used to grungy men.

While she was waiting for Levi's location coordinates to come in, she sat with the compass and map and worked out some more plot courses.

Voodoo said snidely, "Don't forget to take a flashlight."

Meaning he didn't think she could locate Levi and get back before dark. She shrugged and said, "Good idea." If he thought he could get under her skin, he'd have to do better than that.

As the minutes ticked past, she got more and more worried. The farther away Levi chose to be, obviously the longer it would take her to get there and for them to get out, and sunset was getting closer and closer. He wouldn't sabotage her like that, would he?

As soon as she had the thought, both her phone and Boom's dinged with an incoming text: Levi's coordinates.

Her instinct was to hurry, but she pushed that away; being accurate was most important right now. She took the topo map and found his location, then double-checked. She studied the map, then used the compass to plot two courses. He was diabolical. The most direct course, according to the topo map, was also the most difficult, with some steep hills to climb, dense vegetation, and a creek that might or might not be easy to ford. The longer route would bypass most of those difficulties, though that damn creek managed to get in her way.

She didn't ask Boom or Snake, the two friendliest guys, to check her work. She either did this on her own or she failed. She folded the map and stuck it in the zippered pocket on her thigh, slung the bag strap around her neck on the diagonal, and set off at a brisk lope. Running flat-out in this heat would exhaust her fast, but she didn't have the luxury of taking her time, either.

Her feet pounded the pavement as she cut across the parking lot; cutting through the training area would have been faster, but there were people on-site executing training exercises; suddenly darting through the middle of one of them would be a good way to get several people hurt. Leaving the training area behind, she cut through a small field that was knee-high in weeds, then stopped to take her bearings again.

She hadn't gone far enough west to skirt the roughest terrain. She set off again.

At the edge of another field, the weeds disguised a drainage ditch that she didn't see in time to jump it and instead plunged in with both feet. She wasn't hurt, but the green, slightly slimy water in the ditch came almost to her knees and immediately gushed inside her boots, soaking her socks.

"Damn it," she groused as she grabbed a clump of greenery to haul herself out of the ditch. A briar jabbed into her palm. "Son of a *bitch!*" In too much of a hurry to stop and hack the offending bristly plant to pieces, she clambered out, sat on the ground to pull off her boots and empty them of water, then started out again.

A quarter of a mile later, she stopped for another compass reading. This time, she'd gone far enough west. Now she needed to head due north. According to the coordinates he'd sent, Levi should be about five miles straight ahead.

Five miles. She could do that, even though the terrain of the course she'd chosen wasn't as challenging as the most direct route, but neither was it flat. Two months ago she couldn't have done five miles, at least not at the speed she needed, but that was two months ago. This was now, and she was all "I Am Woman, Hear Me Roar." Uh-huh. As if she'd have enough breath for roaring.

Then she hit the woods. She stopped long enough to cut herself a nice, sturdy, five-foot-long stick, both for extra support on the uneven ground and for a means of dealing with snakes. She drank some water, because sweat was pouring off her in rivers in the steamy humidity, and set out again. Gnats swarmed around her head. One actually got in her nose and she had no choice but to stop, because she was jumping up and down and cussing and trying to blow her nose to get the damn thing out. When she finally had her nose gnat-free, she could only thank her patron saint—she assumed everyone had one, whether they were Catholic or not—that she was alone and none of the guys saw that particular spastic fit. She'd never have lived it down. They might have changed her nickname from Babe to Gnat, in honor of the occasion.

As bad as Babe was, she preferred it over Gnat.

With an estimated three miles to go, she realized she had a problem.

Her wet socks and wet boots were doing their best to take the skin off her feet. She could feel the blisters forming on her heels and across her toes as her feet moved up and down inside the boots—and these were her good boots, the ones that fit the best. Damn it, damn it, damn it. She had run miles in these boots, probably a hundred miles, and this was the first time they'd given her any trouble. Of course, this was the first time both the boots and her socks were waterlogged. There was no telling what kind of germs were in that drainage ditch, either. A quick personal inventory told her that she hadn't automatically stuck any adhesive bandages in her cargo pockets, either, not that they'd stay stuck considering how wet her feet were.

There was nothing to do but keep on. She had to keep pounding, pushing through brush, climbing over rocks and fallen trees. Turning back would mean she failed to accomplish the mission, and she couldn't trust that she'd get a second chance. She had to find Levi; then and only then could she worry about her feet.

But, damn, every blister was a hot and growing point of pain. Clenching her toes to move the pressure around didn't help. She thought of stopping just long enough to take her wet socks off, but that would make her feet move around inside the boots even more. All she'd get for that was new blisters.

She stopped to take another compass reading and drink more water. That was two bottles down, and two left. Sweat drenched her; her olive drab tee was as wet as her pants and boots. Her hair clung to the back of her neck, and her eyes stung from the salt in her sweat. Being tough was not for the fastidious, but this was one of those times when she'd rather be fastidious than tough.

By mile four, she was using the stick to help bear her weight. A check of her phone told her she'd been fairly fast, even hampered as she was with painful blisters; she'd get to Levi in time for them to walk out before dark. She wasn't certain how she'd manage the five miles back to the training site, but she'd worry about that after she found him.

The last three-quarters of a mile were the hardest. The terrain roughened from just forest to *uphill* forest, with boulders and rocks and fallen trees, and thicker underbrush where the fallen trees had let in more sunlight. Climbing up a slick rock face wasn't fun, because if a snake was going to sun itself anywhere, on a rock would be the place. Once her boot slipped on some moss and for a moment she thought she was going to slide all the way down, but she managed to catch herself within a foot or so. She skinned one elbow and her hand, but that was it.

Once on the other side of the rock, the terrain smoothed out again. She checked her bearings with the compass, adjusted a little to the left, and five minutes later walked up on Levi, sitting on another large rock, a bottle of water dangling from one hand and a book in the other. He wasn't reading, though; he was watching her approach.

"Whatcha reading?" she asked casually, as if she hadn't almost killed herself getting to him in time.

Instead of answering he said, "You're limping." His tone was curt.

Why did every comment he made feel like a criticism? She tried not to bristle. "Blisters. My feet got wet. C'mon, let's go, we have to get out of here by dark. Your rules."

Instead of getting up, he dug his phone out of his pocket and sent a text.

Jina stared at him, feeling a flash of anger. *Now* he was going to sabotage her by deliberately delaying?

"If you make us late, that's on you," she said sharply. "Or I'll leave and you can stay here. I've found you. If I make it back before dark, I've completed my mission, whether you're with me or not." She gripped her stick and turned around, not willing to waste another minute.

"Sit down and pull your boots off," he ordered just as sharply. "I texted Boom to come pick us up."

"What? No!" She gripped the stick tighter, ready to whale him with it. "I found you. I can make it back before dark. I won't let you knock me out of this by—"

"Stow it," he interrupted, dark eyes cutting through her. "I didn't say we had to walk out, I said you had to find me fast enough that we'd have enough time to walk out. You did. I already had it set up with Boom to pick us up, though he can't get all the way here. We'll have to hike part of the way, so your feet need taking care of. Now pull off your damn boots and socks."

She could have strangled him. She seriously thought about trying, except he'd take her down so easily it would be humiliating. Her stress level was through the roof, her common sense was trying to talk her temper down from the ledge, and she was so knocked off balance that she was dangerously close to crying. She might have cried a time or two once she was home alone, but she'd never cried in front of the guys and didn't intend to start now, especially not with Levi.

"No point in it," she muttered after a moment of struggle with her stubbornness. "I don't have a first aid kit with me."

"Maybe you're not prepared," he shot back, "but I am." He pulled a small yellow kit from his left thigh pocket. She had one just like it . . . in her car. She didn't carry anything she didn't think she'd need, and she hadn't thought to get it from her car before she started out. Of course, she hadn't planned on stepping in a water-filled drainage ditch, either. And it was just like Levi to point out her error.

But her feet were hurting like blue blazes, and some bandages would keep the damage from getting worse. Scowling, she sat down on the rock and began unlacing her boots. She peeled off her wet socks and surveyed the blisters on both heels, and across the tops of her toes on both feet. "Crap." This was going to be a pain for a couple of days.

She held out her hand for the first aid kit, but instead Levi crouched in front of her and lifted her right foot onto his knee. Her mouth dropped open, and a flurry of words crowded into her throat, fighting to come out. "What? Hey! I can do that!" That wasn't all her words, but they were the coherent ones.

She tried to pull her foot back, but he closed his long fingers around her ankle and firmly held it in place. He flicked a glance up at her. "I've got it."

Abruptly her heart was pounding like a sledgehammer. She stared at his big hand, feeling the heat of it burn through her skin. He was so big and muscled that he made her feel overwhelmed, as if he had her flat on her back—*Whoa!* She shut that thought down in a hurry, but she was so unnerved that her whole body jerked.

Again the cutting glance. His eyes were so dark she couldn't tell the difference between his irises and pupils. "Be still," he said, and there was something in his voice, some subtle inflection, that she couldn't decipher but nevertheless went all the way to the bone and froze her in place.

LEVI LOOKED BACK down at the slender foot he held and concentrated on keeping all reaction out of his face. It was just a foot, for fuck's sake—a girly foot, with bright pink polish on the toenails, and a glittery stripe painted diagonally across each nail, but still just a foot. The hard truth remained, literally, that he'd been less turned on by looking at a completely naked woman than he was by holding Babe's bare foot. He was touching her skin. Not the skin he preferred to be touching, but still, her skin.

And it was skin that needed some first aid. The blisters on her heels had broken open and could easily get infected.

"How did your feet get wet?" he asked as he opened the kit and took out a squeeze-pack of antibiotic salve.

"Drainage ditch. I didn't see it until I was in it."

He gave a brief nod. Shit happened to everyone. He'd gotten his feet wet a time or twenty, about half the time on purpose. You had to plan for it, because dry feet were essential. All of them were former military, except for her. The importance of keeping their feet dry had been drilled into them, but he'd overlooked getting her in the same frame of mind. These blisters were his fault.

"I should have told you to always pack extra pairs of socks," he said, trying to ease the curtness of his tone. He fought a constant battle when he was around her, and only by erring on the side of asshole could he keep things completely hands-off. Now, in spite of himself, he was touching her, just like when she'd started to fall off the rope and before he knew it he'd grabbed her to keep her from getting hurt. Keeping his distance was getting tougher by the day. He didn't have a noble bone in his body; his dick was pointing at her like a bird dog toward a nice fat quail, and telling his dick no didn't come naturally to him.

But she looked as if she'd jump like a scalded cat if he barked at her, or moved too fast, so he had to tone it down. Getting her feet taken care of was more important than keeping his distance. "My fault," he said calmly. "I didn't think about it. But in the future, always keep two or three pairs of socks with you if we're in the field—as well as a first aid kit," he added pointedly, squeezing the salve onto the broken blister on her right foot.

"I wondered when you'd get around to that," she grumbled.

Deftly he plastered a bandage over her heel, then took care of the blisters on top of her toes, using one bandage to cover two toes, taping them together, then another bandage on the other two small toes on that foot. Only her big toe had escaped blistering.

On her left foot, all five toes were blistered. He shook his head. "If you're in a jungle and don't take care of your feet, you'll end up with jungle rot, and that's a bad deal." As he bandaged that foot he told her about the time he'd overlooked taking care of his feet in humid conditions, how he'd spent six days in sick bay, completely pissed off because his team deployed without him. All the while he talked, in a separate part of his brain he was thinking what it would be like to crawl up between her legs and put her flat on the big rock. He already had her foot in his hand, all he had to do was move it to the side, stand, and he was there.

With his hands on her foot and ankle he could feel the fine tremors that were quaking her, though when he glanced up she was staring fixedly at her right foot as if she could will it to heal. Her cheeks were pink, though, and he could see her pulse fluttering at the base of her slender neck. Instinctively he looked lower, to where twin little points tented her tee, and his mouth started watering like a damn teenager's. He wanted his mouth on those nipples. He wanted his mouth on her, period, wanted her under his hands, under *him*.

Fuck.

He set his jaw and finished slapping bandages on her left foot. Then, to give himself something to do, shifted around to sit beside her and picked up her boots, running his fingers around the inside to feel for any rough edges. Granted, her feet were soft, but she'd rubbed up those blisters faster than he'd have thought, even after getting the boots wet.

No seams or edges. He frowned and looked at her socks, noticed that they were oddly lumpy. He turned one inside out and pieces of foam fell on the rock. "What the hell?"

"Foam," she said, picking up the pieces and slipping them into her pocket.

"I can see that. Why do you have foam in your socks?"

"To keep my boots from flopping up and down on my feet and rubbing blisters." She scowled. "Doesn't work when everything's wet."

She could effortlessly punch buttons he hadn't even known he had. Just the idea—"Why the hell don't you just buy boots that fucking *fit?*" he snapped. At first they'd all tried to watch their language around her, but as the days had gone by they'd slipped back into their old habits, and she never paid any attention to their language or reacted in any way. But sitting so close to her, being turned on by her and knowing she reacted the same way to him . . . saying *fuck* wasn't the smartest thing he'd ever done, because it took his thoughts right back to the track he'd been trying to get out of.

She whirled toward him, amber and blue eyes spitting fire. "Because they don't *make* these boots that fucking fit," she snarled back at him. Then she caught herself and turned facing forward again. "At least not that I've found. I need size seven narrow, with extra narrow heels. These are medium width."

They looked like a kid's boots to him, but then he wore a size thirteen. Again he felt an unaccustomed surge of guilt, because he should have realized she wouldn't know how to find the proper boots—though, damn it, she could have asked.

"How in hell have you been running?" Because she had. She'd had to work up to their stamina, but now she pretty much ran as much as the rest of the team, unless she was on drone training.

Defiantly she pointed toward the foam. "That and insoles. Low tech, but it's mostly worked. I stuff the foam around my heels. I guess now I'll start putting it over my toes, too."

"No, now we'll find you some boots that damn well fit. Where did you get these?"

"The mall."

He muttered a few more cuss words. "Because it never occurred to you to ask us where to get boots that fit, huh?"

She bristled up at him again. Even though they were sitting side by side, the top of her head barely came to his chin, but that didn't stop her. She had no common sense, he thought; most men wouldn't cross him, but she didn't hesitate. But maybe she sensed he'd rather break his own hands than hurt her. No, that wasn't it, because she fired up at all the other guys, too, and as far as he knew none of them were tied up in knots over her.

"A: Y'all were gone. B: I needed them fast. Running in sneakers was hell, with sand getting inside them. C: I was too tired at the end of the day to do much more than eat a sandwich and take a shower. I found what I could find as fast as I could find it." She bit the words off, clipping each sound with an audible snap of her teeth.

He could chew her out, argue with her, or just cut bait and move on. He decided on the latter, because she'd argue until nightfall. "All right. I'll find you some boots that fit. In the future, damn it, *tell me* if you have a problem. I'm not a fucking mind reader." Again that uncomfortable awareness at his word choice zinged through him. Fuck, was he going to have to stop saying *fuck?*

"Yes, sir," she said so flatly he knew he'd be lucky if she so much as asked him what time it was.

He scrubbed his hand over his face and blew out a frustrated breath. "I don't know how much good it did to put those bandages on your feet when you have to put those wet socks back on, but it's either that or I carry you to the pickup point. Boom should be there soon."

She muttered something that sounded like "cold day in hell," but it was enough under her breath that he didn't push her on it. Instead she picked up the socks and began working them on her feet. After packing the pieces of foam inside the socks, around her heels, she gingerly tugged on her boots and stood. She made a face. "Not great, but I can walk. It's better than before." Then she grudgingly added, "Thanks."

Probably just as well he didn't have to carry her; he'd have liked getting his hands on her again way too much. Better that they keep on the way they were, with her throwing up her temper as a way to keep him at a distance, and him locking away his impulses to go all caveman on her because, God, he'd like nothing better than to throw her over his shoulder and carry her to bed, or to the floor, or hell, against the wall.

And that would destroy the team. Even if the changed dynamics didn't blow everything to hell, if he made a move on her himself after putting her off-limits to the other guys, their resentment would do the damage. He'd done what was safest for her and best for the team, and now he had to live with it.

He could hear the far-off rumble of an engine. Both relieved and annoyed, he said, "There's Boom. Let's move."

SIX

When one was trying to draw a coyote into a trap, one had to be
very careful not to set off any alarms. Coyotes—in this case Axel
MacNamara—were sly and notoriously skittish. Joan Kingsley knew
she didn't have a prayer of getting close to him, therefore he had to
come to her. That was where the trap came in, because he couldn't
know she was involved in any way. If he even suspected, he not only
wouldn't venture into the trap, she was likely to lose her own life.

Sometimes she wondered why she hadn't already been assassi-
nated, but the knife edge of grief had been so keen she hadn't really
cared. He could easily make her death look like an accident, though
really that could be gotten around just by controlling the "investiga-
tion." The fact that he hadn't made her suspect he anticipated having
some use for her in the future, by blackmailing her into cooperating
with whatever scheme he'd concocted. There was nothing she put
past him.

Perhaps she wanted to live, now, though she hadn't at first after
Dexter was killed. Not even their son had been enough to ease her
grief. He was grown, and no longer lived at home; though she loved
him very much, he was no longer a part of her everyday life and she
accepted that he never would be again. Nevertheless, part of her
wanted to stay alive because of him, because of the possibility of
future grandchildren that would be Dexter's grandchildren as much
as hers.

For that, she would live. And to live, she needed to rid herself of the pestilence that was Axel MacNamara.

She had a plan. It would involve moving some chess pieces into place without MacNamara realizing who was doing the moving. At this point Devan was doing all the actual work, because she had to look absolutely uninvolved.

Devan likely thought she was still in the dark about his real identity, and in a sense she was, because she didn't know the name he'd been born with. Nevertheless, since Dexter's murder, from Devan's actions and resources she had concluded that he was a Russian plant, perhaps even Russian himself. Instead of disappearing and protecting himself, he'd remained in touch with her, subtly feeding ideas of vengeance to her. At least, he thought they were subtle. Joan Kingsley was a born politician, and she could spot half-truths and emotional bullshit manipulation from a thousand yards away.

Before Dexter's murder, she had even appreciated the lack of bullshit in Axel MacNamara. That was likely his only good point, but having no subtlety himself meant recognizing it in others was difficult for him. He functioned in D.C. only because those in power saw the benefit of having a rabid wolverine on their side.

But she *would* bring him down. The end game would be his death, but before then she would drive him mad by attacking what he cared about the most: his precious GO-Teams, and using those attacks to maneuver him into position.

Graeme Burger, South African banker, obscure and easily manipulated, was the current chess piece to be moved into place.

The game had begun.

"GUYS," JINA SAID the next day when they were taking a break, sitting on the ground and guzzling water. The September sun was hot, the sky a cloudless blue bowl overhead. "What do you tell your family about what you do? My parents are making noises about visiting." She hated being worried about seeing them, but reality was reality and she had to deal with it.

Boom scratched the side of his nose. "My wife knows, in general. Not the details, but she knows I can get called at any time, and that I can't tell her where I'm going or how long I'll be gone."

"Ditto," Snake added. "No way to hide it, when you're married. My kids are too young right now to ask questions, they just accept whatever we tell them. I don't know what we'll tell them when they get older, just play it by ear, I guess."

Behind her, Levi folded his long length to the ground; she knew it was him without looking around. Her skin tingled, up her spine and neck, and abruptly she felt as if she was being blasted by heat. She was always acutely aware of his location, though they seldom spoke directly to each other. He didn't want her there and she knew it, knew too that proving to him she could do the job was way too important. She didn't want it to be, but it was. The best she could do was keep him from seeing how he affected her, even if only for the sake of her pride.

Crutch tilted his blond head back and poured water on his face, then flopped on his back and folded one arm back to pillow his head. "I told my mom I work for an engineering firm that gets sent all over the world."

"What's weird about that is he doesn't have an engineering degree, and his mom buys the lame-ass excuse anyway," Jelly said, snickering.

Crutch shrugged, as if to say there was no explaining what people chose to believe.

"My mom would never buy that." Jina squinted up at the blue sky. "I told her I was learning a new computer program."

"True enough, as far as that goes," Snake said. "But, yeah, they'd have to be blind and stupid to buy that's all you're doing. Look at you."

Look at her? Jina looked, frowning. Okay, she wasn't dressed like someone who normally worked with computers; she knew computer nerds, given that she had one foot at least halfway into nerdhood herself. She should be wearing jeans and sneakers and a tee from some obscure rock concert. Instead she wore lace-up boots that looked as if she'd run a hundred miles in them—she had—and brown cargo pants. She was definitely wearing a tee, but it was a sweat-stained dingy white. "Not wearing this, no, but I can change clothes. I was talking about the hours I spend with you guys, and how dirty I am when I get home unless it's a swim day." Thank God for swim days; at least then she could shower before she went home.

Trapper snorted, leaning back on his elbows. "The girl doesn't have a mirror," he commented to the others.

"Do too. I brush my teeth and hair every morning."

Several of them chuckled. She slugged back some water, enjoying the level of camaraderie she and the guys had established, with the exceptions of Levi and Voodoo. Voodoo didn't like her, but as far as she could tell he didn't like anyone, so she didn't take it personally. Levi, though . . . he watched her with cold assessment, as if waiting for her to screw up so bad he could legitimately refuse to let her join his team. She knew he could do it, too; the team leaders had a lot of autonomy, because a smooth-working team was so essential to their success. She'd busted her ass for three months to keep from giving him that excuse. Whenever she had the time to think about it logically, she *should* be giving him that excuse, rather than half killing herself trying to do what they asked of her. Because she couldn't think of any logical reason for her illogical actions, she had long since given up trying to explain it to herself.

"You're skinny and tan and have muscles," Jelly explained.

Huh. According to the scale, she'd actually gained about ten pounds, after some initial weight loss. Despite gaining weight, though, all her old clothes were too big for her now, to the point her sweatpants barely hung on her hips and she didn't dare wear them out of the condo. But buying more meant going shopping, and she didn't have the time, energy, or interest. She'd made the effort for boots, but the boots were important. She'd ordered the cargo pants—several pairs—off the Internet. Other than that . . . meh. She'd shop some other time, like maybe next year.

She hadn't been heavy before—the description that kept coming to her was "normal." Not tall, not short; not heavy, not skinny. She kind of wasn't normal, now, and whenever she caught sight of herself in the mirror she was briefly taken aback, but the truth was that beyond the teeth-and-hair brushing she seldom had time to even check what she was wearing. She'd never been blessed in the boob department, but now they were almost nonexistent because she'd lost so much body fat while adding muscle. She did like her arms, though, liked the definition of her triceps, and being able to pop her biceps up. In just three months she was so much stronger that even though she was always tired at the end of the day she could bound up the stairs to her condo.

"Maybe I could tell them I've been working out," she mused. "That's true enough."

Two or three grunts answered that. "They won't believe that, unless they're dense," Boom said. "You don't have gym muscles, and that wouldn't explain the tan."

Well, damn. Her folks weren't dense. They hadn't successfully raised five kids by being either naive or gullible. Three months before, Jina wouldn't have known the difference between gym muscles and the kind of muscles achieved by hard work, but now she did. Gym muscles were for posing; work muscles were for doing, and there was a definite difference.

"Maybe they won't come," she said, feeling guilty because not wanting to see them felt awful. She loved her family and normally saw them four or five times a year—until now. Maybe she could go home around Christmas, and by then her tan, attained despite a liberal application of sunscreen every morning, should have faded. And she'd still have to run, even on vacation, because staying in shape was a constant effort. When the guys weren't on a mission, they were either working out or going through training exercises, keeping their skills sharp. She'd be expected to do the same, so her family would see her running and assume her weight loss and muscle gain was because of that.

"Do your families ever meet the other team members?" she asked, unable to contain her curiosity. To date, she hadn't met any of their family members or outside friends. Maybe they were like her and were too tired when they got home to hang out with friends.

"Sure," Trapper said. "There are cookouts, things like that. Boom and Snake both have kids, and their wives do things together, take the kids to do stuff."

Jina wondered if they'd had any cookouts in the past three months, because if they had, she hadn't been invited. She didn't let herself feel hurt; though she'd been assigned to Levi's team, she wasn't yet an official member because she hadn't completed training. If—*when*—she was cleared and began going on missions, and they still didn't include her, then she'd let herself brood about it, but that time wasn't now.

While they were in a talkative mood, she pressed on. "Do your families call you by your team nicknames?"

"In a way," Snake said. "My wife calls me by my name, but everyone else's family members call me Snake."

"Why Snake? Do you crawl fast on your stomach, or something?" She'd wondered about all their nicknames but was usually so busy trying to keep up and stay alive that she hadn't asked.

In answer, he pointed to the two round scars on his forehead, rolling his blue eyes up as if he could see them.

She gaped at him. "A snake bit you? Really? What kind?"

"A rattler. I guess the only reason I'm alive is it didn't eject any venom. I about pissed my pants, though."

"You'd probably be called 'Snake' even if you weren't on a GO-Team," she muttered. "Why do we need nicknames anyway?" She didn't like "Babe" at all, would never like "Babe," and wouldn't like it even if she *was* a babe, which she wasn't.

"'Technically, we don't.' After their heart-to-heart talk in his truck on the first day, when he was making it plain to her she was the most expendable person on his team, Levi seldom spoke directly to her except in command. Hearing his voice behind her made her heart jump, and her stomach went into the jitters. She didn't turn to look at him, though, instead holding herself as still as a rabbit being eyed by a cobra. "But we aren't military so we don't have the protection of a military structure behind us. We're civilian, and officially unauthorized, no matter how *un*officially authorized we are. It's safer for us not to have our real names broadcast over a radio."

She sighed. Unfortunately that made sense, which meant she wasn't going to be able to jettison the "Babe." Calling her that was probably already too ingrained, anyway. She wasn't certain any of them even remembered her real name.

"What about you?" she asked, moving on to Jelly. "What's behind your name?"

"Nothing as special as a snake bite, I just like jelly." He gave her one of his beatific smiles that made him look about sixteen.

"On almost everything," Snake pointed out.

"I like what I like."

One by one she got the stories behind their nicknames. Boom got his nickname by falling on the top of a vehicle and making a loud boom; Voodoo's name was because he was from Louisiana; Trapper once constructed a small trap out of sticks and caught a mouse; Crutch had broken three toes the first day of training and gimped around on crutches for a couple of weeks; and Levi was called Ace because he'd once played in the World Series of Poker. He hadn't won the big pot, but he'd walked away with a couple of hundred thousand. Jina was impressed despite herself; she didn't play poker, but she'd—out of boredom—actually watched some of the tournament the year before, so she wasn't completely ignorant. Yeah, she could see him sitting stone-faced at a poker table with a bunch of other stone faces.

"You get the nickname trophy," she said to Snake, smiling. "Getting snake-bit on the forehead is kind of exotic. Everyone else's nickname is boring compared to yours."

"Break time's over," Levi said brusquely. "Let's get back to it." He two-pointed his empty water bottle into the trash bin nearby and rose effortlessly to his feet, his powerful leg muscles and abs doing all the work.

Hah! Jina could do that too . . . now. She'd even practiced doing so at home, so no one would see her when she gracelessly collapsed to the floor. Getting up unaided required all sorts of muscles, muscles that she now had. She got to her feet, and per his instruction got back to it.

She could do this. She could handle anything he threw at her, and she was far more confident now than she'd been three months ago. She had this.

TWO MONTHS LATER, she regretted even *thinking* those words. "Say what?" she said in horror. Surely she hadn't heard him right. She couldn't have heard him right. This was so far out of her capabilities it might as well be in outer space.

"Parachute training," Levi repeated.

"Uh-uh. No." Jina began backing away from him, as if distance would help; her hands were up as if she could ward off the words. "I can't do that. I can't jump out of a plane. That's unnatural. Only crazy people do that."

"Are you resigning?" he asked neutrally, though his cold dark eyes were boring into her. The other guys stopped what they were doing to listen; Voodoo snickered, but she didn't expect anything else from him, the jerk, so she ignored him. In turn, they all ignored that she'd just called all of them crazy. Hey, if the tinfoil hat fit, wear it.

"No." The word was thick on her tongue, but she managed to get it out. "Resign" was another word for "quit." And though she'd stuck it out this long—five months now—climbing a freaking rope and running for miles and all sorts of other crap wasn't in the same category as jumping out of a plane. Her survival instinct was too strong for that, and her need for an adrenaline rush way too weak. Pain and bone-deep fatigue had become her new normal, but jumping out of a plane . . . she didn't know if she could.

"I'll try," she said, hearing the doubt in her own voice. She wanted to run screaming, because she knew—she *knew*—she wasn't going to be able to do any suicidal leap out of a plane, but pure cussedness kept her in place. She was already beginning to shake in dread, just at the idea. God only knew what would happen when she was actually in a plane faced with the imminent prospect of plummeting to her death—pass out, maybe. Yeah, that would work. Maybe. She wouldn't put it past him to pick up her unconscious body and toss her out of the plane.

Levi had thrown that bombshell at her while they were all kind of winding down after a long day of small-arms training, running, lifting weights, then swimming in the Olympic-sized pool in the gym the GO-Teams owned—or rather, that the government owned, unofficially and completely off the books.

While they'd been off doing other stuff she'd also spent a couple of hours with the drone, too, the real drone, a thing so miniaturized it was the size of a small bird, but equipped with high-definition cameras in both infrared and live-feed digital. With the equally state-of-the-art laptop and highly classified program, she could finesse Tweety, as she'd come to think of him, into a small pipe if she wanted to. She could perch him on a limb, peek from behind a rock, evade a diving hawk, which had taken her by surprise, but she had since learned raptors tended to see her little Tweety as prey. She was determined that Tweety would stay safe on her watch.

Sometime along the way, she had started hanging out some with the guys after training was over for the day, nothing social but sitting around afterward and shooting the shit. There had been some other socializing away from training because she'd heard them talking about it, but she still hadn't been invited, and she'd noticed she was being excluded even if she hadn't let herself react. She was damned if she'd let them know it bothered her.

Until now, swim days had been her favorite days of training, but she didn't know if they could recover that ranking after being linked in her mind with parachute training. Still, good old swimming had a lot going for it; at least when there was swimming involved there were also showers, both before and after the swim, and she now took a change of clothes—or two—in her car wherever she went. She didn't have to go home filthy and tired, just tired. Being clean made a big difference. And she liked swimming, in a way she would never like climbing a rope or running in weather so hot she felt as if her skin was melting.

Other than the times when they were gone on unspecified missions, almost all her awake time was spent with the guys, so it was a good thing they were on better terms now. For better or worse, they were a team . . . for the most part. She was still sometimes taken aback by their guyness. She didn't know a single woman who would think it was hilarious to dump a bucket of mud over the top of a teammate's head, but Crutch and Jelly had laughed themselves sick after doing that to Trapper. Then they'd eyed her, and she'd given them a stony look and said, "Whoever dumps mud on my head will have to wash my hair *and* blow it dry." Considering how long her hair was now, because she hadn't had time to even get it trimmed since starting training, they had immediately disavowed any intention of getting mud on her. Uh-huh, sure; she believed that like she believed in the tooth fairy.

But because she liked them—for the most part—and because she wanted to shove Levi's conviction that she couldn't do the job down his throat, she had worked her ass off for the past five months. To become worthy of being on the team she had pushed herself so much further than she'd ever thought she could go. She could run an easy eight miles now, ten if she pushed herself, which she constantly did. She could do a hundred push-ups, though chin-ups still gave her problems and her numbers went way down with them. She'd mastered the technique of hook-and-pinch on the rope, though they called it brake-and-squat, and could go over the wall almost as fast as they could. She had qualified with small arms, learning how to handle a variety of weapons even though her job description didn't call for that, but as Levi put it, every day things happened in the field that weren't planned for in the book. She hadn't turned a hair at handling weapons; being a country girl from south Georgia had made her comfortable with rifles and such long before she was old enough to drive.

She had changed; there was no way she could have avoided changing. She was far more sure of herself when it came to her place on Levi's team. The woman she saw in the mirror was slimmer, harder, refined down to muscle and bone . . . and she liked it. She liked being able to do things, liked feeling capable.

She'd paid a price for working so hard to be here. Once upon a time, she'd had a few girlfriends with whom she'd seen movies, gone to bars and concerts, a little bit of shopping. She hadn't heard from them in months. Come to think of it, she hadn't heard from her mother in . . . maybe a month? The threatened visit hadn't materialized, and abruptly she felt a wave of homesickness. She needed to call home tonight, because Levi was going to kill her tomorrow. He was going to throw her out of a plane.

Reading her expression, Trapper bumped her shoulder with his fist and said encouragingly, "You can do it. You know how it is when you're afraid of something; you're nervous only until you actually jump, then after that you're too busy doing what you need to do to think about it."

Yeah? She gave him a dubious look. He was assuming she wouldn't pass out, but she wasn't assuming anything. Everything else she'd done had been physical effort, pushing and pushing and not letting herself stop, but this . . . this was different. This was terrifying.

"When do I do it?" she asked, too terrified to be embarrassed that her tone was so thin.

"Tomorrow," Levi said.

Oh, shit.

Jina called her mom that night, and managed to sound normal, managed to keep the conversation general and light even though she felt as if she might vomit from nerves. She slept in fits and starts, unable to ignore the jitters in her stomach or her sense of overwhelming dread. She even handwrote a will—not that she had a lot to leave anyone, but still—and left it on the table, dated and signed. Then she wondered if the existence of the will would make someone think she'd suspected she was in danger, and her parents might be tormented for the rest of their lives wondering if she'd been murdered. Sighing, she wadded up the sheet of paper and tossed it in the trash, then got it out and held it over the lit eye of the gas stovetop until it caught fire. Then she spent ten minutes cleaning up the damn ashes; burning something wasn't a tidy way of disposing of anything.

JINA'S EYES WERE hollow with fatigue and dread when she showed up at training the next morning, but she was so wound up she could barely sit still. She hadn't eaten breakfast, because she was so terrified she couldn't swallow anything solid.

They were all standing in a clump, arms crossed, waiting for her. Over the months she'd gotten used to how big they were, but now felt like the first day all over again, when she'd felt insignificant and pretty much useless compared to them. Everything she'd done, all the effort she'd made, would mean nothing if she failed now. She'd be kicked out of training and likely she'd never see them again, because even if she was assigned another job with the agency, she wouldn't have any actual contact with the team. They had become her life, to the exclusion of almost everything and everyone else. Nevertheless, she either managed this or they'd walk away from her and not look back, because a smoothly functioning team meant more to them than any individual.

She walked up to them, her boots crunching on the gravel, the chilly morning air going all the way to the bottom of her lungs. "All right, let's do this," she said, trying to sound tough. She failed at pulling that off because her voice wobbled.

The seven of them looked at her woebegone face and burst out laughing, even Voodoo and Levi, who laughed about as often as a blue moon rolled around.

"What?" she asked, stuffing her hands in her pockets and feeling self-conscious.

"You thought you'd jump out of a plane without knowing what you're doing?" Jelly asked, snickering.

"No, I thought y'all would throw me out of a plane without knowing what I'm doing," she retorted. "The word 'jump' implies I'd do it willingly."

"Ground training first," Levi said. "Then we throw you out."

There were a few more snorts of laughter, none of which belonged to Jina. She tried to look as stony as he did. "What's ground training?"

Jelly smiled a big, completely distrustful smile. "It's where we teach you how not to go splat."

SEVEN

"Ground training sounds good," Jina said fervently. That meant she'd be on the ground, right? She liked being on the ground.

"Step over here with me," Levi said shortly, turning and walking a good thirty feet away.

Jina hid her astonishment—and trepidation—and trudged in his wake, trying not to show her reluctance. Whatever induced Levi to break his normal behavior with her, meaning mostly ignoring her, had to be fairly important.

He stopped and turned so he was facing the rest of the team, folding his arms across his chest. His impassive dark gaze fastened on her as she approached, each step slower than the last because she really didn't want to have a one-on-one conversation with him, given how well the first—and only—one had gone. She stopped a good five feet away, crossed her arms in the same posture he'd taken, and waited. On the theory that she didn't want to look him in the eye, she stared instead at his nose; it was close enough to his eyes that maybe he wouldn't notice she wasn't exactly meeting his gaze.

Her theory didn't work. She could *feel* him looking at her, so intensely it was almost like a touch that sent waves of heat washing over her skin. She shifted uneasily, wondering what the odds were that he'd give up and tell her what he wanted. Those odds had to be long, because he simply waited, silently, until she couldn't stand it any longer and made eye contact. Immediately all her nerve endings jolted, as if she'd grabbed a live wire. His dark gaze bored into her, an invisible force field battering at her, scouring her from the inside out, frying her blood in her veins.

Shit. Silently she acknowledged that she let him get to her way too much, but she didn't know what she could do about it. He was the team leader, for now the ruler of her universe. She wanted to poke at him until she broke through that iron control of his, see what she could stir up, and dear God she had to be absolutely crazy to even think of such a thing.

"What?" she asked, unable to keep the truculence from her tone. *Damn it.* She really needed to work on her attitude, she thought, annoyed at herself. Her brothers had always said her mouth would get her in big trouble one day, and she'd spent years proving them right.

His eyes regarded her as remotely as if she weren't a sentient, carbon-based life-form. The twitch at one corner of his mouth told her she was about an inch from overstepping her bounds; she sucked in a deep breath and braced herself for whatever he was about to unload on her, but a small, deeply buried part of her quivered with excitement that finally, *finally*, she was getting a reaction from him.

"You just don't have any stopping sense, do you?" he finally observed.

"Sorry," she muttered. "And, no." Like he had to ask. She'd spent the past several months demonstrating to all of them that she and stopping sense had nothing more than a nodding acquaintance.

"One of these days you're going to push too hard, little girl, and then you'll be on the road of no return," he said in an eerie echo of her brothers' predictions.

Little girl? She swallowed her ire at the dismissive phrase, because she'd pushed and she knew it. Levi was the boss, and they didn't have to be in the military for his orders to count. The team leaders were the badasses, and what they said went, at least as far as each leader's own team. Axel MacNamara might run the entire agency on the administration side, but he listened to his team leaders and got them everything they needed. Without them, the GO-Teams were nothing.

Levi waited, giving her a chance to spout off again. Jina pressed her lips together. She could feel words pushing against the back of her throat, but she bore down, called on her seldom-used smart-ass control, and kept them there.

After giving her time to verbally hang herself, he gave a brief nod indicating satisfaction that he'd sufficiently slapped her down—for now—and moved on to business. "Here's what's going to happen, and why. Your group is the first bunch of trainees who've had no prior jump experience, which means we aren't set up to do training the way you'd get it if you'd been in the military. We've had a short tower built, and a swing-landing trainer in a big Quonset hut, but a big tower would call too much attention to us, so your first jump will be an actual jump. Has to be."

An actual jump. Her stomach didn't wait, it jumped right then, up into her throat. If she'd needed to answer, tough, because she couldn't have managed to say a word. And what the heck was a swing-landing trainer? She didn't want to swing while she was landing. For that matter, "landing" meant she was in the air heading down, and she didn't want to do that, either.

"Boom is a certified jump instructor," Levi continued. "He's going to be in charge of your training, and it's going to be fast. In the military, jump school takes three weeks. We're going to have you jumping in less than a week, but it's individual training instead of instructors handling a whole group, so it'll work out to about the same. But don't fucking waste our time—got it? If you can't do it, walk out now."

That was what he wanted. She could see it in his eyes, hear it in the gravel of his voice, see it in his body language. He wanted her gone.

Okay, damn it, she hadn't wanted to be here any more than he'd wanted her here, but she'd committed her time, a lot of energy, and a buttload of pain, to doing this. She'd become provisional friends with most of the guys—provisional because they joked around with her, teased her, sometimes deliberately making themselves targets of her ire because they liked winding her up, but they were all still aware that she hadn't made the final cut yet. She didn't want to be provisional, she wanted to *do this*. She wanted to meet their friends and families, she wanted to be invited to their cookouts, feel as if she belonged.

She straightened her shoulders and squared up with him. Even standing as tall as she could, he was so damn big her head barely reached shoulder level on him, but she refused to show that she was intimidated—just a little—by him. "I want to do it." *Lie.* "I don't like giving up." *Truth.* "I'll do my best." *Maybe.* No, she'd try her damnedest, because she didn't know any other way, so change that last one to *truth*. Two out of three wasn't bad.

The corner of his mouth did that twitching thing again. She did a quick mental check to make sure she hadn't subconsciously crossed her fingers and he'd noticed, but no, her fingers were doing what they were supposed to do, clutching her own biceps to mimic his position. Maybe that was what was annoying him, that she was mimicking him. If so . . . tough.

Typical Levi, he instantly went back to being all about the work. "Today you'll learn about the different types of parachutes, how and why they're different, and you'll get into harness. It's possible to harness yourself, but mostly buddies or instructors help because it's awkward. When you're getting in the harness, Boom will be passing straps between your legs for you to buckle in place. It's not a big deal and he won't be copping a feel, so don't squeal and do something silly."

"I don't do silly," she growled, which might not be completely true in all situations but in this one she was serious. There were a couple of the guys who might let their hands go places where they shouldn't, but Boom wasn't one of them. She trusted him, and he wouldn't do anything to make her uncomfortable.

"Just letting you know what will happen. After you get through ground training, then you'll do tower training, jumping off a thirty-four-foot tower into different ground conditions like sand or pebbles, learning how to land, how to roll."

"Won't jumping from that high break my legs?" Or possibly kill her. She might not live long enough to die in a failed parachute jump. She'd read once that most lethal falls were from something like fifteen feet.

"You'll be harnessed to a safety line. If we didn't know what we're doing," he said impatiently, "none of us would survive training."

She had to give him that, so she nodded.

"Then you'll do the swing landing, learning how to handle the parachute swinging from side to side, prepare for the unexpected. In three days, you're jumping."

Three days. Jumping. Her. Out of a plane.

Oh God.

Her lips felt numb, so she didn't try to talk, just gave another brief nod that she hoped looked curt, instead of simply being as much as she could move because she was mostly frozen stiff.

"Your first jump will be tandem," Levi continued. "Normally I'd hook a first-timer to a static line and kick his ass out, but he'd have already done tower jumping. Like I said, you aren't military and that's getting you a couple of breaks here."

Lucky me. Your kindness is astounding, she thought sarcastically, but still kept her mouth shut. Now was not the time to get him pissed off, not when he could still hook her to a static line, whatever that was, and kick her ass out of the plane. A tandem jump. Maybe she could handle that. The idea still made her stomach twist, but at least if she died she wouldn't be alone. Yeah, she could find some comfort in that.

"We'll need the other guys to pull the ropes on the swing-landing trainer, but until then I'm pulling them off and having them do different stuff. They don't need to be standing around watching you; they treat you like a spectator sport, anyway, and that shit needs to stop."

Spectator sport. Jina stiffened. She'd been cold, but now a flash of outrage sparked through her veins. She also found her tongue. "Spectator sport?" she asked carefully. She'd pushed herself so hard she'd been on the verge of collapse more days than not, and they thought of her as *entertainment*?

"Don't get your ass on your shoulders," he advised shortly. "There's no benefit, and if you blow up at them, you'll lose their support. Just suck it up, and keep going."

That was what she'd been doing, and she hadn't found any fun in it. But he was right; there was no benefit to getting angry. On the final analysis, she'd rather they enjoyed having her around than be actively looking for ways to get rid of her, because that could get ugly, fast.

"Let's get started," she said, trying to sound positive, and headed back to the other guys.

LEVI WATCHED HER walk away from him and allowed himself a brief moment of purely male enjoyment at the view. He missed the softer curves she'd had at the beginning of her training, but there was nothing wrong with the rounded muscles of her ass now. She'd worked hard to get those muscles, so damn straight he was going to admire them. He just had to make sure that she didn't catch him at it, and that his expression wasn't as horny as he felt.

He'd hoped that with time he'd get accustomed to having her

around, that maybe he'd find something about her that killed or at least muted the attraction he felt. Hadn't happened. If anything, she appealed to him more every day. How could she not? She had bone-deep grit and determination, way more than he wanted her to have. None of them, from the top down, had thought she'd make it this far, but she'd had the highest score on Mac's spatial games and they couldn't exclude her just because she was a woman. He'd waited not so patiently for the day she washed out; no one could say she hadn't tried, because she'd kept at each phase or exercise way past what they'd thought she could do, and Mac would have put her back in her old job. That was the best-case scenario.

If she'd washed out, then he could have seen about having some personal time with her, find out if she kissed with the same sass and pepper she threw at them every time she opened her mouth, find out if she was half as aware of him as he was of her. He thought she was; no, he was *sure* she was. Levi was neither naive nor inexperienced, and he knew when a woman was attracted to him. She tried to hide it, but the color in her cheeks deepened whenever he was near. She tried like hell not to look at him, not to speak directly to him, and he knew why: she didn't want to feel the attraction any more than he did. She wanted to control it, and above all she didn't want any of the others to know.

They'd both succeeded in keeping the others in the dark, but damn it, with everything else, he felt as if they were sliding down a slope with no brakes, no way to keep them from a hard fall. Just being near her made him feel as if the air between them was arcing with hot electricity; she felt it, too, and betrayed herself by getting as restless as if she had ants in her pants. She fidgeted, she twitched, she shifted back and forth, she'd start nervously feeling her long ponytail. Maybe she hadn't admitted to herself yet how aware she was of him, but *he* knew. He was damn good at reading people; he had to be.

This damn jump instruction would likely be the death of him. Boom could handle everything on the ground, but he wasn't a certified tandem instructor, and Levi was. A tandem jump wasn't anything to leave to someone inexperienced, no matter how many solo jumps that person had made. Strict professionalism was needed in a tandem jump, because hell, two people were harnessed together in spoon fashion. Given their height difference, she might need to sit on his lap to get her harnessed in the correct position, and the prospect made him feel grim while at the same time he couldn't help anticipating it. He'd try getting her positioned without doing that, but safety won out over discomfort. She had to be in the right position. If the harness was too long and she was hanging lower instead of snugly against his chest, both steering the parachute and landing were more difficult. She was already so scared about trying, she needed a jump that went as smoothly as possible.

If he was the double-crossing kind, he could scare the shit out of her and force her to quit, clearing the way for them to get up close and personal. That was dirty pool, though. He wouldn't necessarily go out of his way to help her, but neither would he sabotage her. He'd be pissed as hell if someone did him that way, so he wasn't going to do it to her. Fail or succeed, she'd do it on her own.

If she succeeded—and she was damn close to finishing training ahead of everyone else—he'd have to tough it out and ignore how attracted he was to her. If she failed, then hallelujah, he was unleashed. Until then he was between a rock and a hard place. The rock was his own ironclad rule that placed her off-limits, and the hard place was in his pants.

He rejoined the group and gave the guys their assignments. Jelly, predictably, groaned. "Ah, Ace, we wanted to watch her."

Levi saw her give them a quick, sharp glance and knew she hadn't liked being regarded as their entertainment. He couldn't help kind of agreeing with the guys, because, damn, there was no telling what might come out of her mouth. Still, no one wanted to be the comic relief.

"We have other things to do," he replied. "Boom will let us know when he needs our help."

Boom scowled at them. "Get outta here. Babe and I won't need any of you until the tower training starts."

JINA GAVE THE parachutes her undivided attention, because her life was going to depend on these nylon things. Boom had printed matter for her to refer back to, let her take notes, paused occasionally to look things up on his phone for her to watch. The harness was impressive, and far more complicated than she'd expected—not that she'd ever expected anything about parachuting, because she'd never thought she'd be required to do it. She studied the webbing and straps and buckles and rings; at first everything looked like a hopeless tangle, until Boom showed her how to step into it.

"Don't expect a harness to be comfortable," he said, "though they're better now than they used to be. The leg straps are a bitch. Women don't have the problems there that men do, but when the canopy opens and jerks you back, you feel it. After you're under canopy, you can adjust the straps across your boobs some, make them more comfortable."

She didn't react to the boobs comment, because it hadn't been made salaciously; he'd been giving her information, nothing more. Besides, her boobs were barely there, so she didn't expect she'd need much strap adjusting.

But the harness itself . . . damn. Jina saw now what Levi had meant about needing a buddy to get it strapped on. Doing it alone was possible, but she was glad she didn't have to figure it out by herself.

A question gnawed at her and finally, after looking around to make certain no one was within earshot, she said, "Boom, give me a straight answer on something."

He was bent over straightening the harness, preparing to guide her again through the process of putting it on. "Maybe," he said. "I don't commit to anything without knowing what it is."

"Fair enough. Do the guys make fun of me when I'm not around?"

He straightened abruptly, giving her a startled look. "Make fun of you? Hell no! What made you think that?"

"Something Levi said." She quickly amended, "Ace," because that's what everyone else called him—except she couldn't make the nickname stick in her head. She didn't have that trouble with any of the others; some of them, she didn't even know their real names. "That they looked at me as their comic relief."

To her dismay, Boom laughed. "Not in what you *do*, because you try so hard sometimes you put them to shame. It's what you *say* the whole time you're doing it, cussing under your breath like you think we can't hear it, yelling that we're insane morons, little things like that."

"Oh." She did tend to mutter to herself, and after that first horrendous day, she might have gotten in the habit of telling them what she thought of them and the ordeals they put her through, but what was the point in saying they were syphilitic sadists if they thought it was funny? "I thought maybe y'all didn't like me."

He put his ham-sized hands on his hips and scowled at her. "What makes you say a stupid-ass thing like that?"

Jina sighed. She was beginning to feel like a moron herself. She never should have brought up the subject, because acting needy wasn't cool. "I don't get invited to the cookouts," she mumbled. God, how lame! She might as well be in middle school again.

Boom's mouth fell open, and he looked thoroughly befuddled.

"The cookouts?"

"Yeah. When y'all hang out together."

Funny; as she watched, his dark skin took on a sheen as he began to sweat. He rubbed his jaw. He looked left, then right, as if some elusive answer lurked off to the side. "Uh," he said.

Yeah. *Uh.*

She sighed. "Never mind. I know I'm not a real part of the team, I'm a tech FNG you've been saddled with."

Boom was beginning to get the panicked, slightly crazed look a lot of men got when confronted with things like female feelings and etiquette. "The wives do it," he finally blurted.

"You're blaming it on the wives? The same wives who—I'd like to point out—I've never met?" It was probably mean of her, but she was beginning to have fun. Boom looked so totally helpless and at sea, and it was kind of funny because after Levi, he was the one the others on the team looked to for guidance, because he was the oldest and most experienced.

"You haven't?"

She snorted. "Nice try. You know I haven't. I'm fairly sure you'd have noticed if I'd been sitting at your dinner table."

More jaw rubbing. He shifted his feet. "Uh," he said again. Then he rallied. "The wives plan the barbecues. If any of the single guys are dating anyone regularly, they're welcome to bring their girl-friends, but most of them don't unless it's starting to feel serious. I, uh, I guess we didn't introduce you, did we?"

"Not that I remember."

"Hmm. Okay. My wife's name is Terisa, Snake's is Ailani. She's Hawaiian. She does some catering on the side, so when she cooks, we like to be there, because she's damn good. Terisa's a nurse. That means she orders a mean pizza."

"I'm going to tell," Jina blurted, because for sure he'd get in trou-ble if his wife knew he'd said that. She relished having something to hold over any of the guys, even the nice ones. Well, they were all nice, except for Voodoo. And Levi.

He glared at her. "You better not. No way in hell am I arranging for you to come hang out with the team if you're gonna start tattling."

"Are you? Arranging, I mean."

"I guess. I'll tell Terisa you've been left out. She'll get mad at all of us, then she'll call Ailani, then they'll get something planned."

Jina had a second thought. "How about I throw together a taco bar or something like that at my place?"

If she'd taken the time to have a third thought, she'd have kept her mouth shut, because Boom jumped on that like a duck on a june bug. Evidently he'd thought twice about informing his hardworking wife she needed to put together a cookout. A split second after, she remembered how small her place was. If all the guys brought dates, if Boom and Snake both brought their kids, she'd have about twenty people crammed into her little condo. She didn't even have enough chairs for twenty people to sit down. Oh, what the hell; she could buy some cushions and throw them on the floor. The kids, at least, wouldn't mind, and she'd make sure she was one of the floor sitters herself.

She forced herself to concentrate on the rest of the parachute lessons, but damn, if anything could distract her from her terror at the idea of jumping out of a plane, throwing a kind-of impromptu party for the guys—and two wives, an unknown number of girlfriends, as well as some little kids—did the job.

Then, the next day, the weather gods smiled on her. Rain didn't stop them from training, it just made the training more physically miserable. Oddly enough, it gave her the courage to take that first jump off the tower, because she figured the ground was muddy enough to give her some cushion. Looking up, the tower didn't seem that high; looking down was a whole different perspective. Even in harness, knowing she was hooked to safety ropes, her stomach was knotted up. But this wasn't much different from zip lining, and she'd done that a bunch of times. Well, the *first* part, the stepping off into thin air and trusting your harness, that was like zip lining; the landing and learning how to hit and roll was something new. Twice she face-planted in the mud, much to the guys' amusement; even Voodoo laughed out loud. "So glad I can make y'all happy," she snarled as she picked herself up the second time.

"We've all done exactly the same thing," Jelly said cheerfully. "You're doing good."

The rain was still coming down when she went to the swing-landing training, but at least for that she was under a roof. The concept behind swing landing was that she was pulled from side to side, mimicking wind, and she had to learn how to guide a parachute under those conditions. *Zip lining, zip lining,* she chanted to herself as they ran her through the exercise again and again. She was safe; her harness was connected to ropes, she wasn't going to fall; she might land wrong and break a bone, but that was true of zip lining, too, so she handled the swing-landing training just fine.

That left only actually jumping. Out of a plane. From a couple of miles up. Oh shit.

But, thank God, the rain didn't let up, and the weather system that produced the rain added some healthy wind gusts to the mix. Levi made the call to postpone the last phase of jump training, and Jina lurched from one panic-inducing scenario to another: the taco bar at her place. The food, and the lack of space, were the least of her problems.

A date. She needed a date. She was a woman, she knew the wives would be more friendly to her if she had a man of her own on the scene, so they'd know she wasn't poaching on husbands. And that wasn't all; she needed some protection so Levi—

She shut that thought down before it could form. Some paths weren't meant to be traveled, and some ideas were better left alone.

Discretion wasn't her strongest point, but her survival instinct was nice and healthy.

Date, date . . . who to ask? She hadn't had a date since—damn, she didn't remember, but definitely not since she'd started training to join Levi's team. She and Donnelly had never managed—*Donnelly*. Of course. How obvious could it be?

Her own guys had so effectively separated her from the herd that she seldom saw any of her fellow trainees these days, outside the computer-training sessions with the drones. For all she knew, Donnelly had landed in a relationship since the last time they'd tried to get together for a movie. As soon as she was headed home, she pulled up his cell number in her contacts list.

"Hey, Babe, what's up?"

Jina curled her lip at her heartily disliked nickname, but got straight to business. "Hey. Listen, are you seeing anyone now?"

"Not really. Who has the time?"

Amen to that. "Good. If I throw together a taco bar this weekend"—oh shit, the time had slipped away and the weekend was on top of her now—"*tomorrow*, actually, for my guys and their wives and girlfriends so we can get to know each other, would you be available as my date?"

"Sure. That's assuming neither of us breaks something between now and then."

"Always. Okay, that's set." She told him the time, gave him the address.

"Got it. By the way, congrats."

"Yeah? For what?" She couldn't think of anything she'd done that warranted congratulations.

"Word is you're starting jump training."

Just like that, the bottom dropped out of her stomach again. Why would he congratulate her on her impending death? "Oh.

That. Yeah, kind of." Kind of, in that she'd completed two-thirds of it and the only thing left was actually jumping.

"I heard the teams don't jump very often."

Lord, please, let that be true. "I hope not."

"It's the last phase of training, right? After that, you'll be mission active."

Jina's eyes widened. "Really?" *Mission active.* No one had told her that. Maybe they thought she knew, maybe it was common knowledge among the other trainees. Same deal as before, her contact with them was limited, and when they were together, they were all so intensely focused on what they were doing then that there hadn't been much conversation. Or maybe Levi hadn't told her because he hoped if she didn't know she wouldn't have the motivation to try harder. She couldn't stop herself from circling back to the truth that no matter how hard she tried or what she accomplished, he still didn't now, and never would, want her on his team. The knowledge was acid in her veins.

She couldn't let herself dwell on it, she had to get in the right mind-set, focus on the right outcome. The jump training was do or die. This was it, the last hurdle. No pressure, right?

"I'm not looking forward to it," Donnelly continued, "but at least I have a couple more weeks before I reach that stage. You're ahead of the rest of us."

"I am?"

"Yeah, smart-ass," he said, and she could hear the smile in his voice. "You're damn good with computer games and you know it."

"But so are you, and all of the others, otherwise we wouldn't have been targeted. Uh—picked."

He laughed. "I hear you. I signed on for a nice inside, sitting-down job, and instead I got this. But I'm never bored."

Who had time to be bored? "That's for sure. Listen, thanks for bailing me out." She started to say bye and end the call, but a detail popped into her head. "Wait. What's your first name?" She'd have to know in order to make introductions; how would it look if she was barely acquainted with her own date?

He snorted. "Now I know for certain why we never managed a date."

She supposed that was true enough. If she'd been truly interested in him, she'd have made time somehow—and she'd have found out his first name.

"It's Brian," he said.

"Bye, Brian."

Throwing together even an informal group thing took a lot of planning. Even with the jump hanging over her head like a sword, she'd made lists: a grocery list, a list of who she was inviting, a list of cleaning chores that needed to be done. She needed extra seating, some music, maybe a movie to stream, and something to keep the kids occupied. She put all her lists on a clipboard and carried it around with her, putting check marks beside each item as she took care of it, or each name as she asked each team member.

They all said yes, even Voodoo, which surprised the hell out of her. He barely glanced at her as he muttered a brief, "Sure," but it wasn't as if she wanted to have a conversation with him, so she was okay with that. She checked off his name.

"Are you bringing a date?"

"Probably not."

Big surprise there. She wondered how hard up a woman would have to be to go out with someone that surly. Still, she wasn't going to play favorites and not invite him. He was part of the team.

She left Levi for last. She hated being a coward about it, but she had to gear herself up for any encounter with him. He was too everything that made her uncomfortable: too grim, too intense, too big, too . . . just *too*. And he made her feel insignificant, nervous, jumpy, insecure—all the things she wasn't. No, she had to be honest with herself: he didn't *make* her feel that way, it was something in herself that was susceptible to whatever it was about him. Her weakness, her problem.

Finally she ran out of time and couldn't put it off any longer; everything was set up, the other guys were all coming, so he'd likely already heard about it and might be wondering why she hadn't invited him, kind of the way she felt about not being included in *their* social things. Uh-huh, right; the day Levi Butcher worried about his popularity, or lack of it, would be the official end of the world. She was just trying to psyche herself up by imagining him with feelings.

Finding the opportunity was more difficult than she'd thought. She didn't want to ask him in front of everyone else, because what if he said no? He wouldn't, of course, but if he did they might all rethink their acceptance of her invitation. Even worse, she might do something embarrassing, like blushing. Maybe she could just text him, because everyone on the team had everyone else's phone numbers.

Because she really, really wanted to go the text route, she mentally snarled at herself for being a coward. She had to just do it, regardless of the circumstances. The next time she saw him, she'd suck it up and do it.

"The next time" turned out to be as she was leaving a session of drone training. He was coming out of a room that she knew housed the evil demons who devised the training scenarios for the drone operators; Levi had likely been giving them ideas on how to trip her up. Swiftly she ran through this last session, trying to see any mistakes she'd made. The mission had been accomplished and all operators were home safe, but she couldn't give herself any pats on the back because she could have handled the drone more smoothly. There was always something; no session was ever perfect.

Levi gave her a cursory glance as if registering her existence but nothing more and turned in the opposite direction.

Mentally girding her loins—though what the hell was "girding," and weren't there more important body parts that needed protecting?—she called, "Levi, wait up!" Clutching her clipboard with its all-important lists, she trotted down the hallway toward him.

He turned, planted his booted feet apart, crossed his arms, and with hooded eyes watched her approach.

Jina clutched her clipboard as if it were a dependable barrier between them. "Ah," she began, then her mental gears engaged and she looked down at the topmost list as if double-checking something on it. "I'm having a taco bar at my place Saturday night. Would you like to come—"

"No," he said.

She hadn't expected that. She'd had the thought, but she hadn't really expected it. Maybe an excuse, maybe he already had a date and they'd made other plans, but his flat refusal was a slap in the face.

"Okay." She looked down at the list, trying to keep her expression casual as if she'd asked him nothing more important than if he wanted coffee.

He made a low sound, kind of like a growl, and seized her arm, then immediately released her as if she'd burned his hand. "Let's go someplace more private," he muttered, turning and striding off, not once looking back to see if she obeyed.

She thought about not following him, about turning around and marching out of the building. A hard lump in her throat made her think about making a dash to the bathroom, before she did something embarrassing, like cry. She would *not* cry. No way would she ever let him know that he'd in any way upset her.

But he was the team leader, and she'd spent months doing exactly what he'd said, when he'd said it. Her feet might have dragged as she followed him, but they moved, because Levi had said so.

He looked into a couple of rooms before entering what turned out to be a small office; whoever belonged there had either already gone home or was taking a bathroom break. It didn't matter; Levi claimed the space. As soon as she entered the room, he closed the door and locked it.

Locked it.

The hair on the back of her neck stood up, and she stopped in her tracks. Her breath seized in her chest, but the alarm she was feeling wasn't one of fear. She wasn't afraid of Levi, not like *that*. She was afraid of him on a much more feminine level, one she didn't let herself examine because there was no way she was going there; that road was too fraught with emotional land mines, and she was neither crazy nor self-destructive.

He gave her an impatient look and ran his hand over his stubbled jaw, the rasping sound like sandpaper against her nerves. "Shit," he muttered.

She relaxed a little at his expression of mingled impatience and disgust, but she was alone in a small space with him and her lizard brain was on red alert. Then that dark gaze zeroed in on her and for a split second, before he could control it, she saw a flash of heat as potent as a volcanic cauldron, bubbling and ready to blow. Then he shut it down, leaving nothing in his expression for her to read.

"I don't shit where I sleep," he said bluntly. "I know you've got the hots for me and it won't go anywhere. It can't go anywhere. So, no, I won't be your date or your fuck buddy or anything else. Got it?"

For a moment Jina was blinded by shock. She could feel herself fumbling with the clipboard, but she didn't know what she was doing. Her whole body was numb, her lips incapable of moving. He'd slugged her with words, but it felt as if he'd used his fist.

Then rage hit, rage so white and searing she felt incandescent with it. Her mind was blank. She looked down at the clipboard, and the list of names swam into focus.

"Okay, let's see," she said as if to herself. "Boom and his family, check. Voodoo, check. Snake and family, Brian, Jelly, Crutch, Trapper—" As she ran through their names she made little check marks beside them. "Looks as if everyone is coming except Asshole." Vigorously she marked through his name, digging the pen so hard into the paper it tore holes.

"Who's Brian?" he interrupted in a growl.

"Brian?" She looked up, managed to give him a megawatt smile. "He's my date." Clutching the clipboard to her chest, she strolled to the door, flipped the lock, and left. She didn't know how she managed to put one foot in front of the other. She was reeling from his words, not just the crudeness but the lethal accuracy.

Because he was right. The son of a bitch was right.

EIGHT

Jina didn't sleep that night. Her mind wouldn't shut down, wouldn't let her forget the searing humiliation. Levi had seen through her, likely from the start; she'd wasted all that time and effort staying away from him, not talking to him if she could help it, not even *looking* at him, all for nothing. Damn it, it wasn't as if she were in *love* with him—God forbid—so she should have been able to play the situation better. The good Lord help any woman who loved Levi Butcher, because she'd need the backup.

What she felt was just potent physical chemistry, and she wasn't a fool; she knew that acting on it would be a disaster between team members. Moreover, that strong survival instinct of hers warned her to steer far, far away from him, at least in a personal sense. Levi was intense; controlled, but intense. Sex with him might be incandescent enough to render *her* blind, but at most he'd walk away thinking, *Okay, tension relieved, that was good, hey isn't it almost time to change the oil in the truck?* They came at life from two different levels. She was normal, and he wasn't. He was like Rambo with Kama Sutra training, considering what he did to her hormones, and it wasn't fair.

How classic could the setup be? In a team of alpha males, he was the most alpha, the super-high-octane alpha. As the only woman—and by default the alpha female—on the team, according to biology and anthropology and probably a lot of other -ologies, within their little group she had no other option than to choose him as her mate.

Except she had an option, all right, and her option was to say no. "I don't want to mate," she growled into the darkness of her bedroom, though she had to acknowledge that wasn't strictly true. She didn't want to *mate*, as in form a bond and procreate, but she sure wouldn't mind trying him on for size. She'd never had sex just for the sake of having sex, but for him she'd be happy to make an exception . . . if circumstances were different. And if he wasn't such an asshole.

Except not now. Now she wanted to geld him.

How was she supposed to function with the team now, when she dreaded every minute she'd have to spend in his company? This wasn't not liking someone; she'd worked with people she didn't like before, and she'd made the best of it because her parents had always told their kids that life wasn't perfect and they'd have to deal with problems all their lives, so deal with them and stop whining. This was different; this was so uncomfortable and humiliating that she wanted to punch him and be done with it. Punching him would get her kicked off the team, right?

Since this whole deal had started, over five months ago, she'd often comforted herself with the idea of quitting, knowing the whole time that she'd rather eat maggots than quit because her streak of stubbornness was so ingrained from years of keeping up with her brothers that she didn't know *how* to quit. But she could have if she'd wanted to, and having that as an out had been nice because she liked having options.

Now she had no option. None. She couldn't quit under any circumstances, because that would mean Levi had won and she'd rather break every bone in her body than give him the satisfaction. No way would she let him think she couldn't take the stress of being near him and not being able to have him—hah! If she'd been chasing after him and embarrassing herself, she could understand why he'd felt the need to say what he did, but she hadn't. She'd kept to herself, never let herself even *think* of flirting with him. He could have maintained the status quo; he didn't have to rub her nose in her hormonal insanity. She hadn't acted on it, wouldn't have acted on it.

Her only path now was to stay the course, to try not merely because she couldn't bear to quit, but because she wanted to become a real member of the team. Her focus had to be on something more than just getting through the next day, something bigger, something more important.

As of right now, she swore savagely, Levi was nothing to her other than a team member. He could take his damn overflowing testosterone and entice some other woman, and she hoped he developed *erectile dysfunction*. Maybe he could be in one of those television commercials, sitting in one of those stupid side-by-side bathtubs in the middle of the woods.

The ridiculousness of that thought so entertained her that she chuckled out loud in the darkness. Ah, hell; she wasn't sleeping, at least not until she calmed down some, so she might as well get up and do what she could to get ready for the taco bar tomorrow. She checked the time, saw it was almost one-thirty A.M., and changed that "tomorrow" to "*today!*" What on earth had possessed her to invite everyone to her little condo?

Oh, well; she'd get to know the wives, mainly because everyone would practically be sitting on top of each other. And as her mom always said, it wasn't the surroundings, it was the company. And the food. She couldn't stretch her condo and make it bigger, but she could make sure the food was both fun and good.

And thank God, because the event was right on top of her, and that gave her something else to focus on; otherwise, she'd have lain in bed and wallowed in fury and self-pity all night long. As it was, she got up and muttered irritably to herself the whole time she cleaned the condo. After all, it was one-freaking-thirty in the morning—now two in the morning—and she was cleaning instead of sleeping, and it was all Levi Butcher's fault, damn his black heart and eyes and every other part.

She wanted everyone who came to have a *great* time and spend the next day telling Levi all about it. And she might even indulge in a little PDA with Donnelly . . . Brian . . . no, that wouldn't be fair to him, not when she knew there'd be no romantic relationship with him, ever. Damn.

She went back to bed at four and was so tired she slept like a rock for all of three hours. After months of getting up early, her body evidently thought that was what it was supposed to do. Supposedly the guys had perfected what they called the "combat nap," so they could grab a quick nap whenever they needed it, but that wasn't something they'd taught her yet.

Because there would be kids—and men, even if the kids were left with babysitters—she made a big sheet cake with her mother's special chocolate frosting. She got fancy and made another batch of frosting, colored some of it red and some green, and piped some roses and leaves onto the cake. Baking was something she enjoyed, and she was the only one of three daughters to have inherited her mother's touch with cakes. Then to make the kids laugh, she piped some big red lips and a tongue sticking out, right in the middle of the cake. There—something for everyone. She would have added teeth, but she didn't know the ages of the kids and she didn't want to scare them.

She'd told everyone to be there at six, but she was dressed—such as it was, in jeans and sneakers and a lightweight sweatshirt—at five-thirty, because she didn't trust the guys not to show up early. They were guys, after all. "I must be psychic," she said smugly, when the doorbell rang at exactly five-thirty-eight.

After a peek through the peephole, she opened the door to Jelly and Crutch. "Hi. Did y'all come together?"

"Naw, we stopped dating a year ago," Crutch said, then laughed at his own joke. "We always have our own wheels, and our gear, in case we get called out on a mission."

"I'll have to do that, too," she said in dawning realization. She was on the brink of full membership on the team. She'd been so engrossed in training she hadn't thought it through to all the ways, big and small, that her life would change.

"Yep." Jelly put his hands on his hips and looked around. "Nice place."

It wasn't, not really. For starters, it was an upstairs unit, which wasn't ideal. It was on the small side. Her furniture tended more toward comfy than stylish. But they were bachelors, so what did they know? Some framed prints on the walls, a rug or two, window treatments other than plain blinds, and the place likely seemed almost luxurious to them. Oh—and clean. Clean went a long way.

"Glad y'all could come. Can I get you something to drink?"

"You have any beer?" Crutch asked, looking less than hopeful.

"Beer, soft drinks, bottled water, fruit juice for the kids. Come on into the kitchen." She'd stocked some popular brands—Bud, Coors, Corona—and had them all iced down in a cooler. She'd barely gotten the beers opened and in their hands before the doorbell rang again. Donnelly stood in the small entrance alcove, a six-pack of beer in his hand.

"I didn't know if you'd have enough," he said, holding up the beer.

"Thanks. Want to take it to the kitchen and put it on ice? Crutch and Jelly are already here."

"Cool." From his eager look, she thought he was looking forward to hanging with some of the team guys. None of the other team leaders had followed Levi's lead and involved themselves in their training, so she was the only one who so far had had any real interaction with them.

Only a minute behind Donnelly was Snake, with Ailani and their three kids, ages seven, five, and two—boy, girl, boy. Ailani held a dripping umbrella, and Snake held the two-year-old with a firm grip around the kid's legs, which was a good thing because the toddler had thrown himself backward and was hanging head down, shrieking. Jina laughed; all of a sudden, the noise felt like home.

"Ailani, Jina," Snake said in brief introduction. The decibel level from the upside-down kid went up ten points, and he shifted his grip until he was holding his son by both ankles.

"Don't drop him," Ailani warned and gave Jina a polite smile. "It's nice to meet you. Thanks for inviting us, though I'm not sure you knew what you were getting into."

"I did," Jina reassured her. "I'm the middle one of five kids, so to me family means a lot of people and noise." Ailani struck her as somewhat reserved, maybe a little tired and not exactly pleased to be there, so she didn't overdo the friendliness. "Let me take everyone's coats, and the umbrella. Drinks in the kitchen, Crutch and Jelly and Brian are already in there."

"Who's Brian?" Snake asked as he passed her.

"My date. He's assigned to Kodak's team."

"He is? I can tell him a thing or three about Kodak."

Next was Trapper, then Voodoo, who for some reason seemed to be wildly popular with Snake's two oldest kids. There was no accounting for taste, especially at their ages. Boom and his wife, Terisa, were last, with a gap-toothed eight-year-old boy and a big-eyed three-year-old girl who was so cute as she clutched Boom's leg and peeped around it that Jina couldn't help squatting down and trying to entice her to talk—a useless effort, because she merely shook her head and clutched Boom's leg even tighter.

"Her name is Mia. She'll warm up in a while, and then you'll regret trying to get her to talk." Terisa smiled, but her eyes were even more tired than Ailani's and she was in scrubs, which meant she'd either met Boom and the kids here or they'd been so pressed for time she hadn't taken the time to change. "Thanks for inviting us; saved me from ordering another pizza."

Jina couldn't help shooting a quick look at Boom, who narrowed his eyes at her in warning. Terisa caught the look. "What?" she demanded suspiciously, sending her own narrow-eyed look at Boom. "Have you been throwing off on my cooking again?"

"No," he said with absolute honesty and beat a path for the kitchen, ignoring the snorting noise Terisa made at his back.

With two tired wives and a bunch of men who were attacking the beer, Jina deemed that the sooner she got food in everyone, the better. She had the taco beef keeping warm in two slow-cookers, and all the other components had been chopped and diced and were ready to set out. Within fifteen minutes, everyone had tacos except the two youngest kids, and she'd had the foresight to get chicken nuggets for them.

Snake's toddler had stopped shrieking to run around the condo with a chicken nugget clutched in each hand, yelling, "Chee! Chee!" at his mother.

Ailani gave Jina a harassed look. "Sorry. Do you have any cheese other than the shredded? He's a cheese hound."

"I do," Jina said, and got a bag of cubed cheese from the fridge. The cubed cheese evidently called to all the kids, and before she knew it the bag was empty, but the toddler was quiet and happy.

Once everyone had food and drink, the noise level dropped dramatically. The guys were in the kitchen, either seated at her small table or standing with their food on the counters; Donnelly seemed to be having the time of his life. Jina and the other two women claimed the living room, where the kids were on the floor pillows, which they thought was great fun. Jina got her own taco and drink and settled on the floor kind of in the middle of the kids, so she could keep an eye on them and give their mothers a break. "I'm glad you could all make it," she said. "I know it was kind of last minute."

"No way we were going to pass up a chance to finally meet *Babe*," Terisa said, her tone neutral.

Yeah, there was some sticky ground to cover. Jina made a face. "Ace saddled me with that name. It isn't my favorite, so of course no way would they change it."

Ailani looked around, as if just now noticing there was someone missing. "Where is Ace? Normally he'd charge through a minefield to get to food."

"He said he couldn't make it. Maybe he already had a date." Except he could have used that as an excuse and hadn't bothered. Instead he'd slapped her down like smashing a fly with a flyswatter. Under the circumstances, she was proud her tone was nonchalant.

"Have you been seeing Brian very long?" Terisa asked.

"Not all that long." She wasn't going to lie, but neither was she going to be specific. "We worked in the same department before we got reassigned to this project. Seeing each other while we're both in training has been a real challenge."

"What exactly are you doing? Unless that's classified, of course."

"Basically I'll be providing additional surveillance on-site. Covering their butts," she added. She put her taco down and blew out a breath. "I'm already having nightmares about maybe missing something and one of them gets hurt." *Or worse.* But she didn't say that, because the reality of what could happen was something they lived with every day. Just like a military wife, or a cop's or fireman's wife, they knew that any day could be the day their man didn't come home.

Ailani glanced toward the kitchen. The condo had a fairly open design, so she could see almost all the guys. She watched them for a moment, her expression saying without words that she, too, had nightmares. "They're a tight-knit group; I imagine all the teams are, have to be. How are you fitting in?"

Jina made a face and rocked her hand back and forth. "They weren't happy to be saddled with the only woman," she said quietly, not wanting the guys to hear. "For my part sometimes I feel so choked on testosterone I want to run screaming down the road. Other than a checkout clerk or my mom, I think y'all may be the only women I've talked to in months. I've been training such long hours I haven't been able to make any time for my friends, and they've stopped asking. It's a wonder I'm sane."

Terisa chuckled at that, and her tone warmed a little. "And here I thought they'd be falling all over themselves making things easier for you."

That was so genuinely funny that Jina hooted. "They fall all over themselves *laughing* when I face-plant in the mud. And they don't help me up, either."

The doorbell rang again. Surprised, Jina started to set her food aside and lever herself up from the floor. Donnelly had just stepped out of the kitchen and he said, "I'll get it," winking at her as he went past. That was perfect, not only the wink, but him acting as kinda-host, as if he was accustomed to being here. She admired his sharpness. But who was doing the ringing now? She not only didn't think the kids had been all that loud, but she knew for certain her downstairs neighbors were out for the night; they were a young couple who went out with their friends every Saturday night. She began getting up, anyway, because whatever had come to her door was likely some problem she'd need to handle.

Donnelly opened the door and Levi stood there, rain glistening on his dark hair, his big frame filling the doorway. Jina had been enjoying herself—not ha-ha great time, but nice enough—but at the sight of him the bottom dropped out of her stomach and cold dread spilled in, crowding out pleasure. "Hey," Donnelly said, stepping back for Levi to enter, because of course he recognized him.

The room immediately felt suffocating and small, with Levi taking up all the space. He wore a battered brown leather jacket that was spattered with rain across his shoulders, faded jeans, and scarred boots, the first time she'd ever seen him in anything other than fatigue pants and T-shirts. Come to think of it, this was the first time she'd seen any of the guys—other than Donnelly—in civvies, but she hadn't really noticed with them. With Levi, she was sharply and unfortunately aware of everything.

Because it would look odd if she didn't speak to him, she said, "Hi. Thought you couldn't make it." Then she tilted up her water bottle and took a couple of swallows, unable to think of anything else to say.

"Turns out I could." His dark eyes were as expressionless as always. "Hi, ladies and munchkins." There was a chorus of welcomes.

"Plenty of food and beer in the kitchen," Donnelly said, his easy manner bridging what might have been an uncomfortable silence from her.

Levi shed his jacket, hung it on the hall tree beside the door, and followed Donnelly to the kitchen. As he passed by her Jina felt the weight of his gaze, but she didn't look up. What was he doing here? He'd made it plain he didn't want to associate with her in any social sense at all.

She couldn't think of any scenario that would have prompted him to show up, because the one thing she didn't expect from him was that he would change his mind. Not only that, even if he did, *she* hadn't changed hers. Even if she couldn't quite nail down exactly what he thought of her—not good enough? slutty? stupid?—she knew how she felt, and "angry" didn't begin to cover it. Even worse, she knew she'd have to suck it up and swallow that anger, because that was the only way she could continue on the team.

The seven- and eight-year-old boys finished their tacos and, being young boys, immediately started looking for something to do. They dashed into the kitchen, and in short order found the balcony, which was accessed through sliding doors in the kitchen, and cold damp air swept through the condo. Knowing exactly what had happened, Terisa called, "Marcus!"

"I'm on it," Boom said.

"I didn't know Boom's name was Marcus," Jina commented.

"I think I'm the only one who calls him that now."

The three smallest kids somehow knew something was afoot, and in a flash they were gone, leaving behind juice boxes and a few chicken nuggets. The two-year-old was amazingly fast, darting past Ailani's outstretched hand. "Eric!" Ailani called. "Catch him."

"On it!" Snake called.

Terisa and Ailani remained in their seats, taking their time with their meals. Ailani sent Jina a smile. "There are eight big men in there," she said, "and just five kids. They can handle it. We don't get the chance to hand the kids off all that often, so I'm staying right here."

The noise from the kitchen was just short of an uproar, with kids shrieking for some reason, and orders being barked in a distinctly military manner. Jina scooped up some guacamole and munched while she relished the relative quiet of her small living room. She had missed being with other women. With the guys she usually felt as if she had to act tough—okay, so she didn't actually do it, but she felt as if she should. But the training was so physically demanding that she had to make a big effort to do something simple like painting her toenails, and wearing makeup had gone by the wayside. All she wanted was fast and easy, and at the end of the day she was happy to just be relatively clean.

For tonight, she liked leaving her hair loose instead of pulling it back in either a braid or a ponytail, liked sitting and talking with people who didn't stink of sweat and dirt. Thinking that made her realize how much she missed her mom and sisters, all her family, and that turned her thoughts to the upcoming holidays. Thanksgiving was just a week away, and her mom had sounded annoyed during their last phone call when Jina couldn't give her a definite answer about going home.

"How are holidays handled?" she asked. "I just now realized none of the guys have said anything. Do they usually get to spend holidays at home?"

"Sometimes yes, sometimes no," Ailani replied. She settled back on the sofa, her face relaxing as the piercing shrieks from her youngest turned into giggles. "There's no way to plan because we can't predict what might happen that calls them away. It is what it is. During the summer vacation, I take the kids to Hawaii to see my folks, and that's a nice break from the heat and humidity here."

Jina laughed. "Hawaii? Yes, that's definitely what I'd call a nice break."

"Where's your home?" Terisa asked. "You're definitely southern."

There was no mistaking that, not with her accent. "South Georgia."

"Are you going home for Thanksgiving? This will likely be your last chance for a while, because you'll finish training soon and then heaven only knows where you'll be."

Evidently Boom had told Terisa that jump training was her last phase, and then she'd join the team full-time, which was more than any of them had told *her*.

"She can't go home until she finishes jump training," said Levi from the kitchen, proving that he was keeping track of conversation in both rooms.

"You won't be doing training on Thanksgiving," Terisa retorted, raising her voice to make sure he heard her. "Marcus won't, anyway."

There was a rumble of laughter from the kitchen. "Guess you got your orders," Voodoo said.

"No argument from me. I like Thanksgiving." Boom stuck his head around the corner and winked at his wife.

"I like this," Ailani announced out of the blue. "Us in the living room, and the men in the kitchen. Usually it's the other way around. I could get used to this." She settled back against the cushion with a blissful smile on her face. "After dealing with clients, some days the last thing I want to do is see another kitchen."

"We need to schedule some regular breaks for you two," Jina said. "It's a win-win. Everyone comes here, y'all can rest, and I get to be with women. I miss my family." She tried to keep her tone neutral, but all of a sudden she did miss them so much she ached. Getting away from them was good, that was why she'd moved to the D.C. area to begin with, but she hadn't seen any of them in months and months and that was way too long. If she could go home at Thanksgiving, she was going, even if it was for just that one day.

When she got up to cut the cake, the kids all came running. "I want the tongue!" Boom's son—his name was Matthew—shouted, and Levi said drily, "Son, don't we all."

Everyone except Jina laughed, but Levi joking around was almost more than she could take. She was tolerating him being here, but that didn't mean she was comfortable with it. After flaying her with words, here he was eating her food and destroying the peace of being in her own space. She didn't want him here, didn't want to be able to picture him standing in her kitchen.

"I think I can cut it so all of you get a piece of the mouth," she told the kids, and did just that, making a circle in the middle of the cake and then doing some artful cutting that allowed each kid some of the red frosting. Snake stepped in and took the small plate for his toddler, who set up a bellow of rebellion. Over the noise he said, "Sit in my lap, buddy, and I'll help you eat the tongue cake, okay?"

"No! No! Mine!"

He scooped the struggling, protesting kid up under his arm. "It's yours, I'm not going to eat it, I'm just going to help you. Now settle down." The last three words were said sharply enough that the rebellion subsided to a quivering chin and damp eyes, which changed to contentment as soon as the first bite of cake was in his mouth.

It was amusing watching Snake deal with his little hellion, but it did make Jina think twice about wanting kids sometime in the amorphous future. Now, if she could be assured her kids would all be cute charmers like Mia, that would be different. Not that she had to worry about kids now, with not even a hint of a romantic relationship anywhere in her life.

The whole cake soon disappeared; she felt lucky to be able to serve some of it to Terisa and Ailani and grab the last small slice for herself and retreat to the living room. The rest of the evening went pretty much the same way, with the men grouped in the kitchen with the kids running around. Deep voices rumbled, bursts of laughter came and went, but with the kids around there were limits to the raunchiness they could descend to. The women were content to sit in the living room and chat. When Mia sought out Terisa, climbed into her lap, and promptly went to sleep, Jina took that as a sign that the families would generally have an early departure time. She had no idea what time the single guys were thinking about leaving, but she didn't mind shooing them out. She'd fed them, she had given them beer; her social obligations had been met.

There wasn't much food left to put away, but she got up and took care of that chore. Ailani and Terisa of course offered to help clean the kitchen, but Jina refused them with a smile. "There isn't much to clean, just some spoons and such. I worship at the altar of disposable plates and cups."

"Amen, sister. I'm trying to remember the last time I ate on a real plate," Terisa said.

Snake came in with the wild child asleep on his shoulder. "We should get these kids in bed," he said. "Thanks for having us over, Babe." He paused. "Where did you get that cake? Brody wants a 'tongue cake' for his birthday."

"I made it."

"Liar."

"Am not. I can make cakes, and my mom taught me how to decorate them."

He turned and raised his voice so he could be heard in the kitchen. "Hey, guys, Babe made the cake!"

She saw right away where that was going. "Doesn't matter," she said. "I'm not baking cakes for y'all. Just not."

"Aw, come on."

"Feeding the bunch of you is not my job. I didn't take you to raise."

They left kind of in a group, a few of the guys still trying to talk her into baking for them. Levi wasn't one of them. She had no idea why he'd come, unless he was just looking for free food and hanging with the other guys. He went out without looking at her or saying good-bye, which was fine with her. Donnelly stayed behind, which was also fine; that's what a boyfriend would do.

"Thanks for coming," Jina said as she began loading the few dishes into the dishwasher. "This was nice." Not great, but nice. He was a good guy to help her out the way he had.

"I enjoyed it. The guys are cool, aren't they? I'm looking forward to joining my team, though I wish Kodak had made an effort to work me into the team the way Ace has with you."

She snorted. "Even though they've worked my butt off, trying to get me in what they think is acceptable shape?"

He lounged against the cabinet beside the dishwasher, watching her work. "Yeah, even then. When you go on the first mission, you'll already be part of the team. You know them, and they know you. The rest of us will be going in cold, not knowing what to expect."

He paused. "Maybe you should send a memo to MacNamara that he should make integrated training par for the course."

"Maybe *you* should send the memo. Bring yourself to his attention."

Now it was Donnelly's turn to snort. "Yeah, right. Like I want him to notice me."

"Then why are you trying to throw me into the cage?"

He grinned at her, not the least abashed. "Better you than me, right?"

He hung around a few minutes more, making small talk, then yawned. "Sorry," he said sheepishly. "This program has turned me into one of those mutants who go to bed early."

Jina barely kept herself from yawning, too—and it was just nine o'clock. She saw Donnelly out and locked the door behind him.

Blowing out a breath, she surveyed the condo. Not much damage had been done; she'd have to stack the cushions on the floor in some corner to get them out of the way, but for the most part things were in fairly good shape. The parents had ridden herd on the kids and kept them pretty much under control. Nothing had been broken, a few things were out of place, and that was it. She'd been to parties with her friends that resulted in way more chaos.

She'd been straightening things for a few minutes when the doorbell rang. Muttering under her breath because Donnelly must have forgotten something and she was already out of the mood for company, she nevertheless took the time to check through the peephole.

Levi.

She stood frozen, her heart thundering in her chest. His effect on her was instantaneous, and maddening. What in hell did he want? A second later she decided she didn't care and left him standing out in the small foyer while she returned to her neatening. He could stand out there all night for all she cared.

The bell rang again. "I saw you check the peephole," he said, his deep voice barely muffled by the wood. "Open the door."

"Go away," she retorted. "I don't want to see you, I don't want to talk to you."

"Tough shit. I have something to say and it's going to get said tonight, even if I have to kick your door in."

"I'll have you arrested if you do."

"No, you won't, because that would screw with the team."

She knotted her fists and clenched her teeth, caught with the truth of that. Working as hard as she had to join the team had made the team a whole lot more important in reality than it had ever been in concept. The guys weren't just guys, they were teammates.

She unlocked the door and opened it, but kept her hand firmly on the doorknob and herself planted in the doorway, denying him entrance. If he really wanted in, she wasn't physically able to stop him, but she sure as hell wasn't going to *invite* him inside.

"What?" she demanded truculently, trying to ignore the almost overwhelming physical presence of him, man mixed with the scent of rain and the chill of a November night.

He looked down at her, dwarfing her with his height and muscularity, his mouth thin and his dark eyes with that flat expression. "I came to apologize."

"I don't accept your apology," she shot back. No way was what he'd said all right, and he couldn't make it right.

"Then don't. I waited in the parking lot to see if Donnelly left—"

"Stalkerish, much?" she muttered. "You could have sent me a text, so I could ignore you. I prefer that approach. Honest."

"What I said—it was true. I should have phrased it better, but it was true."

"Fine. You aren't good with the English language. I don't care. You can leave now."

When she started to close the door, he slapped his left hand out and stopped it. "You're going to listen," he growled, taking a step forward so she would have to tilt her head back if she wanted to look at his face.

She didn't. She kept her gaze straightforward, staring at his chest. He was so close she could feel the heat coming off his body, feel the fury and frustration almost boiling in him. A hard pulse was pounding in the hollow at the base of his throat, like a visible hammer.

He waited, but when she didn't say anything else, he inhaled, blew out the breath. "I left out an important piece of information."

"That you're an asshole? I already knew that." She couldn't relent, couldn't make herself retreat to a more civil position. She had never in her life been so angry and humiliated and, yes, hurt, and she hated feeling like that, she hated herself for being susceptible to him, hated him for knowing.

"It goes both ways." His tone was deep and as full of anger as she felt. "You need to know that. It goes both ways."

Then he turned around and left, his lithe stride taking him down two steps at once; he turned the corner of the landing and she couldn't see him anymore, though she stood there in the open door listening to his booted steps, the sound of the outer door opening and closing.

Numbly she closed her door and locked it, then slowly sank to the floor with her back against the door, staring sightlessly at nothing.

He could have gone forever without telling her that. She wished he had. Because nothing had changed, except now regret was added to the pain in her heart.

NINE

Jina picked herself up from the floor, both literally and figuratively; sitting there was accomplishing nothing and she needed to finish putting her space back in order. If she couldn't quite push him out of her mind, she could at least occupy herself by doing something useful.

Damn him, she thought yet again; that phrase seemed to come to mind a lot whenever she thought of Levi. Why hadn't he just kept his mouth shut? She'd been doing a good job of not letting herself acknowledge how attractive she found him; it was that good old survivor instinct of hers at work. Levi wasn't a man who would even be a comfortable casual date, much less anything more serious. She hated being so aware of him, hated the way her pulse rate shot up like fireworks whenever he was near, or when he spoke to her—even if he was barking an order. She could easily become obsessed with him, and she hated that kind of weakness so she hadn't let herself, hadn't let herself do a lot of things.

She hadn't let herself daydream about when she'd blistered her feet and he'd tended to them, or how he'd ordered the perfect boots for her feet. Well, why should she? She'd *paid* for the boots, it wasn't as if they were a gift. She felt silly for liking them because Levi was involved in getting them for her. The boots didn't mean he cared, regardless of what he said about "it going both ways." What he cared about was the team functioning as a well-oiled unit, all parts of it healthy and able to do the job. So she turned him on. Big deal. He wouldn't let that intrude on the team dynamics, and she agreed with him. That was why she'd kept herself to herself.

She hadn't let herself dream about him, hadn't let herself wonder about his taste or what it would be like to have that laser attention focused on *her*, hadn't let herself flirt, had been strictly business in her dealings with him.

That was what hurt. He'd slapped her down for no reason. Or maybe he thought she was weak, and he'd just been waiting for her to . . . what? Tackle him and ravish him?

Her cheeks burned with anger, because she *had* entertained a fleeting speculation about the size of his dick. How could she not? Once when he'd squatted down, the angle had been just right and she'd seen that big bulge and she was human, of course she'd enjoyed a brief fantasy. Evidently the fantasy hadn't been brief enough, because he must have seen something and it was her fault, because the other guys had also done some squatting and all sorts of other positions and not once had she checked out their packages. Just Levi's. Damn him.

Her thoughts kept circling back to the same path, the same words, and finally she was so annoyed with herself she went out on the balcony without a jacket, to stand in the dark and let the cold damp air chase the frustration out of her brain. Being cold and shivering refocused her thoughts in a hurry, and for some reason put things in perspective.

She didn't have to let this throw her. She'd carry on as usual, do her job, finish her training—*dear God, jumping out of a plane!*—and take her place on the team. She hadn't busted her butt all these months to blow it by boohooing over hurt feelings. So screw him. No matter how hateful he got, she wouldn't quit.

She slept well that night, despite him. Still, when her phone dinged with a text at five o'clock the next morning, she wished she could have gotten another couple of hours in bed.

Groaning, her heart pounding because what if something had happened to some of her family, she switched on the lamp and fumbled for the phone. "Ah, hell!" The text was from Levi, **ACE** showing big and bold in the screen. She rubbed her eyes, focused on the text, and suddenly who it was from didn't matter at all, because the text itself made time stop.

Weather cleared. Meet at training site 0800.

No! Oh God, no! Not today. Not on a Sunday. Sundays were off days, except for running. She'd expected to have more warning, so she could hunt down a sedative, or, failing that, somehow land herself in the hospital. God, if you're listening, joking not joking.

She got up and hit the shower, because if she died, she wanted to be clean, not that it would matter, because if she went splat, there wouldn't be enough of her left to tell if she'd been dirty or not. Still, the impulse was strong. Running water was supposed to be soothing. It failed on that count. After her shower she braided her hair, because long hair flying all over the place couldn't be good while arrowing toward Earth at a gazillion miles per hour.

She choked down half a slice of toast, smeared with peanut butter, though maybe an empty stomach would be a better idea. What if she threw up in midair? Would the vomit descend at the same rate, so she'd go the whole way down surrounded by her own puke? Bummer. On the other hand, if she didn't eat, her blood sugar might bottom out and that wouldn't be good, either. She drank just half a cup of coffee because she didn't want to pee on herself in midair, either.

Another dilemma presented itself. How was she supposed to dress for plunging to her death? A quick check of the weather confirmed that the sky was clear and the temperature was chilly, though it would warm up all the way to mildly pleasant by the middle of the afternoon. This wasn't a question she was going to text to any of the guys, because they'd never let her live it down. That was based on the assumption that she'd survive the day, so that thought was vaguely reassuring. In the end she put on some long silk underwear she'd bought her first winter in D.C., then dressed mostly as usual for a training day, in cargo pants, a sweatshirt, but sneakers instead of boots because her boots were speed-laced and jump boots weren't. She tried not to think of things the hooks on her boots could get hung on, during a jump. Finally she grabbed her North Face pull-on snow cap and thought she'd done the best she could.

Trying to focus on the pros and cons of being clean and well dressed while she was terrified out of her mind and might be dying soon didn't work very well as a means of distraction.

She arrived half an hour early and sat in the car with her head resting on the steering wheel, praying under her breath and wondering if she should call her mom, in case she never had another chance. No, because if she talked to her mom now, she might lose it and blurt out everything, about the GO-Team and the drone, which was way classified, and being forced to parachute, and that would be bad.

A tap on her driver's-side window made her shriek and jump and bump her knee hard on the steering column, which made her cuss.

Levi stood there, laughing. She hated him, hated the way his laugh lit up his face, white teeth flashing, dark eyes crinkled at the corners. How dare he laugh, after everything? She opened her car door and shoved it hard, banging it against his knee.

"Ow!" He moved out of range, leaning down to rub his knee and glare at her. "Watch what you're doing."

She returned the glare as she got out and slammed the door. "I did, and I enjoyed it very much, thank you. It was funny. You know, like when I banged my knee and you laughed."

For some reason he seemed to be in a good mood. The right side of his mouth quirked up in a half smile, and he said, "Fair enough." Maybe he was in a good mood because he thought today would be her swan song, and even if she survived, she might say she was done.

As if she would give him the satisfaction. She might die, but she wouldn't quit.

Boom arrived in his big king-cab pickup and interrupted whatever might have followed, whether it would have been an argument or stony silence. Could have gone either way.

Levi said, "We're riding with Boom," and strode toward the truck. Jina trudged along behind him, not willing to trot to keep up with those long strides. She walked differently these days, using longer, more efficient strides herself, but no way could she keep up with someone who was six-four. He should have stopped growing at a reasonable height. Damn him.

She didn't even like the way he breathed.

He got in front with Boom, and she boosted herself into the backseat. Boom's truck wasn't as high as Levi's, maybe because he had a wife and two kids who also rode in the truck, but these days she wouldn't have had any problem, anyway. *Legs of steel*, she thought triumphantly, and although that was an exaggeration, she was in the best shape of her life. Maybe the legs of steel had enough coil and strength to them to keep her from breaking her neck when she landed. Or maybe she could use them to kick Levi out of the plane.

"I like your truck," she chirped to Boom, knowing her tone would irritate the shit out of Levi, and maybe Boom, too, but Levi was her target and Boom would have to be collateral damage. "It doesn't look like a pouty Darth Vader owns it."

Pouty. Boom coughed to disguise what was likely a laugh, and Levi slowly swiveled his head to give her a basilisk stare. She gave him a sweet, very insincere smile. This was fun. For a few seconds she could forget that her knees were knocking together.

The landing strip Boom drove to was in rural Virginia, surrounded by farmland. The strip wasn't busy, not this early, though a few planes were tied down beside a large, rusty Quonset hut with a rough but serviceable wooden addition jutting out to the left. Two other vehicles were there, but no one was in sight. A Twin Otter sat on the strip, and a fit-looking guy in jeans and a leather jacket was slowly going around the plane, examining every exterior detail.

Just a few months ago she'd have thought a Twin Otter was a pair of cute critters, but now she not only recognized it, she knew it was considered one of the best planes for jumping. Yay for her. If only her test was on paper instead of practical experience, she'd ace the damn thing.

"I rigged the chutes myself," Boom said to Levi. "Most I've ever done at one time."

"We'll probably need them all," Levi replied.

Meaning they were going to keep at it until she either made a jump or died? Probably. Surely they wouldn't have time for more than two or three jumps . . . would they? She was the only trainee, though, and they were the only jumpers on the plane. They'd be limited by the time it would take the plane to take off, climb to altitude, then land again, plus however much time it took to pick them up from the landing zone. Her heartbeat kicked into another gear, hard and fast. They were really going to do this.

"Where's the landing zone?" she asked, hoping it was miles away because that would slow everything down.

"Next field over," Levi said, jerking a thumb to the right. "I would've made it here, but there'll be other planes landing and taking off. I've arranged for us to be picked up."

Of course he had. Why couldn't they just wait in the field until the plane landed and he could pick them up? That would have killed some time. But no, Levi had to be efficient, so they could get in more torture sessions.

Frantically she pulled up the memory of zip lining. Her stomach had been in her throat then, too; stepping off into nothing and trusting the line to hold her had required all her nerve and gumption, but once she'd taken that first step everything had been okay. Maybe this would be like that. The guys had said it was, though they could have been lying. Maybe she'd automatically focus on what she was doing rather than what was happening. Maybe it would be okay.

The sky was a big blue bowl, completely cloudless, as if trying to make up for the days of rain. Too bad, because she had really prayed hard for that rain to continue for the next year or so. There was a chilly breeze, but nothing that would interfere so there was no help on that front. The weather was not cooperating. Jina forced herself to take slow, steady breaths, trying to slow her heartbeat. The air smelled fresh and crisp, tinged with the smell of fuel. A few birds were calling back and forth, not the mad singing they did in spring but a kind of desultory "we're here" notice.

Boom got the harnesses from the back of his truck and Jina began gearing up. She was concentrating on getting the straps straight and in the right place, so it took her a minute to realize Levi, not Boom, was putting on the other harness. She stopped. "I thought Boom was jumping with me."

"I'm not certified for tandem jumps," Boom replied. "Ace is."

"Oh, shit," she said, so dismayed that she said it aloud.

"Got a problem with it?" Levi asked, his tone hard.

"Well, I *do* trust Boom not to cut me loose in midair if I vomit on him." Oh Lord, she was going to be harnessed to Levi. She didn't want to be even this close to him, much less strapped so closely to him they'd essentially be spooning.

Boom snorted a laugh, and even Levi gave a quick grin. "You won't vomit," he said, and it was as much of a command as it was a reassurance.

She pulled on her knit hat and Boom said, "That won't stay on."

Sighing, she tucked it back into her pocket and instead stuffed the thick braid of her hair down the back of her sweatshirt.

"Why won't it stay on?"

"Because we'll be going a hundred and twenty miles an hour when we leave the plane," Levi said.

She blanched and tried not to think about it. Her heart started that pounding again. Was it possible to die from fright? She might not have to go splat; Levi might flare his parachute for a perfect landing with a corpse strapped to his chest.

The idea was ghoulish enough that she felt a bit comforted, and the panic subsided. With luck, the experience would scar Levi so much he'd never be able to jump again. Would that be justice, or what?

She was kind of in a daze as they boarded the plane and the two engines coughed to life. The Twin Otter was roomier on the inside than she'd expected: benches lined each side, and she slid onto one of them, buckled herself in. Boom closed the door, and he and Levi took their seats. Levi was right beside her, so close his left leg was touching hers. Silently she shifted her legs away from him.

The pilot, who Boom had introduced as Air Bud because his nickname really was Bud, released the brakes, the engine noise changed, and the plane began moving. The copilot was Bud's wife, a jumpsuit-wearing redhead with a broad grin and a lot of freckles. Jina wanted to go forward and commiserate with her about what jerks men were, but Boom wasn't a jerk and she didn't know about Bud so she clenched her hands on the edge of the bench and stayed where she was.

The plane lifted away from the earth and began a steady climb. Levi got to his feet and he and Boom began making preparations that Jina didn't watch. She was too busy trying to catch regular breaths and talk her stomach down out of her throat. Her mouth was dry, her legs trembling. She didn't have to watch to know when the door was opened, because cold air rushed through the cabin.

She had dreaded a lot about all the training stuff, but she hadn't been actively frightened. Now she was. No, "frightened" was too mild a word; she was terrified, and it wasn't something she could talk herself out of.

Then Levi sat down beside her again, tapped her on top of the head, and said, "Time."

Mutely she looked up at him, the details of what she was supposed to do lost somewhere in the fog of silent panic. He waited, but no matter how frantically she searched her brain, no details surfaced. She was here. She was about to be forced out of the plane. Nothing else came to mind.

An unreadable expression flickered across his face. Silently he scooped her up and sat her on his lap, her back to him, her legs straddling his.

Whoa!

Jina jerked, as shocked as if he'd thrown water in her face. Physical sensations rushed in—the heat and hardness of his body against her back and under her butt and thighs, his breath on her hair—all of it tangling with fear and numbness and throwing everything off-kilter because no one component fit with any of the others. What the hell was he *doing?* And right in front of Boom!

Clumsily, none of her muscles working in coordination, she tried to shove herself off his lap. He grunted and clamped his right arm around her hips and hauled her back down. "Be still," he growled. "This is the easiest way to get us harnessed together."

Harnessed . . . together. Right.

Shaking, breathing hard, she tried to relax as he fastened their harnesses together in four places, on each hip and each shoulder. She was pulled back snugly against the muscled wall of his chest. Glancing down, she saw his spread legs between hers, which spread *her* legs that much wider. The visual was another shock to her system, sharpening her awareness of him to the point of near pain.

"I'll be handling everything," he said in her ear. "You're just along for the ride, though after we're under canopy, you can take the toggles and steer us to the LZ. Remember, tuck your head back into my shoulder and curl your legs upward between mine. Got it?"

He was telling her things she'd already gone over during the ground training, but the repetition was good because she wasn't able to think. She had never been so scared in her life, and the dread was getting worse, not better. Maybe the actual jump out of the plane was the worst, like the guys said, and once she was in the air everything would get better.

Or maybe her heart would explode from the terror. That seemed more likely.

"We'll free-fall for about a minute. It's like floating, you'll have no sense of speed other than the wind. When we get to twenty-five hundred feet, I'll pop the chute. It'll jerk like hell when it opens, pull us up and back, so don't panic. I'll ease the straps so it's more comfortable for you. Then it's an easy ride down."

Don't panic? Was it possible to panic more once one was already panicked? Like a re-panic, or a double layer of panic?

"Goggles."

A pair dangled in front of her, and she put them on. Goggles. So it was really about to happen.

"You'll do fine," Boom said reassuringly. "Ace has you." Then the traitor helped Levi shift with her over to the open door. Lips trembling, she looked up at Boom and started to say something, maybe even beg him to help her, but before she could make a sound, Levi heaved them through the open door of the plane—

Plunging into hell.

Face-first.

Jina jerked and stiffened, instantly engulfed in a screaming wind, her head forced back against Levi's shoulder while her eyes rolled wildly around so that the brown and green of the earth flipped sick-

eningly with the merciless blue bowl of the sky. She was screaming, too, along with the wind, deep hoarse screams that scraped her
throat raw. It was all too much, worse than she'd expected, more
than she could handle. The fear she'd been halfway controlling
seemed to explode inside her, a great black force that blew out of her
chest and expanded in a split second to swallow her whole, and she
fell into the black.

"Jina! Babe! Wake the fuck up!"

The black didn't want to give her up. She didn't want it to give
her up, she wanted to stay right there, insensate and safe. She slowly
resurfaced to the distant sound of Levi bellowing the command to
wake up at her. The sound got closer and closer as consciousness
returned, and she opened her eyes to stare dazedly around. Her
head bobbled to the side, but she was able to catch herself, and
she realized they were still in the air, still going down. She jerked
again, pushing herself back against him as if she could force herself
through his body, anything to put distance between her and the approaching ground.

"It's okay, we're under canopy, we aren't falling."

He kept repeating that, the words meaningless at first, but after a
few times they began making sense and she tilted her head back to
stare at the huge white mushroom blooming overhead. The movement moved her head against Levi's chest and she saw the underside
of his chin, his strong jaw, deeply tanned and bristled because he
hadn't shaved that morning. Odd how that seemed so obvious, and
why she noticed at all, when she felt so sick. Her heart was slamming against her rib cage with such force she could feel her bones
vibrating and she thought she might vomit after all. The fear seemed
to come in uncontrollable waves, barely giving her time to catch a
breath before she was swamped again. A high-pitched keen of dis-
tress vibrated in her throat.

"Babe. You're all right." His deep voice was right beside her ear, so close she could feel his breath in her hair. "Here, take the toggles."

"*No!*" She thrashed her head back and forth, shrinking from the suggestion. The toggles represented this whole experience, and it was as bad as she'd feared it would be. It was awful. She'd never passed out before, but now she felt as if she might faint again, and she didn't care what Levi thought or if this got her booted out of training. All she wanted was to be on the ground, and all in one piece. Normally her determination would carry her through a sticky situation, but this wasn't just sticky, it was horrifying beyond her imagining. She'd felt the same way about bungee jumping—not going to do it, no way, no how.

"All right, all right, you don't have to." That rough voice was oddly soothing. Maybe he thought he could afford to be kind now that she was very likely out of the program.

Strange how now that they were actually floating instead of plummeting, she could tell they were moving, going down. At least she was upright instead of facedown, staring at her death. She could look out at the horizon—but she didn't, because what was below her had her in an unholy grip. To escape it she closed her eyes, not wanting to see the ground getting closer and closer; her whole body felt limp, her muscle tone gone, and despite herself she let her head fall back against his shoulder again. Oh dear God, she was held in place by four buckles. Four. *Levi* was the one who wore the parachute harness, not her. If the buckles failed, or the straps broke, she was gone.

"When I tell you, lift your legs straight out so they aren't in my way when we land," he said. That kind note was still in his tone. She hated him for being nice in the face of her failure. If he'd been this way from the beginning—no, it was probably better that he hadn't. She didn't want to like him at all.

She forced her eyes open, because it seemed cowardly not to. The minutes crawled, but at the same time the ground was coming up way too fast. Her breath began hitching in her throat again, and her heartbeat was so fast she was essentially limp in the harness. Details on the ground began to take on sharp clarity, individual leaves on the trees swam into focus, and Levi said, "Legs up!" in that bark of command she was more accustomed to.

Her body obeyed, as she had obeyed so many of his orders. Her thigh muscles shook, but she lifted her legs so she was in an L shape.

It was like seeing her car was about to crash but being unable to stop it. The ground was rushing toward them now, a blurred impression of the black asphalt road, the brown grass, a red cross painted on the ground to make the LZ. A jolt shook her in the harness as Levi touched down, his powerful legs absorbing most of the shock. He made a couple of running steps, then stopped as casually as if falling thousands of feet through the air was an everyday occurrence, and began unhooking them. She was so numb she couldn't quite absorb that they were on the ground, safe, without any broken bones or anything. She hadn't smashed herself into red mist.

The harness latches released, and she began dropping, sliding down his body; he caught her, one steely arm around her waist, and said, "Put your feet down now."

Okay, she thought, everything feeling distant, even herself, as if her mind had disconnected from her body. Still, she put her feet down and he bent down enough to stand her on the ground, then immediately turned around to begin gathering in the canopy.

Jina sat down. She didn't have any choice about it because her legs folded like noodles, but at least she sat instead of collapsing full-length. The chill damp of the ground soaked into her pants, and in the length of time it took Levi to gather and secure the canopy she began shivering. *Wet ground was soft*, she thought, *and soft ground was good.*

She pulled off her goggles and drew her knees up so she could rest her forehead on them and close her eyes. Shutting out the world was a relief; if she could have deafened herself, she would have, to create a total cocoon, but she couldn't and sound still intruded. She could hear Levi talking—at first she thought he was talking to himself, then realized he was on a headset talking to Boom. Likely they'd been in communication the whole humiliating, terrifying time. Boom knew how pathetically she'd failed.

She didn't care. For once in her life, she didn't care that she hadn't been able to make herself handle what was in front of her. Parachuting was going to be her Waterloo, because she couldn't make herself go through that again.

I have to.

The inner whisper came up from her depths. She tried to push the words away, because there had never been anything she'd run into before that had so terrified her beyond functioning. Sure, she'd been scared before, she'd hit obstacles before that she hadn't thought she could get over, but she'd kept at it with dogged persistence that maybe went beyond the bounds of good sense. This was different. This was fear on a primal level she hadn't experienced before. This almost reached the level of *I'd rather slit my wrists than do that again.*

But even below that at the cellular level was something that made her take a deep breath and face the awful truth.

She had to.

She heard Levi's footsteps come closer, felt him looming over her, blotting out the faint warmth of the sun and leaving her even more chilled, there on the wet ground.

Forcing her lungs to pull in enough air to speak, she raised her colorless face from her knees and looked up at the big man who stood looking down at her. "Let's go again," she said.

TEN

Levi squatted down in front of her, his powerful thighs stretching the fabric of his cargo pants, those dark eyes boring into her as if he wanted to pin her to a board like he was some bug collector and she was the bug. "You fainted." Accusation number one; she knew there were more coming.

And she hated the way he said that. "Fainted" sounded so much more wussy than "passed out." She put her cheek down on her knees again, picked up a small stick, and scraped at the winter-dead grass with it. "I won't again."

"Really? How you gonna stop it?" He sounded derisive.

"Same way fighter pilots do, I guess—grunt and stuff like that." She was kind of vague on the procedure, but she could look up the details on the Internet. She knew there was grunting involved.

"They grunt to force oxygen to their brains. Lack of oxygen isn't your problem."

No, sheer terror was. She didn't know if she could grunt long enough and deep enough to overcome that, though maybe if she focused intensely on the grunting she wouldn't pay attention to being in midair and falling at a hundred and twenty miles an hour, with the possibility of both the main chute and the reserve malfunctioning, in which case she and Levi would die together, and the equal possibility that he'd undo the harness buckles and let her drop. Yeah, she had to stop thinking about that last one.

"You screamed, too." Accusation number two.

Had she? Oh, yeah, she kind of remembered screaming as if she were being dismembered. Dang. There was no denying it; she hunched a shoulder as if to say *So what?* and kept her mouth shut.

"You didn't tell us you're afraid of heights." Accusation number three.

Annoyed, which was nice because it meant she was feeling something other than terror and humiliation and the even-worse fear of failure, she lifted her head and glared at him. "I'm not afraid of heights, I'm afraid of falling to my death. Big difference."

His mouth quirked again in the way she couldn't tell if it was a smile or a smirk. Going with "smirk" was a safer bet, because generally Levi didn't smile at her. She both wished he would and wished he wouldn't. Nothing was simple where Levi was concerned.

"Your ass is getting wet sitting on the ground."

Was that an accusation, or an observation? Maybe both. "There's no 'getting' to it, it got wet right away."

"Is this your way of hiding that you pissed your pants?"

Not as outraged as she normally would have been, she still mustered the spirit to shoot out a foot and kick his boot. "I passed out. I didn't pee my pants, and neither did I vomit! So there!"

He laughed and effortlessly rose to his feet, extending a big hand down to her. "Come on, here comes our ride."

She didn't need his help getting up. Even though she felt shaky and weak and numb and grateful all at once—the grateful was because he'd made her mad with the last comment and she had so needed that relief—she tucked her left foot under her, pushed up with her right, got her left leg under her to balance her weight, and stood without aid. Back at the beginning she'd practiced that move over and over because she'd seen how easily the guys got up from the ground, not holding on to anything, just getting their feet under them and standing. Part of it was just technique, but the rest was pure muscle tone—and now she had that muscle tone. What she didn't have was nerves of steel, as witnessed by the last ten hours.

Just to check, she pulled out her phone and looked at the time. Crap, barely half an hour had passed since the Twin Otter had lifted off the runway. It *felt* like ten hours. Maybe part of hell was that the time seemed to pass so slowly, in which case she knew that hell involved both Levi and parachutes.

A pickup truck pulled up to the LZ and she straightened her spine. *She had to do this.* She had to ignore the nausea in the pit of her stomach, and the way her heart had started that sickening *pound-pound-pound* again, because the only other option was unthinkable. Silently she followed Levi, every movement so weighted with reluctance that her legs felt as if they weighed a hundred pounds each.

There was something genetically wrong with men, she thought as she watched Levi striding in front of her, every inch of his big body infused with confidence. It likely never occurred to him to be petrified at the thought of parachuting; it would have been just one more skill to acquire to make him as self-sufficient and lethal as possible. Sometimes jumping out of a plane would be the best way to get to his target; therefore, he would jump out of a plane. She'd seen him practice his hand-to-hand skills, practice live-ammo shooting, push his body to what seemed like superhuman lengths. He dedicated himself to being as well trained and prepared as possible.

All the team members trained constantly, so they'd be ready for whatever mission came their way. Sometimes it was nothing more action filled than surveillance or intelligence gathering, but they trained at that with as much dedication as they did everything else.

She too had devoted herself to the training. What she did with Tweety the drone would help keep them alive when they were in dangerous situations, as well as doing some of the normal surveillance missions. But she got the sense that during a mission the guys would push themselves to and past the point of death, kind of like racehorses. She'd read that stallions would run themselves to death in a race, but mares wouldn't, that they had the good sense to stop before they reached self-destruction.

The revelation exploded in her brain. *That was it!* She was a mare, and Levi was a stallion. He'd willingly jump out of a plane, and she had better sense.

She felt much better about herself now—except for the fact that she had to forget she had good sense and jump out of a plane like the stupid stallions did.

They climbed into the pickup and the driver took them back to the airstrip. The Otter had just landed and was maneuvering back into position for takeoff again. The bottom dropped out of her stomach, just watching it. *Pound-pound-pound.* Was it possible for her heart to beat so hard it bruised itself against her sternum? Icy sweat drenched her. Could Levi smell her fear? Could he tell how utterly helpless she felt, or was she somehow projecting a can-do façade that kept him from seeing the truth?

The Otter swung around, propellers a blur, and she saw Boom crouching in the open door; even from where they were she could tell his expression was grim. Maybe he'd expected her performance to be better, after his tutelage. She squirmed inwardly, because she hated being a disappointment to anyone, especially to someone she liked as much as she liked him.

She approached the plane with her head down. Ahead of her, Levi effortlessly vaulted into the plane. Boom leaned down and extended his hand; she took it and he pulled her up. Levi gave her a long, cool look and she remembered how she'd declined to take his hand. Well, tough. It would take a long time before she forgot how nastily he'd declined her invitation, and showing up anyway didn't make her feel any better about him. Neither did anything about the current situation.

"I passed out," she mumbled.

"I heard." Boom shook his head. "You should have said you're afraid of heights."

She didn't feel like going into the difference between being afraid of heights and being afraid of falling, so she just shrugged. "I can do this." Even to herself her voice sounded weak, kind of like a sickly frog, more raspy than usual. Maybe that was from all the screaming.

"Let's get this over with," Levi said and closed the door with a loud *thunk*.

Meaning it was her last chance? It couldn't be. Boom said he'd packed more parachutes for today than he ever had before, so just two attempts wouldn't use up the supply. She didn't know which was most terrifying, the thought of having to do this whole thing again, or Levi tossing her out of training.

Realistically, what would happen if she crapped out of training? She'd go back to her old job and earn good money, though not as great as what she was currently pulling down. She'd get her weekends back. She'd be able to go to movies again, and hang with her friends, and see her family on a regular basis.

And she'd be a failure.

Jina began shaking as she slid onto a bench and strapped herself in.

Once again Levi took the seat beside her. His scent had changed, he had a more outdoorsy smell now, like cold fresh air. Guess that was appropriate, given that they'd just fallen through a couple of miles of fresh air. He seemed invigorated by it, his energy level up so far electricity was practically snapping around him. His big gloved hands rested on his thighs, relaxed despite the situation. Maybe he was happy. Maybe he was looking forward to this.

She felt nauseated; hot moisture pooled in her mouth, forced her to swallow.

All too soon, they were in the air again.

Pound-pound-pound. Her own heartbeat was loud in her ears, the force of it vibrating through her body. She couldn't breathe; her chest seemed to have tightened, preventing her lungs from expanding. Was she hyperventilating, or suffocating? How could she tell the difference, and did it matter anyway?

"Time," Levi said.

What? No! They'd just taken off. They couldn't be more than a couple of hundred feet—except when Boom opened the door she saw the earth far below.

Why couldn't there be a group of them jumping? Maybe if she saw other people doing it before her turn, she wouldn't be so terrified? Not only that, there would be a delay before her turn. But, realistically, even if there were a thousand people who jumped before she did, she'd still be as terrified. Watching other people do it wouldn't help at all.

"Come on, let's get hooked up," he said, giving her thigh a light slap.

The bottom dropped out of her stomach. Resentment burned in her, that *now* he said something that could be construed as flirtatious, *now* he was treating her more like a team member than a team intruder. He must be confident she wouldn't make the cut, that she was going to crap out, and the prospect of getting rid of her put him in a good mood.

She'd like to twist his dick off.

And throw it out of the damn plane, a dick without a parachute, and see if he'd dive out after it.

Of course he would. Men would march through hell for their dicks. But wouldn't it be funny if a hawk or something caught the falling dick and carried it off to be eaten?

She was so distracted by thinking of the adventures of the flying dick that she didn't move despite his prompt. Should she be ashamed she was thinking of mutilating him? It was just that the part of her that wasn't terrified was so angry at him for everything, for the situation, for being who and what he was, for denying her

attraction to him for months now and throwing it in her face anyway so all that effort had been for nothing. Anger and terror didn't
make a good mixture, leaving her nauseated and exhausted.

Levi's patience lasted a few seconds, then he hauled her in front
of him with her straddling his legs like before and hooked their
harnesses together. The heat of his body warmed her butt and legs,
banishing the wet chill from sitting on the ground. Jina catapulted
from thinking of dismemberment to wanting to lie back against that
hard hot strength and let him cradle her while she rested. She was
so tired, so scared, and so damn tired of being so damn scared.

He began moving them toward the open door. Jina stiffened,
planting her feet against the floor and pushing back against him, even
though she knew resistance at best would gain her only a few seconds.

"Just trust me," he said in her ear, his tone rough and low. "I won't
let anything happen to you."

She tilted her head back and looked up at him. His dark gaze
bored into her, intense and . . . something else that she couldn't read.
Trust him. She wanted to. She wanted a lot of things where Levi
was concerned, and she was suddenly crushed under an avalanche
of half-formed thoughts and wants and needs that sent her mind
spinning. Before she could process any of it, he muscled them out of
the plane and into nothing.

It was worse than the first time.

The wind tore at her. She knew she was screaming because she
could feel the strain in her throat. She tried to take a deep breath,
tried to control the terror that had exploded through every cell in
her body the moment Levi took them out of the plane, tried to stop
screaming. She tried to orient herself, to make sense of sky and
earth. She could hear Levi yelling at her but couldn't tell what he
was saying, not that it mattered, because her body had overruled her
mind and, screw reason, was in a battle for survival.

She fought him. She fought him with everything she had, her

lizard brain telling her that he was the cause of her terror, her impending death, and logic had nothing to do with it. So what if he was the one with the parachute strapped to his back? She fought him anyway, tangling her legs with his, trying to flip him, trying to get *away*. That was all she wanted, just away, away from this horror of an experience and the complete lack of control. The pressure in her chest was enormous, crushing her, and she was too far gone to tell it was his arms wrapped around her trying to control her struggles. With his arms down instead of spread for wind resistance they were an arrow plummeting earthward, a bird without wings, without guidance, without control.

An eternity later, exhausted, her body simply gave up and she went limp. Only then did she dimly realize that he had her wrapped up, legs and arms clamped and controlled by his steely limbs. She sucked in a shuddering breath just as they were jerked violently upward. The straps of her harness dug painfully into the jointure of her thighs, and across her breasts. The universe swung sickeningly and then settled into proper position, with earth below and sky above, and instead of falling at full speed they were now swaying under the billowing canopy.

"We're off course to the north," she heard Levi say tersely. "I don't have the altitude to correct. If I try for the LZ, we'll go in the river. There's a field just to the east of the country road, we'll land there."

What was she supposed to say? It wasn't as if she had a choice in any of this. Then he said, "I'll radio our exact position," and she realized he was talking to Boom.

Everything felt very distant, as if she had disconnected, and Jina realized she had crossed an invisible boundary between terror and numbness. Some people might look around and enjoy the view from their altitude, but she had no interest in the view other than noting the ground seemed closer than it had the first time they'd gone under canopy.

Silently Levi reached across her chest and loosened the strap with a quick, economical movement, easing the pressure and giving her more comfort in the harness. The backs of his fingers unavoidably brushed against her breast, and she couldn't work up any kind of reaction, good or bad. He wasn't copping a feel, he was . . . he was taking care of her. Then she saw his gloved hands on the toggles, turning them away from a river that was on the left and toward a small overgrown brown field bordered on two sides by trees, the green of pines mingled with the bare leafless limbs of hardwoods. The field was coming up fast. Levi said, "Legs up," and obediently she lifted her legs a couple of seconds before they were on the ground.

It was a rough field, not a clear, level landing zone. They went down, with Levi twisting them to the side so he didn't land on top of her. Weeds scraped her face, hidden rocks and lumps and sticks dug into her side. So what? They were on the ground. The condition of that ground didn't matter, so never mind the boggy smell and the dampness soaking into her clothes.

He said, "Are you hurt?"

Mutely she shook her head, and pulled off her goggles, let them drop. He unhooked their harnesses and said, "We're down, A-okay." He rattled off some instructions and distances, then removed his headset and goggles and laid them to the side with her goggles. She closed her eyes and rested, listening to him release the parachute straps and haul it in.

What now? She had failed again, miserably, even more miserably than the first time. She hadn't passed out, she'd fought him, which was worse because she could have killed them both. Nausea churned in her stomach, thinking of the possibilities, all of them bad. He'd kick her out of training now; he had to. Even if she could somehow convince him to give her another chance, she wasn't at all certain she'd live through another attempt. Even if she was doing a solo jump, at some point her heart would give out, had to, or she'd pass out again and though the automatic activation device would deploy the parachute if she was unconscious she wouldn't be able to steer it and she might slam into a tree or power lines or even come down on a road in front of a semi.

Tears burned against her closed lids and fiercely she banished them. He might tell her she was finished, but damn if she'd cry over it.

His big hand closed on her shoulder and rolled her onto her back. Her eyes flared open and she stared up at him, silhouetted against the pale blue sky. He was close, so close, leaning over her until there was barely a hand's width between their faces. His body heat seared her through their clothing, tempting her to roll closer, to cuddle against all that heat and strength and just for now let him be a buffer between her and the world. Her pupils expanded until all the amber ring that surrounded them was swallowed up, leaving only the blue outer edge; her heart rate, which had settled down, began pounding again.

"You could have killed us." His face was hard and fierce, no give in him at all.

"Ready to go again?" she asked in a thin, watery voice. She couldn't manage a smile, but she tried. "Maybe I can do it the next time."

"Which? Kill us, or make the jump?"

"I'll let it be a surprise," she fired back.

He glared down at her. "Fuck," he growled, then jerked her against him and kissed her.

A dam broke inside her.

For months Jina had buried her femininity, not letting any hint of flirting or sexuality intrude during the long, long hours and days of training. She hadn't traded on her lack of muscle, she'd concentrated on building some. She hadn't let the guys help her because she was a woman; she'd had to do it on her own for just that reason. For God's sake, she hadn't even worn *mascara* in so long the tube had probably dried out and needed to be thrown away. She hadn't worn a dress, or pretty shoes, or had her hair styled. She had made herself as sexless as possible, trying to fit in with the guys and not cause any disturbance in the team force.

Then Levi kissed her, and all those inner controls and barriers melted to nothing. The relief was overwhelming, everything in her giving way and reveling in the sense of womanhood that flooded through her. His mouth was everything she hadn't let herself think about, hot and male, his taste going to her head faster than wine on an empty stomach. Pushing him away never entered her mind; from the first moment she met him, something primal and powerful inside her had wanted him, wanted this moment, and from the center of her being she responded. She wound her arms around his shoulders, one hand sliding around the nape of his neck, and her mouth opened under his to give him what he demanded as well as making demands of her own. A little hum vibrated in her throat, a sound of pleasure and want and need, sending the call into his mouth.

He lifted his head and his gaze burned as it raked over her face. "Shit. Fuck. I shouldn't do this."

Now she thought about pushing him away, and maybe delivering a punch or two in the process. Damn him, he didn't get to jerk her back and forth like this. But in any physical contest he was going to win, unless he deliberately let her hit him, and where was the satisfaction in that? Instead she stretched a little, moving her body against him, and smiled a faint, ironic, and utterly beckoning smile. "Then don't. I'm sure you're strong enough to get away from me." As she spoke she burrowed her fingers under the hair at his nape and lightly stroked.

If anything his eyes got even hotter, more intent, and his gaze moved down her body. She didn't have to glance down to know her nipples were tight and fully erect, the points showing even under her sweatshirt. She could feel their tightness, and the way every breath she took rubbed them against the fabric.

A dull red flush darkened his cheekbones.

He lifted his gloved hand, clamped the tip of one finger in his teeth, and pulled the glove off. He let the glove drop out of his teeth onto her chest, then slipped his big hand under the band of her sweatshirt, moved up to clasp one small breast before sliding over to the other, then back. His rough palm rasped over her tender nipples, making her gasp, bite off a moan.

"From day one," he said roughly, and she knew what he meant. From day one, this had been between them. She'd tried to ignore it, stifle it, forget about it. Evidently he'd been fighting the same attraction. "If you weren't on the team, we could—" He broke off, shook his head. "You're too damn good with the drone. Having you there will give the team a layer of protection we didn't have before. I could have made things so tough for you that you couldn't make the cut, but that wouldn't be fair to either you or the other guys."

"That hasn't changed," she pointed out, her breath coming faster as he continued rubbing her nipples. She turned her head against his shoulder, inhaling the utter maleness of his scent, the warmth of his body heaven on her chilled skin. *Pound-pound-pound.* He had to feel her heart slamming against his palm, and she didn't care. Months of bruising herself against his hostility and coldness were abruptly washed away as if they'd never been.

Frustration darkened his face. "As long as you're on my team, this can't happen."

"Then get your hand out from under my shirt," she snapped, and kissed his throat.

A primal sound vibrated in his chest. In one rough movement he was on top of her, one muscled thigh pushing between her legs to spread them wide, then he took his place between them. His mouth crushed down on hers again, his tongue making forays that she welcomed with her own tongue. Why should she make things easy on him? He hadn't been easy on her. She wanted him to suffer a little, wanted him to think about what he wasn't getting. She welcomed him with her entire body, wrapping her legs around his hips and lifting her hips to cradle the hard ridge of his erection against her softness. A purely sexual pleasure speared through her, an effervescent joy that despite everything she was in his arms and he was in hers, that his hand was on her skin, and for these few stolen minutes there was nothing else.

She strained against him and his hips moved in rhythm as if there were no layers of clothing between them. He was so heavy despite bracing some of his weight on his arms, and she loved the pressure of him. Everything spun away; the fact that they were lying in a wet field of weeds, that their ride was on the way and would soon arrive, that the only way they could be together was if she failed in the training and despite herself she would try again, try her best *not* to fail. For now there was just *this*, the hard jut of his penis against her just where it needed to be, the fast spiraling lash of pleasure that started between her legs and spread upward, hot and liquid and so intense she moaned.

Briefly she tried to control her surging response but just as quickly surrendered to it because she wanted this moment, this pleasure. She came, driven by months of denial, of being painfully aware of him and having to keep it all under a lid nailed down so securely none of the other guys had any hint of it. *He* had known, though, maybe by animal instinct, and now like any predator he was moving fast on his prey. That was how she felt, like his prey, at his mercy, and she turned the tables on him by giving him all her sensuality, her femaleness, the wildness and completion of her response. She cried out, her voice hoarse from screaming, and dug her nails into his neck.

He swore viciously under his breath but cupped her ass in both hands and lifted her, grinding her, giving her more pressure, more pleasure, riding her through it.

She knew what he wanted. He wanted to strip her pants off and get inside her right there in that wet, muddy field, uncaring whether or not their privacy could be interrupted at any minute. She knew because that was what she wanted, with a degree of sexual madness she'd never before experienced.

And she wanted more—more Levi, more time, more of his companionship, his touch, his taste, more everything. The hunger she felt couldn't be satisfied by occasional stolen moments; she wasn't built that way, to be content with a clandestine relationship.

He rolled off her, breathing hard and scowling at the sky. Helplessly she stared at him, devouring every detail of his features, the strong bone structure of his lean face, the level dark brows, the curve of his mouth. He was a breathtaking man, not because he was handsome but because he was so damn masculine he practically oozed testosterone. When she thought the word "warrior," he was the image she saw, muscled and lethal. He would look as natural with a sword strapped to his back as with a rifle slung over his shoulder. Civilization was a light cloak that he could throw off as needed; he was one of the rough men, as were all the men on the GO-Teams, ready to do whatever needed doing.

She wanted to reach out and touch him, but despite what had just happened between them, she felt constrained. Their make-out session hadn't changed anything. He was still the leader of the team, and he'd do whatever was necessary for their operational stability because their very lives depended on it. Her job was to safeguard them as much as possible, to provide an extra set of eyes looking for trouble or gathering information without exposing them to unnecessary danger.

If she were in an arguing frame of mind, she'd yell at him that the guys wouldn't mind at all if she and Levi began a relationship, but she'd be lying. It *would* make a difference. The others would subconsciously begin looking for signs of favoritism, which would foster resentment and a lack of trust. Any argument between her and Levi would necessarily cause tension among the others. That was just how team dynamics worked; a disagreement between any two members was one thing, but throw sex into the mixture and it became combustible.

She turned her head and stared at the sky as grimly as he was, and for the same reason. As things stood, she had two choices: she could quit training and have Levi—for how long was up for debate—or she could stay on the team and deal with the bitter truth that they couldn't be together.

She. Couldn't. Quit. Doing so would betray everything she was, every sense of self. Maybe she drove herself past what a sane person would do, but didn't the guys also do that? Being who they were, doing what they did, required more of them than, say, a regular nine-to-five job.

She had been happy with that nine-to-five job, but now *this* was her reality, and she wouldn't, couldn't, turn her back on it.

She rolled to her knees and picked up her goggles. Her clothes were wet all along her back, and on her right side. Her elbows and knees had mud on them, evidently from when they'd landed and skidded along the ground. Her forehead was beginning to sting, and she suspected there was a scrape there. Bits of weed clung to her braid, which was no longer stuffed down the back of her shirt. Fingering her face, she found some dirt and debris and wiped it off as best she could.

Silently Levi got to his feet and began gathering in the parachute, pulling it the rest of the way to him. She picked up his goggles, and the glove he'd discarded. "Here," she said and tossed the glove to him. He released the parachute with his right hand and fielded the glove one-handed, pulled it back on.

The pickup rolled to a stop on the shoulder of the road, about a hundred yards away. Jina began trudging toward it, gearing herself up to do this one more time—and one more time after that, if necessary.

Whatever it took.

ELEVEN

She was as white as the clichéd sheet.

Levi had to stop himself from picking her up and lifting her into the plane. She looked so damn *little* and dispirited, not that she truly was either of those things, but his protective instinct was kicking in harder than ever. He'd kissed her, he'd held her under him and felt the slenderness of her bones, he'd made her come; his dick and balls and brain, and hell, yeah, he realized his brain was third on that list, were all joined in a savage fight because two of them were insisting she was now *his* and his fuck-ass stupid brain was telling them they couldn't have her. His sense of frustration was so great he wanted to go all Hulk and pick up the damn plane and throw it.

At the same time—God, it had been good, even though his balls were aching. The taste of her, her breath on his face, the way she caught on fire and responded with everything in her, no holding back, no games, just Jina-Babe as honest and straightforward as ever. At last he'd gotten his hands on her, on those sweet little breasts. She wasn't wearing a bra. He'd almost come in his pants when he'd felt nothing but smooth skin and tight nipples. If he ever got that far again, he swore to God nothing would stop him, next time he'd get her naked and get inside her, and to hell with the consequences.

Which meant he didn't dare take that risk again, not as long as she was part of the team.

Fuck!

As soon as Boom saw her he shot a concerned look at Levi as they climbed aboard the Twin Otter for the third time. Levi knew how he felt. As bad as she'd reacted the first time, at least she hadn't done anything worse than faint. An unconscious Babe was hell and gone better than a Babe who was fighting him as hard as she could. He'd been on the point of knocking her out so he could safely deploy the parachute and get them both down alive, but at almost the last second she'd gone limp, too tired to fight anymore, and he'd been able to get them into the proper attitude and pop the chute.

"Hey!" she said to Boom, catching the look and scowling at him. "At least I stayed conscious this time." Her voice was raw from screaming, not much more audible than if she'd had laryngitis. She looked pretty bad. She had dirt smeared on her face, her clothes were wet and muddy, and her body language screamed *dispirited*, which was so unlike her Levi wanted to hold her on his lap and comfort her, the last damn thing she needed.

Boom scratched his jaw. "I'm not sure that's a good thing," he replied.

"I know." Wearily she sank onto the bench. "I could have killed both of us."

The plane started moving and Levi called out for Air Bud to wait a minute; no questions asked, Bud simply eased back and the plane stopped rolling. Boom sat down on one side of Babe and Levi took the other side, both of them dwarfing her. She had her head down and she looked even smaller than usual, as if she was trying to draw into herself.

Levi started to take her hand, lace her fingers with his, and caught himself to change the gesture to a backhanded tap to her forearm. "Babe, you can do this. You know how. Boom's taught you everything you need to know, just trust him and your training. You know how to steer, you know how to land, and if there are any malfunctions you know how to handle them."

She gave a tiny nod, her head still down.

A big, primal part of him wanted her to say she couldn't do it. Or he could pull the plug himself, right now; likely any of the other team leaders would have as soon as they were on the ground after the disaster of that last jump. Boom would back him if he did. But she had tackled everything else with so much stubbornness and determination that he knew how she'd feel if she failed at this, knew how devastated she'd be. She deserved another chance.

"All right," he said, making a swift decision. "This next jump, you're wearing the parachute." Boom looked at him over the top of Babe's head and gave a brief nod.

Her head snapped up and she stared at him with huge, rounded eyes, white showing all around the irises. Her lips were bloodless.

"Boom and I will jump with you," he said. "We'll hold on to you, but you're the one who'll have to deploy the chute and steer it to the LZ." The way it worked, he and Boom would also have chutes and they would hold on to her until her chute deployed, then they'd release her and once at a safe distance pull their own cords. He didn't think she was grasping all the details, though, because she looked panicked.

"What if I kill us all?" she asked, sounding like a terrified frog.

He shrugged. "You'll be dead, too. At least you'll escape prosecution." Coddling wouldn't do, not now. Let her think she was responsible for all three of them making it down safely.

Boom snorted, called to Bud to let it roll; the brakes released, and they started down the runway.

LEVI AND BOOM were moving around, getting things ready. Jina concentrated on breathing, inhaling to the count of four, holding for seven, exhaling to eight counts. If she could control her breathing, maybe she could control something else. The results on breathing were mixed. She felt as if she was gasping for air, her lungs functioning in jerks and starts, and she never made it to the holding for seven, much less exhaling for eight.

Total panic lurked just beyond the next breath. They were jumping with her. *She'd* have the parachute. That seemed like a completely stupid situation for them to set up, but she knew they meant business. When it came to their training, the GO-Teams didn't mess around, it was serious as a heart attack. Levi was forcing her to do this, or else. She had to get her head straight and either quit before they went out that door, or, once they had, function and do her job.

"Take off the tandem harness," Boom instructed, and numbly she began unhooking and shucking out of it, then getting into the harness with the parachute container. At least Boom had packed the parachutes himself, so she trusted that it was properly folded and would deploy correctly, if she could just keep her head in the game and remember to *pull the freaking cord.*

She knew how to do this. She just had to keep the panic at bay and remember what she'd been taught. As she geared up she ran through the parts in her head, picturing them, naming them: the container that held the D bag; the deployment bag, which actually held the parachute; the risers; the pilot chute; the toggles; the reserve chute; the automatic activation device that would deploy the chute at a certain altitude if she hadn't already done it. Thinking of the AAD gave her a bit of relief; the parachute would open regardless of what she did . . . unless she started fighting them, and they were in the wrong position when the parachute deployed, meaning they'd be hopelessly tangled.

She couldn't panic. Their lives depended on it. Mentally she walked herself through each and every thing that could go wrong, and how to handle every situation, immediately, no hesitation and no trying to fix it. Don't analyze, *act.*

Boom opened the door. Again. She was beginning to hate that

sight. No, there was no "beginning" to it, she hated that open door with every fiber of her being. Freezing cold air was blowing through the cabin, like being caught in a winter storm. She didn't want to be cold, she didn't want that door to be open, and she desperately wanted to be on the ground.

"Let's go," Levi yelled. Resigned, she pulled her goggles into place and the three of them shuffled to the door. Boom gave her a thumbs-up sign and she gave him an *are-you-crazy* look. Bookended by the two men, Levi on the left and Boom on the right, she crouched with them.

Tears blurred her vision, ran hot against her eyelids. *Dear God, please don't let me kill them*, she silently prayed. They each took firm hold of her harness, and heaved themselves, and her, out the door.

Damn fools! she thought wildly, including herself in the sentiment.

Her vision went black. She still felt the horrendous wind, though strangely it didn't feel as cold once they were out of the plane as it did while they were still in it. It tore at her skin, slapped at her. She tried to breathe, tried to do the counting thing, four in and hold for seven, but she couldn't inhale for a four count; she could barely gasp, not much oxygen getting past her constricted throat. At least she wasn't screaming this time, but that was because she *couldn't*, not because she had any choice about it.

"Open your eyes!" Levi bellowed, barely heard above the roar of the wind.

Doh. So that was why she couldn't see. Squeezing her eyes even tighter, vehemently she shook her head. She didn't want to see. She'd already seen that view twice today, and that was twice too many times. It didn't improve with repetition.

Boom tugged on her harness. "We have you!" Like Levi, he was yelling as loud as he could.

"You have to do this!"

Levi again. She had stereo nagging.

But he was right. She had to do this.

At least her brain hadn't turned off this time. She was at least capable of thinking, even if her teeth were chattering in fear and her bones felt as if the terror had turned them to water. Her breath was hitching in her throat now; her lungs were burning in their need for oxygen. How soon before she did pass out, from lack of air?

Oh, *God*.

She had no idea what their altitude was, hadn't looked around in the basic security check for other aircraft or any of the obstacles she was supposed to be aware of. She just knew she couldn't pass out, at least not without pulling the pilot chute that deployed the main chute. She had to do that one thing, because Levi and Boom were with her. They were relying on her to get them all out of this hell alive. She had to function.

Clumsily she reached behind her back. Boom had had her do this time after time; she knew where the pilot chute was, she had to pull it free.

She pulled it.

For an agonizingly long time that was really only a couple of seconds, nothing happened; their plummet down was as fast as ever, and her heart sank, because it hadn't worked, the parachute hadn't worked. Then there was a whoosh that she *felt*, a vibration that shivered through her harness, and they were jerked violently upward as if attached to a bungee cord. Somehow she had air in her lungs now and she screamed because surely, surely Levi and Boom would be jerked away from her. She grabbed for their hands—

She felt them lose their grips on her harness.

The horror she'd felt during the first two jumps was nothing compared to the awful sense of disaster that overwhelmed her, smashing into her chest like an avalanche. A guttural scream tore out of her throat, long and agonized, and her eyes popped open as she searched frantically for their falling bodies even though she knew there was no way she could reach them, nothing she could do to stop their headlong plunge to their deaths. Here she was swinging under that damn chute, and they were gone.

Levi! Sobs choked her. She tried to scream his name, tried to turn her chute so she could look for them, tried to—

The world stopped. Two canopies were floating down near hers, one slightly behind and below her, the other slightly above. Levi. Boom. With their own freakin' parachutes.

Rage filled her like whiskey, hot and potent. They'd tricked her. They'd made a fool of her. Yeah, they'd gotten her to control her own jump, but she freakin' *hated* them for this whole miserable day and this was the cherry on top of the whole shit shake.

Her arms were shaking violently as she grabbed the toggles, so violently that her parachute began swinging back and forth. Terrified, she turned them loose, then grabbed them again when she remembered she had to hold them. Looking down, she saw her feet swinging and way, way below them was the patchwork of the earth, thousands of feet down. The shaking got worse and desperately she switched her gaze to the horizon, the blur where sky met earth.

She had to get down. She had to safely navigate all those thousands of feet of nothing but air, she had to steer this stupid parachute—and what *moron* first thought it was a good idea to jump out of a plane with nothing but a glorified umbrella to float him down like he was Mary Fucking Poppins—to somewhere close to the landing zone and then actually make it down without breaking a leg, her back, her neck, or any other bone, because she had to be relatively whole and unhurt in order to *kill* them, not just for scaring her to death but likely laughing while they did it, and on top of all that they'd made her dis Mary Poppins. People went to hell for less than that.

Tears kept pouring down her face. She tried to stop crying, tried to wipe her face on her hunched shoulder, but every time she did the motion started her parachute swinging and she'd just now gotten the damn thing fairly stable. She could hear both Levi and Boom yelling encouragement and instructions at her, but she didn't acknowledge them in any way, didn't look at them, didn't even scream at them to eat shit and die the way she wanted to.

She had several minutes before they were on the ground. Technically she knew that was how long it took, though the descent had seemed so much longer the first two times—and this one felt even longer. In that short length of time she had to wipe away any sign of tears because damned if she'd let them know they'd made her cry, that she'd been so terrified for *them*.

On the other hand, pride would carry her only so far, and in order to wipe her face she had to release one of the toggles. Not going to happen.

Besides, the effort would have been useless. She couldn't stop crying. Through the blur of her tears she identified the landing zone, jerkily pulled on the toggles to steer herself toward it. The ground was coming up fast, gaining in speed. She started to pull her feet up, then remembered she wasn't tandem with Levi now, she had to land on her own feet. She choked on a sob, flared the parachute the way Boom had taught her, and her feet hit the ground.

Her landing had none of the powerful grace of Levi keeping his balance and taking a couple of steps, it was more that she stumbled and went down, hitting knees first then tumbling flat on her face before the billowing chute pulled her to the side. She wanted to just lie there and sob, but there were things she had to do. She struggled to her knees and unhooked, scrabbled around to begin hauling in her parachute, which was streaming across the ground like some kind of giant amoeba. It felt as if the fabric was fighting her, trying to catch the wind again and pull free.

She wanted to let the damn thing go, but controlling the parachute and pulling it in had been drilled into her by Boom. She hauled on it, scrabbling on her knees, throwing her weight back, digging in her heels. Her movements were clumsy, or the chore wouldn't have been nearly as difficult. She was bad at this, spectacularly bad.

Then she had the damn thing under control. She sat on her ass on the ground, pulled a handful of the nylon to her, and buried her face in it while sobs choked her and her whole body shook.

She knew Levi and Boom were both on the ground, knew they had gathered in their nylon; she heard steps as one, maybe both, of them approached her. She didn't look up.

"Babe." It was Levi. A hard hand grasped her shoulder. She twisted away from his touch, scrambled to the side, and managed to get to her feet even though she had to put a hand on the ground to brace herself. She felt a rock under her fingers and before she knew it she'd whipped her arm around and hurled the rock at him.

He jerked his head aside barely in time to keep from being brained with it. He was too close, and she'd thrown thousands of rocks during her childhood. She saw him scowl, saw him start to bark something at her, then he saw her face and closed his mouth. Behind her Boom laughed; Levi held up a warning hand and Boom cut off the sound like slicing it with a knife.

She stood there, crying and angry, clutching a fistful of nylon in one hand and her other hand knotted into a fist. She wished she had a whole supply of rocks to throw at them. She wished she had a hammer to throw at them. She wished she had her car here so she could just drive off and leave them standing here, because she wanted to do a lot of damage to both of them and there was no way she could unless they let her, which took all the fun out of it.

"You jerks," she gasped in a wobbly voice. She could barely talk, her throat was so raw.

Carefully Levi said, "You should have known we weren't stupid enough to jump without a parachute."

"*I did!*" she shot back, glaring at him through her tears. "On your orders! So evidently I was stupid enough."

Boom winced. "Got us there."

Levi was watching her as if she were a rabid squirrel, about to pounce on him. She'd had all she could take today, she was *done*. Swallowing hard, she turned her back on them and began gathering the parachute up in her arms.

Their ride was there, and silently Jina marched toward the pickup. Logistically she assessed her options: if she got in the back of the king cab, she'd be riding beside one of them, and she didn't want either of them that close. If she got in the front with the driver, they'd both have to get in back. Good enough. That's exactly what she did, climbing into the front passenger seat and slamming the door before they even reached the truck. She held the parachute bundled on her lap and stared straight ahead.

She expected to be taken back to that godforsaken Twin Otter—she was ready to blow the damn thing up, except they probably had a replacement—but when the driver asked, Levi said, "We're done for today, take us to the truck."

The relief was overwhelming.

During the short ride to the truck, Jina accepted the bitter realization that she had to do something. As much as she felt her dudgeon was justified, that wasn't the way team dynamics worked, especially not a paramilitary team. Likely none of the guys would feel the way she did, or even if they did, they'd bury it under their guy-camaraderie reaction, with cussing and some insults, then laughing. She felt up to the cussing and insults, but laughing was beyond her right now.

She couldn't be a girl about this. If she wanted to be part of the team, she had to put up with a certain amount of bullshit. Besides, yeah, if she hadn't already been so mentally exhausted, she'd have realized the obvious, that they had chutes. They'd even put them on in front of her. She just hadn't been capable of paying attention right then, and that was on her.

That didn't mean they wouldn't pay.

They had nothing to say as they got into Boom's truck, which suited her fine. She got in back, positioned herself in the middle, which if they'd given that a minute's thought would have alerted them to the possibility of retaliation. But she'd cried and made them uncomfortable, and they were inclined to leave well enough alone. She wished she hadn't cried, but she had, so now she'd use the advantage.

She waited, biding her time, looking for the right moment. She wanted some traffic around them, but nothing close behind.

Levi took out his phone and started texting. They stopped at a traffic light; Boom lightly drummed his fingertips against the steering wheel, looking off to the left. The traffic light changed, and they started forward. Jina made a quick check behind, saw the coast was clear; she drew up her knees, yelled, "*Look out!*," as loudly as she could, and with all the strength in her legs kicked their seat backs.

Boom slammed on the brakes. "Shit!" Tires squealed and smoked. He and Levi were both thrown forward against their seat belts, and both braced for impact while wildly looking around for whatever was about to T-bone them. Jina was already braced, her legs against their seat backs. The truck slid a little sideways, then rocked to a stop.

Silence.

Slowly the two big men in the front turned their heads to glare at her.

She smiled, buffed her nails against her sweatshirt, and said, "Payback."

AFTER DRAGGING HER weary butt home, Jina showered, washed her hair, put antibiotic salve on her scrapes, drank some hot tea with honey to soothe her throat, then put on clean sweats and crashed on the couch. She had the energy of a noodle, and she didn't want to think about the day, not even the Levi-kissing-her part. With the TV on and a light blanket over her, she even napped for a couple of hours and woke feeling hungry, so evidently the emotional trauma hadn't been bad enough to affect her stomach.

Holy shit. She'd jumped out of an airplane—three times. Okay, so she hadn't jumped so much as she'd been thrown, but still. If she added the altitude three times, today she'd fallen more than the distance from the top of Mount Everest to the bottom. That was quite an accomplishment, but she didn't think she'd tell her mom about it.

The sun was going down and she was thinking about ordering in a pizza when her doorbell rang.

A quick look through the peephole revealed the guys, or at least five of them. Even Voodoo was there, though not Levi or Boom. She opened the door, gave them a puzzled look. "What's up?"

"You made the team," Snake announced, grinning. "We came to take you out and get you drunk."

What?

"I did?"

Trapper grabbed her, tugged her out of the door. "Yep. Jumping was the last segment, and you passed it."

"Mostly they threw me out of the plane and I lived to tell about it . . . barely." She tacked on the last word in the spirit of being honest. "Wait! I'm not going out wearing sweats. I need to change clothes."

All five of them got that look that said they didn't understand, then Crutch hitched a shoulder and said, "Girls."

"Undeniably," she countered, and let them in to watch TV while she hurriedly pulled on jeans and sneakers, and a bra. Deciding her sweatshirt was good enough, she grabbed her phone and wallet and keys and rejoined them within three minutes, start to finish. Because she was cautious, getting drunk wasn't likely to happen, but she'd have a drink with them. She'd made the team!

She didn't know how that made her feel, other than giddy and scared all at once. The training was over, or at least the preparatory phase was. The guys constantly trained to keep their skills sharp and she'd be expected to do the same, but now it was all maintenance instead of proving herself.

Going down the stairs, she said, "Ace and Boom nearly killed me. I'm not speaking to them."

"Yeah, we know," Jelly said cheerfully, giving her his deceptively sweet smile. "You'll have to get over it. They're waiting for us at the bar."

All of them? That sounded ominous. She skidded to a stop, holding on to the railing in case they tried to drag her the rest of the way down. "Wait. If this is any kind of initiation, I'm going back upstairs and locking the door."

Snake snorted. "You're kidding, right? Boom and I had to tell our wives about this. My orders were you can't be hurt, embarrassed, or humiliated. That leaves getting you drunk."

Jelly shook his head. "Sad but true."

Reassured, she released the railing and went down the rest of the stairs. "I've already been hurt and humiliated today, but I was too scared to worry about being embarrassed. I don't know why anyone goes skydiving for fun."

"Not Voodoo's favorite way to exit a plane, either," Trapper said. Voodoo just looked surly and shrugged.

Oddly, that made Jina like Voodoo just a tiny bit more, because not liking skydiving proved he wasn't an idiot, at least in her book.

The bar and restaurant they took her to was on the lowbrow side, which made her comfortable with her jeans and sweatshirt; she hadn't expected fine dining, anyway. The booths and tables were mostly occupied, and to her surprise she recognized more than a few faces; several guys from other teams were there. They lifted their beers in her direction. She'd made it!

A small table had been pushed up to a big booth that would easily seat six people, so there was more than enough room for the eight members of the team. Sure enough, Levi and Boom were already there, beers in front of them. Levi slid out of the booth and somehow she was herded in on that side, he slid back in beside her, and she ended up against the wall with no escape.

His thigh pressed against hers. The booth was large enough that even with Voodoo taking a seat beside Levi there was enough room that they didn't need to touch, but there his leg was, and she had nowhere to go.

"I don't want to sit next to you," she said. "You tried to kill me."

"You got back at us," he replied, then told the guys what she'd done in the truck. "Scared the shit out of us."

Boom blew out a breath and shook his head. "My heart's still pounding." There was a lot of laughter and joking, a waitress came to take their orders, and to her relief there was a lot of food ordered as well as drinks.

In short order a burger and fries were in front of her, as well as a lemon drop martini, which the guys called a sissy drink, but she didn't like beer, so tough; that was her celebration drink, the one she'd gotten when she turned the legal age to drink, as well as when she'd finished college.

It was also a *strong* lemon drop martini.

Like any made-the-team celebration, this one involved a lot of toasts, not just from her guys but from the other team members, too. By the fifth toast, she was feeling the martini, though she tried to be careful with her sips. By the time the drink was gone, she was very happy indeed, so much so that she'd stopped worrying about Levi's leg touching hers.

A jukebox was playing and one of the other team members—she

couldn't remember his name—had the balls to approach and ask if she wanted to dance. As happy as she was, Jina started to accept, but then realized something.

"I'm trapped," she announced to her would-be dance partner. "I can't get out."

"They'll let you out—"

"No," Levi said. "We won't. There's a reason she's where she is, and that's to keep assholes like you from hassling our girl."

"Aw, c'mon, Ace, it's just a dance."

"I've seen you dance, you damn octopus. She stays where she is."

"Damn right," Trapper added, smiling his calm, sniper smile. "Go dance with your own trainee."

There was some good-natured griping back and forth, but the guy left smiling. They were generally a good bunch of guys, all the teams, she thought. They hadn't been recruited because they were criminals or didn't play well with others, they were recruited because of their abilities and how they functioned within the team framework.

Another drink appeared in front of her. Her fries were salty, and the drink was welcome.

Somewhere around eight-thirty, her phone buzzed in her jeans pocket. She pulled it out, blinked until the name and number came into focus, and announced, "It's my mom!"

She swiped the phone and happily said, "Hi, Mom!"

There was a pause, and her mother said, "Hi, honey. Where are you? There's a lot of noise."

"A bar. I finished training today, and the guys are getting me drunk."

There was a symphony of groans and rolling eyes around her, and she blinked at them in surprise. She lowered the phone a bit. "What?"

Deftly Levi snagged the phone away from her, heaved a sigh, and put it to his ear. "Mrs. Modell? I'm Levi Butcher, Ba—uh, Jina's boss. She's safe. The whole group is here." He listened a minute. "Yes, ma'am, I'll personally guarantee her safety."

"Hah, that's a joke!" Jina muttered. "You tried to kill me today."

"Shhh!" came from several big men.

"Don't shush me. I want to talk to my mom." She scowled at them.

Voodoo popped a fry into his mouth. "Let this be a lesson," he commented. "She's a lightweight."

She leaned around Levi to shoot him the bird. Levi slapped her hand down and continued talking to her mom. "Yes, ma'am. No, ma'am. She's had a drink and a half. We fed her first, but—you got that right. Yes, ma'am. I'll have her call you when she's safely home. I'll send you a text right now. Good night, ma'am."

He pulled his own phone out, his face grim, and looked at the contact info on Jina's phone while he thumbed in a text.

"What're you doing?" she demanded, grabbing for her phone. "Give me that. I want to talk to my mom."

"She's already hung up. As for what I'm doing—" He shook his head. "I just texted your mother my contact info, because she's holding me personally responsible if anything happens to you."

There was dead silence around the table, then Snake said, "That's a first."

TWELVE

Her mother called first thing in the morning—*really* first thing, meaning five-thirty. It wasn't even daylight yet. With the hours of daylight so short now, Jina had barely rolled out of bed and hadn't made it to the kitchen for the first cup of coffee. "Hi, Mom," she said around a yawn. "You're up early."

"Thank goodness you sound all right," her mother said grimly. "Your daddy and I were prepared to be called to D.C. to identify your body."

"Oh." She yawned again. "I won't say there was nothing to be worried about, because I guess if I was a mother I'd have been worried, too." Even half asleep, Jina was too smart to dismiss her mother's concerns. The woman had eyes in the back of her head, spies everywhere, and a built-in lie detector somewhere in her belly, close to her uterus.

"Well—" Momentarily taken aback, her mother rallied. "That was *not* a great situation for you to be in."

"I had seven companions, two of whom are married, and their wives—"

"Oh, thank goodness," her mother said fervently, not letting Jina finish her sentence, which had been that the wives had given their okay. "Because it sounded like all men."

Jina didn't correct the assumption that the wives had been there, because she wasn't that sleepy or that stupid. Thinking back, she remembered seeing a number of women in the bar, so she didn't have to lie. "Not even close. Anyway, I'm the first one to finish training, so they took me out to celebrate. Kind of. Hamburger and fries, nothing fancy."

"And alcohol."

"And alcohol. I had one and a half lemon drop martinis."

That earned a chuckle. "Your celebration drink."

"I don't even have a headache this morning, so I didn't drink that much, though I was a little happy when you called."

"Your boss was reassuring. Thank him for me, for understanding that I was worried."

"The funny thing is, when you called, he'd just finished running off some guy who asked me to dance."

"Good for him. Tipsy women shouldn't dance. No good can come of it."

"I thought that was how you met Daddy."

"And I have five kids. Point made."

"Which ones of us would you give back?"

"There have been times in the lives of each one of you that I'd have jumped at the chance. I'm just glad last night wasn't one of your nights."

"Love you, too, Mom. Before I forget—unless there's an emergency, it looks as if I'll be able to come home for Thanksgiving. While I was still in the training program I was nailed down, but now I can probably wiggle free for a few days."

"Hallelujah!" Delight warmed her mother's tone. "It's been too long. If you hadn't been able to come, I was planning on making a trip the next weekend to see you."

Wow, talk about dodging a bullet. Jina could just imagine marching to Levi's orders and trying to entertain her parents at the same time, because there weren't enough hours in the day.

"I'll send you my flight information. I won't have time to drive down, that would use up half of my time off."

"I'll have your favorite cake waiting."

German chocolate! Jina's salivary glands activated. "I've been working out like crazy, just to buy myself some leeway for the holidays. I love it when a plan comes together."

Jina thought about that cake while she was drinking the all-important first cup of coffee and making herself a small protein smoothie, followed by a small bowl of oatmeal for the warm and homey feeling. After yesterday, she needed some comfort food, and there wasn't any meatloaf available. To have that cake, she'd have to run even more miles. Heck, she'd have to run whether she had cake or not, because that was how this gig worked: stay in shape, or else.

Because she had time, she got on the computer and checked flight times. She lucked out and found a single seat on a Wednesday night flight out of Reagan to Atlanta, then she checked for an available seat to either Albany or Brunswick, her family home being about equidistant between the two. Then, on second thought, she arranged for a rental car, so she'd have her own wheels while she was there, in case the team got sent out on a mission and she had to leave in the middle of the night.

Pride filled her at the realization she'd really done it: she was a member of a GO-Team now. She not only had an important job where she could make a difference, she'd lasted through some tough training. A couple of the other trainees had gotten hurt, but even more of them had washed out. She hadn't washed out, she was still standing at the end.

As an official part of the team, she should do what the guys did and keep a bag packed and in her car so she could leave at a minute's notice.

There was a plan. Unfortunately, packing a bag with a couple of changes of clothes and some necessities didn't require a lot of brainpower, and she found herself thinking about Levi, whether she wanted to or not. Yesterday had been so traumatic that she hadn't been able to analyze anything; she'd simply tried to live through the day. Last night, she'd been tipsy. This morning, there was nothing to ward him off.

He'd kissed her, damn him. Focusing on that helped her *not* focus on the fact that his hand had been under her shirt and he'd been between her legs, and that even with their clothes on he'd made her come. She didn't know how to act, and most of all she really wanted to avoid him now. After everything he'd said, *he* was the one who hadn't toed the line. She felt resentful about almost all of yesterday—last night had been fun—but in retrospect she was most resentful about that. Kissing her was dirty pool.

In the months she'd known him, she had watched how he pulled this string to get that effect, how he shifted and balanced and analyzed in his role as team leader; given that, she had to consider the possibility that he'd kissed her as an emotional prompt to quit the team—make her think they'd have something, become a couple, if she just quit her job. Maybe some women would have done exactly that. Maybe *most* women would have made that call, depending on the depth of their own emotional involvement. Jina wasn't one of those women. Being physically attracted to Levi wasn't the same as being in love with him, and she didn't confuse the two.

He was known for being ruthless in his pursuit of the mission, whatever any particular mission might be. It stood to reason that if—*if*—he thought she was a weakness that could endanger the team, he'd have booted her out of training. On the other hand, she was the only woman trainee, and there might have been political pressure for him to "help" her succeed. She didn't think so, because Axel MacNamara wasn't exactly known for his political correctness; rather, the exact opposite. Still, the small possibility existed, and that made her angry. She wanted to succeed because she could do the job, not because someone gave her a pass because of her sex.

Damn it, there was no way to sort out all the variables and possibilities, including the one that Levi might, just might, truly be attracted to her. He hadn't been faking the huge erection in his pants, but under those circumstances, in that position, she'd have been more surprised if he *hadn't* had one.

The unwelcome fact was that no matter how she worried the details or how many possibilities occurred to her, she still ended back at square one, with no options other than to do the job to the best of her ability and handle the moment she was in. That was all anyone could do, just handle the moment.

Her go-bag packed, she set it in front of the door so she wouldn't forget it, then checked the time. Just six-thirty, she had plenty of time to get to the training site. Being a full-fledged team member didn't change certain things, such as staying in shape. She also needed to log some computer time with Tweety, keep those skills sharp, now that she'd actually be using them in the field. She could hardly wait.

ONCE SHE WAS at the site Jina got in some running time, which was easier now that the heat of summer was gone. She kept to an easy lope, because she thought she deserved an easy day after the horror that yesterday had been. Besides, she'd sprinted on Friday—in the rain, no less.

Donnelly fell in beside her around the two-mile mark. His shirt was already dark with sweat, telling her he'd hit the course early.

"Hey, we heard some buzz about you last night."

No mind reading was needed to guess what that was about. "The jump training? Yeah. It was horrible. I was scared to death, and I never want to do it again." She was still breathing easily, so talking wasn't a problem.

"But you did it, right?"

"On the third try—and it wasn't pretty."

"No points for pretty," he said and slapped her on the shoulder. "You did it, you qualified! You're officially on the team."

She grinned. "The guys took me out last night to celebrate, and my mom called in the middle of it. I told her I'd finished training and the guys were getting me drunk. Levi—Ace—had to explain himself to my mom and she made him text her his name and phone number. She held him hostage, in case anything happened to me."

Donnelly laughed so hard he stumbled and had to stop. Jina pulled up, too, walking around with her hands on her hips and breathing deep so she wouldn't get stiff. She had to grin, too, because Levi having to deal with a worried, horrified mother had been pretty good stuff.

They finished the run together, though Jina thought Donnelly probably ran longer than he'd been planning, but he asked her a lot of questions about jumping. She could tell he wasn't thrilled by the prospect of parachuting, either, and he said his training in it was due to start that week, so the experience was rushing at him a lot faster than he wanted. She didn't sugarcoat the experience, nor did she gloss over how horribly everything had gone the first two times. That seemed to reassure him, that she could goof up so bad and still pass. He'd been expecting to get one chance, and that was all.

Kodak was extremely well liked in the GO-Team community, but Jina didn't at all approve of how he was handling the trainee situation; for that matter, none of the team leaders other than Levi had taken a hands-on approach to their training. Levi was also the only one who had been saddled with a woman, which was why he'd done it. She had to admit she was likely in much better shape, and as far ahead as she was, because of his decision. Funny how she hadn't felt honored during any of the ordeal.

But it was *done*, and she was ready to get in the field with Tweety, see what she could do. As the first operator activated with this particular program, a lot of attention would be paid to her results.

There were a lot more people at the training site as they neared the end of the course; neither of them slacked up, because doing so would get some sharp words from Baxter or someone else (don't let up until the job is done), and she saw a few of her guys, including Levi, standing around talking.

Levi turned to look at her, and even from that distance she could feel his gaze boring into her. He hadn't asked her anything about Donnelly, though he'd waited in the parking lot Saturday night to see if Donnelly stayed late. Was he taking it for granted that her "date" had been nothing but window dressing? He might be rethinking that, though if he did she thought she might be insulted, because if she'd truly been dating Donnelly, she wouldn't have kissed Levi the way she had and she certainly wouldn't have allowed the rest of what had happened, but he didn't know her well enough to get that about her. She actually knew more about him than he did about her, because of the scuttlebutt about him.

Any way she looked at it, she was annoyed, angry, embarrassed, and she didn't want to talk to him right now.

She said bye to Donnelly and he continued jogging to join the group of trainees, some of whom waved at her. She felt a little sad that she hadn't gone through training with them, the geeks and nerds with whom she was so comfortable, but that water had long since passed under the bridge. She was walking toward her group, swiping her sweaty face on her shirtsleeve, when she saw Kodak himself pull into the parking lot and on impulse she swerved, heading instead toward him.

Kodak was a big, good-looking blond guy, kind of scruffy in a just-rolled-out-of-bed-after-a-good-time way. He was known to be as cheerful as he was good in the field, and normally being on his team was the best assignment Donnelly could have asked for. Kodak stood in the open door of his truck, reading something, but as she approached he tossed his reading material onto the seat and closed the door.

She probably shouldn't do this. How Kodak ran his team was none of her business. No one had ever told her "Don't interfere with another team" but that didn't mean there wasn't an unspoken protocol about how things were handled. If there was, she was about to violate it.

Damned if she did, chicken if she didn't.

"Hey," she greeted him, then stood there feeling awkward. Eloquent and effective. They had never actually met, though she knew who he was.

A slow, easy smile lit his face. "Babe," he said, making it clear that he knew who she was, too. Or maybe he called all women babe.

"Could I talk to you for a minute?"

"Darlin', you can talk to me as long as you want." His gaze went over her, and his eyes said he liked what he was seeing. "I know a little hole-in-the-wall café that has the best coffee in D.C. Want to go over there and start the morning out right?"

She sighed. His reputation as a hound was evidently well deserved. "No flirting, this is serious."

"I'm dead serious about flirting. It's one of the most enjoyable things in life." That easy, charming smile flashed again. "Can I hope you want to leave Ace's team and join mine?"

"After you've screwed up so bad? No way."

The smile left his face and he straightened, his gaze turning direct. When it came to work, Kodak was serious. "Whattaya mean, I screwed up?"

She took a deep breath and plunged in. Might as well get it over with. "Ace is the only team leader who involved his team in his assignee's training. I've spent months with the guys, getting to know them, becoming part of the team. Brian Donnelly, the trainee assigned to you, is a good guy, but you haven't made any effort to make him a part of the team before you have to go into the field with him."

Kodak took off his cap, slapped it against his leg, replaced it. His blue eyes were steady, narrowed. "You involved with him?"

She scowled at him. "You don't have to be involved with someone to take up for them."

He held his hands up in a surrender gesture. "Just asking, don't take my head off." He grinned. "I could get used to being fussed at, if you're the one doing it. I heard you give as good as you get. You sure you don't want to transfer to me?"

Determinedly she stayed on message. "He's a casual friend. I know him a bit better than I know most of the other trainees, but they're all getting hung out to dry by their assigned teams." She shrugged. "Ace wanted to oversee my training because he figured I'd be more of a liability because I'm a woman. I wasn't happy at the time, but in hindsight that was the best thing he could have done. Time's running out for the rest of you."

He rubbed his jaw, nodded. "You have a point." He cut his eyes to the right, grinned a little. "Looks like you're about to be snatched from my lascivious clutches," he said, winking at her.

"Oh my God, you really said *lascivious*!" She had to laugh. Even when she disagreed with him, he was so damn likable she thought hanging out with him would be one big party. Too bad she felt none of the visceral reaction to Kodak that she had to Levi because he would be so much easier to get along with. Maybe there was something wrong with her, that she preferred the man with the scowl, his roughness to Kodak's smoothness.

"I know other four-syllable words, too," he replied, grinning. "I'm really pretty smart."

All of them were, really. Doing what they did required a certain sophistication of thought and action, all of them spoke at least two languages, they could fly a variety of aircraft and operate computers; sometimes they made her feel almost backwoods.

She was suddenly surrounded by four big men, all the members of her team who had already arrived at the training site, even Voodoo, though he might have come along just for entertainment.

"Stay away from her," Levi said, the words and tone flat; he meant business, and he didn't mind Kodak knowing it. His chin was tucked and his hard gaze was level on Kodak, as if he was ready to start brawling.

Kodak just grinned. "I'm just standing here by my truck," he pointed out. "She came to me, and from my point of view I'm the one who needs protecting. Evidently I've been going about things wrong, but I've now been set straight."

Now Levi's hard gaze switched to her. Jina hitched a shoulder. If she had the guts to do it, she figured she had the guts to own it. "All the other team leaders should have been training their assignees the way y'all did with me," she said, folding her arms and lifting her chin. "That way they're already part of the team when they go out on their first assignment, instead of being strangers."

Levi's jaw clenched and Jina knew exactly what he was thinking, that she'd interfered on her "boyfriend's" behalf, though she knew she'd never referred to Donnelly as her boyfriend. She switched her gaze back to Kodak. "Anyway, think about it, though there isn't much time to do anything about it. Nice talking to you." She nodded to him, slid between Levi and Snake, and walked away. She had to consciously keep from clenching her fists. Boy, it was a good thing Thanksgiving was coming up, because she desperately needed a break from the guys, even if it was just a couple of days.

Sure enough, as soon as the guys rejoined her, Voodoo sniped, "You likely just made things tougher for your boyfriend."

"Bite me," she shot back. "He's a friend, not a boyfriend."

"He was your date Saturday night."

"So?"

"So he acted like he knows you pretty well."

"Like I said, he's a friend. I had a life before I was hijacked into training." She gave him a smile that showed more teeth than necessary. "Not that you'd know anything about having friends."

"Can it," Levi ordered, looking fed up with the exchange. He glared at both of them. Whatever else he might have said was cut off when his phone signaled an incoming text.

Almost simultaneously, four other phones began buzzing, including hers. She pulled it out of her pocket, read the text, then reread it. Her mouth fell open.

"Really? *Really?*" Three days before Thanksgiving, two and a half days before her flight, they were being ordered to Paris. Not even Paris, Tennessee—France. Paris, *France*. She groaned. "I was going home! I booked my flight this morning."

Snake looked unhappy, too. Levi shrugged. "Can't be helped. Someone's holiday is messed up no matter which team gets the call. With any luck we'll be home in a couple of days, but we won't know until the briefing. Come on, let's move."

At least she wasn't caught completely flat-footed, Jina thought morosely as she went to her car. She had her go-bag with her. Normally she'd be excited about her first mission, and normally she'd like to go to France—but not when it meant missing Thanksgiving and her mother's German chocolate cake.

Damn it all. Sometimes life just wasn't fair.

THIRTEEN

Eighteen hours later, Jina and Crutch sat in a not-very-good hotel room in Paris while the other six team members were conducting surveillance on their target. Crutch was keeping in contact with them and coordinating. Jina wasn't doing anything other than waiting. She hadn't expected to be bored but she was; somehow she'd thought the teams did exciting stuff all the time, which if she'd taken the time to think she'd have known wasn't possible, but innocent expectations were what they were—and in this case they were wrong.

"A lot of the stuff we do is boring," Crutch said easily when she mumbled a complaint. "Probably about seventy percent is gathering information. With you and Tweety here, maybe we can cut down on the time spent following people around and getting jack shit for our efforts. Sometimes we're just building a file, looking for patterns, things like that. It's not immediately important, but down the road all of it is."

That was one way of looking at it. Too bad the present was still just as boring. This was an object lesson: always have reading material with her. This was in fact the second object lesson she'd learned on her maiden mission; the first was that she'd packed as if they were going into the field, when most of what they did was in urban settings. Her cargo pants and boots would get her only so far; what she really needed was jeans, a pair of flats, and a warm but stylish sweater, because this was *Paris*. She'd developed a huge inferiority complex just driving in from the airfield and seeing the Frenchwomen on the sidewalks. Not only was she now bored, she was fighting a powerful urge to go shopping, have her hair done, and get a manicure . . . after she visited a pastry shop.

But she was stuck here, with no downtime until Levi said so. The subject of their surveillance was a South African banker named Graeme Burger, who had triggered some flags at the National Security Agency because he'd contacted a Sudanese who had terrorist links. The Sudanese was currently in Paris, and now so was Banker Burger, whose plane had touched down at De Gaulle a couple of hours ago, and whose taxi was now being followed by Levi and the other guys using a tag-team method. They had three cars, two men to each car, and so far so good; there was no indication that they'd been burned, and the taxi driver wasn't making any effort to evade them. Maybe Burger being in Paris at the same time as the Sudanese was a coincidence—and maybe the sun would turn blue. In the dark underworld of terrorism, there were no coincidences.

Despite the NSA's all-encompassing record gathering, so far the reason for the connection between Burger and Nawal Daw was murky. South Africa wasn't a terrorist hot spot, and although the Foreign Service Institute scored the S.A. banking industry as a possible safe haven for tax evaders, again, it wasn't a hot spot. Sudan, however, *was* a terrorist cesspool, and Nawal Daw was involved up to his skinny neck, with ties to Hezbollah, ISIS, and several domestic Sudanese groups. Why a country needed more than one terrorist organization, Jina couldn't fathom, but from the briefing they'd received, Sudan had quite a collection. Nawal Daw wasn't one of the leaders, but he had connections to the leaders.

Of particular interest was that Graeme Burger had applied for a visa to travel to the States for a vacation. The visa had been approved, and a watch on Mr. Burger had been put in place so whatever plans he made could be monitored. If a terrorist group in Sudan wanted to use Mr. Burger in an attack on the States, the GO-Teams had been put in action to find out exactly what was being planned.

And she would miss out on her mom's German chocolate cake. And Mom would be mad at her for missing Thanksgiving.

Jina sighed. She couldn't even play games on the heavy-duty, field-tested, encrypted, top-secret laptop with which she controlled Tweety, because the government evidently didn't want her playing games on their equipment—which was really crappy of them, because playing games on their equipment was what had gotten her this assignment in the first place.

On the other hand, playing more games might end up getting her launched into space, so she supposed she should leave well enough alone. "Why can't I be helping with following the goonie, since I can't do anything else?"

Crutch said, "You aren't qualified."

"I have eyes, and I can drive."

"You might be needed here at any time, and trust me, you can't drive in Paris. It's a nightmare. You don't speak French, you don't know anything about the streets, you'd get lost, and you'd likely cause an accident that would get you killed." He grinned at her. "We're looking out for you."

And boring her to death at the same time. "Does everyone speak French except for me?"

"Some, at any rate. Voodoo's fluent, Ace and Trapper not quite as good. The others get by, but the French sneer at them. You should take some language courses."

"In my spare time." But that was an idea. She'd see which languages were most useful now, and at least get some rudimentary language skills going. Overseas flights were long, and that would be something to pass the time because sleep was hard to come by. She'd been too excited, quarters had been cramped, and she hadn't acquired the guys' ability to nap on a moment's notice whether they were lying, sitting, or propped against a wall. Not only that, Jelly and Crutch were such practical jokers she didn't think she'd ever feel comfortable sleeping in their presence.

Her work cell phone buzzed. She jumped, and her heart rate picked up. Part of the protocol was that anything relating to the drone would be sent by text, instead of a phone call that might be picked up by an audio recording bug. The text was from Levi:

get tweety ready

Adrenaline shot through her system, making her feel almost dizzy. She jumped to her feet and got Tweety ready to fly. Guidance systems for drones originally required line-of-sight communication with the controller, but they were so far beyond that now she could operate him from just about anywhere; the military's Predator drones could be controlled by people sitting in front of a screen thousands of miles away. But that much distance had the built-in lag time that MacNamara had wanted eliminated, so Tweety didn't need that kind of capability. Paris was a big city, with innumerable obstacles, but with Tweety's 360-degree cameras, sensors, and pinpoint GPS, she could zip him around the city as easily as if he were a real bird.

The next text was the coordinates where Levi wanted the drone to be positioned.

Swiftly Jina pulled the coordinates up on the computer and surveyed the area, while the computer plotted the best path. Paris was an old, overcrowded, jumbled city, with almost no straightforward route to anywhere. There were so many variables that had to be considered: wind, pedestrians, buildings, streetlamps; Tweety had been designed to attract minimum attention—he was silent and had awesome battery power—but keeping him unnoticed with so many people around was a priority. The last thing they wanted was to have an incident that resulted in the drone being knocked from the sky and captured. That wouldn't be as bad as the software in the laptop falling into the wrong hands, but still.

She texted Levi that Tweety was on the way and suited actions to words.

It was a rush, watching on her computer screen, seeing what Tweety saw, deftly guiding him over or around obstacles, sending him flying to Levi's location. This was what she'd trained for months to do, though not exactly this; she'd thought there would be more of a "hot mission" feel to it, rather than these rather prosaic conditions. The sky was overcast, the day cold and windy but not drastically so, with the possibility of rain at any time. Paris might be called the "city of light," but it looked dreary on a cold, late November day, and Jina was just as glad to be inside their cramped, run-down hotel room, exploring Paris from the all-seeing eyes of her Tweety.

There was an art to the flight, choosing ways that allowed her to blend the drone in with the background. She had practiced making his motions look like those of a bird, sometimes darting and swooping, sometimes flying straight, sometimes pretending to "roost" by hovering close to a ledge or anything else appropriate. Now she opted for more speed, because the faster she got to Levi's coordinates, the better.

Getting him there on surface streets would have taken over an hour. Flying him there, she had him close in fifteen minutes and texted Levi for further instructions.

Crutch was quietly talking on his headset, coordinating the six guys on the ground, making sure everyone knew what everyone else was doing and no piece of information went by unnoticed. Jina half listened to him while she mostly concentrated on her eyes and fingers, seeing what Tweety saw, immersing herself in the program the way she did when she played computer games.

Tweety's software was programmed to recognize the team members, and one of his cameras immediately locked in on Levi, showing him standing under an awning that protected him from the light rain that had started falling. Even from Tweety's viewpoint, Levi's physical presence was like a punch in her sternum, making her feel breathless and dizzy. He was so tall and powerful that people instinctively glanced at him, which wasn't the best thing for covert work but perversely made others in the same field disregard him *because* he was so noticeable. His features, though, blended in with the native French; his hair and eyes were dark, his facial bone structure was chiseled enough that he could belong to any number of nationalities.

She didn't want to notice, didn't want to think about what had happened between them Sunday afternoon. Staying busy was the best antidote to depression and frustration.

She sent a text that Tweety was in position. Levi took out his phone and read the message, but was too professional to look around for the drone. Instead his thumb moved over the keypad, and her phone buzzed again. **Across street in cafe, get photo of file** was followed by a brief description of the men in question. Then Levi pocketed his phone and walked off down the street, not once glancing at the café or his quarry.

Okay, it was up to her now. She positioned Tweety and located her target. The two men were sitting at a table against the window, protected from the elements but able to watch their surroundings. With Tweety's fast, high-resolution camera recording, she flew him past the window, high enough to look down. From what she saw on the laptop, the file was an actual file folder, which struck her as ridiculous. If they were up to something nefarious, shouldn't they be sneakier about it, rather than meeting in the open with a real file folder? She gave a mental shrug. Maybe being so open and acting innocent was the new thing with terrorists. She'd been told to get photos, so she got photos.

The two men talked. Graeme Burger opened the file, turned it around, and with the expertise of someone who often dealt with upside-down paperwork, pointed out several things to Nawal Daw. For all the world, it looked as if he was making a presentation, or trying to close a deal, maybe convince the Sudanese to move some money to his bank. Well, at the base of it, terrorism needed money to exist. But what did this have to do with Burger's planned visit to the United States? Maybe something, maybe nothing.

She took Tweety on another pass, photographing the open file. Then she took him to a roosting position on a streetlight, looking down and waiting for another page to be turned. The two men often looked at the foot traffic on the sidewalks, and around them in the café, but neither of them noticed Tweety's roughly bird shape.

Crutch murmured, "Everyone has pulled back, waiting to resume surveillance." His phone dinged, and he looked at the message. "Burger has booked himself on a flight leaving de Gaulle this evening, back to Johannesburg. Given the flight schedule, he should be leaving here and going straight to the airport."

Levi said, "Snake, Voodoo, you're on airport duty. Boom and Trapper, swap out with them. Jelly and I are on Daw."

Two acknowledgments.

Another page was turned in the thin stack contained in the file folder. Jina sent Tweety by the window again. Burger caught a glimpse of movement and glanced up, and smoothly Jina swung the drone higher, out of his view.

The file contained five pages. After each page had been examined, the two men shook hands and parted company.

"That doesn't seem very interesting," she said to Crutch.

He shrugged. "Never can tell."

She sent the intel to GO-Teams headquarters for analyzing. She could have read what was on the papers herself, by enlarging, but she didn't have any way of putting what she read into global context.

On Levi's command, she began bringing Tweety home. The rain was falling more heavily now, and wind gusts kept her busy finessing the drone's balance and direction. Umbrellas popped open on the sidewalks, where pedestrians were rapidly finding dry places to be, meaning she didn't have to be as careful about disguising Tweety's movements. Still, it was nerve-racking. At one point a gust blew him against the side of a building and she hastily recovered his balance, swearing under her breath—or not so under her breath, because Crutch looked up with eyebrows raised—and praying there was no damage. She'd become fond of Tweety. Never mind the drones were all the same, and never mind it was a miniaturized machine/computer; this particular drone was hers. She'd named him. And once things had a name, they developed personalities, even if the personality was wholly in the mind of the operator. Tweety was her bird.

She was sweating when she brought him safely in through the open window. Quickly she closed the window against the wind and rain, shutting out the gloomy day, and checked the drone for damage. There were some scraped places, but the powerful cameras and sensors were all working when she ran the diagnostics. The drone was sturdy; it had to be, to function in all sorts of conditions. Granted, some rainy weather in Paris didn't equal a sandstorm in wherever, but rain and electronics were notoriously unhappy together.

THREE HOURS LATER, they were on a plane returning to the States. Jina couldn't believe it. Just like that, her first mission was over, having been as dramatic as doing her laundry. She was exhausted from lack of sleep, disappointed by the boredom, by Paris in general, by missing Thanksgiving for basically *nothing*—though "nothing" might change to "something" when the photographs were analyzed— and . . . "Wait a minute," she said aloud. She wasn't sure of her math, because she was so jet-lagged, but she was gaining back six hours, right? They would land in D.C. about three hours local time after they left Paris, because of the change in time zones. She scrubbed her face and poked Snake, who was the one sitting beside her this time. "What day will we get back?"

He'd already dozed off in that annoying way they had, but he woke up and scrubbed his face much the way she had. "Ah . . . Tuesday. Maybe early Wednesday."

"So I can still go home."

He grinned at that. "Yeah. We'll be back for Thanksgiving." He gave a rumbling sigh and closed his eyes again. "Grab some sleep, or you'll be worthless for two days."

Grab some sleep, he said. He had already dozed off again. Looking around the plane, the others she could see had already done the same thing. Okay, this was a talent she needed to master, as of right now. She was certainly tired enough, so tired that her brain, which felt slightly buzzed, had separated itself from her heavy-as-lead body. Even if she couldn't sleep, at least she could close her eyes and rest. Wadding her jacket into a ball to use as a pillow, she hugged her arms around herself to ward off the chilly air, curled into herself as much as possible given the constraint of the seat belt, and determinedly closed her eyes without any real hope of catching some sleep.

She was wrong.

JINA STUMBLED BLEARY-EYED off the plane and stood staring at the signs directing passengers to the luggage claim area, to the exit area, to public transport, to parking . . . they might as well have all said "to hell" for all the sense her sluggish brain was making of them. The guys all seemed to be coping with jet lag better than she was, but this was her first time out of the country, period, and she felt as if she'd been body-slammed.

"I need coffee," she mumbled. "Before anything else, I need coffee." There had been coffee served on the plane, but the pick-me-up had already let her down.

Seven masculine grins came her way. Then Levi slung his bag over his shoulder and said, "I'm heading over to check on things before I go home," meaning he was going to headquarters to see if the analysts had come up with anything interesting on Graeme Burger, and strode away.

Looking around for a coffee shop was more important than watching him walk away. Besides, Jina figured she'd see him walking away a lot in the future, so there was no point in letting herself yearn.

"Yeah, let's find some coffee," Trapper said. She hadn't meant for it to be a group thing, but somehow she found herself borne along anyway and that was okay because now she was a real part of the team. However they kicked back and rehashed things, she wanted to be included—though she wouldn't have chosen a coffee shop in a busy airport, but what did she know? They were the experienced ones. She'd stay a short while, get enough caffeine in her to get safely home, then she'd take a much-needed nap before getting up, showering, and packing for her flight home that night. After two trans-Atlantic flights in about forty-eight hours, getting on a plane again so soon didn't appeal at all, but going home did.

They found a place and kind of took it over, dragging tables and chairs to their corner and ordering not just coffee but food, too. "Eat," Boom advised, when she said she just wanted coffee. "You need the energy. Food will get you through."

So she ate, and he was right, she did feel better afterward. To her surprise they didn't rehash; instead they unwound, talking sports and Thanksgiving. They did take a few shots at her for packing like an amateur, but she was one, so she shrugged it off.

Then Jelly smiled the innocent smile that always meant he was up to something and said, "Hey, Babe, this is a landmark day for you."

Instantly wary, she drew back and scowled. "No, it isn't." She didn't know what he was up to, but considering this was Jelly it couldn't be anything good.

"Sure it is," Crutch put in. "You've finished your inaugural mission. Only happens once in a lifetime."

Uh-oh. Jelly and Crutch together was a disaster in the making. Whatever they'd concocted, Boom wasn't in on it, because he was giving them a questioning look. Snake, Voodoo, and Trapper were harder to read, though she thought Voodoo had a slight smirk on his face. "The whole thing was boring," she said, trying to head off whatever they had in mind. "Nothing worth celebrating."

"Boring is good," Jelly said. "We all like boring. Go in, do the job, come home in time for Thanksgiving. Doesn't get any better than that."

"Yeah, speaking of Thanksgiving, I need to go home so I can pack—"

Crutch shook his head. "That isn't what you need."

"Is to. I haven't seen my mom in—"

"What you need," Jelly interrupted, "is a tattoo." The last three words had a dramatic flourish.

"As a commemoration," Crutch added.

Her mouth fell open and her eyes got huge. "No. I do *not* need a tattoo. Strictly speaking, no one *needs* a tattoo. I don't like pain. I'm afraid of needles. A tattoo isn't happening." She'd have been less dismayed if they'd wanted to shave her head—she needed a haircut, and anyway hair grew back. A tattoo was permanent. A tattoo hurt. "Let's just get me drunk again instead."

An unholy light had entered Trapper's eyes, and he slowly wagged his head back and forth. "Getting drunk is nothing. Drunk goes away. You can't look at it and remember the occasion."

"I don't want to remember the occasion. I was bored. Who commemorates boredom?"

"Your first mission," Boom said in a wondering tone. "It's something special."

Boom, too? Feeling betrayed, she glared at him. "I'm telling on you."

He tilted his head as though considering what Terisa might have to say, then shrugged. "There's home, and then there's team. You need a tattoo."

"Do *you* have a commemorative tattoo?" she shot back.

They blew right past that; they all had various tattoos, which they began describing to her, but when she tried to pin them down on which ones had been "commemorative," they ignored her. They were relentless. Before she knew it they were exiting the airport and she was being herded to Jelly's truck despite her protestations that she had to get her car—"We'll bring you back," Snake promised, grinning. She was so telling on him, too.

The only way to get out of being tattooed was to get nasty with them, and she wasn't prepared to do that because they weren't being malicious. This was being part of a rough-and-tumble team, and the way to handle it was to go along then get back at them later. "Three conditions!" she yelled. Some people making their way to their own cars stopped and looked her way, maybe thinking she was in trouble. Her guys stopped and waited, their expressions laughing and expectant.

"One!" she said emphatically, holding up one finger.

"*One*," they echoed.

"The tattoo artist has to be a woman."

They all looked at one another, shrugged.

"Okay."

"No problem."

"Two!" She held up a second finger.

"*Two!*" They bellowed the number.

"I get to pick the design, with no input from any of you."

"Aw, Babe."

"Don't you trust us?"

"We want to be involved."

"You can be involved by listening to me scream," she retorted. "This goes my way or it doesn't go at all, and I'll start screaming and fighting right here and your butts will all end up in jail, because who do you think the cops will listen to?"

Voodoo scratched his jaw. "We could take the cops," he pointed out.

"Yeah, but the publicity would suck." She had to stand her ground on this point in particular, or she could end up with something like a giant purple octopus inked across her back, with tentacles wrapping around her arms and legs. Trust them, she didn't.

"All right," Snake said, looking disappointed. "You get to pick the design."

She moved on immediately after that concession, not giving them time to argue about it. "Three!" She held up three fingers.

"*Three!*"

"None of you get to watch."

"What!"

"That takes all the fun out of it!"

"How will we know you actually get one, then?" That was Voodoo, trying to throw a monkey wrench into the situation.

"Trust, gentlemen. Trust." She folded her arms. "Those are my conditions. Take 'em or leave 'em."

"Ah, hell." Trapper looked aggrieved. "She called us gentlemen."

"And she used the T word." Jelly heaved a disappointed sigh.

"Y'all ate my tacos and my cake," she pointed out.

"All right, all right." Amid much grumbling, they dispersed to their vehicles, though Jelly still insisted she ride with him. Evidently they didn't trust her enough to let her drive on her own, and she couldn't say they were wrong because she could see herself bolting.

Evidently she was getting a tattoo.

FOURTEEN

Levi's phone signaled an incoming text and he glanced at the screen. What he read had him swearing and turning the truck around, never mind that he was almost at team headquarters. What the *fuck* were they up to? "Taking Babe to get a tattoo" wasn't something he wanted to read. For one, he was sure that if she wanted a tattoo, she'd already have gotten one. Two, she had looked completely wiped out, and in no shape to resist being swept along on a crazy idea. This had Jelly and Crutch written all over it, but it seemed as if all the others had joined in, even Boom, though Boom at least had the sense to let him know what was going on.

If she wanted one, fine, that was her business. But knowing what he knew about the two jokesters on the team—he quickly thumbed in a reply to Boom's text asking two important things: **is she willing, and where the hell are you?**

His phone rang. Boom. "Hey, Ace, I think she's seized control. She laid down the conditions under which she agreed. The guys are having fun, and she's going along with it. I'm watching, I won't let them go out of bounds."

"Thank God," he muttered. "Where are you?"

"Almost at Hilda's War Ink. That was one of her conditions, that she have a woman tattoo artist." He laughed. "You can tell she's new at this."

"Where the hell is Hilda's War Ink?"

Boom gave him the address.

Levi calculated distance and time. "Look, I'll be there in thirty. Don't let them get crazy."

"We're good. Babe has this."

She would, too, Levi thought. He was getting alarmed for nothing, and he couldn't be seen as protecting her. He should probably turn around and go back to headquarters, but—on second thought, he wanted to see this.

Hilda's War Ink was an unadorned storefront with the name on a sign and TATTOOS blinking in neon in the window. The number of vehicles parked in front probably made passersby think the place was doing a booming business. He found a parking spot down the street and headed in.

The front room was small and filled to overflowing with his team. There were three chairs, which meant the others were either sitting on the floor or leaning against the wall. From behind a drawn curtain came the buzz of a tattoo gun. "Hey, Ace," Jelly said with a wide grin. "Guess what?"

"I guess you've been up to some shit," he said equably and joined the wall leaners. "I was feeling left out."

There was a rumble of laughter, and from behind the curtain Babe called out, "No one is allowed behind the curtain! That's one of the rules. *Ouch!*"

"And I'm backing her up," came another female voice from behind the curtain. "Hold still, honey. Man, this is so pretty."

Crutch groaned. "Ah hell, you're getting a *pretty* tattoo?"

"What did you think I'd get?" she shot back.

"Something that makes a statement. *Pretty* doesn't make a statement."

"Not your tattoo, so butt out."

Levi grinned. He should have known she'd handle it. She hadn't taken any shit from any of them since day one. His personal opinion and involvement aside, the guys seemed to enjoy having her around. She was good at her job. Wanting to get in her pants was his problem, and he'd keep it that way.

"Tell us what you're getting," he called. "Describe it."

"None of your business. This is my tattoo, and mine alone." There was a quick intake of breath that signaled another stab of pain. Having a couple of tats himself, he knew how that went.

"How big is it?" Trapper asked. "A tiny little tat doesn't count."

"When it's my tat, I decide what counts. You don't get any input, remember?"

The back-and-forth went on, with Babe giving as good as she got, though her comments were interspersed with gasps and ouches and a few breaths sucked between clenched teeth.

"You're doing good," Hilda said encouragingly. "You're not bleeding much at all, and that's good for the longevity of the ink."

"Yay, me." She sounded disgruntled with the whole process now.

Levi crossed his arms and tried not to think about her with her shirt off—or maybe she was getting the tat on her hip and her pants were off. He thought how he'd like to be holding her hand and teasing her. Couldn't happen, and he had to stop this. The last thing he wanted was to get a boner right now. Instead he focused on whether or not she'd been able to get any useful intel with the drone, then whether or not he could try to wrangle a flight out to his own parents' home in Arizona, and damn if the desert heat wouldn't feel welcome. He always waited until the last minute in case anything came up, but given that they'd just got back from a mission—uneventful as it had been—something really big would have to happen for them to be called up. The team that was the most rested would go.

"*Ouch!*"

The disgruntled sound made them all laugh. Even Voodoo was smiling, and that was saying something.

"Not too much longer," the unseen Hilda said in a soothing voice.

Several of the guys checked the time. "About an hour," Crutch said. "Has to be small."

"About quarter sized," Hilda reported cheerfully. "But more ornate than you're thinking."

"Tiny," Trapper grumbled.

"My choice, remember," Babe growled. Her raspy voice went all the way to Levi's groin and he shifted uncomfortably, rubbed his eyes. Maybe this wouldn't take much longer; he was rooting for a *very* small tat, so they could all leave. They were all winding down. As he had the thought, Boom rolled his shoulders and stretched.

"Tiny's good," he rumbled. "The sooner this is finished, the sooner we can all go home and get some sleep."

"That was my original idea," Babe said. She was sounding more and more grumpy. "But no, the two wiseasses out there had to come up with the tattoo idea and the rest of you thought, yeah, let's get me inked and keep us all from getting some sleep. Now I'm the one in pain and bleeding, and all of you can damn well sit your asses there until this is finished!"

They sat. The "almost finished" still took longer than they'd anticipated. Then they listened to Hilda telling Babe how to care for the new ink, what to put on it, how long to baby it, things some of the guys had never heard before—either that or they'd been too drunk to either pay attention or remember. Levi had a couple of ink jobs himself; one he'd been sober while getting, the other he hadn't. He liked the drunk one best. Maybe one day he and Babe could compare their ink—

Shit.

Couldn't happen, at least not in the foreseeable future. He kept tripping himself up. Normally his self-control was better than this. He'd let himself kiss her, and that was his fault, not hers. Since then he'd relived every moment of how she'd tasted, how she'd responded, the sounds she made as she came. He wanted that again, every moment of it, but he wanted it with them both naked and his dick deep inside her. He wanted her, smart mouth and all.

Double shit.

He had to stop thinking about her. He was the team leader, and the cooperation and unity of the team was on his shoulders. This was on him, and he had to step up. Babe was now part of that team and would be for the foreseeable future. Letting sex and what he wanted even enter the equation was letting the team down, and he had to stop himself cold. Right now.

"I'd like to hang around for the finish, but I still need to get some work done," he said abruptly. They would know what he meant, but Hilda wouldn't. "Nothing else going on today, guys, and I mean it." He gave both Jelly and Crutch the evil eye. "Boom."

"Got it." With those two words Boom acknowledged he was on top of things, and Levi escaped out into the morning cold.

HE WAS GONE.

Jina felt Levi's absence as if a fire had gone out. Just knowing he was there had been both warmth and irritant, making her restless deep inside. How twisted was it that having him close made her feel both alive and furious? She wanted to ignore him, turn the page, focus forward, but just hearing his voice hit her hard.

Acknowledging that her own thinking was convoluted made her even angrier. She wanted things to be clear-cut, and they weren't.

Why had he even showed up today? He'd been on his way to headquarters. He—

He'd come to protect her.

The knowledge shot through her, and she forgot all about the sharp stinging sensation of the ink gun.

She could have used him to nix the idea at the airport, but now that she was here she was okay with the cool little tat she was getting. Rapport with the team was important, important enough for her to go along with this and rag at them for it. Levi knew that, too, but he'd still stopped what he was doing to come here and give her backup if she needed it, if the guys had been railroading her—not that Hilda would have done the tat if she'd thought there was anything like coercion going on, but none of them had known that when they chose this shop.

For all his dislike of having her on his team, time and again Levi had stepped up: when she'd fallen off the climbing rope and he'd caught her, when he'd intervened with the boot issue, when he'd babied her through the parachute training—and, yeah, now that she had some distance from it, she could see how he'd done more to help her than he'd had to do. Maybe he'd have done the same with a male trainee, but she kind of doubted it. One tandem jump, maybe, but not three. He'd safeguarded her from outside forces while she was getting drunk. He'd gone out of his way today to be here if she needed him.

Her heart squeezed and quick tears flooded her eyes.

She might be in love with the son of a bitch.

The thought was devastating.

She didn't want to love him. Lusting for him was okay. Lust was temporary, maybe acted on, likely ignored. Love under these circumstances was a recipe for a lot of pain. Maybe she could fight this nonsense down or it would go away on its own, because if you didn't feed something it died, right? She wanted this feeling to die. She didn't want to care what he did or where he was. She didn't want to get blindsided out of the blue by moments like this. The sick feeling in her stomach said that wasn't likely to happen, or at least not any time soon.

The good thing was she was lying on her stomach, so Hilda couldn't see the tears. Even if she had, she'd probably seen a lot of tears in the eyes of those under her ink gun.

Hilda finished with the immediate aftercare and bandage, and

Jina sat up. The stinging in the middle of her back had already mostly stopped. Focusing forward, Jina put Levi away in the back of her mind and instead kind of savored the realization that she, Jina Modell, had a tattoo. She'd always been so vanilla, stuck in the middle, nothing unusual or outstanding, that getting a tattoo made her feel daring even if it hadn't been her idea. Besides, her little tattoo was cool, different, *and* pretty; she'd hit the trifecta with it.

She tugged her sweatshirt down and hopped off the padded table. Hilda grinned at her as she removed the paper covering from the table, wadded it up, and tossed it in the trash. "How does it feel?"

"Fairly okay." She liked Hilda, who had her black hair pulled up on top of her head in a short, brushy ponytail, a single gold hoop in one ear, and technicolor eyeshadow that showcased her vivid blue eyes; she wore an off-the-shoulder tattered sweatshirt that bared one slim shoulder adorned with a snarling lion's head. Hilda was about five-ten, maybe a hundred and thirty pounds, wore so many rings it was impossible to tell if she was married or just liked rings, and exuded a powerfully cheerful sexuality. Crutch had already been eyeing her with intent.

Jina pulled back the curtain and stepped into the main room. The guys who were sitting came to their feet, and the ones who had been standing straightened away from the wall. "What did you get?" Jelly asked.

"None of your business."

"Where is it?"

"On my back. And, no, you can't see it. Don't even ask."

"Then how do we know you actually got one and aren't just tricking us?"

"The fact that I'm charging three hundred bucks," Hilda said, going to the cash register and opening it. "The design is small but awesome, with a color change."

Three hundred dollars. Jina sighed and reached for her bag. Good thing she had the money, because she hadn't thought to ask before-hand.

"We've got this," Boom said, pulling out his wallet. He opened it, then eyed the other guys. "Pony up, assholes. This wasn't her idea, why should she have to pay for it?"

Voodoo scowled a little, but there wasn't any complaining; they each pulled out fifty bucks and handed it over to Hilda. As she was putting the cash away, Voodoo leaned on the counter and said bluntly, "Are you free tonight?"

Crutch looked outraged that Voodoo had beaten him to it.

Hilda laughed out loud. "Honey, I have a three-year-old and a one-year-old. I'm not free *any* night, not to mention my husband might not like you."

"Can't blame a man for trying," Voodoo replied in the most civil tone of voice Jina had ever heard him use. She gaped at him, trying to reconcile grumpy sneering Voodoo with a man some women might actually go out with. He scowled at her. "What?"

"Nothing," she said, eyes wide. "I didn't know you were human. Just startled me, is all."

They trooped out amid jokes and needling, and Voodoo reverted to his surly default setting, which was fine with her. Getting a blast of cold air in her face seemed to trip the switch between functional and exhausted. Making her ride with Jelly had been such a bad idea, now they had to fight the traffic back to the airport, get her car, then she'd have to drive home from there.

She couldn't do it. Her car could just stay at the airport. She was going back tonight, anyway. "Take me home," she mumbled. "I'll Uber to the airport tonight."

"Good plan," Jelly said. "You look dead."

"I feel dead." Not *too* dead, though; as soon as she was in Jelly's truck out of the cold—and turned to the side so her new tattoo didn't scrub against the back of the seat—she took out her phone and texted both Ailani and Terisa. Too bad the others weren't married, but at least Snake and Boom would pay for their part in the morning's events.

Because Jelly was Jelly, she gave him a warning. "If you take me anywhere other than to my home, I'll kill you. Are we clear on this?"

"Jeez, Babe, you sound as if you don't trust me."

"I trust you in certain things. This isn't one of them. Drive."

He grinned and put the truck in gear.

There had been a lot of times since being picked as a trainee when she'd wished she didn't have a second-floor condo, and this was one of them. With Jelly's cheerful good-bye ringing in her ears, she literally hauled herself up the stairs, locked the door behind her, then dropped her bag on the floor and made it as far as her couch before determination gave out on her.

BEING HOME WITH her family made Jina feel as if she could finally breathe after months of not being able to relax. Both her parents, as well as her just-younger brother Taz, who was home on leave from the army, waited up for her that night even though it was after midnight when she finally drove up to her childhood home. The front porch light was on, and light was also spilling from the living room and kitchen windows, which were on the front. Jina got out of her rental car and as she hefted her suitcase out of the backseat the front door opened and all of them came outside.

"Get the suitcase for your sister," she heard her dad say quietly, and Taz obediently stepped off the porch and took the suitcase from her. Then she was enveloped in her parents' enthusiastic hugs and kisses, and the familiar sound and touch of them went straight to her heart.

"Your hair is so *long*," her mother said, touching the dark fall of hair that streamed down Jina's back.

"I know. I've been too busy to get it cut. Maybe you can whack off a few inches for me, while I'm here." She hugged her mother again. "Just like when I was little."

"I trimmed your bangs, I didn't do big haircuts."

Taz thunked the suitcase down just inside the door and gave Jina a peculiar look, which she was too tired to decipher. Instead she said, "Where's Caleigh?" because she knew her baby sister was home from college.

"Out on a date, she should be home anytime now. Come on, let's sit down for a minute and let me look at you. It feels like forever since you've been home!"

Before Jina could sit down, her dad ruffled her hair and pulled her in for a quick kiss on her forehead. "Glad you're here, pumpkin," he rumbled, his voice raspy like hers. Rather, hers was raspy like his.

"I was afraid I wouldn't make it," she replied and tried unsuccessfully to stifle a huge yawn. Her eyelids felt as if they each weighed ten pounds. She dropped into one of the armchairs. "Monday I had to fly to Paris on a last-minute deal, and I had no idea if I'd get finished in time to come home. I made it, but I got back to D.C. this morning with a huge case of jet lag."

"Paris!" Her mother's eyes got big. "I'd love to see Paris!"

"I might, too," Jina grumbled. "But all I saw was what was on the way from the airport, then looking out a single window while I worked." She yawned again. "Maybe someday."

Her mom, Melissa, was a pretty blond woman with an hourglass figure, which Jina's two sisters had inherited and she hadn't. She wore pajamas and a robe, her face scrubbed clean of any makeup she might have worn during the day, but even without makeup she still looked darn good. Jina hoped she aged half as well as her mom had done.

She pulled off her jacket and her mom immediately gave her a piercing look. "What's going on? You're so thin!"

"What?" Jina looked down at herself, trying to marshal her tired mind. Oh, yeah, the working out. "I told you I'd been working out like crazy. My brain is so tired at the end of the day, running helps me relax. I don't have to think about anything when I'm running." None of what she'd said was a lie, which was good considering her exhaustion.

"Well, I'll get some food in you while you're here." From the grim note in her mother's voice, anyone would have thought Jina had been forcibly starved.

"The thought of your German chocolate cake pushed me the whole time I was in Paris," she said truthfully. "Is it made already?" She wouldn't mind having cake and milk before going to bed.

"No, I'm so sorry, I was going to make it tomorrow. Today," Melissa corrected, because it was after midnight.

Jina yawned again. "That's okay. Y'all, I'm falling over I'm so tired. Is it okay if I just go to bed?"

"Of course it is! Your bed is made and ready. Go on to bed and we'll see you in the morning."

That was the most excellent thing she'd heard all day. Escaping to the room her older sister, Ashley, had once occupied in glorious solitude while Jina shared with Caleigh, but which had become Jina's alone when Ashley moved out, she heaved a sigh of relief. A quick shower, a ginger application of Aquaphor ointment to her tattoo, which was damn hard to reach where it was, then she tumbled into bed in panties and tee shirt and went right to sleep, soothed by the familiarity of her surroundings. She was home!

HOME OR NOT, the habit of months was a hard thing to break, even when jet lag was thrown into the equation. Before dawn Jina was pulling on sweats and lacing up her trainers, because she had to keep up her training, and doing so before the holiday got into gear was the best time. After some stretches, she let herself out the front door and trotted down the driveway, hit the secondary road, and turned to the left. A couple of miles down a small road to the right would loop around and cut back into the secondary road, bringing her right back here. She estimated the entire distance at around eight miles, which was a nice run. There was just enough light to see.

She had reconnected to the secondary road, with a mile or so left before reaching home, when she heard footsteps pounding behind her. Alarm skittered along her nerves, and she threw a quick look over her shoulder even as she picked up the pace. Just because she was home didn't mean there was no danger. But she recognized Taz, dressed much as she was, and slowed until he came abreast of her before picking up her speed and running side by side with him.

"You're up early," he said, his breath just a little short though his face was shiny with sweat.

"So are you. Best time to get in a run."

"What the hell's going on?"

Startled, she said, "What?," and threw him a frowning glance. It still shook her some to see her little brother looking so military, with his high and tight haircut, erect posture, and confident way of talking. Taz had been a little shy when he was younger—not with the family, but in school—so the confidence was good. He was also in really good shape.

"You were hauling your suitcase around last night as if it was mostly empty, and I know the damn thing had to weigh fifty pounds. How long are you planning to stay, a month?"

"Just until Sunday. And it was forty-two pounds."

"You were picking it up with one hand."

She didn't pause in her stride, just popped a biceps for him. "Feel," she said proudly.

He obligingly squeezed her muscle. "Nice. What are you doing?"

"You know. Running, lifting some weights. The usual stuff."

"Bullshit."

Like a sister, she rolled her eyes. "What does it look like I'm doing right now? Sleeping late?"

"That's what's wrong. You've never been into exercising. And I've seen gym rats; you're not in gym rat shape, you're in something-else-entirely kind of shape." Taz had always been observant. "What are you *really* doing in this new job of yours that keeps you tied up for months?"

"It's computer stuff, just like I said. Software applications and training." That was the absolute truth, and the annoyed tone was just right. "The running and lifting weights is because I was spending so much time in front of a computer I was turning into a lump. I also took a couple of martial-arts classes. There's a lot of crime in the D.C. area, in case you didn't realize."

"Does the software have military applications?"

She shrugged. "I guess it could. I'm not with the military, though." Again, complete truth.

"And you going off to Paris at a moment's notice—"

"Was troubleshooting. I'm good at what I do. Want to play some games, try to beat me?"

"Forget it," he grumbled, because neither he nor Jordan had ever been able to regularly best her at computer games. Then he said, "Race you!," and took off at a sprint.

He was taller than her, had longer legs, was younger (even if only by a year and a half). He ran a lot, because he was in the army. But he was years out of basic training, and the conditioning the GO-Teams went through was constant, unrelenting. Jina's reaction time had been honed so that she was sprinting, too, before the word "race" was out of his mouth. Top end speed was one thing, and she likely couldn't match him, so she leaped over a ditch and went cross-country. Hah! That would teach him to try to get the jump on her, instead of setting the rules out first. She heard him yelling at her, but when she glanced over her shoulder he was running as if he were in the last leg of a relay with just a hundred yards to the finish line.

She raced over the rough ground of the field, once planted with what looked like soybeans but now lying fallow for the winter, the humps of the rows forcing her to pay attention to where she placed her feet—or at least as much attention as she could, given that she was leaping over them like a deer. She reached a fence and barely paused, bracing her left hand on a post and vaulting over the strands of wire. There had been rain recently and the ground was soft, but not so soft that she bogged down.

This is nothing, she thought as she raced through her dad's small apple orchard, the tree limbs bare now, then vaulted another fence. The land was flat here in south Georgia, unlike the hills where she trained. "Slowpoke!" she yelled, not sure Taz could hear her, but she thought she heard him bellow something in response and laughed. This was how it had always been with her brothers, in constant competition with them, trying to keep up and most often being left behind. She might not win this race, but Taz would know he'd been in a race.

She pelted forward, approaching the house from the left side while Taz turned in from the road and pounded up the driveway. He cut across the yard and was still ten yards away when she jumped onto the front porch. "Hah! I won!" she crowed as she wrenched open the front door and burst into the warmth of family, the smell of fresh-brewed coffee and bacon cooking in the oven. Their dad was sitting at the table enjoying his first cup of coffee; Caleigh was nowhere to be seen, so she was probably still asleep.

"You cheated," Taz charged.

"How? What were the rules?"

He looked frustrated, because he hated like poison to lose at anything. "We didn't make any," he groused.

Melissa eyed them with a long-suffering, will-this-ever-end look in her eye. "You two go shower, because you're sweaty and you stink. After we have breakfast, I'm putting everyone to work. Got that?"

"Yes, ma'am," they both said, then Jina bolted for the Jack-and-Jill bathroom between her bedroom and Caleigh's, so she could get a jump on the hot water. The battle for hot water was an old one, and the loser got to finish showering in the cold.

Just as she closed the door she heard Taz mutter, "Computers, my ass."

Okay, so he didn't believe her. She didn't care. She was home for Thanksgiving, her new tattoo was itching, and the promise of her favorite dessert in the whole world would get her through jet lag, parachute jumps, boring missions—and missing Levi.

She briefly leaned her head against the doorjamb, fighting against the hollow feeling in her chest, then shoved the feeling down and got on with the day.

FIFTEEN

Joan Kingsley punched the remote button that closed the garage door behind her and got out of her BMW SUV. She opened the back and retrieved the small overnight bag she'd taken to visit her son for Thanksgiving. Once she'd had a driver, but now she preferred to drive herself because she would forever be suspicious that any driver she hired would be a spy for Axel MacNamara. Driving in D.C. traffic was a nightmare and occasionally she would Uber if she needed to work during the commute, but for the most part she drove.

The inconvenience was a small one in comparison to all the other changes in her life, but it grated.

To all appearances she was doing exactly as MacNamara had ordered her to do. She knew all mail she sent and received was photographed and opened, though very skillfully. No packages arrived that hadn't already gone through inspection. There were bugs in her house, all her calls on both cell and landline were monitored, and two or more agents followed her everywhere she went. She was nailed down as tightly as they could manage, without actually arresting her—which would be difficult to do unless some evidence was manufactured, because she'd taken care that nothing provable existed.

They underestimated Devan.

It was so simple, really, and perhaps that was what created the hole in their surveillance. Her house was watched—when she was here. When she left, the watchers left and followed her. They trusted that their listening bugs and her own alarm system had the property covered with video as well as the more traditional entry alarms. She knew the alarm system had been hacked into, which gave her an advantage because she knew what they saw. She'd checked her video feed and verified that the view of the bottom of the mudroom door was blocked by a chair on which she sat to change her shoes whenever she went into the back garden.

There were two churches on her block where Devan could park without attracting attention. It was a simple matter for him to approach the house from the rear, using the code she had given him for the back gate so no alarm was raised, and slip a single sheet of paper under the mudroom door. He knew what days her housekeeper, Helen, worked, and what hours; Joan had perfected the art of retrieving the paper without it being noticed. Sometimes she would slip it up her pants leg while she was bent over changing her shoes and read it later when she was in a bathroom. There were other methods, and so far they had all worked. She and Devan communicated with ease, and it gave her enormous gratification every time they outwitted Axel MacNamara.

She never went straight to the mudroom; that in itself could look suspicious. Though she was anxious to find out if the Graeme Burger bait had been taken, the result would be the same regardless of when she found out. The laundry was adjacent to the mudroom, and when she took the day's dirty clothing down, she'd find out then if there was a message.

Instead she took her bag upstairs to her spacious walk-in closet and unpacked it right then instead of putting the chore off until later. The afternoon was fading away and she was tired from traveling; she wanted a shower first, then she would take her laundry downstairs. Waiting was both difficult and amusing, knowing the bugs were picking up the sounds of her moving around her house.

She showered, changed into her nightgown and a robe, gave her distinctive silver hair a good brushing, moisturized her skin. Then she took her dirty laundry downstairs and dumped it in the hamper for Helen to deal with; as she left the laundry room she noticed the note on the floor and her heart thumped. Going over to the door she ostensibly checked the lock, though she knew good and well it was secured, and while she was there glanced down to see the words "Bait taken. One."

So the lure had been a success. "One" designated which GO-Team had been sent to cover Graeme Burger's visit to Paris. She and Devan had devised a simple code, listing the teams in alphabetical order by the team leader's last name, and "Butcher" was number one. She was vaguely disappointed; she'd have preferred that Tyler Gordon's team be the one because that had originally been the team led by Morgan Yancy, the man who had killed Dexter. That would have been poetic justice, but in the end which team didn't matter. All she and Devan needed to do was slowly lure them into a trap. Nothing would hurt MacNamara more, and bait him into the trap she had planned at the end, than the destruction of one of his beloved teams.

THE MISSIONS WEREN'T always boring.

Over the next three months, Jina learned to treasure the ones that were. Likewise, the missions seldom went as smoothly as her first one. There were hiccups in timing, unforeseen circumstances that interrupted whatever they were doing—such as an auto accident happening in front of them and bringing traffic to a halt—minor injuries in training or on the job that interfered with the fluidity of the team, or a glitch in communication. The one time they were in the field with no cell service, the equipment malfunctioned. Tweety worked perfectly; she could hear the guys perfectly. The glitch came with her own communication back to the guys, with breaks in their ability to hear what she was saying. They were lucky in that nothing bad happened because they couldn't hear her, and the whole point of her being on the team was her being able to alert the guys to any approaching trouble. If her throat mic didn't work, then there was no point to her even being there.

Just after Christmas—which they got to spend with their families, hallelujah, but they had to leave the day after—they spent almost three solid weeks in Colombia establishing pattern of life on a bad actor. They had cell service, so the throat mics weren't needed. From Colombia they went back to Paris and she damn near froze to death, partly because she'd just spent those three weeks in a warm clime and her system had no time to adjust. Then it snowed twice, nothing more than a dusting each time, but still—insult, meet injury. From Paris they went to Egypt, spent a grand total of eighteen hours there, then on to the Philippines to fetch a defector. That was the first time Jina got to use Tweety for his designated job, with no cell service out in the boonies, watching the guys' backs for them—and her throat mic wouldn't work half the time.

By the time they got home from that particular mission—having hitched a ride in the belly of a cargo plane, which was *not* comfortable—they'd crossed so many time zones going back and forth that she had no idea what day it was. She assumed it was still January, but she wouldn't swear to it. She was grouchy, sleepy, hungry, had a massive headache, and she was completely pissed off about the throat mic. She grabbed her stuff and stomped off in the direction where she thought she'd parked her car maybe a month ago, though maybe not. No matter that she needed a shower, a cup of coffee, twenty-four hours of sleep, and food, in any order whatsoever because she was beyond caring. No, she did care. She'd last had a shower . . . she wasn't certain. It had been in Paris, though— whenever they'd been there. Didn't matter. She was taking the faulty throat mic to headquarters to start raising hell, and some shit was going to start rolling uphill until whoever was in charge of R&D got this POS *fixed*.

She couldn't find her car. There was snow on the ground, covering the vehicles. And she was brain-dead. She stomped up and down a couple of aisles, because she had a vague memory of parking close to the fence . . . maybe. Maybe that had been the first Paris trip. None of the snow-covered lumps looked familiar. Snow crunched under her sneaks, spilled over the tops and down into her shoes. Yeah, she'd paid attention on that first mission and this time wore something other than boots, and now look.

There were sounds coming from different aisles of the parking lot as the guys found their vehicles and started them. No one moved, though, because they all had to deal with the snow on their wind- shields. Several of them got out and began scraping the snow off. Yeah, she had a snow-scraper in her car, too, a foreign piece of equip- ment to someone from south Georgia, but she'd learned her first winter in D.C. that the gadget was necessary. All she had to do was find her car and she could scrape with the best of them.

Or maybe she'd just stand right here in the middle of the parking lot and sleep, and worry about her car tomorrow.

A truck door slammed, and she heard footsteps crunching to- ward her. She turned and saw Levi, big and imposing in his heavy jacket, a black knit cap covering his hair. "Something wrong?" he asked, coming to a stop beside her.

She had spent the long weeks since Thanksgiving ignoring him as much as possible, which wasn't as much as she'd have liked because he was the team leader and she *had* to pay attention to him. But she tried not to look at him, to keep her head down and acknowledge him only when he directly addressed her, which didn't happen that often because he was doing his part to ignore her, too. *Damn him.* He was better at this ignoring crap than she was, and every night she went to sleep resenting him for ever letting her know he wanted her. Her equilibrium hadn't been the same since.

"I can't find my car," she muttered.

He rubbed his eyes. He didn't look as tired as she felt, adding to her resentment, but he wasn't brimming with energy, either. "I'll take you home," he said, and turned away, the matter settled as far as he was concerned.

Take her home? She was tired, not crazy. "No," she said bluntly. "I need my car."

He turned back and eyed her. "I don't think you're okay to drive," he finally said.

"If the guys are okay, I'm okay. Besides, I need to take this piece of shit throat mic to headquarters and ram it down someone's throat."

His lips twitched. He looked up at the sky, then back at her. Finally he pulled out his phone and looked at it. His lips twitched again, and she got the feeling he was trying not to smile. If he smiled, she'd punch him in the nose. "Uh-huh. What day do you think this is?"

She knew a trap when she saw one, but she couldn't pull out her own phone to check without proving that she didn't know. She thought she'd kept track of the days, despite all the time-zone hopping. "Friday afternoon." She looked at the sky, too. "Latish." Maybe that was wrong, because something didn't look right.

"How about Sunday morning, earlyish."

Oh. That was what didn't look right; the sun was in the wrong place. She shrugged. "I'm just a day and a half off. Not bad."

"Not too bad. But I'll take the piece of shit mic and shove it up someone's ass, not you."

"I said down someone's throat, not up his ass."

"Whatever. I'll be the one who does it."

"It's my mic."

"It's my team."

She wanted to argue but there was no refuting that point, so she pressed her lips together. He was the boss. A complaint coming from him would carry a lot more weight. She dug in her equipment bag and pulled out the offending item, thrust it at him. "Have at it."

He took the throat mic and shoved it in his pocket. Deprived of the prospect of unloading her ire on someone, she could feel what little energy she had draining from her. She needed to find her car and get home; everything else could wait.

An idea sluggishly emerged from the morass that was her brain. Her car keys were secured in an outside pocket of her equipment bag. She fumbled for the pocket, pulled out her keys, and hit the button for the alarm. Obediently, from somewhere close by, a horn started blowing. She turned in a circle, trying to pinpoint the sound.

"Over here!" Boom bellowed from where he was busy scraping his windshield, pointing to the left.

She waved. "Thanks!" She stopped the alarm and started down the row.

"Wait."

Reluctantly she turned back. "What?"

"I was serious. You're barely functioning. I'll take you home."

She considered that for a whole second. "Would you take any of the other guys home?"

He didn't like that. She saw it in the way his eyes narrowed. But he didn't lie. "No."

"Then you aren't taking me home."

He dug in his pocket, came out with a candy bar. "Then take this."

It was a Baby Ruth, chocolate and peanuts, a triple whammy of sugar, protein, and a little bit of caffeine. Oh, thank God. She grabbed it from him, not caring at all that he was the one to provide it, and tore it open as enthusiastically as a tiger on a fresh kill. From now on she'd carry her own supply of candy bars; she learned something new on every mission. "Thanks."

Without acknowledging her thanks he turned back to his truck and climbed in. Jina trudged through the snow to her car, still gnawing on the Baby Ruth. As she passed a couple of the guys she saw that they were chewing on something, too, so evidently this was something they did to give them a last burst of needed energy.

She wondered if she'd taken Levi's only bar of candy.

If so . . . tough.

Because they'd just come home from such a long, convoluted job, they didn't have to show up at the training site again until Wednesday, and she needed every hour of the recovery time. When she got home she fell facedown on the couch and slept four hours, then woke befuddled and annoyed. Not knowing what else to do, she changed to sweats and went for a run. Then she ate some peanut butter crackers, showered, and went back to bed. The fitful, out-of-sync sleep continued. She was awake at midnight, doing laundry. After another nap, she forced herself to stay awake all day Monday, going for a couple of short runs, cleaning out the refrigerator, buying groceries. Her brain felt as if it was made of fog. But she stayed awake until a reasonable hour, then slept twelve hours and woke feeling much better, except for the memory of a vivid dream about Levi.

She didn't want to relive those moments in the field when he'd been kissing her as if he could inhale her, but her subconscious decreed otherwise. He'd given her his candy bar—the bastard. Just when she got a mental wall against him somewhat built, he'd do something like that, or like going to the tattoo parlor to protect her, and BAM! all her carefully placed mind-blocks came crashing down. Her dream wasn't exactly like what had actually happened; in her dream, the entire team stood around watching, and making angry comments.

She woke feeling depressed; how else could the guys be expected to react? Even her subconscious agreed, and hammered the lesson home.

She remained depressed all day Tuesday; even a long run that exhausted her didn't produce enough endorphins to counteract her angry longing. She wanted Levi, not just physically—though that was intense—but the everyday things that cemented life. She wanted to eat breakfast with him, argue with him, bitch at him about leaving the lid up, snuggle against his back at night. Never before had she cared about a man enough to think about a life together, but with Levi . . . yes. She wanted that.

Why couldn't she have felt this way about Donnelly? He was a nice guy. Going through life with him would be easy, and comfortable, with shared laughter. On the other hand, nothing about Levi struck her as easy. He was hard, somewhat grim, uncompromising. He lived a dangerous life, regularly risking injury and death, and he did it without hesitation.

Hard on that thought came the realization that she shared that life, that her part in the missions was mostly in the background but not without risk. She was that extra layer of protection for him and the other guys. What if something happened to him, to any of them, on her watch? A chill ran through her. She should have realized this before, and on a superficial level she had, but until this moment she hadn't *felt* the weight of responsibility for their lives. The heavy mantle of it settled on her shoulders, sank into her pores, and forever changed how she regarded her job.

Levi could die if she screwed up.

No matter how angry she got at him, no matter how much the situation frustrated her, that home truth drove her hard when Wednesday rolled around and they returned to their training routine. After such a long mission they were slated to be home for a healthy stretch, but they never slacked up with the training. For her part she ran harder, longer, pushing herself more than she ever had before, and she'd pushed herself plenty. She put in long hours with Tweety's program, practicing and then practicing some more, honing her skills.

Whoever's ass Levi had crawled up about her malfunctioning throat mic came through with a replacement that was guaranteed to work. The problem had evidently been a bad laryngeal sensor. She put the new throat mic through the mill, making the guys participate despite their bellyaching, on the grounds that it was their butts on the line. The new mic performed the way it was supposed to, with clear and reliable audio into their headsets. Finally satisfied, she gave it a thumbs-up.

"About time," Levi said drily, when he found out. "Now we can go active again."

She was startled enough to look directly at him, something she tried not to do because the impact of his intense gaze was enough to make her falter. He was standing closer than she liked, close enough that she was caught in his gravitational pull; she had to fight to keep from leaning closer to him. "What?"

"All the equipment has to be okayed before we go."

Her mouth fell open. "You mean—we were waiting on *me*?"

"Yep." One side of his mouth quirked. "Not that we minded the down time, but I was beginning to think you were going to design and manufacture your own."

"Why didn't you say something?"

"You're in charge of Tweety. Until you say it's ready to go, it doesn't go. If there had been an emergency we'd have gone without you, but things worked out."

"Go *without* me?" she repeated, horrified by the idea, though logically she knew that if a team member got hurt the rest of the team would deploy without him if necessary.

"We got along without you before," he pointed out, his tone even and a little cool, the way it always got when he wanted to put some distance between her and the rest of the team. It stung, and she tried never to let him see that it stung. Did he think that if he managed to push her out, she'd still want to get involved with him? She'd be mad as hell, because she didn't like to fail at anything. She wouldn't let herself quit, and she'd fought like hell to be good enough, so the only way to get her off the team would be to somehow force her to fail.

The only other option she could see was if she asked to be transferred to another team, and she thought that idea would go over like a lead balloon. Teamwork was essential, and the drone operators had been assigned to the team MacNamara had thought each one would work best with. Moreover, after the long months she'd spent with *her* team, she didn't want to go through it all again with another bunch. She'd tested out at the top of the trainees, start to finish; no one else could protect her guys as well as she could. Damn if she'd transfer. Damn if she'd quit.

No matter how she looked at it, that left them with nowhere to go. One of them would have to bend, and it didn't look as if that was going to happen.

"That was before," she said just as coolly, and left it at that.

Their next mission put them back in Colombia. Her work cell phone went off in the middle of the night, and the shot of adrenaline woke her up as thoroughly as if someone had poured ice water on her. She bolted out of bed, hit the brew button on the coffee maker she'd installed in the bathroom, and threw on her clothes before even checking instructions. She swished some mouthwash, gave her hair a quick brush and secured it in a ponytail, then got her checklist to make sure she didn't forget anything important. Her go-bag was in the trunk of her car, better packed now than it had been on that first trip.

There had been a big powwow over whether or not the drones and the laptops, with their highly classified software, should stay with the operators or be safely stowed in some secure place and checked out only as needed. When a GO-Team was activated it usually had to go, top speed, and wading through protocol to get the drone and laptop would slow things down. On the other hand, Jina hadn't been wild about the idea of having something that valuable in her safekeeping, and neither had any of the other operators. Places were broken into all the time, and laptops stolen. In the immortal words of Forrest Gump, shit happened.

The compromise was that a GO-Team supervisor, one per each shift, was assigned laptop/drone duty. Whatever team was activated, the supervisor had to get the designated laptop and drone and get it to their point of egress. Getting the correct laptop and drone was of the utmost importance, because the drone was programmed to recognize the team members of the unit it had been assigned to. She couldn't specifically alert one team member if she didn't know who it was; she would have to alert all, wasting time and effort as they all reacted to a threat that applied to only one of them. So— individualized drone recognition.

She did, however, have her headset and radio, and the weapon she'd been instructed to carry if they were traveling by a means that allowed the team to go armed. This time the firearm had to go with her, meaning they weren't traveling commercial. She preferred commercial over hitching a ride on whatever military or cargo plane they could wrangle, but so far commercial was the exception rather than the rule.

By the time she had checked all items off her list and was ready to go, the coffee was made. She turned off the machine, poured the coffee into a thermos she had sitting ready, dumped the grounds into a plastic bag placed there just for that purpose, gave the carafe a quick rinse, grabbed the rest of her stuff, and was out the door. She dropped the plastic bag containing the coffee grounds in a trash can at the curb. She had learned, after that horrendously long mission, to not put scraps of food in her kitchen trash can assuming she'd be there to take it out before it started stinking. This type of job required thinking through every detail, mundane or not.

At 2:13 A.M. she ran out of the condo building. Her car was covered with such a thick coating of frost that at first she thought it had snowed since she'd gone to bed. Unsurprised but swearing under her breath anyway, she started her car, scraped the windshield just enough that she had a small clear space to peer through, and was on her way.

She reached the small private airfield they'd been instructed to go to, and the bottom dropped out of her stomach. This was the same airfield where Levi and Boom had forced her to parachute; though it was dark now and deep in winter's grip, she recognized the hell hole. Instead of a Twin Otter idling on the runway, a small jet sat there, lights on, waiting for them.

Levi was the first one there. The second arrival was herself.

She parked beside his truck, took a bracing breath, squared her shoulders, and climbed out of her car. On the other side of his truck, a door opened and slammed shut as he got out. Levi being Levi, there was no interior light to give his position away. Annoyed, she realized all the others likely turned off their interior lights, too; one more thing to add to her never-ending list of things to learn and do.

Silently she got out her gear, her go-bag, her thermos, and locked the car, though considering how cold it was, waiting *inside* the car would be smarter.

"C'mon," Levi said, "we'll board the plane and wait there."

"I need to wait for the air mail," she said, referring to Tweety and its carrier.

"He can bring it to the plane. Same amount of time, and you won't be cold. Besides, first ones on the plane snag the best seats."

"I'm just glad there *are* seats," she muttered. When they'd hitched a ride home in a cargo plane, comfort had been secondary. They'd parked themselves wherever they could, in whatever position they could manage.

Two other sets of headlights were approaching; their opportunity to be the first ones aboard was fast disappearing, so she fell into step beside Levi. She'd never been in a small jet before, and she was curious.

The pilot met them at the steps and eyed their bags. "Anything need to go in the hold?"

Levi said, "No, we travel light."

That was an understatement. Their go-bags were all small duffels, even hers. She had diversified and refined, and her bag now weighed a good five pounds less than it had before.

She climbed the steps and poked her head in. The operative word was *small*. There was no standing in the cabin; it was like getting into a car. The interior had been configured to allow seating for eight passengers, but the jet wasn't a luxury model. Aft were four seats facing forward, two to a row. Then there were two seats facing the other four. The fore seat was a two-seat bench, like a small loveseat, with an arm divider, and it faced the cabin door. Levi pushed her forward, into the plane, and by instinct she started down the narrow aisle to take one of the seats in back.

"Here," Levi said, taking her arm and pretty much depositing her on the loveseat, in the seat closest to the pilot. Then he dropped into the seat beside her.

Not good.

"I wanted to sit in back."

"Yeah, but I need to sit here, and I want you beside me." His dark eyes raked her face. "Don't argue."

"Why do you need to sit here?" she asked, just as Trapper came up the steps and poked his head in.

"Because that's the one seat where he can stretch out his legs,"

Trapper groused. "No matter how hard I try to get here first, he always beats me."

She could see that. Levi was the tallest of the team, and the space between the other seats would be tight even for the other guys. What she didn't see was why she had to sit beside him; shouldn't she take one of the other seats to give someone else more room? She would rather sit beside any of the others, even Voodoo. Voodoo's surliness was easier to take than feeling her nerves frayed by every brush of Levi's arm, or his leg, or feeling the heat emanating from him even across the arm rest. Her senses were so acutely focused on him that she could even *smell* him, that stomach-clenching scent of heat and skin and testosterone. That was all it took to send her senses reeling back to those moments when she'd felt his weight bearing her down, the thrust of his knee between her legs, the hard bulge of his erection just where—

She took a deep, quiet breath, forcing the memory-sensation away. She was warm, now, heat suffusing her entire body, even her finger-tips. Her mouth felt full and soft, as if he'd been kissing her.

This was torture.

She started to move, no matter what he said. But then the other guys were climbing in, filling the other seats. Voodoo was the last to arrive—except for the headquarters guy who ran up with Tweety and the laptop. She got up to take possession of both, signing the three-part form he thrust at her because even off-the-books entities still had paperwork, and when she turned back Voodoo had taken the last available regular seat. She curled her lip in his direction, not that he cared because he didn't see it. Resigned, she sat back down beside Levi, and buckled in.

As soon as they were in the air, Levi nudged his knee against hers. "You gonna share that coffee you've been hiding?" he asked, a twinkle replacing the usual somberness in his eyes. "I saw the thermos when you got out of the car, and I know you didn't fill it with milk."

Six other heads turned in her direction. "Coffee?" Boom said, his tone hopeful.

Now she knew why Levi had wanted her beside him; coffee was the lure. The realization was both lowering and relieving.

"Blabbermouth," she muttered at him. Louder she asked, "Did *none* of you think to bring coffee? Never mind. Of course you didn't. You're men. I lost my head there, for a second."

"It's the job," Boom said. "We just get up and go."

"So did I, but I punched a button on the coffeemaker before doing anything else." Resigned, she looked around. "Anything y'all can use for cups? The thermos top is *mine*, and I'm not sharing."

They began scrounging around. A few polystyrene cups were found. Levi stuck his head through the curtain that closed off the cockpit, and the pilot was good enough to donate a few more. The pilot had his own thermos of coffee, but he didn't offer to share. Smart man.

Dividing the coffee eight ways, there was no way for any of them to get much more than an ounce each, maybe an ounce and a half, but when it came to coffee an ounce was better than nothing. Reduced to sips, she savored every one of them. It wasn't much, but it would get her through.

After the coffee was gone, she hauled out the laptop and checked the program. There wasn't any real need to, but it kept her busy.

Levi's long legs were stretched out, and he reclined his seat, settled into a more comfortable position, and tipped his cap forward to cover his eyes. Jina glanced around; because the two seats closest to them were facing backward, Crutch, seated on the opposite side of the aisle and facing forward, was the only other team member whose face she could actually see, and he was already asleep. All of them had reclined their seats and were doing their combat-nap routines, grabbing sleep while they could.

They were the experienced ones, so she should follow their example. She took off her coat and pulled it over her like a blanket, then reclined her seat, curled on her side away from Levi, and closed her eyes.

Maybe she dozed. At the least she created a cocoon for herself, with her head almost covered by her coat. She could still feel Levi beside her, hear his deep breathing as he slept. That was worse, infinitely worse, than if he'd been awake. This was what it would be like if they were together, having him beside her as they slept. She wouldn't be curled away from him, she would have her head pillowed on his broad shoulder, and his rough hands would reach for her every time they changed positions. Sometimes her back would be against him and he'd cup her breasts, his penis would be nestled against her bottom, and if she wiggled just right the head would slip inside her a little. Levi would wake up, and—

Behind her, he shifted position. His arm dropped heavily from the dividing armrest onto her hip, his fingers resting against her butt. She froze, listening, but his breathing remained as deep and even as before. Carefully she lowered the edge of her coat enough to peep at him. His eyes were closed, his features relaxed. Slowly, moving in increments, she pulled one arm out from under the coat and hooked her finger in the cuff of his sleeve, lifted his arm—

His eyes opened.

She froze. That dark gaze roamed sleepily over her, starting at her face and moving down, taking in the way the back of his hand rested against her butt, how gingerly she held his sleeve. Slowly, ever so slowly, he moved his fingers—back and forth, caressing, rubbing, as if he savored even this small contact. His sleepy gaze was raw and naked and hungry, slamming her with the focus of his need. Then his gaze shuttered and silently he moved his arm back to his side of the seat.

Just as silently she turned away from him again, pulling her coat up to shield her face.

From the protection of the coat she stared at the dark cockpit curtain, her heart heavy.

SIXTEEN

Swearing silently because cussing out loud took too much breath, Jina raced along the rough ground with the equipment bag banging against her back. Tweety was safe in the padded compartment made specifically for him, laptop, sensors, cameras, and power unit protected. Her back was neither padded nor protected, and all that banging damn well *hurt*.

They were all pelting headlong through the Chocó rain forest, because the double agent they'd been sent to rescue had chosen there to hide from the FARC insurgents pursuing him. Colombia was ostensibly more stable now, with an official agreement between the government and rebel forces, and a much ballyhooed "disarmament" of FARC, but a lot of hostile undercurrents were still running through the country. Insurgents, rebels, drug lords, government forces, and foreign elements still made for a volatile mix.

She hated Chocó. She felt guilty for hating a rain forest, but yeah, she despised it. Rain forests were great for the environment, but not for people. This place had freaking poison *frogs*. Touch one of the little devils and you went into cardiac arrest. At least they were neon colored, so they were easy to stay away from—except they were so tiny they could hide under a leaf. Even if there hadn't been any frogs, running through the rain forest wasn't a picnic in the park. Sundown was just a couple of hours away and the damn place would get dark like someone turning out a light. In the meantime, she had to leap over giant roots, fronds slapped her in the face, monkeys howled as if mocking them and alerting predators to their intrusion (*Hey, jaguars and snakes and whatever bad things live here, there's human meat on the ground!*), and she had to keep trucking. And keep a lookout for those damn frogs. She didn't know about the jaguars, but if she'd ever been in a place likely to have jaguars, this was it.

They were in a long, single-file line, separated by just enough distance that they could keep each other in sight, which because of the vegetation wasn't truly that far. Levi was leading. The double agent was behind him, followed by Trapper. Boom, Snake, and Crutch were next, then Voodoo, then Jina, with Jelly on rear guard.

They'd made contact with the guy, Ramirez, without any trouble. The rain forest had lit up her screen with heat signatures, but none large enough to be human except for her guys and Ramirez. She didn't like all the visual static, but she could work through it. She sat on a rock that the guys had made sure was clear of snakes and frogs and ants and carefully guided Tweety through the dense foliage. She watched their backs, weaving in wide circles around them, making sure no one was lying in wait to ambush them, or approaching unseen. With all of Tweety's available "eyes," getting anything by him was difficult. Someone would have to know how to disguise their thermal signature to slip past Tweety.

It was when they'd started out that they'd run into trouble. They were supposed to rendezvous with a couple of Jeeps that would take them to an airfield to be picked up. The timing had to be tight, so that any unfriendlies in the area had only a narrow window of opportunity to get to them.

Unfortunately, sometimes pure bad luck overrode the most careful planning. She couldn't deploy Tweety while they were on the move, so they had no warning. There was a shot from the right; she couldn't see what was happening because of the vegetation, but training kicked in and she hit the ground.

Levi's voice in her ear comm was as calm as if he were in a church. "Trapper, do you have a location?"

"Affirmative."

There was another shot, this one from a rifle. "Target down," Trapper said.

Jina's throat constricted so tightly she couldn't have made a sound. Knowing she could be in a violent situation was different from actually *being* in one. Someone had just died. One of *them* could have died. Ramirez was logically the target, but in reality the shooter could have been aiming at any of them, and with Tweety not in deployment she had no way of guarding their backs. She felt as if she'd personally failed them, because this was precisely the situation she was supposed to be working.

"Cover me," Trapper said.

"Affirmative," Levi said, and Boom echoed him. They were on each side of Trapper, and literally the only two who could see him. Jina tried to stay motionless and keep her breathing absolutely even and silent, while she listened for any unusual rustles around her. She could see Voodoo in front of her, weapon in hand, alertly scanning his surroundings. Jelly was somewhere behind her, making no sound that would betray his location, doing the same thing.

She should have pulled her own weapon. She was required to carry one, required to be reasonably proficient with it, and though she'd practiced like heck to meet the minimum standards, she'd hit the ground without once thinking about using it and now she couldn't get to it without making noise.

Mistake number two.

In her ear Trapper said, "Confirmed kill."

"Babe, deploy Tweety and take a look around."

"Affirmative," she replied, trying to replicate the dead-level tone they'd been using, and not knowing if she succeeded. Levi still sounded so damn *normal*, as if this was no more stressful than crossing the street. She rolled to a semisitting position, trying to keep herself as much under cover as possible, and swiftly unpacked the equipment bag. She had done this so often that getting Tweety in the air was a matter of seconds, rather than minutes.

She eased the drone in a three-sixty, looking for any other unwanted company. She used the thermal imaging, found nothing humanlike, though there were ways to thwart a heat signature. Because of that she took her time, examined every hint of a heat signature she could find to make certain it was animal.

"Babe." Levi was showing some emotion in his tone now; unfortunately, it was impatience.

"Hold your horses," she replied testily, and she took Tweety higher, into the understory where the monkeys lived—monkeys that were uncharacteristically quiet, and she wanted to know why. But the ones she found were going about the normal business of monkeys, paying no attention to the human contingent on the forest floor.

Relieved, she brought the drone home. "Clear," she finally said.

"Medic," Levi said, back to the emotionless tone.

Medic? *Medic!* Someone was hurt, someone at the front of the line where the shot had come from. Her blood began rushing through her veins, making her hands shake as she got Tweety and the laptop safely stowed once more. Jelly was there as she climbed to her feet, his sharp gaze constantly moving over the vegetation-clogged forest floor. A rain forest floor wasn't a thicket—the canopy restricted light and kept the going relatively clear—but "relatively" didn't mean "open." Fallen trees, ferns, tangled vines, all meant a short field of sight and provided a lot of cover. An army could hide behind the huge tree trunks, except she had already peeked around them with Tweety and the team was alone—for right now.

Now she drew her weapon, feeling like both a fool and a fake, but at least it was in her hand instead of her holster as they moved forward as quietly as possible. Voodoo was already up and moving, his head swiveling back and forth like Jelly's.

In less than a minute they joined up with those in the front of the line, who had formed a guard circle, each on one knee, around Levi and Snake. A long splinter of wood—if something at least six inches long and half an inch wide could be called a "splinter"—stuck out of Levi's right scapula, and a dark stain of blood was seeping down his shirt. Jina skidded to a halt, her stomach leaping into her throat.

Common sense told her the wound wasn't particularly serious; he'd be okay with some stitches and antibiotics. Still—this was Levi. She wanted to shove Snake out of the way and take care of him herself, an insane reaction because Snake was a trained medic and she wasn't, but one that was so strong she had to look away to keep herself from acting on it. She forced herself to do what the others were doing and focus on their surroundings.

A grunt from Levi jerked her gaze back to him, in time to see Snake use forceps to pull the splinter out. He dropped the bloody piece of wood on the ground. As soon as the splinter was out, Levi jerked his shirt off over his head and twisted his neck to try to get a look at the injury.

"Cut that shit out," Snake said as he mopped at the blood, which was trickling in rivulets down Levi's muscled back. "Just hold still." He pressed the wad of gauze against the wound and with his other hand searched for something in his bag. He didn't carry a military-issue kit, but a long, narrow bag that he packed himself and carried quiver style across his back. "Shit," he said again. Quickly he looked around, and his gaze settled on Jina. "Babe, come over here and get a QuikClot out of the bag for me. Things must have got a little disorganized when I hit the ground."

Knowing she'd been chosen because she was the least effective team member when it came to hitting what she was shooting at, she swallowed her chagrin and slid her weapon back into her thigh holster, then secured it before approaching and kneeling beside the medic bag. While she searched through the disordered bag, Snake squirted the wound with saline solution to wash out any trash, then did more mopping before pressing the wad of gauze against the wound.

Jina located the QuikClot pack and tore it open. "Slap it on," Snake said, and she did, holding the gauze pad in place while he quickly tore off strips of tape with his teeth and secured the pad. She tried to keep her eyes firmly on what she was doing, though she was acutely aware of smooth tanned skin and heat and a lot of hard muscle that made her mouth water. She tried—and she failed. She'd never seen Levi without a shirt before, for which she could only thank God, because if she had, she might have lost her fight with temptation. Some of the guys had gone shirtless in front of her, and though they were all in extremely good shape, they hadn't appealed to her. How could they, when all her senses had been focused on Levi?

He was kneeling on his right knee, leaning forward a little with his left forearm propped on his left knee, his weapon in his right hand while Snake tended to him. The broad expanse of those powerful shoulders made her heartbeat stutter; she was so acutely aware of him that she noticed everything: the tufts of dark hair under his arms, the tattoo of the ace of clubs on his left shoulder, another tattoo of the letters *PBJ* (the initials of an old girlfriend?) on his right shoulder, the deep furrow of his spine, the hot scent of his sweaty skin, the thick layers of muscle. He was on high alert, head turning back and forth as he surveyed the surrounding foliage, his dark eyes narrowed, searching.

"Okay, that's enough," he said, surging to his feet. Snake efficiently stuffed his supplies back in the roll bag and slung it crossways across his back, morphing from medic to operator in the matter of a half second. Jina wasn't as fast getting back into mission mode; she forced herself to look away from Levi so she could regain both her breath and her composure. Still, he moved back into her line of sight as he jerked his bloody shirt back on over his head; she saw the dark patch of hair spread in a tree-of-life pattern on his chest, and her mouth filled with drool again.

Stone-faced, she returned to her position between Voodoo and Jelly.

"I know who this is," Ramirez said, looking down at the body Trapper hauled into the open. "He's one of the Restrepos, three brothers who belong to FARC. They're known as 'the hounds,' because finding people is their job."

"Hunting you specifically?" Levi asked.

"Seems likely." Ramirez was from Chicago but spoke a couple of the Colombian dialects like a native. He shoved his sweaty hair out of his face. "They spread out when they're hunting. The other two will have heard the shots and will be converging on us."

"Then we have to move," Levi said sharply. "Babe, move to the center. Crutch and Boom, fall back to the rear. Double time."

Jina opened her mouth to protest, then shut it. He wasn't moving her to protect her; he was moving her so the team members most accurate with their weapons were both in front and in the rear. They had to move now and move fast. They might run straight into one of the remaining Restrepo brothers, but that was a chance they had to take because what they couldn't do was sit in ambush, maybe for hours, and miss their ride out. They had already lost precious minutes, and the timing had been tight to begin with.

They began double-timing out of the area, Levi still taking point. As before, Jina soon lost sight of everyone except Voodoo in front of her, but he would have eyes on the team member in front of him just as Jelly, behind her, kept her in sight. The heat and humidity pressed down on her, making every breath an effort because the air felt so thick. She was coated with sweat, sticky sweat that made dirt and insects stick to her. Damn, why couldn't they ever go somewhere with a *temperate* climate, like maybe Seattle?

Abruptly she noticed that Voodoo wasn't in sight. She could hear him, but she'd lost line of sight, and that was bad.

Shit. She couldn't let them get separated, or there'd be hell to pay. She dug deeper, pushed harder, reached for every bit of speed she could muster. Her thigh muscles ached, her lungs burned. She ignored them; she'd breathe later, when they were on the plane. Air was overrated, anyway.

She pelted around a huge tree, leaped over a giant protruding root—and slammed headlong into the side of a man who popped out of thin air, his head turned toward Voodoo, whose back was just visible as the man raised a rag-wrapped weapon and pulled the trigger.

Simultaneously:

The sharp *crack* oddly muffled by the vegetation and thick air, out of balance because her left ear was protected by the communication bud she wore, but her right ear was unprotected.

Whump! as she collided with the shooter.

Sick shock reverberated through her. Voodoo had likely been hit, maybe killed. The shard of sorrow that pierced her gut was unexpected. Voodoo was an asshole—but he belonged to her the way the other guys did. He was a part of the whole.

The impact of the collision rattled her teeth, jarred her bones— twice, because she hit the guy at full speed, bounced off, then hit the ground flat on her back. She landed on the equipment bag, knocking her breath out.

The shooter staggered sideways, swung around to face the unexpected attack. She saw slanted dark eyes, a mop of matted, dirty black hair, bad teeth, his weapon coming up, and she knew she was dead. The realization was staggering and brought a sort of numbness with it. Then there was another *crack*, this one from behind her, and clots of red sprayed out of his chest. He staggered back, still bringing his weapon around toward her, and a second shot hit him square in the forehead. He went down like a rag doll, falling across her feet and legs.

Jina gasped for breath, too much happening in a couple of seconds for her to process. She couldn't get her lungs to work, or her brain to move faster than wet mush. A body lay heavily across her legs, brain matter leaking out of the massive exit wound on the back of his head. She couldn't push it off, couldn't even sit up.

Jelly ran up. Keeping his weapon aimed, he hooked his foot under the shooter's armpit, rolled him over, mostly off Jina's legs but with her left foot still trapped. His expression was grim and set, no sign of the incorrigible team joker on his face now. He slanted a fast glance at Jina. "You all right?" he asked, then snapped his attention back to the guy's body.

No. Maybe. She didn't answer, couldn't answer. All she could do was move her lips like a guppy, trying to somehow get air into her lungs. Her brain said she was okay, she'd just had the wind knocked out of her, but her body was in a panic and the two were miles away from agreement. She totally took back the thought that air was overrated, because she couldn't *breathe*, and all of a sudden that was damn important.

She had a confused sense of being converged on, the rest of the team surging around, weapons drawn and ready. She saw Voodoo, not only alive but evidently unhurt, though she wasn't sure how that had happened. Levi's face swam into view, his expression so savage she'd have run if she could. Fat chance of that; she was dying here, lying on the forest floor with damn bugs crawling on her, and they were too busy to *notice*. But he stood astride her like an avenging angel, holding an HK MP7 instead of a flaming sword, his head on a swivel as he looked for additional threats. Snake slid in beside her, as if he were a runner stealing second and she were the base; before he could do anything, Levi must have realized what was wrong because abruptly he leaned down and grabbed the waistband of her pants, jerked her up and shook her, let her drop—and blessed air rushed into her lungs.

That *hurt*. For a minute all she could do was suck in deep, shuddering breaths. Awkwardly she rolled to the side as much as she could, what with Levi still standing astride her, Snake on her left, and the dead guy still lying across her foot. She was surrounded by men, and none of them were doing anything helpful—well, except for Levi practically body-slamming her to the ground and knocking the air back into her. Her throat hurt. Her chest hurt. Her right ear rang.

She coughed, gagged, then managed a groan.

"Are you hit?" Snake was asking urgently, when she could pay attention to something other than her body's desperate need for oxygen.

Still unable to make a sound anywhere resembling an actual word, she coughed some more while she vehemently shook her head.

"What the fuck happened?" Levi snapped. "Ramirez, is this another one of the Restrepos?"

Ramirez crouched by the dead man, examined the face distorted by the head shot, then shook his head. "No. I don't recognize this one. This means it isn't just the three of them, they have others with them."

Jina needed to sit up, so she could cough and gag more efficiently. She tapped Levi on the knee. He didn't move. She felt as if she was going to choke to death if she didn't get *up*, but no one was paying attention. She glanced at Snake, but he was busy keeping surveillance on the forest around them, now that he knew she hadn't been shot.

Damn it *all*. She punched Levi on the knee as hard as she could, then shoved at him. That predatory gaze swooped down to her; she shoved his leg again and understanding flashed. He stepped over her, releasing her from the cage of his stance, and leaned down to grip her forearm and haul her to a sitting position.

"Thanks," she managed to say, though the word was so strangled it sounded more like "hgnsks." She coughed violently, bent over from the waist, but finally her lungs and diaphragm and throat were all on the same page and air was moving in and out, and her brain decided she wasn't in danger of dying. She'd seen football players get the wind knocked out of them before, but she hadn't realized how weird and awful it felt. In retrospect, she had a lot more sympathy.

"I repeat: what the fuck happened?" Levi's tone sounded like the first step into hell, with worse awaiting.

Jelly said, "Babe all of a sudden kicked into high gear. I didn't see the bastard until she hit him broadside. She looked like a fucking linebacker—a *little* linebacker, but still. He had Voodoo square, if she hadn't plowed into him when she did. She bounced off him, hit the ground. He came around on her and I plugged him in the chest, then the insurance tap to the head."

Eight men looked at her. Jina wiped her watering eyes. "It was an accident," she croaked, and tried to get up but the dead guy still had her left foot trapped. Annoyed, frustrated, she half yelled, "Would someone get this dead guy off me?"

Maybe she should be more upset that she'd just seen someone killed. Maybe she should be in hysterics that the guy's body was lying across her foot. Maybe in an hour or two she *would* be upset, but right now Voodoo was okay and no one else had been hurt—her included, because for that frozen moment when everything happened she'd been sure she wouldn't survive—and all she wanted to do was get up and punch a tree or something.

Boom and Ramirez rolled the dead guy onto his back, off her foot. Freed, she pulled her knees up and rested her head on them, breathing hard and trying to get herself back. Being on the team was no longer an adventure; even though she'd known in her head that people could get killed, actually seeing it happen was something else entirely. She gave herself maybe five seconds, then set her jaw and rolled to her feet. Like before, the gunfire would bring anyone in the area down on them, and they needed to get moving.

She settled the equipment bag back into place and hoped Tweety and the laptop had survived her landing on top of them. "I'm ready," she said, though she wasn't certain of that. Her chest still ached, and her emotions felt numb.

No one moved. Levi still looked like a thundercloud. "You *tackled* an armed man?"

"No. I ran into him; big difference. I told you, it was an accident."

They didn't believe her. She could see it in their expressions, in-credulity blended with something else she couldn't read. She shifted uncomfortably and said, "Let's go."

Crutch said, "I dunno, Babe. Maybe instead of tackling the guy you could have whistled, or something, to give Voodoo a heads-up?"

Oh, for pity's sake! Angry, upset, and growing more hostile by the second, Jina shouted at them, "I'm a girl! Girls don't whistle! We don't spit or scratch our balls, either. Those are guy skills. Now can we get the hell out of here before I throw up on someone?" To her chagrin her eyes began burning, and she turned away before the burning became actual tears. It didn't help that she really couldn't whistle, and Jordan and Taz had teased her relentlessly about it when they were growing up. Even her baby sister, Caleigh, could whistle. It was dumb for such a little thing to surface now and upset her, especially given that she knew Crutch was teasing.

"You heard her," Levi snapped. "We need to get the hell out of here."

So they did, falling into line and resuming their sprint through the green hell. She noticed Voodoo checking over his shoulder a couple of times, as if making sure she was still in sight. That was so unlike him it unnerved her, especially given that she knew her speed was slower than before. Her energy level had dropped, and she couldn't seem to do anything about it. Even worse, Jelly was sticking closer to her than before, too. She didn't want them babying her, because that might undermine her fragile self-control.

When they were finally on their way back home, she'd have to set them all straight on what had really happened.

Despite their previous bad luck, they didn't encounter any more of the FARC hunters and reached the designated clearing just a half minute after two Jeeps roared to a stop. They all hopped on board, the drivers floor-boarded the gas pedals, and they bumped and swerved and tempted fate at a dangerous speed until they reached an airstrip with another small plane waiting for them. This one didn't hold a candle to the small jet that had brought them in, but this one wouldn't need as much runway and Jina didn't care if they all had to pack themselves in like sardines, as long as that engine had enough power to get them airborne.

It did. Even better, it took them to another airstrip, where a cargo plane awaited. As uncomfortable as cargo planes were, at least she'd be able to stretch out her legs, which was more than she'd been able to do in the small plane. She was exhausted. Everything that had happened had drained her dry, and the run through the forest was the least of it.

Levi and Boom went to talk to the pilots. The other guys stowed their gear, grabbed some bottles of water, began winding down. Jina stood alone for a minute, still trying to ground herself, and finally boosted herself into the cargo hold and found a flat place to sit. Wearily she unbuckled the equipment bag, took out Tweety and the laptop, and checked both for damage. They were fine, so she re-packed them and settled back, letting the momentary solitude sink in and relax her. She would have only a few minutes, if that long, but by the time the guys began loading up she had regained a measure of equilibrium—enough, at least, to last until she got home, where she could truly be alone.

The guys began boosting themselves into the hold. Levi tossed her a bottle of water and said, "Hydrate," just the way he had that very first day, months ago. She caught the bottle and began drinking, only then realizing how thirsty she was and how good the water felt on her strained throat.

Ramirez climbed aboard, and his dark eyes swept the interior of the cargo hold. His gaze lit on her and before she knew it he was lowering himself to sit beside her. "Real introduction," he said, giving her a slight smile. "My first name is Joseph. And you're Babe . . . ?"

"Modell," she said, a little bit at a loss.

"When we get to D.C. and I've been debriefed, would you be interested in—"

From across the hold, Levi said, "Get away from her or we'll break both your legs." He was stretched out, his eyes half closed, but the dark gleam under his thick lashes was hard and direct.

Trapper looked up from where he was wiping down his weapon. "That's if I don't shoot your ass first."

Ramirez's eyebrows shot up, and he held up both hands in surrender. "I was just—"

"Yeah, we know what 'just' is," Boom muttered. "You heard the man. Get away from her."

Confused, stunned, Jina looked around at all the guys as Ramirez did what he was told and moved to another spot. They all looked pretty ragged and lethal, and none of them were smiling. What the hell?

"We heard about your rep," Levi said to Ramirez, which explained their sudden hostility. She was tired, but not so tired that she couldn't figure out Ramirez was evidently a player. He was good-looking enough, but she didn't have time to play. Besides . . . he wasn't Levi.

Voodoo settled into the spot on her left that Ramirez had vacated. He sat silently for a moment, then held out his left fist toward her. Her sense of surprise was so great she almost gave him a "what the hell?" look, but she recovered after a split second and silently bumped his fist with hers. Okay, the social stuff had been taken care of; now she could close her eyes and maybe grab a nap—

"That's it?" Crutch demanded. "He's been an asshole to you since day one, and all he has to do is offer a fist bump and you're letting him off the hook? He owes you big-time, Babe."

Jina forced her eyelids to at least half-mast. "I know he's an asshole," she snapped. "But he's *my* asshole. One of them, anyway." She paused and thought about what she'd just said. She heaved an exhausted sigh. "That didn't sound right."

There were some snickers going around the cargo hold, tired laughter that was drowned out as the engine noise built to a roar and the plane began moving. Jina didn't care. They knew what she meant, and so did she. They were all her guys. They were a team.

SEVENTEEN

Levi opened his eyes a slit and looked across the cargo hold to where Babe lay curled on her side, fast asleep. She was using her equipment bag as a pillow. The roar of the engines drowned out even the snores he knew would normally rattle the rafters of a building, but cargo planes weren't built to be quiet inside. About two feet away, on her far side, Voodoo was slouched against some boxes, his chin on his chest as he too grabbed some sleep.

Sleep would have been nice, but Levi couldn't quite get there. His shoulder hurt just enough to be annoying, especially when he leaned back. Not only that, he was still too rattled from those brief nightmarish moments when he'd thought Babe had been shot. He could see she was alive and moving—he'd have sworn she was glaring at him—but fuck, for a minute there he'd been ready to burn the fucking rain forest down and destroy everything in it. Reining himself in hadn't been easy.

But she was okay. The relief hollowed him out, knocked him sideways. And somehow she'd kept the FARC asshole from shooting Voodoo, though she'd said it was an accident. How she "accidentally" tackled someone was beyond him, but maybe it was, maybe it wasn't. With her thought processes, it was tough to tell. However it had happened, she'd finally won Voodoo over so at least now they wouldn't have to listen to his bitching. What rattled Levi most of all was that "accident" or not, she'd thrown herself into the middle of a hot situation. Being heroic wasn't in her job description, and he had a hard time handling the idea.

Then he got on the damn plane and had to watch Ramirez coming on to her. He'd barely been able to change the "I" to "we" when he'd threatened to break the bastard's legs.

Shit. Keeping his distance kept the team working smoothly, but on another fundamental level it wasn't working at all, because it didn't do anything to lessen his attraction to her. He'd hoped that like most of the time when he was attracted to a woman, after a while the attraction would start fading, whether or not he did anything about it. The fact was no matter how much he'd enjoyed the various relationships he'd had, in the end the work had always been more interesting. But he'd been around Jina for months now, and he still got off on it. Damn, he liked looking at her, liked being with her.

She was sexy, with those two-toned blue-and-gold eyes of hers, all that long, heavy hair, the way she laughed and cussed and tackled life. Her expression was usually that of someone who was about to get up to some mischief, or at least enjoyed the *thought* of mischief even if she didn't do anything about it. She was funny, gutsy, and had a level head; she finessed keeping that fine balance between being friendly with the team members without letting anything sexual intrude. She treated them like brothers. She got along with Terisa and Ailani. She did her job and did it well. She laughed and joked, and sometimes he didn't pay attention to what she was saying because he was too busy just watching her. To keep any of the guys from noticing, he tried not to look at her all that often, but sometimes he let himself tease her because all of them did, on one level or another.

All in all, he couldn't find a damn thing about her that he didn't like, except that she was off-limits.

And when he relaxed, like now . . . that was when he couldn't stop his imagination from stripping her naked and pulling that fine, toned body of hers under him. In his mind he ran his hand over the curve of her ass, then reached lower to where she was hot and wet, pushed his fingers in and got her ready for his cock. The one time he'd had her under him, touching her, kissing her, she hadn't tried to hide anything. She'd been honest, and real.

She was the only woman he'd ever felt jealousy over. He hadn't been kidding about breaking Ramirez's legs.

The truth was, since he'd met her, all he'd been doing was marking time: waiting for her to quit, then waiting for her to fail, and now just waiting.

He could feel his patience stretching thinner and thinner. He was fighting to maintain the status quo, and the internal battle was turning all his inner barricades to rubble. Nothing had ever broken him; he'd always maintained that inner surety of his center. He knew what he wanted out of life, knew his own guidelines, his strengths and weaknesses. Doing what he did gave him the kind of challenge and satisfaction he needed. This was different; Jina was different. Sooner or later, he'd break under the strain.

Restlessly, he changed positions, finally managed to get halfway comfortable. He was able to grab some sleep, waking when the thunderous sound of the engines changed. He'd been on so many planes that his subconscious recognized the altered pitch as a signal that they were slowing in preparation for approach and landing.

He stretched and got more water; around him, the others were stirring, too, alerted by the change in the noise level. Jina slept on, her soft lips barely parted, but she didn't look particularly blissful; faint, fleeting expressions gave her a troubled look. He watched her for a minute, then nudged her sneaker with the toe of his. She gave a quick little frown, pursed her lips, and that was it. He nudged harder. Another frown, and this one looked as if it meant business. On the third try, he gave the sole of her shoe a light kick and said sharply, "Babe! Wake up!"

She sat up with a jerk and blindly threw a punch that would have de-balled him if he hadn't jumped back, but he'd been halfway prepared for that sort of reaction. The other guys started laughing. Scowling, she looked around at them all, then scrubbed her face. "I was dreaming," she muttered. "About the dead guy on my foot."

"Thought you might be," he replied, keeping his tone neutral. "We'll be landing in a few. There's a forward lav, if you need to go."

Without a word she jumped to her feet and headed forward, weaving her way through the secured pallets and boxes. She needed to piss more often than the men did, so over the months they'd all adjusted to stopping for more piss breaks and letting her go first. Levi sat down again, thinking philosophical thoughts about the realities of traveling with a woman.

Actually landing took them another half hour; according to his watch, there were a couple of more hours until sunrise. At least they'd had some sleep and none of them were as jet-lagged as they had been the previous mission. He and Ramirez would go straight to debriefing, but the rest of them could catch a little downtime.

The plane rolled to a stop and the big ramp lowered. They got their gear and wearily trudged down the ramp and toward where they'd left their vehicles. As soon as they were off and clear, the ramp was raised again and the plane taxied around to take off for its final destination.

"C'mon, you can ride with me," he said to Ramirez, striding past him toward his truck.

Ramirez gave him a wary look. "Will my legs be okay?"

"As long as you stay away from Babe," he replied equably. He unlocked the doors, leaned in to insert the key and start the engine, then began scraping frost off the windshield.

"Like seven big brothers, huh?" Ramirez said as he slid into the passenger seat.

"She has brothers. We're the mean-ass guys she works with." He didn't want to be her damn brother. He wasn't content with being the mean-ass guy she worked with, either, but for now he'd have to settle.

As he drove the mostly deserted pre-daylight streets to headquarters, Ramirez—evidently he had more balls than brains—said, "She's a grown woman."

Levi grunted. "Noticed that, did you? Did you also notice that she's more than capable of telling us to shut up and mind our own business if she was interested? What does that tell you?"

Ramirez frowned. "Okay. Shit. I get it. She wasn't interested."

"She'd have thrown something at us if she had been."

They reached headquarters and entered the nondescript building, signed in. Ramirez went one way, Levi went another. They would be debriefed on different aspects, Ramirez on what he'd learned while undercover, Levi on the exfil mission itself.

Two cups of coffee helped him get through the debriefing in a relatively benign mood, but he was damn hungry by the time they finished. As he was heading out of the building, he heard his name called and turned to see Kodak striding toward him.

"What's up?"

For once, Kodak's easygoing expression was absent. Instead he looked tired and grim.

"Thought you'd want to know. We lost Bingo day before yesterday."

"Lost" meant "dead." Bingo was the nickname Kodak's team had given Brian Donnelly almost as soon as he joined the team.

"Shit," Levi said under his breath. Losing any member of any team was always a kick in the gut, but Donnelly was not only one of the drone operators, he was Jina's friend. That one time Levi had been around him, he'd had to like him even though he'd been jealous as hell over Donnelly's status as Jina's date. "What happened?"

"Things went sideways," Kodak said wearily. "We were doing a hostile exfil, the LZ was hot, and Bingo took one in the head."

That was a very brief description but Levi knew exactly what the exfil had been like, having done more than one himself. Chaotic, violent, bad shit going down. It happened.

And now he had to tell Jina.

EVEN THOUGH SHE was tired and would have liked to sleep for half the day, Jina had already learned that the best way to get back on schedule was to stay awake for the rest of the day and do normal stuff. Besides, she didn't want to sleep just yet. The dead guy's face—even though he was a bad dead guy—wasn't far enough away from her subconscious. She didn't want him to bother her, but he still did.

On the way home she stopped at an IHOP and had breakfast, taking care to sit well away from other customers because she figured she stank. If she did, at least the waitress didn't make a face. Coffee, bacon, and eggs went a long way toward making her feel human again. Gray daylight was peeling back the shadows of darkness as she drove the rest of the way home.

When she unzipped her go-bag to dig out the dirty laundry, however, the smell nearly knocked her down. Her head turned aside, she dumped all the contents out in front of the clothes washer. Whether she'd worn everything or not, all of it was contaminated beyond what she could bear. If the source of the extremely bad smell hadn't been her dirty socks, she'd have thought the guys had pranked her by maybe spraying the inside of her bag with sulfur mixed with skunk— and maybe dead possum thrown in for variety. Her Merrell sneakers smelled really bad, too, though the footbed was supposed to have odor control; maybe rain forest funk outstunk the control factor.

She stripped off where she stood, determinedly ignored the blood on her jeans, and started her laundry, even tossing the sneakers in, too. If being washed ruined them, then they were ruined. She could buy more sneakers, but she couldn't stand that smell.

After that she took a nice long shower, shampooing twice, conditioning, and sighing with relief because her skin could breathe again, without all the dirt and sweat. Doing girl stuff felt so *good*. She moisturized, put on scented body lotion, then pulled on a pair of cuddly flannel pants and a long-sleeved thermal shirt. She removed her chipped toenail polish and put on a pair of moisturizing socks to pamper her feet.

There! Human again.

She was on the couch catching up on some programs she'd recorded when the doorbell rang. She scowled at the door. No way should her doorbell be ringing, unless maybe the downstairs neighbors had a dead battery and needed their car jumped off. That was the only possibility that got her to her feet.

But it wasn't either of her neighbors she saw through the peephole, it was Levi.

I don't need this, she thought. This wasn't how to keep his distance. She could get angry at him, she could sometimes hate him, but what she could never do was be indifferent to him. She needed his help, she needed him to stay *away*.

"Go away," she said aloud, leaning her head against the door.

"It's important."

Of course it was. *Damn.* She unlocked the door and opened it, standing in the threshold so he couldn't come in. "What?"

He came in anyway, simply stepping forward and putting his hand on the side of her waist, muscling her back, then closing the door behind him. Jina's heart tripped at his expression, both grim and remote. She knew he'd gone first to debriefing, but evidently he hadn't had an opportunity to shower and change clothes. He still wore the grimy clothes he'd had on when he drove away a few hours ago, he still had a two-day stubble darkening his jaw. Whatever had happened was bad enough that he'd come straight here.

Her thoughts flashed to her family. If anything had happened to one of them, was it somehow set up that Levi would be notified first if the team was on a mission? They weren't on a mission *now* but they'd just returned, so that was possible. She hadn't checked her personal cell phone for messages or looked at Facebook. She had no idea what could have happened.

She kept on moving back, putting distance between them. "What?" she asked again, but this time there was alarm in her voice, because she'd never seen him look like that.

"There's no easy way to tell you," he said, striding forward and gripping both her elbows before she could back even farther away. "Babe—Donnelly got hit."

"Hit" could mean slapped. "Hit" could mean struck by a car. But in their world, "hit" meant something else entirely. She felt as if she'd been hit herself and would have reeled back if he hadn't been holding her, his big hands like clamps on her arms. His dark gaze was steady on her face, reading and assessing every thought and emotion that flickered past.

She looked around, as if her condo could give her some safe, reassuring answer. Donnelly was her friend. Donnelly had the same job she did; they stayed out of the action—though hadn't she almost gotten "hit" herself, about fifteen hours ago?

"Is he . . ." Her voice was faint and faded away. Her lips felt numb, barely able to move. She swallowed, tried again. She couldn't ask if he was dead, couldn't make herself say the word. Instead she said, "Will he be all right?"

Levi slowly shook his head. His voice was quiet. "No."

She stood very still, staring at his chest, about three inches from her nose. She didn't want to look up into his eyes, she wanted to pull into herself and not move at all for a very long time, until she could process this and handle it, get her emotions under control.

Donnelly was dead. *Donnelly.* He was a nice guy, everyone said, and he had been. Good-looking, good-humored, intelligent, friendly, sharp—what wasn't to like?

She wished she could have loved him.

Very gently Levi eased her forward until she was resting against him and closed his arms around her.

Gentleness from him was devastating. It shattered her self-control, allowed the grief to come roaring up. A sob caught in her throat, broke free, and she began crying. Levi pulled her even closer, his big hand coming up to cradle the back of her head, his strength wrapping around her as if giving her permission to turn to mush within that sturdy framework of protection. She still tried to resist, for maybe a second, then she rested her forehead against the hard muscle of his chest, circled his waist with her arms, and gave in.

Even when the sobs dwindled down to sniffles and trickles of tears she stood there in the circle of his arms, tiredly astonished that he was holding her and just letting her cry, because Levi didn't strike her as a man who was very patient with shows of emotion. The hand on the back of her head was slowly rubbing, his fingers sifting through her damp hair, his fingertips brushing the nape of her neck.

"Where were they?" she finally asked, her voice nasally and thick with tears.

"I don't know. I can find out, but does it matter?"

She felt something brush the top of her head. Had he kissed her, or had he rubbed his chin against her hair? But as he'd said—did it matter?

"No," she said, to both questions, and fell silent again.

After a while she withdrew her arms from around his waist and gently pulled back. His arms tightened briefly, then he released her and stepped back. She scrubbed her hands over her damp cheeks, wiped her eyes on the hem of her shirt. "Have you had anything to eat?"

"Haven't had time."

Meaning he'd come straight here to give her the news before she could find out from someone else. She nodded and managed to look at him. "Are you hungry?"

"As a bear." A small quirk curled one corner of his mouth.

"Have you had that shoulder looked at?"

"Haven't had time."

Okay, that settled that. He'd offered her comfort, likely against his better judgment, so she felt obligated to offer him something in return. He was tired, he was hungry, he was hurt. She couldn't just push him out the door.

"If you want to grab a quick shower, I can have eggs and bacon on the plate by the time you're finished. You likely need stitches and I can't help with that, but I can put a clean bandage on your shoulder." She paused. "And you'll have to put your dirty clothes back on, because I don't have anything that'll come close to fitting you, other than a sheet."

He didn't say anything right away, making her brace herself for a rejection; he surprised her by finally saying, "Both the shower and food sound great. You don't mind me using your shower?"

"I wouldn't have offered if I did. I doubt you're dirtier than I was. The fresh towels and washcloths are in the linen closet in the bathroom." She showed him the way through her bedroom to the connecting bath; once she'd have been embarrassed by her unmade bed, but he knew she'd jumped out of bed in the middle of the night and his bed likely wasn't made, either. "How do you like your eggs?"

"In pancakes."

She snorted, but said, "Got it," and left him to it, hurried back to the kitchen. As it happened she was short on eggs—she had one—

but she did have a Shake 'n Pour pancake mix, and a couple of packs of precooked bacon. She got out her griddle pan and began getting it hot while she nuked some of the bacon. Because she was smart that way, she also started some coffee brewing.

Poor Donnelly. She tried to think of the last time she'd seen him . . . maybe two weeks ago? They'd run into each other briefly, stopped to chat, nothing special. He was enjoying being on Kodak's team. Some last meetings were humdrum, completely forgettable. The same with last words; she couldn't remember what they'd said, specifically. The last time you saw someone should be special, marked in your memory by a sense of importance, but no; last words were special only in retrospect.

The dead guy in the jungle didn't seem nearly as important now. Someone very much like him had killed Donnelly.

The sad realization that she'd never see him again settled inside her. If he'd quit, moved to a different part of the country, she wouldn't even have truly missed him, she'd have shrugged and moved on. Knowing that he was no longer alive was different, because he was truly *gone*; the part of the world that his soul and spirit had occupied was now empty.

She had the first two pancakes plated and buttered when Levi came into the kitchen, dressed in the same pants and shoes but bare chested. She knew why; putting that dirty shirt on over his uncovered wound wouldn't be smart. She wasn't in the mood to ogle his naked chest anyway, despite how impressive it was. The sadness in her filled up the space that was normally occupied by lust. She lifted her brows at him. "Which do you want first, food or bandage?"

"Food," he replied, no hesitation.

She poured two more rounds of batter onto the griddle pan, then took the plate with the two pancakes to the table, along with a fork, the bottle of syrup, and the plate of bacon. "Go ahead and get started, I'll bring these two when they're finished." Then she took a cup of coffee to him, not asking if he wanted sugar or creamer be-cause as far as she knew all the team drank it black; they kept things simple.

"Thanks," Levi said, his gaze on the pancakes. She understood; she'd felt that way about her plate at IHOP earlier.

He was taking the last bite of the first two when she brought the second two to him. "Two more coming," she said. "Tell me when you're finished."

"Six should do it."

He was slower on the second two; there was still some left when she brought the last pair. She liked feeding him, she thought. She liked that he'd used her shower. If they were together this was how it would be . . . ah well, no point in dreaming.

After setting the plate down, she took the time to look at the wound on his back. The piece of wood had left a jagged puncture that would definitely need stitches; the wound was deep, the area around it swollen and discolored, red and deep purple. "Hope you're up to date on your tetanus shot," she said. "You should have had that wound taken care of before you came here. But I know why you didn't . . . thank you."

There was something of the predator in the fierce darkness of his gaze that slanted toward her. "I am. You're welcome."

While he was finishing she fetched her first aid kit, then he sat while she plastered an antiseptic pad over the wound and taped it. Afterward he pulled on his dirty shirt, took his dirty plate and fork to the sink. She let him, though a proper hostess would have pro-tested. She wasn't a proper hostess; she was a teammate, and team-mates could take their own dirty plates to the sink.

"Thanks for breakfast," he said, turning toward her. His gaze flickered to her mouth, then his eyes shuttered; he turned and went to the door. When he reached it, he looked back at her.

"I'm sorry about Donnelly. I'd tell you not to let it eat at you, but it will. It's eating at me, too. You drone operators are supposed to be in safe places, but the truth is, on a mission, there aren't any safe places."

No, there weren't. After he left, silently closing the door behind him, she crossed the room and secured the locks. The irony wasn't lost on her. She could lock the door, but when it came down to it, Donnelly hadn't been safe, and neither was she.

EIGHTEEN

In April, the South African banker, Graeme Burger, cleared Customs with his family and for four days gave every appearance of being nothing other than a tourist, hitting all the usual historical sites in D.C. None of the GO-Teams were deployed to follow him; Axel MacNamara preferred to keep a level of separation between his teams and any domestic issues. Let the FBI handle it. That way any triumph was theirs, but so was any failure.

Mac's policy was proved to be a smart choice. On the fifth day, Mr. Burger somehow managed to ditch his surveillance. In D.C., where cameras were everywhere, that was an impressive feat for even the most experienced agent. For a banker from a foreign country to do it sent alarm flags flying at every intelligence agency in the federal government. He connected with his wife and children four hours later, smiling, and resumed doing touristy things.

Joan Kingsley, alone in her big house, smiled too as she imagined all the intensifying interest being focused on Graeme Burger. The banker was garnering all sorts of attention, and as of now Axel MacNamara would double down on his efforts to find out what was going on. The bastard always assumed the worst, assumed massive, complicated conspiracies were going on all around him—and sometimes he was right. Like now. Only national security wasn't the target this time, *he* was.

She knew how it worked, because she had seen the system in action so many times. Now Devan would begin feeding them bits of crucial information that would pull Ace Butcher's GO-Team into an ambush—the big step that would hook MacNamara himself.

She could hardly wait.

JULY CAME IN hot and humid. Jina realized it had been a little over a year since she'd begun training, but whoop-de-do, something like that didn't call for a celebration. It was a guideline for marking time, nothing more.

On one level, everything continued as normal. Another drone operator was being trained to join Kodak's team, and this time Kodak and the rest of his team were involved from the beginning. She thought that would become the accepted way of doing things from now on. Donnelly's death had brought it home to everyone that the drone operators were only as safe as the situation allowed them to be, and that the situation could change at the drop of a hat. What could be done to ensure their safety was already being done, and when it came down to it, it was the *team* operators' safety that was the most important, not the drone operators.

As Levi had so pointedly told her on the first day of training, she was the least important member of the team. There was far more money and training invested in the guys, and their expertise was off the charts in comparison with hers.

In the middle of July, they were notified of an upcoming mission in Syria.

At the news, a heavy sense of dread settled in Jina's stomach. Syria was one of the most dangerous places on Earth. She was more politically aware now than she'd ever been before, and she knew Syria was a war zone. Government forces had lost control of most of the country, battles continued with ISIS, and, boy, she did not want to get in the middle of that.

At least they didn't have to leave in the middle of the night. The mission required meticulous planning and timing, because of the uncertainty of the ground situation. They were to meet up with a Syrian sympathizer who would lead them to where an informant was hiding; their mission was to get the informant safely out of Syria, because he wouldn't tell them what he knew until then. The first reaction had been to leave him there; if he wanted to play games when his own safety was ostensibly at risk, then his information likely wasn't that valuable. Then he'd mentioned a name that had gotten their attention: Graeme Burger.

What they knew about Graeme Burger was getting murkier, rather than clearer. First he had ties with the Sudanese Nawal Daw, and now his name was cropping up in Syria. Someone who had at first seemed to be low tier was assuming more and more prominence. His ties and influence were looking like a spiderweb, with far-reaching consequences. The world of terrorist groups was Byzantine. They were as often enemies with each other as they were with the Western governments; they were less effective because of that. No one wanted them to link together and begin working as a cohesive force, and it was beginning to look as if Graeme Burger might be trying to do that very thing.

Jina completely understood *why* they were going to Syria. What she hated was the *how*—because they had to parachute in.

As soon as she heard the plan during their mission briefing, she got the familiar sick feeling. She'd done more jumps—she'd had to, to keep current with her training—but at best she'd learned how to function. That was it. She dreaded each and every jump, was sick with nerves beforehand, panicked when she first left the plane, and her landings were clumsy at best; usually she landed on her fourth point of contact, namely, her butt. Still, she did it, and hated every second of it.

Sitting in the briefing room, she could feel each team member giving her a quick, concerned glance, because they all knew how much she hated it. And because they were concerned, she had to do it. She couldn't let them down.

They were lucky in that the new moon was in thirty-six hours, so at least they'd be jumping in the dark. It would have to be a high-altitude jump, to evade radar; the region they were jumping into was sparsely populated, but the Russians had supplied the Syrians with mobile radar/missile batteries that could be anywhere. Theoretically the batteries were deployed near the ports, but "theoretically" was the key word.

Parachute in, meet the sympathizer who would take them to the informant. Then they'd have to get out. That was the hard part. There would be nine of them; a truck would be easier, stealthier, as long as they didn't encounter any ISIS forces. A helicopter would be faster, but would have to fly the nap of the Earth to stay under the radar horizon, and would attract more attention. Neither option was great, in Jina's opinion.

But the GO-Teams were built to take such difficulties in stride. Every operation had problems peculiar to it, and their job was to solve those problems and execute the mission. How they did it was up to them.

"Our LZ is here," Levi said, pointing to a spot in the southern Syrian desert. "Our contact will have a truck fueled and ready to go, here." He pointed to another location, about two kilometers from the LZ. "Babe, there're some ruins there where you'll set up. We'll collect our package, haul ass for Iraq where we'll have transport home." He paused. "We're operating with one eye closed, here, because we don't know exactly where the informer is holed up. He could be close, he could be several klicks away, and we don't know in which direction. Regardless of where he is, if the situation goes tits up, our secondary exfil point will be here. A bird will come in low from Iraq and pick us up." He gave the coordinates, and everyone made note.

It was understood that, in the event they had to use the secondary point, it would likely be an emergency situation and they wouldn't have the truck. They'd possibly be under hostile fire, double-timing it on foot across the desert in miserable heat, at night, for—Jina did some rough conversion of kilometers to miles in her head—over twenty miles. Closer to twenty-five miles, likely, which was almost a freakin' marathon. If they were military, a helicopter would fly through hell to pick them up, but they weren't military and they had to do the best they could while keeping as low a profile as possible.

Summer. Desert. It was going to be hellishly hot.

"Go home, get ready, get some rest," Levi finished. "We leave at oh three hundred."

Getting some rest sounded like a good idea. When Jina climbed the stairs to the small landing outside her door, though, a tall man was sitting on the floor against the wall and got to his feet as she approached.

"Taz!" she gaped at him. "What're you doing here? Why didn't you call?"

"Just passing through, had some time to kill, thought I'd come see you," he said, which didn't at all explain why he hadn't called.

She gave him a sisterly get-real look. Just passing through? He was military, he didn't just "pass through" anywhere. He was in fatigues, and his camo duffel bag was at his feet. "Where are you being deployed to?"

He shrugged, meaning he couldn't say.

As she unlocked the door, Jina thought the military had been good for her little brother, giving focus to what had been a lot of energy and an inclination to try anything with the possibility of breaking his neck. He was a man now, not a boy; the staff sergeant's stripes on his sleeve said so.

She eyed the stripes. "When did you make E6?" He'd been an E5 the last time she'd seen him, at Christmas.

"Couple of months ago." He shut the door behind him. "When did you learn what the stripes mean?"

Oops. Civilians without prior military service wouldn't recognize most ranks by the insignia. "I live in D.C.," she pointed out, thinking fast. "You can't walk ten steps without running into someone who's in the military."

He gave her his own version of a get-real look. "C'mon, sis, fess up. I'm not Mom and Dad, I know you aren't working on software." His encompassing assessment started at her head and swept down to her feet.

"What?" She looked down at herself. She was wearing a T-shirt, jeans, and her latest pair of sneakers, which in her view was pretty damn normal. "I do too work with software. Do you think I should have a pocket protector, or something?"

"You look hard as a rock. You were never as girly-girl as Ashley and Caleigh, but you always had on some face stuff." He circled his finger around his eyes. "Lipstick and shit. Not now, though. Yeah, running a lot will tone you up, but it won't give you those arms."

At least he hasn't mentioned that my boobs have gone away, too, she thought in exasperation. "I work out, I don't just run. My job is classified, I'll give you that, but do you know how many people in the area work on classified stuff?" She glanced at her phone, checked the time. "Do you have time for dinner?"

"I do. You cooking?"

The get-real expression came out again. "I'll treat you—as long as your taste runs to a pizza joint, or maybe Italian."

He hooked his arm around her shoulder. "Now you're talking."

Taz had six hours to kill before he had to report for duty and seemed determined to spend every minute with her. Normally she'd have loved his company, but not when she needed to get her gear ready and get some sleep. She watched the clock the whole time they were at the pizza joint, mentally counting down how much sleep she could get. When he finally left at eight P.M., she figured she was good for a solid four, then more on the flight.

She wanted those four hours, though, so she intended to zip through repacking her go-bag. Then her phone rang: her mom, who had just talked to Taz. Jina chatted while she packed, grabbing her boots because they were going to the desert, extra socks, a change of clothes, some wet wipes and sunscreen, lip balm, extra water, some protein bars and hard candy. By the time she got off the phone and got showered, she was a little short on those solid four, but—family. What could she do? She loved them anyway.

ABOUT EIGHT HOURS into the flight the next day, Jina wasn't so certain about loving them. She'd slept, she'd read some in the book she'd brought along, and time was still dragging. There was nothing about a long flight that was enjoyable, even on a chartered jet. She changed out of her sneakers into her boots—and as soon as she shoved her foot into the first boot she knew.

"Ah, crap!" Completely disgusted with herself, she leaned her head back against the seat. Yes, Taz and her mom had distracted her, but bringing the right gear was *her* responsibility.

"What's wrong?" Boom asked beside her.

"I grabbed the wrong boots."

He opened both eyes, looked at them. "They look okay to me."

"They don't fit as well as the others." She scowled, dug an extra pair of socks out of the bag and put them on, too. When they got home, she'd drop these boots in a donation box, get them out of her closet so she didn't make the same mistake again. She'd already thought about doing so, but hadn't gotten around to it. Now she was stuck wearing boots that were too big. Well, she'd made it through weeks of training with them, so she supposed she'd live through a single mission wearing them. Lesson learned.

Besides, if she could focus on fretting about the boots, maybe she wouldn't fret so much about jumping out of a plane. In the dark. Into Syria.

Nope, needed something worse than the boots.

JUMPING FROM A high altitude required oxygen. Jumping at night required night-vision goggles. Jumping at all required either nerves of steel or the brain of a hamster. Her nerves definitely weren't steel, so Jina figured her brain was rodentlike.

The equipment bag went first, rigged for an automatic HALO, so it would be on the ground waiting for them. Then one by one the guys went out of the lowered ramp, disappearing into the night. Jina was next to the last; she would have been last, but they never let her take that position because they weren't certain she'd actually jump if there wasn't someone behind her. Tonight, the last one was Snake.

Tweety and the laptop were strapped to her back, along with her regular bag. She had her oxygen mask in place. She had her NVD, night-vision device, on. She took a steadying breath, closed her eyes, and took a small leap into the night.

The experience was still terrifying; the cold and the wind tore at her, almost pulled her oxygen mask off. With one hand she secured it, resettled the goggles, looked for the rest of the team. She couldn't see them—wait, there was movement. She maintained her body position, monitored her altitude, kept an eye on the team member she could see. The only available ambient light was starlight, and the NVD turned everything green, but if she could see one, then she figured Snake, above her, could see her. That made her feel more secure, which was asinine when she was plummeting through nothing, in the dark, toward Earth.

At the proper altitude she deployed her chute, so prepared now for the violent jerk upward and the straps cutting into her legs that she barely noticed them, other than as a signal that everything was working as it should. Immediately she looked around for the others so she could steer away from them. They were more visible now, the billowing parachutes like giant green mushrooms. She checked above her, located Snake. His chute had opened without problem, too.

The arid air made for a slower descent, which extended the time they were sitting ducks for anyone with a firearm, and there was nothing they could do about it. Jina's nerves were in shreds by the time she saw the ground coming at her. She flared the chute, tried for the one-point landing, and as usual failed miserably. She got off her butt and reeled her chute in, wadding it up and securing it.

"Babe."

She turned toward the whisper and located Levi, joined up with him and Crutch. They went down on one knee to provide a smaller target; there was virtually *no* cover that she could see. There were some rocks, a few bushes, some dark slits in the ground that she assumed were wadis, but that was it. The others shortly joined them, all of them accounted for. Boom, the first on the ground, had located the equipment bag and their weapons were distributed.

They moved as silently as possible toward the contact point, communicating by hand signals and whispering into their comm units. Even though it was night and a wind was blowing, the heat was oppressive. She was sweating within seconds; thank God they'd be gone by daybreak. The crumbled ruin where she'd be stationed came into view. It had been . . . she couldn't tell what it had been. The ruin was too large to have been a hut, but what else could it have been, out here literally in the middle of nowhere? Why would a hut be here anyway? Behind the ruins was the dark gash of another wadi, so maybe at one time the place had been more habitable.

Levi signaled everyone to take a knee, then Trapper and Voodoo silently circled the crumbled pile. A truck was tucked into the shadows on the other side of the ruin, a beat-up Toyota pickup truck that was so covered in dust it blended in with the surroundings. Maybe it wouldn't collapse under the weight of nine people.

Trapper reappeared and gave a thumbs-up. Levi rose to his feet and the team fanned out behind him, approaching the ruin from the front while Trapper and Voodoo covered the back. When he was closer, he crouched, picked up a rock, and tossed it into the ruin.

Ten seconds later, a small figure appeared in the shattered doorway. He wore the traditional loose trousers and a shirt, his thick, untidy black hair blowing around his face. He looked about twelve, though he was likely older. He gave a low, warbling whistle.

Levi whistled in return, but none of them advanced any closer.

The boy stepped out of the doorway and waved his arm. He wasn't carrying any weapons—at least none that they could see.

Cautiously the team approached. Per Levi's instructions, Jina stayed at the back of the group and kept her jump helmet on, though her hair was plastered with sweat under it. With all the gear she was wearing, no one would make her as female as long as her head was covered and she wore the NVD.

"I am Mamoon," the boy said when they got close enough to hear him, his English understandable. He had a quick, shy grin, though it faded somewhat when he looked up at Levi, towering over him. "You are here to pick up a package, yes?"

"Yes," Levi affirmed. "A large package."

Mamoon's grin flashed again, perhaps at the description. "Very good," he said happily. Behind him, a man appeared out of the shadows and every weapon came up. Mamoon's eyes got big and he stepped back, raising one hand. "This is my uncle, Yasser. He will take you to the package."

"We were to meet one person," Levi said, his tone hard.

"I am Mamoon's only relative," Yasser said with dignity. Like Mamoon, his English was more than passable. "He lives with me."

"This is your home?"

Yasser looked around at the crumbling ruin. "No, of course not. Please to enter?"

Jelly slipped past them, sliding along the perimeter of the remaining walls. Only when he reappeared, signaling the OK, did Levi, Boom, and Jina enter.

They pulled down their NVDs, and Levi shone a narrow penlight around the interior, examining it. Over half of the exterior walls were down, and most of the interior ones, but at the very back of the rough structure was a small room that was mostly intact. A black curtain of some thick, rough material closed it off. The heat inside the stone walls was somewhat less, but still stifling.

"Here," Jina murmured, knowing her raspy voice would help disguise her sex. She didn't want to run afoul of any cultural differences, but at the same time she was here to do her job. If she could do it without stirring up any trouble, fine.

The black curtain would block out the light from the laptop screen, giving her a measure of cover while she worked. At the same time, she would pretty much be trapped, in the rear of the ruin, with only one way out.

Levi said quietly, "Get set up." He ducked back through the black curtain, letting it fall, and began talking to Yasser. Their voices faded away as they walked toward the front of the ruin.

Jina put the equipment bag down and took out her own penlight to better explore her surroundings. The little room, no more than eight feet wide, wasn't completely solid. At the back the wall on the left had partially collapsed. She could feel air moving, and when she got down on her hands and knees to look for the source of the breeze, she could see a deeper darkness. She moved a couple of pieces of rubble and saw a jagged hole at the base of the wall, too small for a man to fit through. Mamoon, perhaps, could do so—and she thought she could, too.

She felt slightly better. This whole situation made her uneasy. Everyone was uneasy, and with good reason. The least hiccup could spell disaster.

NINETEEN

Levi said, "How far away is the package?"

"Far enough to feel safe," Yasser answered drily. His eyes weren't friendly, but Levi didn't expect friendliness, just cooperation. Many moderate Arabs didn't care for Westerners, but cared even less for radicals or their own governments. For his part, Levi wasn't concerned with whether or not Yasser was sympathetic; all he wanted was cooperation.

"I need a time frame."

Yasser shrugged. "Fifteen minutes."

About a mile, then, well within Tweety's range. Levi looked around. He didn't like leaving Babe here, but the whole point of her job was to squat in a safe location and keep an extra eye out for the rest of the team. Taking her with them defeated the purpose, because she couldn't walk and operate the drone at the same time. That left him with a choice to make: split the team and leave a couple of guys here with Babe, or take them all with him to maximize the odds of mission success. His training said mission success was the most important. If the informant was so afraid that he was hiding even from his rescuers, then he likely had reason to be, which meant there could well be others out there looking for him. This could still turn out to be a simple retrieve-and-go, but experience told him otherwise.

"I'm leaving one of my team members here," he said, "to handle communications." That was true, as far as it went. He wasn't telling anyone about Tweety, and it would be up to Babe to deploy the drone unnoticed. She likely already had. Looking around, he could see Boom and Jelly kidding around with Mamoon, which meant she was alone in the ruin, doing her thing. The little drone was virtually silent and wouldn't be noticed at night.

"Ah," said Yasser. "I see. That is good. I will be able to leave Mamoon with him, then. I did not want to take the child, because there could be danger, but did not like to leave him here alone."

Levi nodded an affirmative. He liked the idea; that way Babe wouldn't be by herself. The kid seemed bright and friendly and spoke English as well as his uncle. He said, "I'll have a word and be right back," and entered the ruin to talk to Babe, picking his way through the rubble.

She looked up as he pulled aside the black curtain and stopped beside her. She already had the laptop booted up, as he'd expected; she'd made a mostly level place on top of the half-collapsed wall where she'd set the laptop and stood in front of it, tapping on the keys. The illumination of the screen was the only light, giving her a ghoulish look. She'd removed her jump helmet, but even so her hair was dark with sweat and her skin was shiny with it. He liked the look on her, but then he liked how she looked regardless. Smart girl; she'd taken her pistol out of the holster and placed it by her hand, saving her a second of time if she needed it.

She glanced up at him, then back at the screen. "Yeah?" She never maintained eye contact for longer than she had to. He understood that boundary, respected it. He'd love to smash it to pieces, but he respected it . . . for now. How long that would hold true was anyone's guess.

"The kid is going to stay here with you, so you aren't alone."

"Fine." Another quick glance. "Not necessary, though. I've been alone before."

"This could get hairy. You gotta figure the informer has someone hot on his ass, or he wouldn't be so jumpy. There's no telling what we might run into out there, retrieving him—and that's assuming he doesn't get cold feet and rabbit on us."

"Nothing we can do about that. He's either there or he isn't. And if anyone is out there, Tweety will see them."

He looked at the screen. As he'd figured, Tweety was in the air. She had the drone hovering silently over the ruin, slowly rotating as she checked on each teammate, one by one. Yasser and Mamoon were standing together, Yasser's hand on the kid's shoulder. They appeared to be having an earnest conversation, the kid nodding his head as he got his instructions.

"Be careful," she said. For a second their eyes met, then she looked down again before he could get a read on anything, given the dimness of the light.

"You too, babe," he said, knowing she wouldn't hear the faint difference in how he said the word, without capitalization. His palm tingled; the impulse to smooth his hand over the back of her head, her neck, was so strong he could actually feel the sensation even though he wasn't touching her.

Ah, shit. He needed to get his head off this dead-end path and back on the job.

He ducked through the curtain and back outside, though "inside" was a loose description to use for a structure that was mostly in ruins. "Lead the way," he said briefly to Yasser. Yasser pulled a fold of his headdress across his nose and mouth, to filter out the dust blown by the hot wind. Levi and the rest of the team pulled their balaclavas up over the lower halves of their faces, for the same reason. With their NVDs in place, their faces were almost wholly obscured.

The direction Yasser chose was north-northeast, toward rougher terrain, but that was a logical position for the informer because it offered more concealment. A mile there, make contact, a mile back;

Babe would be alone for no more than forty-five minutes if everything went smoothly, but there were no guarantees. Shit happening
was such a given that Levi planned for it. The only unknown was
what shape the shit would take.

JINA TOOK TWEETY in slow circles around the fanned-out line of
men, looking in all directions. She spotted a gazelle once, standing
motionless and watching the humans pass by. She'd done her home-
work, knew there were gazelles and jackals and other mammals in
the desert. There were also, surprisingly, scraggly shrubs and small
trees, rock piles, jagged and barren mountains, and lots of flat space.
Bedouins roamed the region, though in the heat of July it made
sense that they were likely closer to water sources than they would
be during the winter months.

She wouldn't mind a little winter right now—or even a water
source she could be close to. Sweat was dripping off her. But which
was worse, cold misery or hot misery? Hot misery, she decided,
because she felt as if she could barely breathe. The hot wind kept
the dust and sand stirred up, getting in every crevice, making her
eyes and mouth feel gritty, her nose clogged. None of it was a happy
feeling.

She watched the screen, controlling Tweety with both keystrokes
to bring up his various cameras, and the mini roller-ball mouse that
ruled the drone's movements, which she had attached to the laptop.
Her communications headset was in place, earbud and throat mic,
her NVD, equipment and gear bags, pistol, and jump helmet right
beside her, so she could grab and go if necessary.

For the most part the guys were silent, communicating by gesture
or low-pitched comments when necessary. She too was quiet, because she had nothing to report. Idle chatter was distracting.

She heard Mamoon enter the outer part of the ruin, moving

around, singing a little under his breath. He'd been outside for a while, which suited her fine. If he was like most kids, her solitude back here wouldn't last long, because his curiosity would get the better of him.

No sooner had she had the thought than the black curtain moved, and he slid behind it to join her in the small room.

He stared at her in shock. "You are a woman!"

She nodded, maintaining communications silence, keeping an eye on the screen. She feathered the roller ball, turning Tweety in a slow circle.

"You travel with men?"

His tone was scandalized. Jina clicked off her communications mic and indicated the pistol by her hand, though she kept watching the screen. "I'm armed," she said briefly. "They leave me alone." There was no point in getting into any long discussion about anything, just let him know how such a thing was possible, then get back to her job. She clicked the mic back on.

He watched her for a minute, her nimble hands in the fingerless black gloves moving over the keys, "fuzzing" the track ball in minute adjustments. He looked at the screen, tilted his head a little, watched the view change as she surveyed the surroundings. The thermal imaging picked up a very small signature and she zeroed in, enlarged, found some kind of weird rodent going about its ratty business. It looked like a mash-up of rabbit, rat, and kangaroo. Backing out again, she resumed her area surveillance.

Mamoon gasped as the line of men came on-screen. "How are you doing this?"

Crap. She wished he'd shut up and let her do her job. She clicked off the mic again. "I have a flying camera I'm controlling."

His eyes got big, and he looked back at the screen. "You saw the jerboa!"

"The rat? Yes, the camera is very sensitive." Mic back on. She moved Tweety to the other side of the team, searching, watching.

She tried not to sound as impatient as she felt, just keep it businesslike, but the kid must have picked up on something in her tone because abruptly he darted back through the curtain and left her alone. Maybe he remembered something he was supposed to be doing. Maybe he was going to get something. Definitely he was a kid, so who knew? She was just glad he was gone, so she could concentrate.

Checking the time, she saw that the men had been moving for twelve minutes; they should be getting close to where the informant was hiding. She wondered if there were any caves. There were jagged and rocky mountains and such, so logically there had to be caves. It was time to take Tweety farther in advance, see what he could see.

Mamoon had gone outside the ruin. She could hear a faint thunking sound to the left, as if he were fooling around the truck, maybe getting inside it and pretending to drive. Could be he already knew how to drive. Maybe he was getting in it to take a nap, out of the blowing sand, though she thought the interior of the truck would be too hot for comfort.

She focused on Tweety, taking the little drone ahead, looking for the heat signature of the informant.

She heard something else outside—a voice. A man's voice, hushed, too indistinct for her to make out words. At first she couldn't tell if she was hearing it in her earbud, or in her uncovered right ear. She frowned, concentrated, listened.

Then she heard Mamoon's lighter tones, as hushed as the other.

Someone was out there, someone they hadn't expected. Had Mamoon heard him, gone out to deflect attention?

No. It was the middle of the night, and they were in the freaking desert. People didn't just wander around and visit, especially not a ruin where no one was likely to be anyway. Whoever was there wasn't there by accident.

Alarm tingled her spine. She started to let the team know she had company when Tweety's cameras picked up a thermal signature, a man-sized one. Then another. Then another, and more, easily ten or fifteen, concealed on either side of the route the team would take. She forgot about the threat outside the ruin, focusing entirely on her guys.

"*Ambush! Ambush—*" she said urgently.

There was no time for anything else. As she got the second word out a thunderous explosion sent rock and dust flying through the ruin, the percussion knocking her to the right. Her head and right elbow banged painfully against the wall and she went down in a heap, with debris raining down on her.

Coughing violently, dazed, she nevertheless did what her training had taught her to do and pushed the debris away, immediately scrambled back to her feet. The darkness was absolute, the computer screen gone black.

Assume the worst.

The guys were too far away; whatever attack was happening, she had to save herself. She couldn't see. Her night-vision goggles . . . they'd been beside her and were now God only knew where. She couldn't find anything. Blindly she groped, touched something warm and metal, recognized the smooth edges of the laptop.

The laptop was made to withstand being dropped, submerged, and any number of other insults to the sensitive workings. She had to assume it was still operable, which meant she couldn't let it fall into anyone else's hands. She couldn't hear anything, her ears were ringing from the explosion. She couldn't tell if whoever had been outside was even now coming through the ruin in search of her.

Assume the worst.

She had to destroy the laptop. That had been drilled into her over and over, into all of the drone operators. The software was highly classified and *could not* be allowed to fall into anyone else's hands. Before she did anything else, even before she tried to save herself, she had to do her job and destroy the laptop.

Feeling along the edge, she located the switch on the upper left of the casing, and toggled it down. There was a bright, brief flash as the hard drive was destroyed. She had to trust that the destruction was complete because she had no way of checking.

Now she had to save herself.

Her scrabbling fingers couldn't locate her bag, the NVD, anything. Ahead, a flashlight beam . . . two beams . . . were slashing through the dust and smoke. She couldn't go out that way, couldn't hear if they were talking, if they thought she was dead and were looking for her body, or if they assumed she'd lived through the destruction and was waiting for them, possibly injured but definitely armed.

Armed. Her pistol had been lying beside her. Now it was God knows where, and she didn't have the time to feel around for it.

The hole, the one she'd located in the back wall—that was her only chance. Her gut instinct to not be trapped in the back with no escape had been completely on point. A flashlight beam flashed too close and quickly she ducked to the floor. She had seconds, literally less than a minute, before they would be back here unless by some miracle she found her pistol and shot in their direction. She wasn't waiting for that miracle, she had to move and move now. She half crawled, half slithered back and to the left, holding her breath so she wouldn't cough and give away her position, assuming the people searching for her could hear better than she could.

She reached the back of the ruin, couldn't go any farther. She scrabbled around, searching for the opening, and finally found the partially blocked hole. More stones had fallen, slowing her down. She shoved some rock out of the way, got down on her belly, tried to wiggle through. The stones scraped on her arms, caught on her shoulders. No. Desperately she turned on her side, worked her head through, pulled with her hands, pushed with her feet, and her shoulders were free. She was half in, half out, completely helpless if anyone saw her. She sucked in a breath and dust clogged her nostrils, her throat. Quickly she covered her mouth with both hands and tried to muffle the harsh cough she couldn't stifle.

Out. She had to get *out*. She pushed some more, got her hips free, and pulled her legs out. Quickly she turned, on her belly, and reached back through the wall, pulled some debris back in place to hide the hole. Maybe that would buy her some time before they realized she'd escaped rather than being buried under the rubble. Staying flat, she belly-crawled to where she remembered the wadi being, though she couldn't see a damn thing and could only pray she was going in the correct direction.

The ground fell out from under her and she slid into the wadi, rocks and sand going with her. *Found it.*

She had to move, she couldn't stop and assess the situation until she was in a safer location. All they—whoever *they* were—had to do was walk to the edge of the wadi and shine one of those flashlights down, and they'd see her.

Her heart was pounding so hard she could feel her fingertips throbbing. She knew what direction the team had gone in, but when she thought about what she'd seen through Tweety's cameras, she remembered that the wadi went roughly left to right, not on the diagonal she wanted. But it wasn't as if she had another to select, she had to go with the wadi she had. She chose to go right, stumbling along the rough bottom, tripping over rocks, falling again. *Shit!* The delay and possible noise dismayed her more than any pain she might have felt if she'd thought about it.

On her feet, move, keep moving.

Her eyesight was adjusting, clearing, now that she was away from the smoke and dust. She could see deeper shadows, tell that the wadi curved back to the left, taking her more in the direction she wanted and the curve effectively hiding her from anyone still at the ruin. She stumbled along, unable to run because the bottom of the wadi was so rough, but at least she was moving.

She realized there *was* light, a strange light, with an odd flicker to it; she glanced back and saw the night sky lit by the red, pulsing glow of fire, at least a hundred yards behind her. Whatever had exploded was now burning. What? Couldn't be the ruin, stone neither exploded—on its own, anyway—nor burned. *The truck.* Had to be. There was nothing else there.

The pieces fell into place. Mamoon. He'd been talking to someone. The little bastard! He and his uncle—if Yasser was indeed his uncle—were part of the ambush. When he'd seen on the laptop that she was surveilling the area ahead of the team, and that she could see them in the dark, he'd left immediately, likely to warn the others. Then whoever he'd told had faced the problem of both alerting the ambush waiting, and preventing her from giving the alarm to the team. He'd failed in the last, but succeeded in the first.

Levi. The team.

The ringing in her ears was fading a little, enough that she could hear rapid, muted sounds. It took her a few seconds to identify gunfire, but where? Blindly she spun in a circle, oriented herself by the glow from the fire, focused in on the distorted sound.

There.

Yes. The gunfire was coming from the direction of the team.

Her stomach clenched. At least she'd been able to give them warning. Her headset had been knocked askew but was still around her neck; she fumbled for the earbud, put it in place. Through the ringing in her ears she could hear disjointed curses, grunts, the cracks and booms of gunfire, but she couldn't distinguish individual voices.

She started walking again. Her headset was out of place, wrenched sideways by the explosion, or when she'd pushed herself through the jagged hole. The strap was twisted, the throat mic . . . her fingers ran over it. The mic was damaged, she could tell just by touch. Shit. *Shit!* She couldn't make radio contact with the guys.

She tried anyway, clicking on the mic—no, the mic had been *on,* she'd at least gotten out a warning about the ambush, so she had just turned it off. She clicked again, opened her mouth, then shut it. Anything she said right now, assuming her mic worked, would be a distraction.

The wadi turned sharply to the right, once more taking her away from their direction. She didn't dare climb out of it, not yet, she wasn't far enough away from the ruin, and they were in the middle of a firefight.

She couldn't get to them.

Sick with worry, she continued cautiously following the wadi; in some places the dry creek bed was shallow enough that she could see around her, plainly see the blaze in the distance, though it was beginning to die down. She had to bend double to not offer a silhouette in case Mamoon or the man—men?—with him was scanning the area with night-vision goggles. An NVD had fairly limited range of vision and she thought she might be beyond that now, but she wasn't certain.

The wadi continued to bear to the right; if she continued following it, it would take her farther and farther from the team. Uneasy, she stopped, trying to make sense of the cacophony she could hear from the earbud.

The rapid *RAT-TAT-TAT* of automatic weapons in the distance died down. Anxiously she waited, her heart pounding, sweat pouring off her. *Please, God, oh please, let them be all right.*

AT BABE'S TWO sharp words, "Ambush! Ambush!," they all hit the ground. Simultaneously behind them was a *boom!* and Levi snapped a look over his shoulder to see, in the distance, a spreading glow exactly where the ruin would have been.

The internal shock wave that hit him was staggering. *Jina!* Before he could process anything else, Yasser wheeled, holding a weapon he must have had hidden beneath his loose clothing, and began firing while he ran to the side. Yasser didn't have an NVD so he was shooting wildly toward where he thought Levi's team was, which came close enough. A bullet zinged overhead with an angry whine. Levi rolled, aimed, and stitched a line of shots across Yasser's torso. The man staggered, shook, went down. He twitched a time or two, then was still.

Not taking anything for granted, both Levi and Trapper took almost simultaneous head shots at Yasser. Careless people got killed by other people who weren't quite dead yet. Levi wasn't careless, and Yasser was now completely dead.

Jina.

He did a quick surveillance and saw nothing, urgently surged to his feet. Had Jina been telling them there was an ambush at the ruin, or warning them of Yasser? Maybe both. Already moving, he jerked his NVD up and stared in the direction of the ruin. Even at this distance, the glow had become a noticeable fire, pulsing skyward, bright enough to have blinded him if he'd kept the NVD in place.

The entire team was on their feet, looking back toward the fire.

Another shot, this one from the direction where the informant had been hiding. They hit the ground again. Cursing silently, Levi pulled his NVD back into place. The white flare of muzzle flashes revealed the location of the new attackers; they were running, advancing fast.

The good news was, that drastically affected their accuracy, which in his experience wasn't great anyway; it was more blast away until they ran out of cartridges. The bad news was that the team was outnumbered by at least two to one.

He began squeezing off shots, carefully placing the rounds for maximum effectiveness, moving after each shot because his muzzle flash revealed his position, too. The rest of the team was returning fire, doing the same thing he was doing, looking for what cover they could find before the attackers overran them. They scrambled, looking for indentions in the terrain, a pile of rocks, anything. He saw Voodoo get hit, go down, get up, and keep moving.

Then some of the attackers began diving for cover, too, proving that they had at least some training. *Shit!* He was pinned down by these assholes when every cell of his body was being eaten by urgency to get back to Jina. Never before—*never*—had he had to force himself to concentrate during a firefight.

By his count six attackers were down and unmoving, seven if he counted Yasser. There were nine more, unless a couple had hung back to maybe flank them and come up behind them. He did a swift check of his six—clear—and also checked on Voodoo, who signaled a thumbs-up.

Using hand signals, Levi sent Jelly and Crutch snaking around to the left. He and Boom shifted to the right—not too much, didn't want to get in the line of fire from Jelly and Crutch. Snake and Trapper, along with Voodoo, held the middle, but Voodoo was a worry despite the thumbs-up because Levi didn't know how mobile his man was.

"Let's take care of these fuckers," he said.

"REPORT."

Levi's voice. Even though her hearing was still muffled she recognized that rough tone, and tears of relief sprang to her eyes. She wiped them on her grimy sleeve, then had to blink away the dust. She thought she'd heard him say something before, but the sound had been garbled.

"Crutch and Voodoo are down." That was Snake.

Ah, no. No no no. Down didn't mean dead, but they were a long way from the secondary pickup point, and that wasn't good.

One by one the team reported, except for Crutch and Voodoo. Then Levi spoke again. "Babe, report in."

She tried. She clicked the mic, said "here," but the silence met her effort. She tried again, then faced facts: she couldn't. Automatically she reached for her holster so she could fire a shot to let them know her location—she'd also be alerting the bad guys who might or might not still be at the ruins, but that couldn't be helped—and her hand slapped an empty holster.

Damn it, damn it! Why had she ever taken it from the holster? She'd felt uneasy, yeah, and with good reason, but she wished she'd ignored that impulse.

"Babe!" His tone was sharp now. "Report in."

"Shit," Boom said softly, a few seconds later.

"Trapper and I will go back—"

"No." Levi cut Jelly off.

"She might be alive—"

"Snake, what are their conditions?" Again Levi's voice overrode Jelly's.

"Crutch has an abdominal. Voodoo was hit in the leg and upper right torso. They're both bad."

"Find something to make litters. We're carrying them out of here." There was both ice and steel in Levi's tone. "Snake, do what you can to stabilize them. We have to move fast."

"Ace . . ." That was Boom, his voice shaking a little, then it steadied. "Do what he said, guys, and double-time it."

"But I'm here," Jina whispered into the night. "Don't leave me."

TWENTY

Jina scrambled out of the wadi, no longer caring if she was exposed to anyone at the ruin who might have been looking for her. The fire had burned down to a much smaller blaze now and was farther off than she'd thought it would be. Wildly she looked around, but without Tweety and the laptop she couldn't pinpoint the guys' location, and without the night-vision goggles she had only the starlight to see by.

She could hear the guys in her ear, as if she were there with them. They made litters with the materials they had at hand, scavenged from the bodies of those they'd been in the firefight with, and within an impossibly short length of time they were moving. Boom and Jelly were carrying Voodoo, Snake and Trapper were carrying Crutch, and Levi was on point. They would swap out positions, to give each of them in turn a rest.

She tried yelling, only to find that the dust she'd inhaled had scratched her throat so much she couldn't get much volume. They were too far away to hear, anyway, but she tried.

They were gone. *They were gone.*

She was alone.

They'd left her.

The realization was like a knife, slicing into her gut. Knowing why they had—two of the team were seriously wounded, and they had to get them out—that was accepted by her logic. Her heart, though, felt as if a giant hand was squeezing her. They'd left her behind, hadn't even sent someone back to check.

She was the least valuable member of the team.

Knowing that and feeling it were two different things, and feeling it was shattering.

Despite the heat her teeth chattered, and her breath hitched in her throat. They thought she was likely dead, but they hadn't checked and now she *would* die. She had no weapon, no water, no shelter. She would die out here tomorrow, or the next day, assuming someone didn't capture her and she thought she'd rather die first, all things considered.

Mom! The single word echoed in her brain, brought all of them, her family, into sharp focus. They would never know exactly what happened to her, never have a body to bury. At best they'd be told that her remains were unrecoverable.

But the guys hadn't even tried. They'd left her behind.

No! She had to get past that, push it away. She couldn't just stand here and wait to die, she had to do something, and she couldn't function if she let herself get sucked into despair. They'd done what they had to do. Now she had to do what *she* had to do.

Inaction wasn't an option. She refused to accept defeat, refused to give up. She had a chance, because she knew where they were going, knew the coordinates of the secondary exfil point.

Willfully she fought down the thought-clouding panic; she needed every brain cell she had to get out of this alive. Not only did she know where they were going, but she had that damn compass in her cargo pocket, because months ago, almost a year now, they had insisted she learn it, use it, keep it with her, because sometimes phones and GPS didn't work. Like now.

"I can do this," she said aloud, and hoped she wasn't lying to herself.

Cautiously she slid back down into the wadi and pulled out her

little penlight, something else the guys had impressed on her to always keep with her—not in a bag, not nearby, but *with* her, just like
the compass. They might have left her behind, but perhaps they'd
also given her the means to survive.

She had to plot her course. She had nothing to write on other
than the ground, and her finger to scratch in the sand with, but
she could do this. She opened the compass, figured the variables,
and set her course, as much in her head as in the scratching on the
ground. Then she stood and rubbed her boot over the scratches,
because she didn't want to give anyone who might look for her in the
morning, in daylight, an idea where she had gone.

If she let herself think about what she had to do, she'd be defeated
before she even started, because this was so much more than she'd
ever asked of herself before. She took some deep breaths, both calm-
ing herself and gearing up for what she had to do, then climbed out
of the wadi again, and set out across the desert in a trot.

Panic lurked, nipping at her heels. She wanted to run, she wanted
to set a blistering pace across the sand, but she couldn't. She shoved
it down, forced herself to focus on what was real, on the now and
perhaps the next five minutes. If she thought about the future, or
the what-ifs, then she was done.

Reality was that she was in the dark and she didn't dare turn on
the penlight to see better, because not only would she use up the
battery way before daylight, but if any unfriendlies were out there,
the light would pinpoint her location for them. Light was visible for
long distances, even tiny pinpoints of light.

But—what if the guys were close enough they could see the light,
too? Would they investigate?

They might shoot her. They had their NVDs, but the range of
their weapons was greater than the visual range of the NVDs.

There was no safe way to reunite with them en route. She had to
get to the secondary location.

She had to keep going. Focus, push, keep going. Set a steady, easy pace, and keep going.

The heat and the night and the wind pressed down on her. Even at a trot, soon sweat was pouring off her. Her lungs burned, her mouth was cotton dry. No matter how easy the pace, in this kind of heat she needed water, water that she didn't have and had no way of finding. Without water, she had no chance of surviving the daytime heat.

Do this or die. Do this or die.

She stepped on a rock that slid out from under her foot and she went down, sprawled on the sandy, rocky ground. Her fingerless gloves protected her palms, but her knees scraped. She ignored the pain, got up, resumed her pace.

She didn't let herself think. This was big, maybe bigger than she could handle, and if she got caught in the details, she'd falter. She had to be a machine, she had to run the way she'd trained to run—*beyond* how she'd trained, because this was farther than she'd ever run before. This was hours and hours in the dark, in the heat, unable to avoid pitfalls or vipers or anything else. One of those weird rabbit/kangaroo rats—what had Mamoon called it? She couldn't remember—might jump on her and trip her.

Don't think, Jina. Don't worry about the rat. Just move, keep moving.

WAS SHE STILL alive?

The possibility, slim as it was, ate at his guts. Levi set a brutal pace when he was on point, driven by the need to move, to get his men to safety and good medical care before it was too late, before they were carrying two corpses instead of two teammates. The faster he got to the pickup point, the sooner he could go back.

He had to. He had to find her.

Even if she hadn't survived, he had to bring her body back. *No man left behind*. No woman, either. That was the creed he'd operated under when he was in the military, and nothing had changed when he joined the GO-Teams. He wouldn't leave her for the jackals, the rats.

Only Voodoo and Crutch, saving them, kept him focused. Every time he thought about Jina, hearing the explosion and seeing the fire glow in the distance, he nearly buckled under the despair that gutted him. He hadn't kept her safe.

He'd done what he thought he had to do, for the cohesion of the team, and kept her at a distance, always thinking that things would change, that he'd have time later to explore this thing between them. Now it was too late. She was gone. All the things he thought he'd have time for, holding her and laughing with her, fighting with her, those were gone with her.

"Hold up!" Snake said and did a quick check of the wounded men. Voodoo was in danger of bleeding out, and Crutch had an abdominal wound that could be fatal even if he'd had instant medical care. The massive infection from wounds to the gut was difficult to overcome, period.

Unable to help himself, Levi turned and looked behind them, as if he could conjure a small figure emerging from the night, blue-and-amber eyes flashing while she called them morons for going off and leaving her.

He'd left her.

Boom's hand closed on his shoulder. Levi didn't look at his friend and teammate, because sometimes not looking was easier.

"You couldn't have done anything," Boom said, his tone rough with emotion.

"Doesn't matter." Guilt and regret, grief and rage and despair, all balled together in his chest until he felt as if he could barely breathe. "When we get Voodoo and Crutch on the bird, I'm going back."

"I'll go with you," Boom immediately volunteered.

Levi shook his head. "No. You have Terisa and the kids to go home to, so you go. The mission is done, it was an ambush. Fuck if I know how it was set up, or why. You can report as well as I can."

"Two doubles the chance of success," Boom retorted.

"I can go," Trapper said. "I'm not married."

"Or me," Jelly offered.

Snake had a savage expression on his face. Not only did he have a family, too, but he had to stay with Crutch and Voodoo, keep them alive if he could.

Again Levi shook his head no. "This is on me. I won't risk any of you. I made the decision to leave her, and I'm going back for her."

THE GROUND WENT out from under her. Jina gave a hoarse shriek as she tumbled down the rough side of a dry wadi. She hit hard, narrowly missed a large rock. She scrambled away from the rock, in case a snake was using it as shelter. Or maybe snakes were using the night to hunt, and sheltered during the searing heat of the day.

The impact *hurt*, but she hadn't broken any bones. Was this the human version of having a beat-up chassis but a good motor? *She don't look like much, fellas, but she runs good.*

She ran good. Hours and hours and hours of running. Legs like steel. Lungs like . . . lungs like jellyfish. Breathing hard, she decided now was a good time to recheck her course. The short rest would keep her from overtaxing her stamina.

Shaking, she pulled out the compass and penlight, and replotted. She'd gone a little off course, but not too bad. Okay. Really, she was doing pretty good. She'd covered some ground, not as much as she'd have liked because what she'd have liked was to be there *right now*, but a decent distance.

What time was it? How could she not have thought of that before? She roughly estimated the distance, then looked at the luminous hands on her heavy-duty wristwatch like all the guys wore. The world's top marathoners could run that distance in two-something hours, but she wasn't a top marathoner, and they ran in daylight, in sneakers on city streets, with people giving them water along the way. She figured her speed would be less than half that, so . . . at best she had, probably, another five hours of running, and that was if she didn't fall and break a leg or crush her skull, though in the case of skull-crush, her worries were over.

Covering that distance in five hours was a reasonable expectation, she thought. A nice brisk walk would cover a mile in fifteen minutes, four miles an hour, twenty miles in five hours.

Five hours would at least be nautical twilight, and she'd be able to see.

What kind of time would the guys make? They were by necessity traveling slower, but had a shorter distance, and she knew they would push themselves to get Crutch and Voodoo to medical help as fast as possible. They were strong, they could see, and they had water. They might not be much slower.

If they got to the exfil point ahead of her, Levi would call in the helicopter for pickup, and they might be gone before she could get there. It was a short hop for the helicopter, across the Iraqi border just into Syria, then back. It wouldn't wait; as soon as the guys were on board, it would lift off.

She had to go faster.

She climbed out of the wadi and set off again, picking up the pace. The boots rubbed up and down on her feet despite the two pairs of socks she wore. She was sweating so much her socks were damp, anyway. Nothing she could do. She felt the blisters rubbing, felt the pain burning. She ran. She had to cut that time down.

She ran. She fell. She got up and ran again. Over and over. Her gasping breath burned in her chest. But every time she fell she used the opportunity to recheck her course, to catch her breath. Veering off course would be disastrous.

God, her feet hurt. The pain was crippling, so debilitating that tears stung her eyes, rolled down her cheeks. Furiously she ordered herself to stop crying, because she couldn't afford to lose even that much moisture. She stopped, stood weaving back and forth. Could she pull her boots off, run barefoot? Yes, there were rocks and rough shrubs and all sorts of other things, but could that hurt worse than scrubbing her feet raw?

Yes, it could. Her feet were already raw, she could tell by the sharpness of the pain. If she tried running barefoot she'd be inviting massive infection in her feet. Her fault; she'd grabbed the wrong boots.

Run anyway. No matter what, she had to run anyway. Forget her feet. One step after another, that was all she had to do, take the next step, and the next, and the next. Five hours. She could get through five hours. She could focus only on the next step, the next yard, the next mile. She could because she had no choice.

She ran.

What was Levi thinking? Did it bother him that he'd left her behind, was he thinking of her at all, or only about getting his wounded men to safety?

She began crying again.

He'd told her, in words so plain there was no misunderstanding: she was the least valuable member of the team. And now he'd proven it to her.

How many miles? She stopped, tried to calculate how far she'd gone, but the numbers didn't make sense. She couldn't remember, but she knew the coordinates, knew the time. She felt the minutes passing, tick-tock, closer and closer, later and later. Any minute could be one minute too late. She concentrated, dug deeper.

Her feet were agony.

The next time she fell, she lay facedown in the gritty sand, the sudden transition from upright to prone so overwhelming her entire body went limp in relief. She thought about closing her eyes and going to sleep. How blissful that would be, and how easy, just go to sleep and forget about this pain, this spirit-breaking struggle.

The temptation was so strong that she forced herself to sit up and dig the compass from her pocket. She opened it, stared at it with blurred vision, unable to make the dial make sense. Blinking hard, she tried again. Still blurred. Shit. She closed her eyes and sat, sucking in deep breaths, trying to gather her thoughts. She had to do this or she'd die. She couldn't quit, not now.

When she felt a little steadier, she opened her eyes and made herself focus. She painstakingly checked the compass, replotted her course, then did it again to make sure she had it right. Okay. She could do this. She clicked off the penlight . . . and realized the darkness wasn't absolute any longer. The black was becoming gray—a dark gray, but still a definite lightening around her.

Daylight was coming. She was running out of time.

She got up and ran.

Her feet pounded in time with her thoughts. *I can do this. I have to do this. Left behind. Left behind. Left behind.*

Staying upright was harder now. She kept listing to the side. She stopped, sucked in air, focused once more.

"Don't quit," she chanted to herself, under her breath. "Don't quit."

She'd never quit anything. She couldn't start now.

She ran. Her mind felt as if she was running, but her body seemed to be rebelling, going slower and slower. Hours. How many hours had she been running? Was it five hours yet? She'd estimated five hours, that was her target. If she could keep going for the full five hours, she'd be there. She couldn't let herself think anything else.

The dark gray became a light gray, the rocky sand took on a reddish hue, like blood. She puzzled over the color, finally realized that she could see. She wasn't running in the unending darkness now, time had worked its unending magic and unending hell, because it was running out, time was running out.

The terrain was rougher, there was more vegetation—not much, but enough to matter, because that meant if the guys were close by she might be blocked from their view.

Don't quit.

"I won't," she promised, her tone broken, breathless. "I won't."

Something . . . a noise, barely heard over the harsh rasp of her breathing. A strange rhythmic *whump-whump* that made her frown, because it seemed familiar but she couldn't place it. Her instinct said to keep moving but the noise bothered her and she stopped, her head tilted as she listened to it. What *was* that? She'd heard it before, she knew she had.

Because she'd stopped, she dragged out the compass; it was habit now. Frowning, she stared down at the dial, the reading, concentrated.

The compass was wrong. She must have broken it. It said she was almost there, but she wasn't, she was still alone and in Bumfuck Egypt, wherever the hell that was. No . . . Syria. She was in Syria. Bumfuck Syria. Ha! Egypt had a better ring to it.

But if the compass was broken, then she'd be here forever because she didn't know how to find her way out.

Whump-whump-whump.

She looked up and saw a giant black insect thing, silhouetted against the horizon, and then it settled down to the earth.

Helicopter! Her dazed brain seized on the word, screamed it at her. It was the helicopter, *their* helicopter. She'd made it!

No, she hadn't, because she was still standing there. Clumsily she began to run toward the helicopter, her legs not working quite right so that she lurched more than ran, but she was moving.

"Wait for me," she croaked, her voice barely audible. "Here! I'm here! I'm coming. Don't leave me. Please don't leave me."

TWENTY-ONE

"Hostile approaching!" one of the Blackhawk gunners urgently sang out.

They had already loaded Crutch and Voodoo, and Snake was checking them. His face was tense, knowing they were on borrowed time and things could go south for them at any minute. The whole march to the secondary pickup point had been tense, a battle against time and distance in the effort to save them, and underscored by the sick knowledge that they'd lost Babe and been forced to leave her body behind.

Levi's head snapped around. He'd seen his men loaded, and he was getting ready to do what he had to do, knowing he might not ever see them again. Going back was a huge risk, with maybe a fifty/fifty chance of getting out alive. He'd take what water and food they had with them; he couldn't travel during the day, on foot, in heat that would likely be in the 130-degree range. He'd been awake all night and would have to shelter during the day, get some sleep, then start out when the sun went down and the heat dissipated some. The bodies they'd left behind would have been sniffed out by the desert predators by now, and they might have gotten into the ruin— He shut that thought down, fast, because he couldn't let himself go there.

He'd find her, find his Babe, bury her if he couldn't bring her remains out.

But first they had to deal with one more piece of shit in a shit-filled mission.

The gunner had brought his barrel around. Levi narrowed his eyes, gripping his own weapon, moving for cover. Then—something. Something about the distant approaching figure made him shoot his hand out, grab the barrel, and push it up. "Wait," he muttered, staring hard through fatigue-blurred eyes. The unknown lurching toward them was small, a woman or a kid, and thin, and so completely covered with dust that making out individual features was impossible. But the clothes were . . . not Syrian, and there seemed to be a long mop of hair swinging—

"It's her," he said, blurting the words before his brain could catch up to his mouth.

"What?" Boom whirled, already halfway on the helicopter. All of them turned, staring hard at the stumbling figure approaching them. But Levi knew, knew somehow in his gut, and relief hit him so hard he almost staggered himself.

Then he was running, bent low under the whirling blades of the helicopter. "Wait, man," the gunner said sharply, but Levi charged across the sand and rocks toward her. If anyone was chasing her, she'd need cover. If no one was chasing her, she'd need help, because she was lurching wildly, unable to keep a straight course. Boom caught up with him and the two of them closed on her.

His throat clogged, choking him with a massive wave of emotions he couldn't identify. It wasn't joy, it was as if he'd been thrown into hell and suddenly jerked back, as if his life had been over and now it wasn't.

He and Boom reached her, reached out to support her. If he hadn't known it was Jina, he wouldn't have recognized her. Her face was gaunt, coated with sweat and dust, her eyes blind and staring. It was as if she didn't see them, as if she was so focused on keeping her feet moving that she plowed right into them. Levi caught her, then caught the feeble punch she threw at him because she was who she was and never stopped fighting. "Easy, babe," he said, then dipped his knees and tilted her over his shoulder, stood upright with the slight burden of her safe in his grip. The scent of blood hit him, made his stomach twist.

He and Boom loped back to the helicopter. Boom climbed in, reached out, and Levi handed her over. The helicopter had room for eleven combat personnel or six stretchers; with Voodoo and Crutch on stretchers, space was tight, but there was room to lay her down.

"Leave me alone," she muttered, the words barely legible.

Levi vaulted aboard, yelled, "Go!" to the pilot, and they lifted off in a storm of dust and debris. He reached out and gripped one of her ankles, knowing what kind of shape her feet were in, to ease her boots off.

She kicked out violently, her heel catching him on the shin. "Leave me alone," she said again, her tone fierce, then she turned on her side with her back to them, curling up in a protective ball, and he saw her go limp.

With a quick check on the two wounded, Snake scrambled over to her, shook her. She didn't respond.

"She's out!" Levi yelled as he swiftly began unlacing her boots.

Snake put two fingers on her neck, checked her pulse. "Heart rate's too fast!" he yelled back. Quickly he pinched the back of her hand, watched the skin stay pinched. "Dehydrated, bad! We need to get some fluids in her!"

Voodoo and Crutch were already getting fluids, in an effort to keep them alive until they could get to a field hospital. There were no more IV lines available. Severe dehydration was critical; she might go into cardiac arrest. Abandoning her boots, Levi grabbed one of the remaining bottles of water, poured it over her head and the back of her neck. She didn't move, even when the water ran down into her face. She couldn't swallow; she was unconscious, and she'd choke if they tried to pour water down her. Pouring it over her wasn't much, but it was all he could do to cool her down with the supplies they had. He held his hand out and Boom slapped another bottle of water into it.

He slowly poured more water over her head while Snake cut her boots off. Her socks were bloody—not just a little, but bloody from her toes up to her ankles. Snake cut the socks off, too, exposed her raw and bleeding feet. There was almost no skin left on her heels or across her toes, just exposed meat.

"Ten minutes!" the copilot bellowed, aware that every minute counted.

Ten minutes. They were almost there, if Voodoo and Crutch could hang on. In ten minutes, they'd have help, blood, and antibiotics to support them while they underwent emergency surgery. In ten minutes someone would start an IV line, get some fluids in her before she started convulsing.

Ten minutes.

It felt like a lifetime.

JINA WOKE IN a white tent. She stared around, her vision blurry. She was lying down; her tired brain deciphered that much. But she didn't know where she was, and she didn't care. She wasn't alone; she could see what seemed like a row of people . . . maybe. Or maybe she was alone.

She didn't care. Everything was at a distance, and that was okay. She didn't want to think, or feel. She closed her eyes and drifted off again.

The next time she woke, she was more aware, but still not quite with it. The white tent was gone, and there was a droning noise that annoyed her. She moved fretfully, frowned when her hand caught on something, lifted it to stare at the IV in the back of her hand. She frowned again, because her hand was stained and dirty.

A big hand caught hers, lowered it beside her. Levi crouched beside her, his face swimming into focus. He looked terrible, unshaven, dirty, his gaze somehow savage. "You're okay," he said.

She considered that. She remembered running through the desert, remembered the desolation and despair. She remembered a lot, she just didn't care about most of it. "Voodoo?" she croaked. "Crutch?"

"They're holding on. We're on our way to Germany."

That was all she needed to know. Escaping was easy, because she was tired, so very tired. She simply had to close her eyes to shut him out, and she did.

TWENTY-TWO

She was treated in a military hospital in Germany. Jina lay quietly in bed, mostly staring at the ceiling and not interested enough to even look out the window. A massive exhaustion weighed down on her, killing her desire to do anything other than breathe.

Maybe she should call her mom. Vaguely she felt as if she needed to, just to connect with someone or something again, but not only would she have to figure out how to make an international call, she'd have to talk. She didn't want to talk, not to anyone. There was an invisible wall around her and she felt safe inside it, safe and empty and alone. Too many words would dissolve the wall, leaving her vulnerable again.

Maybe she'd call later, when she could stand words again and isolation didn't feel so necessary.

A brief hard tap on the door caught her attention, followed immediately by Levi pushing the door open and entering, as if it wouldn't occur to him to wait until she said, "Come in." Maybe he knew she wouldn't say it. More likely, he simply didn't care.

He looked better than he had on the flight; he'd showered, shaved, had on clean clothes, and had gotten some sleep. The expression in his eyes was still not civilized. Something angry and violent lurked just below the surface, bubbling against his iron control.

She wanted to be left alone. Why was he here? She didn't want him here.

There was a chair for visitors, but, being Levi, he didn't take it. He hitched his ass on the side of her bed, half sitting, and bridged her body with one muscular arm braced on the other side of her hip. Now Jina moved her gaze to the window. Funny—somehow she'd expected to see the stark, desolate landscape of sunbaked Syria, and instead she saw a gray sky and a drizzle of rain on the glass. Germany; she was in Germany. Her body was here, but her mind hadn't caught up.

"They're both out of surgery," he said after a long moment of waiting for her to look at him. She could feel him willing her to obey his will, as if he could use some Jedi mind trick on her eyeballs.

Crutch. Voodoo. For them, she slowly turned her head, looked at him. "Will they make it?" Her voice was thin and scratchy, her throat still dry feeling despite all the fluids that had been pumped into her.

"Touch and go." He scrubbed a hand over his face. "They're both in ICU. Voodoo has a better shot than Crutch, but he took a lot of damage to his leg."

She nodded, and once more looked out the window. Who knew devastation felt so empty? She'd always thought it was great pain, but instead it was . . . nothing, all emotion gone. She felt as empty as the desert, bleak and scorched.

"We're flying out in a couple of hours," he said. "We have to get back ASAP. You'll be released tomorrow, and I've arranged a flight home for you. Everything is taken care of."

She nodded again. So they were leaving her behind again. Different circumstances, and illogical on her part to think that, but there it was. They were leaving, and she wasn't. She could have traveled with them, with some help.

All in all, she thought, she was in fairly good shape after going through the ordeal she'd faced. Her feet would heal. She didn't have any broken bones, and a wonderful nurse had washed her hair for her. She hadn't had a shower yet, because of her feet, but she'd washed off several times and had finally felt clean.

She'd been treated for severe dehydration and she felt much better. Her feet were bandaged and walking wasn't fun, but she could manage to hobble around, get to the toilet by herself. At least the catheter was out, now that they no longer needed to measure her urine output to make certain her kidneys hadn't shut down.

She could have handled the flight, gone with them, even if they were hitching a ride on another cargo plane. Instead he'd opted to leave her to fly by herself, twenty-four hours later.

Been there, done that, forget the damn T-shirt because she didn't want it.

He took her hand, the one that didn't have the IV needle in it, rubbed his thumb across the backs of her fingers. "I'd take you with us if I could," he said.

Sure.

"That's okay." She pulled her hand free and looked down at the sheet. Why was he touching her? He shouldn't be touching her, there was no point. He needed to leave, go do whatever he was supposed to be doing. She was positive holding her hand wasn't on that list. "Can I see Crutch and Voodoo?"

He paused. "I'll see if they'll let someone wheel you in."

"That's okay," she said again. "I'll ask a nurse." *Don't do me any favors, Levi.*

He checked the time, then stood. "I'll see you when you get back." He stood beside the bed looking down at her; she could feel that Jedi thing again, compelling her to look at him, but she set her jaw and kept her gaze on the sheet. She'd already seen enough of him, so damn big and tough and battle-weary, that intense dark gaze on her, his presence almost like a punch in the stomach.

She wanted him to go. He was the one she most didn't want to see. None of the other guys had come back for her, either, but Levi was the one who had kissed her and held her, and he was the one who had made the decision to leave her behind. When she thought of the others, she was okay; when faced with Levi, everything in her wanted to shut down.

Because he was Levi and his will was a force of nature, he cupped her chin in one big, rough hand and turned her face toward him. She stubbornly kept her gaze down, though it felt stupid, but neither did she feel cooperative. His thumb rubbed over her mouth and he made an impatient sound, then bent down and pressed a quick, hard kiss to her mouth, staying just long enough to give her a touch of his tongue. "We'll talk," he said—was that a promise, or a threat?—and strolled out, his broad shoulders barely fitting through the door.

Maybe, maybe not. Three days ago—a lifetime ago—that touch, that kiss, would have had her heart pounding and her thoughts racing around like a crazed squirrel.

He'd left her behind. He'd kissed her and put his tongue in her mouth, then he'd left her anyway.

And she was so tired. She didn't want to think about anything, deal with anything, not even that something about Levi had changed and she didn't have the energy to figure out what it was. Maybe when she got home she'd feel more like herself.

The next time a nurse came in, Jina asked about going to critical care to check on her pals. "I don't see why not," she said, then looked at Jina's bandaged feet. "I don't think you want to walk that far on those puppies, though, so I'll see what I can do about a wheelchair just before the next visitation period."

But then she forgot, and Jina had to ask someone else. Finally she got that wheelchair, though, and an orderly took her to the ICU. Voodoo's cubicle was first. He opened his eyes when she wheeled inside, and she almost collapsed with relief. He was pale, he had tubes running into his chest, an oxygen cannula in his nose, an IV stand strung with multiple plastic bags, and his left leg was immobilized.

Still, he said, "Hey." He sounded heavily drugged, which he was, barely out of sedation.

"Hey, yourself." So far this was a very profound conversation.

His bleary gaze went to the wheelchair. "What's up . . . with that?"

"Oh. I hurt my feet. Not bad. I'm going home tomorrow."

"Damn boots."

"Yeah, the damn boots. They won't cause any more trouble, though; they're gone." That was positively chatty of her, the most she'd said at one time in . . . had it really only been a *day?* A little more than a day? She felt as if weeks had passed.

He lifted a hand, reached for her. She rolled closer and took it. "I was . . . mostly out," he said with difficulty, "but I know . . . you were . . ." The words drifted off, then he rallied and finished, "Glad you're all right."

"I made it. Now you have to make it, too." She laid his hand back on the bed.

"Planning on it." A barely there smile touched his mouth. He lifted his hand again, made a fist. She smiled, too, as she fist-bumped him.

"See you back home, buddy."

She rolled herself down the corridor to where Crutch was. He was asleep, or unconscious. Jina watched him for a minute. He was breathing regularly, but his temp was a hundred and three and his blood pressure was up. Crutch had gone long hours before he was treated with anything but the most basic care. He was strong, but it was still touch-and-go.

Looking at him, looking at Voodoo, she didn't know if either of them would ever be able to rejoin the team.

Life changed on a dime. Even people who lived ordinary lives were at the whim of chance: an auto accident, a fall, a walk in the wrong place at the wrong time, and nothing was ever the same again. For them, the members of the GO-Teams, fate was tempted every time they answered the phone.

Donnelly was dead. Voodoo and Crutch had come close. She herself had come through the disastrous mission without any lasting harm, but the balance could so easily have tipped the other way and she could have died in the Syrian desert. She'd been terrified during parachute training, at the time more than half convinced she wouldn't survive, but that had been a walk in the park compared to the desert. Another mile—even another half mile—and she wouldn't have made it. Five more minutes, and she wouldn't have made it. The helicopter would have lifted off and she wouldn't have been on it.

The orderly stopped chatting with the ICU nurses and took her back to her room. Once more lying in bed, her feet aching, she looked out the window and thought about the mission. A spark of interest lit, and she seized on it with relief, glad to feel something other than sad emptiness. When she got home and talked to the others, she'd find out what they thought had happened, but she'd gone over it herself and it was obvious Yasser and Mamoon had been hostile. When Mamoon had seen the computer screen and realized she would be able to alert the team to the ambush, he'd gone outside and consulted with others who had been well hidden, perhaps in the very wadi she'd used for escape, but somewhere Tweety hadn't been able to see even in infrared. Perhaps they'd been able to contact the ambush team. Or they *hadn't* been able to contact them, and their solution had been to set off the explosion that burned the truck and hopefully killed her, as a way to warn them something had gone wrong. Maybe they'd thought the team would immediately turn back, leaving them vulnerable to attack from the rear.

She didn't know why the attack had been planned as it was, if there had truly been an informant or if he had already been dead. There was a possibility they'd never know exactly what had happened, or why, but the GO-Teams had analysts who would go through every bit of information and advance the most likely theory.

In the end, she didn't have to know why. She had information from her part of the mission, what had happened and how, but she didn't know why, and in a way she was done with it. It was as if there was a line of demarcation in her mind, and what had happened in the before didn't matter in the after.

THE NEXT DAY, she was put on a hospital flight home. Her feet were completely wrapped in what she considered a surplus of gauze, the bandages extending halfway up her shins. She wore the shapeless paper booties surgeons wore and was taken on board the plane by wheelchair. Her feet were better, still very sore and achy and no way would she have wanted to put on a pair of shoes, but she thought the wheelchair was a little bit of overkill, kind of like the bandages. She could have walked on board, though slowly.

It was a long flight. Pretty much they all were, because the GO-Teams didn't operate domestically. She slept some, read some, and still felt like crap when the plane landed at Andrews. She was rolled off the plane, then kind of abandoned while the more seriously sick or injured were unloaded.

She'd been officially released, so really she'd hitched a ride on the med flight and wasn't one of the patients. She was pondering the logistics of getting home—she had no cash for a taxi, her car was elsewhere, and she wasn't exactly in good-enough shape to drive anyway while she was still on pain meds for another couple of days. She'd have to borrow a phone and call . . . someone, though she didn't know who—

"Babe!"

She turned toward the call and saw Terisa coming toward her, a visitor's tag clipped to her blouse. A few seconds later she was enveloped in a warm hug, and for the first time since being rescued she felt tears sting her eyes. Fiercely she returned the hug. "I'm so glad to see you," she said into Terisa's shoulder and blinked back tears.

"It's my off day, so I volunteered to meet your plane," Terisa said. "The guys are all tied up at headquarters. The shit hit the fan over what happened, though Marcus has been his usual lock-jawed self and I don't know any of the operational details, just that Voodoo and Crutch were hit bad, and your feet are hurt and you can't walk. Your car has been collected and taken home, I've gone shopping and stocked your fridge with food—girl, seriously, you had nothing to eat but crackers. Anyway, if you want to stay at home and rest for a few days, you can, or if you want to get out of the house, all you have to do is call. If I didn't have to work tomorrow, I'd take you home with me, though I figure you'd rather have peace and quiet and a chance to get yourself back."

"You don't know how much I appreciate this." Had Terisa somehow guessed how she felt? As a nurse she routinely saw people who had been through traumatic experiences, so maybe she knew getting back to normal took time. Had Boom told her that she'd saved herself by running for hours, on bleeding feet, through the desert?

She didn't want to think about that. And she didn't want to get back to normal, she preferred the disconnect.

Instead she focused on the mundane, because that was safer. She hadn't gotten as far as thinking about the food situation at home—usually lousy, these days—or how she would function until she was cleared to drive, which would be when she no longer needed pain medication. She could always order in pizza, she supposed, but the driving would have to wait. "Have you heard how Voodoo and Crutch are doing? I saw them yesterday, talked to Voodoo some, but Crutch wasn't awake."

"Voodoo has been upgraded from critical to serious, and if he keeps improving, he'll be moved to a regular room tomorrow. Crutch is still critical, his fever is still up, but his vitals are stabilizing." Terisa's tone was the businesslike one of an experienced nurse. She shook her head, her gaze worried. "He has a long way to go before he's out of the woods. Whether or not either of them will be able to work again . . ." She gave a brief tilt of her head, indicating that was unlikely.

Unspoken was the reality that the team was on stand-down for the foreseeable future, at least for the missions that required full strength, because a third of the team was injured and unable. Jina thought of the team without those two, and it didn't feel right. A team was a whole, and family of sorts; losing them would leave a huge gap.

Losing her . . . wouldn't leave as large a gap. She had been an add-on. She'd thought she'd become completely accepted as a teammate, but she'd been wrong.

Terisa took Jina home, fixed a sandwich for her, and made her eat. When she was satisfied that the basic needs had been met, she left and Jina tumbled into bed. She didn't care about resetting her internal clock, because she didn't have to hit the training field tomorrow. She could sleep if she wanted to, and she did.

She slept for hours, woke up hungry, and hobbled her way to the kitchen to eat a cinnamon roll. Thank God Terisa had included some junk food, because even nuking some instant oatmeal was beyond her. She went back to bed then woke up in the early hours, made some coffee, took a basin bath, and put on regular clothes. It was good to wear something other than the hospital scrubs she'd been given in Germany.

At seven o'clock, her phone rang. She reached for it, recognized Levi's number, and jerked her hand back. But he was still her team leader, and now that she was home there was likely debriefing to be done, debriefing that wouldn't wait for a little thing like not being able to drive. Reluctantly she answered.

"Can you be ready in fifteen minutes?" He didn't even say hello, but she gave a mental shrug; it wasn't as if she didn't know who was calling.

"Yes." She didn't tell him she was already dressed.

"Mac is sending a car. There'll be a wheelchair."

She disconnected, and wondered if seven A.M. was too early to start drinking. She didn't feel like doing this and hated like poison to be rolled through headquarters as if she was an invalid—though technically she was an invalid. Okay, literally she was; that didn't mean she liked it.

She also didn't like wearing the paper booties, which were getting ragged anyway, so she tried to put on her only pair of bedroom slippers. Forget that; besides, Caleigh had bought them for her a couple of Christmases ago, and they had moose heads bobbing on the toes. Better she wear paper booties than moose heads.

Ten minutes after Levi's call, she gingerly made her way downstairs. She couldn't flex her toes because of the bandaging, so she had to go down sideways, like a toddler, clinging to the banister for balance. The car Mac had sent pulled to the curb just as she went outside, and the driver, a burly guy in dress pants and a polo shirt, gave her a perturbed look. "I was coming up to get you," he said.

"How? Wheelchairs don't work on stairs," she pointed out.

"My orders were to carry you."

Carry her? She must have looked as appalled as she felt, because he mumbled something about not knowing she could walk yet. She hobbled around the car and got in the passenger seat and hoped he wasn't chatty.

He wasn't, though she could feel him giving her occasional glances as if he was trying to size her up. When they reached headquarters, he jumped out and got the wheelchair from the trunk, unfolded it, held it steady while she transferred from the car to the seat. She already felt tired; despite her dislike of the chair, she was happy not to be walking the distance required.

He pushed her along the sidewalk, up the handicap ramp, into the building where the air-conditioning was already cranked up to maximum, as if trying to get a head start on the day's heat. Headquarters interior was very humdrum, deliberately so. Anyone who entered the building by accident would see a drab lobby, a single receptionist who would kindly direct them away and who would be holding a pistol under her desk, pointing at them. The door leading back to the business part of the building was armored and accessed only by a facial recognition program and a key card.

Beyond that, the hallways seemed to have been designed by a drunk troll, though she knew they were deliberately laid out for defense. Finding her way around, when she'd first been hired, had been a challenge. After a while she hadn't noticed the mazelike layout and navigated the building without any problem. Now she saw things with different eyes and recognized the effectiveness of the design.

Every time they met someone in the hallway, whoever it was stepped to the side and stopped to stare at her. Jina began to feel uncomfortable. Was it the wheelchair? Then they met a woman she recognized from her days in Communications, though she couldn't remember the woman's name. Whoever it was stopped and said, "Jina!" Grabbing both of Jina's hands she said, "I admire you so much. When we heard what you did—running for hours like that . . . well, I couldn't have done it. That was amazing."

"Ah . . . thank you," Jina finally managed. So that was it. Should she tell them she hadn't done anything heroic or amazing, that she'd been operating on blind desperation and the will to survive? In the end she let it go, because doing otherwise would take too much effort and she didn't care enough.

He wheeled her to one of the secure conference rooms. Mac was there, looking as impatient and ill-tempered as always. Levi was also there, and three others, two men and a woman, who she took to be intelligence analysts.

"I have her," Levi said, taking control of the wheelchair from the driver he'd sent.

"Sure thing."

Levi pushed the chair up to the conference table, then poured a cup of coffee and set it in front of her. She murmured a thanks and was sincere about it—the coffee, anyway.

No one introduced the three strangers, which didn't matter to her. She'd likely never see them again, anyway. Mac paced around, scowling. "Okay, we know this mission was in the crapper from the get-go. Ace has been debriefed. What happened on your end?"

"The kid, Mamoon, came in and watched me while I was operating the drone. I picked up a thermal signature, zoomed in on it. I thought he was amazed, interested, but now I know he was alarmed because he knew I would see the men who were waiting to ambush the team. He left, and a few minutes later I heard a voice outside, probably at the truck we were supposed to use to exfil. Whoever it was, Mamoon was talking to him. They were trying to be quiet, probably thought I couldn't hear them."

"Did you understand what they were saying?"

"No. I don't speak Arabic. Even if I did, the words weren't distinct. I could hear just enough to know there was someone with Mamoon."

"What happened next?"

"I flew the drone ahead of the team's position, looking for the thermal signature of the informant. Instead I saw a group of signatures, I'm guessing about fifteen. I didn't have time to count them. I immediately alerted the team to the ambush, then the truck exploded and I was knocked . . . not unconscious, but dazed. I could see two people picking their way through the ruin, toward me. I destroyed the laptop, per instructions, and managed to work my way outside through a hole in the wall."

"Why didn't you contact the team to let them know your location, that you were alive?"

Ah. There it was, the question she'd hoped they wouldn't ask, because that was what she most didn't want to discuss, or even remember. "My throat mic was damaged," she said steadily. "I could hear what they were saying, but I couldn't respond."

She could feel Levi's hooded gaze on her, fierce and intense. He hadn't known that, hadn't known that she could hear him. She couldn't say that he'd made the wrong decision; looking at it unemotionally, she knew he'd made the correct one, the only one he could with the information he had. Unfortunately, though her head knew he was right, her heart couldn't join in the applause.

Mac said, "You didn't have your comm headset with you when you reached the secondary exfil point." It was an accusation, as if he thought she might be lying.

She hadn't known that, hadn't thought about it. "I fell a lot, running in the dark. It must have been torn off. Deduct it from my pay." The last was said with a coldness she hadn't known she could muster.

Levi must have thought Mac was capable of doing just that, because he said sharply, "It was damaged anyway. Forget about the inventory."

Mac gave them both an intensely annoyed look, but he didn't argue.

The debriefing continued. How odd that so much could be compressed into so few words. If anything, telling them about it made everything feel even more unreal, made her feel even more distant from events.

The analysts grilled her for over an hour, going over details, asking for her impressions, what she thought could have happened.

Why did she think the truck had been exploded? Was it possible there had been more than one person outside with Mamoon? Why hadn't they simply come in and shot her?

"My guess is the only way they could make enough noise to warn the others was to set off an explosion."

And, "Possible, but I heard only the one other voice."

And, "I'd taken my weapon out of my holster, had it lying beside the laptop. Maybe they thought I wouldn't be an easy kill, and a shot inside the ruin might not have been loud enough to serve as a warning, so they opted for the warning explosion first, then came in to take care of me. I don't know. Parts of it just seemed like poor planning."

Mac interrupted at that point. "Part of it seems damned Machiavellian. A team was sent to the Syrian interior because of the informant's supposed intel about Graeme Burger. That's a hard place to get into, a hard place to get out of. It looks as if the purpose of the whole plan was to bait a team into a hostile environment and eliminate the entire team."

"More likely the informant was captured, interrogated, and that was the best plan that could be put together on very little time," the woman analyst said. "I agree with Ms. Modell. Parts of it are either poorly planned or poorly executed, or both."

"Or there was no real informant to begin with." Mac scowled. "The intel we could put together on him was thin. Everything about Graeme Burger is thin, a hint here and there. But then he pulled that disappearing act, and—" He stopped, rubbed his eyes. He looked tired, as if he'd been up all night. "From my perspective, it looks as if a deliberate attempt was made to eliminate an entire team, a team that had been focusing on Burger." He said abruptly, "All right, that's it. You're through for now, Modell. You can go."

She wasn't cleared to hear any further intel that might be discussed, so she wasn't surprised. She started to wheel herself away from the table, but Levi took control of the wheelchair and pushed her out of the room, down the hall.

I can do it. She thought it, but didn't say it. If she could run the equivalent of a marathon at night, without water, and with bleeding feet, she could damn well handle a wheelchair. For the first time she felt a flicker of emotion, and it was anger.

She didn't want the anger, didn't want to feel anything. She pushed it away and sat silently as he wheeled her back to where her taciturn driver waited.

"Thanks, Terrell. Take care of her. I owe you."

"No problem," Terrell the driver said, though from the exchange Jina figured his job wasn't driving.

Terrell drove her home, where she refused his somewhat awkward determination to carry her upstairs, and made it under her own steam. *Carry* her in? What the hell had Levi been smoking?

Late that afternoon, Ailani called. "Hi, you," she said warmly. "Do you feel up to some company?"

"Sure," Jina said, though she really didn't. A pain pill—the last one she'd take, she had decided—had eased the pain in her feet and made her feel dull and drowsy.

"I've been cooking today, trying out new recipes. I'll bring you a few meals to put in the freezer, just heat them when you get hungry instead of making do with a sandwich. See you in an hour!"

It wasn't just Ailani who came, though; Snake was with her, though they were kidless. "We hired a babysitter for the hellions," he explained. He was holding a cardboard box, which freed Ailani to give her a big hug. He hefted the box. "Food. I wanted some of it and Ailani said no, so I want you to think of me every time you eat."

"I won't," she assured him. "You can find your own food."

She slowly made her way to the kitchen and stowed the meals in the freezer compartment of her refrigerator. If her fridge had been mostly empty, the freezer was worse, containing only a half-eaten carton of ice cream and three Popsicles. Normally she had a frozen pizza or a microwave dinner in there, but Terisa had been right about her food situation being pitiful. "These look great," she said, and meant it. She felt the stirring of an appetite. "Have the two of you had dinner yet? We can order in a pizza or—"

"Already handled that," Snake said. "The other guys are bringing food. If you don't feel up to having all of us around, say so, because otherwise we're taking over."

What she felt was taken aback, and, no, she didn't want a bunch of people around, but she didn't say so. Sending them away after they brought food would require a level of rudeness she couldn't muster. "As long as no one expects great conversation from me," she said. "I took my last pain pill a little while ago, so I'm a tad fuzzy."

"Your last one? I can get you some more," Snake said, frowning at her.

"No, I have more, I meant that's the last one I'm going to take. I can't drive while I'm taking them."

"You don't have to drive. One of us can take you anywhere you need to go. If you're in pain, take the damn pills."

"Maybe at night, so I can sleep," she said, though she had no intention of doing so.

One by one the guys showed up, all of them bringing something: doughnuts, a bakery pie, chips and dip. Boom and Terisa also arrived sans kids, so evidently they'd all agreed not to overtax her with little people running around, climbing on her, and maybe stepping on her feet. Levi was last to arrive, laden with four large pizzas. Jina hadn't been particularly hungry, but the smell of the pizzas made her mouth water.

She could handle being around Levi more easily when there was a crowd. After all, she'd spent the last year trying to mostly ignore him, except on team matters. She hadn't succeeded, but she'd tried. Ignoring meant not paying attention to him, and no matter what she was always acutely aware of his presence. That held true now; she could mostly keep her focus on the others, but he was like a big, bright thermal signature on Tweety's infrared camera, front and center in her awareness.

"I checked for an update on the guys," Levi said when they were all crammed into her small living room. There weren't enough chairs for everyone, so Jelly and Snake had settled on the floor, with Snake leaning against Ailani's legs. Somehow Levi had ended up sitting closest to Jina, though at least she was in a chair by herself instead of on the couch. Everyone's attention turned to him. "Voodoo is better, they may get him up on his feet tomorrow. Crutch is still critical, but holding his own." His mouth was a grim line. He knew, they all knew, that the likelihood of either of them being able to return was very slim, and that was if Crutch survived at all.

Jina was braced for a rehash of the mission, but perhaps because of Terisa's and Ailani's presence the men avoided the subject. Whatever the reason, she was glad for it. Other than for debriefing, she hadn't deliberately thought about any of it. That didn't mean she could avoid thinking about it, but she didn't go out of her way to relive it. Once had been enough.

She was mostly quiet while everyone else talked, but gradually she realized that despite her initial reluctance, she was grateful they were there. The team had been a huge part of her life for the past year, almost completely taking her over, and abruptly being cut off from them had felt . . . wrong. She'd halfway expected them to carry on as if she'd never been assigned to them, out of sight out of mind, but instead they were making an effort to keep her included. After all, her wounds were relatively minor; they expected her to rejoin them after her feet healed.

The only problem was, she didn't know if she could.

TWENTY-THREE

Over the next week, she was pretty much house bound, but there was no need to go anywhere. The guys were dropping food by every day. Terisa or Ailani called every day to check on her, see if she needed anything other than food. Levi was mostly keeping his distance, unless someone else was there, which suited her fine. She needed the solitude to get settled back into herself.

Gradually the sense of disconnect faded, except with Levi.

He'd left her behind.

If he hadn't kissed her—but he had.

If he hadn't protected her and made her feel wanted even when they couldn't be together—but he had.

Despite everything, she'd felt as if someday the status quo would change and they'd be together, that no matter how frustrating and hurtful it was to put barriers in place between them there would come a time when the barriers weren't needed. Now, she couldn't let herself believe that he felt the same at all, because he'd left her. The attraction that had so consumed her must not have been as strong for him. She tried to put herself in the same position, and couldn't imagine that she would ever leave him behind, not knowing for certain whether he was dead or not.

Maybe she was wrong about that. She'd never had to make that decision. That was the problem; because she didn't know, her heart couldn't accept what he'd done.

The days rocked on, became a week, two weeks.

She healed. Her feet weren't in pretty shape, but the swelling was down and she needed only bandaging around her heels and over her toes. Flip flops were out, because she couldn't get the thong between her toes, but she could tolerate the mule style of bedroom slippers, which Ailani thought of and brought to her so she wouldn't have to wear the moose head slippers. Jina thought she might be recovering, mentally, because she was amused at the idea that, if any of the guys had injured their feet in the same way she had, they'd be wearing fuzzy mules, too.

For the most part, though, she wasn't amused. She watched TV. She read. She puttered around doing small chores, getting her kitchen organized, doing some online shopping for a new bedspread and shams. She'd devoted herself to GO-Team stuff for over a year now, and she wanted to do feminine stuff, get back the part of herself that had been put on the back burner while she dealt with the intensity of training and being a part of the team.

The daily updates said Crutch was finally improving, enough to be moved out of critical care. Voodoo was transferred to Walter Reed, and in another couple of weeks he was scheduled to begin therapy.

She could drive now, so she visited him almost every day. So did the rest of the team, but they were back to the normal training schedule and came at the end of the day; she didn't run into them at the hospital. Because of training her contact with them now was mostly texts, asking if she needed anything, but given that she could drive again she was handling everything herself.

She graduated from bandages to Band-Aids, and was able to walk normally. She tried on her sneakers every day to see if she could tolerate them, and one day she could. She was mostly back to normal—whatever normal was.

The day she was released to resume training, Jina knew she

couldn't stay in stasis any longer. Getting herself back to top level would be an effort.

If she *wanted* to get back to top level.

That was the sticking point, the idea that circled around and around her brain, night and day. She'd never quit on anything. If she'd been a quitter, she wouldn't have made it out of the desert alive. Nevertheless, the idea of rejoining the team almost made her sick.

She cared about them all; she did. When it came down to it, even though she knew they'd had no choice other than to take care of Crutch and Voodoo, try to save their lives, even though she understood they'd thought she was dead, in the end she couldn't get past the fact that they'd left her behind. Reason be damned, emotion was trumping reason. She didn't want it to, she wanted to close the door on yesterday and face forward again, but she couldn't.

If it were just the rest of the team, she could do it. Levi . . . Levi was the one she couldn't come to grips with. Her thoughts circled endlessly around the subject, and she couldn't force herself past it. She was the least important member of his team, and in the end he'd proven it to her. She was desolate inside, knocked down, hollowed out with despair. Levi had left her behind.

Taking a deep breath, she called headquarters and told MacNamara's assistant she had to talk to him. She'd expected to have to wait a month or so—he was never accommodating—but instead she was told to get there immediately.

MacNamara's normal expression was a blend of surliness, impatience, and downright hostility, but when Jina sat down in his office he regarded her seriously. "You went through some tough shit," he commented, leaning back in his chair.

She shrugged, not wanting to talk about it. But for him to even acknowledge her situation was unusual, because normally his attitude ran along the lines of suck it up and do your job. She had, way past what she'd thought she could do, but now she couldn't. "I want to transfer back to my old job," she said.

Instantly MacNamara morphed back into his normal self. "Sorry. We've spent a lot of money on your training, and I'm not going to throw it away. Request denied."

She'd expected that, accepted the course she would have to take. She gave him a level stare, then stood and said, "In that case, I quit."

She'd never said those words before. She'd had to fight with herself to come to this point, because it was so alien to her. She could return to the team, she could force herself forward . . . but she didn't want to. Hearing herself say the words broke a barrier inside, one she'd never let herself cross before. She was in unchartered territory, but abruptly she felt free and calm. This was her chosen path. She was done.

To her surprise, instead of instantly tossing her out the door, MacNamara leaned back and steepled his fingers, studying her over them. "Don't be so hasty. Think this through."

"I have. Through, over, under, around. I'd prefer doing one more mission—with someone else's team, which isn't going to happen—just to prove to myself that I have the guts to do it, but for the most part . . ." She shook her head. "I'm finished."

"Ace made the right call, the only call he could have made with the information he had."

"I know that. I'm still done." Knowing and accepting were two different things. *She* couldn't even argue that he'd made the wrong decision. He'd thought she was dead in the explosion. She got that. That didn't alter what she still had to deal with, the emotions she'd felt when she stood alone in the desert and known he'd left her behind. She wasn't a computer; she couldn't reboot and start fresh. She couldn't shove all that into a different compartment of her brain and ignore it as if it had never happened.

MacNamara shrugged. He wasn't the type who kept beating

at something, he had too much going on. "You still don't get your old job back. I'm not wasting your training. I'll switch you to drone training, you can be an instructor in that, but not communications. Your choice."

Her mouth fell open. To say she was flabbergasted was putting it mildly. She *loved* working with Tweety, loved every bit of the nerdy software stuff and how absolutely cool the little drone was. The flabbergasting part was that no one who knew MacNamara ever expected him to be accommodating. "What? Are you sure? I mean—thank you."

He scowled at her. "Get out before I change my mind."

She did. She left in a daze, knowing she had just walked out of one part of her life and entered another. She had quit. And she had begun.

TWENTY-FOUR

She cried a little bit as she drove to the training area, knowing that she had to tell the guys in person, she couldn't just let them hear about it from someone else. Maybe they already knew, maybe Mac-Namara had immediately called Levi, but that didn't matter: she'd quit, but she couldn't let herself be a coward about it.

Her heartbeat hit double-time as she parked, looked around at a place that, for the past year, had been more familiar to her than her own condo. There was nothing glamorous about it: the dirt, the sand, the buildings for practicing shooting situations, the obstacles and pits and soul-destroying humidity, the coolers of bottled water placed at strategic points, the dust kicked up by pounding feet, the groups of sweating and swearing men working through different rotations. She spotted Kodak and his team, working with the new drone trainee whose name she didn't know because she still couldn't get past the ache that Donnelly was gone and this was his replacement, so she'd been ignoring the man's existence. She wouldn't be able to do that now, though; she'd be training him in the drone program.

What she didn't see was her own team—correction, her *former* team. The thought made her heart ache, but she knew she'd made the right choice. She took out her phone and shot a text to Boom. Maybe she should have texted Levi, but today she was taking the easiest path she could—because she was now a quitter.

Quitter. The word jolted her down to her bones, knocked her world askew, and she had a feeling it would never be on quite the same plane again. She'd spent her life measuring herself against Jordan and Taz, pushing herself to keep up with her brothers, and when she'd been assigned to the teams she'd carried that compulsion to the point of insanity. She had even jumped out of freakin' planes, and what sane person did that? Pride and stubbornness had kept her plugging away at something she didn't want, until she'd become fond of the guys, of Terisa and Ailani, of the kids, and made a place for herself in their world—never mind that their world had never been anything she'd wanted.

Training the drone operators was so much more in her wheelhouse; she'd look forward to going to work every day, instead of dreading what she'd have to put herself through to prove that she wasn't a quitter. There had been days she'd enjoyed; she'd learned to like being in good shape. She would never look at running the same way, not after the desert, but the truth was if she hadn't done so much running here in training, she never would have been able to survive that brutal run. Being on the team had put her in a desperate situation, but it had also given her the ability to handle it.

With a sharp pang of surprise, she realized she wanted to keep up part of what she'd been doing. She wouldn't have a team she could train with, but she could run, she could join a gym and lift weights, do some rope climbing, keep those skills sharp and her conditioning up.

Who knew? Someday she might have to run for her life again. If that kind of situation ever arose—maybe running from a mugger— then she wanted to be able to *do* it. She wanted to leave any mugger in the dust.

Her phone buzzed with an incoming text. She glanced at the screen to see Boom's short reply that they were on the way.

She would have gone to them. Did they think she wasn't able to make it that far under her own steam? Or did they already know she'd quit, and she was no longer allowed on the training site?

Tears burned her eyes again, because likely she *wouldn't* be back on this site unless something came up with one of the drone trainees. Making this change was tough, and not just because she'd had to turn her back on how she'd always defined herself, though perhaps it was equally true that she'd let the challenges of others define her. Regardless of that, the guys on her team meant a lot to her, and not having them in her everyday life from now on would leave a huge hole.

Her world had changed drastically the day she'd been assigned to the GO-Team, and now it had changed drastically again because she'd left them. Before, she'd had friends with whom she shopped, went to movies; she'd dated, though not seriously. She had gone to museums and plays, to ball games. She'd had a life. Now she hadn't touched base with any of those friends since she'd been assigned to the team, because she'd barely had time to do her laundry and every other minute of her day had been taken up with training, eating, and sleeping.

If the guys didn't want to associate with her anymore—what then?

She'd handle it, that was what. She hadn't had any friends when she'd moved to D.C., but she'd made them. She was friendly, and social. She could start over.

She could, but she didn't want to. She wanted the best of both worlds. She wanted to stay friends with them, but she didn't want to go out on missions; she wanted to train Tweety operators.

Likely she wanted more than she could have.

Through her dusty windshield she watched Boom, Snake, Trapper, and Jelly approaching. Levi wasn't in sight. Either he didn't want to talk to her because he was furious she'd quit the team, or he wasn't here. She marked the odds at fifty/fifty.

She climbed out of the car and went to lean against the hood, waiting for them. The scorching August sun beat down on her bare head, sent waves of heat against her sunglasses and forming sweat where the frames touched her face. Maybe if she sweated enough they wouldn't notice any stray tears.

As they got closer she could see the tension in their expressions, and her stomach twisted. But as they neared, Boom tossed a bottle of water at her and said, "Crutch?"

Automatically she caught the bottle and twisted the cap off, another internal organ affected by the one-word question. "Not Crutch," she said hurriedly. "Me."

They formed an arc around her, four big men standing with their boots firmly planted, sweat dripping off them, guzzling from their own water bottles. "You?" Snake asked, sending a quick look down at her feet. "What's up? You having problems?"

She could just say that she'd been reassigned, which was true as far as that went, but definitely not the whole story. She took a deep breath and sagged against the hood. "I . . . I quit," she said, almost strangling on the word. Then she looked down at the ground, because she couldn't bear looking at them and seeing the disappointment on their faces.

Trapper was the first one who spoke. "Quit? Babe, you never quit anything. A couple of times I thought you'd kill yourself rather than back down."

"I quit this," she said in a small voice. "I'm sorry. I can't do it anymore."

Boom moved to her side, leaning his bulk on the hood. His deep voice rumbled as he asked, "Is it because of what happened in Syria? You don't trust us now to take care of you?"

"I could hear," she said hurriedly, sidestepping the issue of trust because she hadn't worked through that yet. "My comm was damaged and I couldn't transmit, but I could hear y'all. I knew Crutch and Voodoo were hurt, I knew you had to get them out. It was on me to get myself to the extraction point. And I did. But I don't want to do it again."

They were silent, shuffling their feet a little. She swallowed hard, fought back the impulse to bury her face in her hands and sob. "The thing is . . . I loved being a part of the team, being with y'all, but the rest of it was something I had to force myself to do. I'm a nerd. I want to do nerdy things, like working with Tweety. I don't want to be in situations like Syria. I don't want to be a moron who jumps out of planes, no offense to you morons who think doing that's normal. I'll always be a liability to y'all, because deep down my heart isn't in it." She sucked in a shuddering breath. "So I quit. Mac reassigned me to training the drone operators."

More silence. Then Jelly said, "So . . . now that you aren't on the team, does that mean I can ask you out?"

Jina's head snapped up, and her mouth fell open. Her expression must have been one of shock and horror, because the other three men started laughing. Jelly wiggled his eyebrows at her, then Snake gave him a quick slap on the back of his head. "Dumb ass," he said.

"What?" Jelly rubbed the back of his head. "Ace said no fraternizing when she joined the team, but she isn't on the team now, right? So—fraternizing."

Aghast, Jina pointed an accusing finger at him. "You made me get a tattoo," she said. She liked her tattoo, but still. "No. Way."

He assumed an innocent expression. "You could have said no to the tattoo."

"I know that. Doesn't matter."

Boom straightened away from the car, heaved a sigh. "I wish you would still be with us," he said. "Damn."

"I know." And she did. "Being a part of the team was great; it was doing what the team does that wasn't great."

Boom blew out a breath. "Does Ace know yet?"

"Not unless Mac has contacted him. I thought he'd be here. I was going to tell everyone at once." But he wasn't here, which meant she'd have to go through all of this again, but with someone who wouldn't be as accepting.

Boom looked at her, studied the misery in her expression. "I'll tell him for you, if you want me to."

Relief flooded her and she said, "Yes, please," the two words tumbling on top of each other in their hurry to get out of her mouth. Quitting was hard enough as it was. Dealing with Levi was still more than she could handle.

THE DOORBELL RINGING at night signaled nothing good. Jina glared at the door. She knew who it was, because no way could she end this day without another confrontation. Boom had to have told him hours ago, but her phone had stayed silent and she'd begun to hope that he either wouldn't contact her or he'd put it off until tomorrow, or even that the team, depleted as it was, would be tasked with something easy like a pattern of life mission and they'd already left the country. She wanted time before she had to deal with Levi, time to settle into her new job, time to get squared away with *herself.*

No such luck, though. Just for form she checked the peephole, and as seemed to be the norm in their interactions she considered not opening the door. She was in her pajamas; she could stuff cotton in her ears and go on to bed, leave him out there leaning against the door frame. But he'd want to know why she'd quit his team and the showdown had to happen sooner or later, so it might as well be now.

She jerked open the door and barked, "*What?*" at him. He wasn't her team leader now; she didn't have to do what he said. She wasn't just prepared to fight with him, she *wanted* a fight, wanted some outlet for her resentment and emotional turmoil.

What she wasn't prepared for was the glitter in his eyes, or the duffel bag at his feet.

Taken aback, she looked down at the bag. "Another mission so soon?" She'd hoped, but she was still surprised.

"No." He kicked the duffel across the threshold, and followed it inside, forcing her to step back.

From day one he'd been forcing her back. He was good at that, she thought, annoyed. Being annoyed felt good, it felt normal. "Then what's with the duffel?"

"I figured I'd be here a while." He wasn't smiling; his expression was as hard as she'd ever seen it.

What? His dark gaze was so intensely focused she backed up some more to get away from him, then went still, the way a rabbit froze hoping the predator wouldn't notice it. He was a blast force of energy; her skin prickled all over in reaction, overwhelmed by his size and heat. Just like that her condo felt too small, too crowded, and she had nowhere to run to.

He kicked the door shut, reached behind him, and locked it. "You aren't on my team anymore," he said, looming over her.

She stared up at him, so full of boiling emotion she didn't know what to do first. She resented him, she wanted to slap him, she wanted to scream at him until she emptied herself of all the pain and anger she felt. She wanted to throw herself at him and take everything he could give her, because he was *more* than any man she'd ever been attracted to before and the competitive part of her needed to know that she could match him. She wanted him; she wanted what he'd come there to do.

But she hadn't quit the team so they could be together, she'd quit because she didn't trust him anymore.

Logic, emotion; she hated them both. Why couldn't the two *match*, instead of being opposites?

Quitting had been so hard she didn't feel as if she had anything left over, but here he was, pushing and demanding, not giving her time to think about anything. What she felt about Levi was very like how she'd felt about quitting the team, her feelings for him all tangled with her stubbornness and competitiveness and resentment.

"You left me to die." The words were low and hard, full of everything she'd been feeling for the past few weeks.

"I thought you were already dead," he shot back, moving forward, forcing her to fall back. She realized she'd once again stepped back from him and jerked to a halt, glaring up at him. "When the truck blew up and burned, from our distance it looked as if the entire ruin had gone up. Nasser had started shooting at us and we took him down, turned toward the ruin, and that's when the fuckheads hit us from behind and—shit, meet fan. Voodoo was hit first. By the time we got that handled, Crutch was down too, and they were both bad. I tried to raise you on the comm and there was no answer. What the fuck was I supposed to do? I had to get Crutch and Voodoo to the helicopter, then I was coming back to search for *your body.*"

The last two words were raw and vicious, powered by a year of want and denial, by the gut-wrenching grief that had almost destroyed him when he thought he'd lost her. He reached out and gripped her upper arms, shook her a little. "*I. Was. Coming. Back.*"

"*I know that!*" She knew that he'd thought she was dead, anyway. She knew, and she still wanted to *hit* him. Some feelings were too big to contain, too painful to calmly examine. She saw the violence in his expression and it lit something violent in her. He might have wanted for a year, but for a year she'd not only wanted, she'd put up with so much crap from him she could barely hold herself back. She'd been a yo-yo that he'd jerked up and down, hurting her feelings, kissing her, enraging her, tempting her, and by God it didn't matter whether or not he'd had good reason or she'd agreed with him, or any shit like that, because more than anything now she wanted him to be as miserable as she'd been. *Love?* She couldn't love him because there was no way he could make her so angry if she "loved" him.

She wanted him to feel as unimportant as he'd made her feel.

There. That was it, the core of what had been eating at her for weeks, since the horrible night in the desert. She'd staggered and limped and fought her way through agony, exhaustion, terror, feeling the knowledge burning in her heart that she was the *least important* to him.

She jerked away from him, moved out of his reach. Angrily she rubbed her hands up and down her bare arms, trying to erase the scalding sensation of his touch. Because she couldn't handle her emotional turmoil yet, she put it aside and focused instead on the bitter temptation of his presence here. "I suppose you took my quitting the team as a sign I wanted you to come here for a quick hook-up? Scratch the itch and get it over with?"

His jaw was set, his eyes narrow and fierce. "Adjust your expectations, babe. There won't be anything *quick* about it."

Her entire body tightened, her memory supplying in vivid playback how it felt to have him on top of her, his mouth and hands on her, the hard ridge of his erection rubbing against her crotch. She felt torn in two by the warring needs to throw him out and to have him inside her, to feed the gnawing hunger she'd held at bay for a year and couldn't control for even a minute longer.

"Then let's do it," she snapped, and whipped her tee shirt up and off, tossing it to the floor. The cool air hit her, instantly tightening her nipples to points. "Let's get it over with, then you can *leave* and I can get some sleep—"

"Fuck leaving," he snarled. "And fuck sleeping." He looked down at her and his expression changed, hardening with sheer lust, color flagging the carved plane of his cheekbones. "Just look at those pretty little things," he murmured as he moved closer, then his big hands closed on her bare breasts, cupping both of them, his rough thumbs rubbing over her nipples; the sharp sensation brought her up on her bare toes, gasping, and she seized his thick wrists—perhaps to steady herself, perhaps to hold his hands where they were. The heat of his palms seared the cool satin of her skin, making it feel as if her breasts swelled toward him, wanting more.

Because she wanted more, because she wanted everything, she released his wrists and stepped back. Fury and want and need burned in her; if she could control her emotions she'd shut them down, reduce everything she felt for him to ashes, but she didn't have that superpower. What she had was . . . now. She had now.

She stalked to the bedroom, unwilling to make even the slightest soft or flirtatious gesture. This might not be war, but neither would she let it be lovemaking. It was sex, nothing more. She wouldn't let it be more. But there was unfinished business between them, and she knew part of her couldn't move on as long as she had doubt. She was on birth control, they were both healthy—there was no reason they couldn't have this out.

He seized her arm, hauling her around and against him. With his other hand he pulled his own shirt up and off, then pulled her so close that her bare breasts nestled against him, soft against hard, delicate against the roughness of his chest hair. Mutely she stared up at him, body-slammed by the shock of being body to body with him like this, wishing she didn't feel so small next to him but perversely reveling in his strength. The look in his eyes scorched her with intensity and suddenly she felt breathless, knowing what was about to happen. Dreaming about him, thinking about having sex with him, was far different in the abstract than in reality.

He didn't kiss her; he simply picked her up and pushed her cotton pants down, tugged them off. Then he set her down; his gaze locked on her and he didn't look away, didn't blink, as he stripped off his clothes. She stood frozen, taking in every detail.

She'd seen him without his shirt; seeing him completely naked was on a whole other level of arousal, both his and hers. His clothing disguised how muscled he truly was, the thick pads on his shoulders and chest, the ridged six-pack of his abdomen. Her breath began coming faster as she looked at him, and those powerful legs and narrow hips, and the thick penis jutting forward, bigger than she'd expected. Her breath tangled in her chest, making her fight for every inhalation. She heard the soft panting sounds she was making and her cheeks burned. Because everything was moving so fast—at her own instigation—and she couldn't handle everything at once, she turned away again.

She heard a low, rough laugh, then one finger traced a spot on her back. "Pretty," he murmured, "and appropriate." He traced the outline of the small, exquisitely detailed and shaded tattoo of a grenade on her back, a grenade that had been given winsome, seductive eyes with striking amber and blue irises. Way back at the beginning she hadn't wanted to be called Babe and had suggested Grenade, and this way she had Grenade forever. It was a sly poke, an "I'll show you" gesture. Despite herself she liked that he'd remembered, and got the meaning.

His finger trailed down her back, then he turned his hand and smoothed his rough palm over the cool, sleek curves of her bottom. She closed her eyes and stood very still under his touch, concentrating on the moment. Her nipples were so tight they *ached*, and she clenched her thighs together because she ached between her legs, too.

Tonight. She had tonight, this once. She had to indulge herself, this once. He had other plans, obviously, or he wouldn't have brought a bag, but she was very much in doubt that there would *be* more moments after this. She'd spent over a year wanting him and denying herself and no matter what else happened she wanted this one time of completion, of being naked with him, of having him inside her. She wanted to know how he looked when he came, how he sounded, what it felt like to hold his convulsing body in her arms and body during that most intimate of moments. She would take that, and to hell with what he wanted.

He moved close behind her, so close she felt his heat at her back, his breath on her shoulder as he bent his head to rub his chin against her hair. His hand slid farther down, into the heat and damp and softness, a softness he violated with the slow push of two big fingers into her.

Jina gasped, rising up on her toes, quivering under the lash of sensation. He anchored her with an arm around her, and probed deeper. She couldn't stop the moan that reverberated in her throat, didn't try to stop it. Her head fell back against his shoulder and he took advantage of the sensitive, vulnerable curve of neck she presented, bending down to bite her, his teeth clamping on the sensitive cord between shoulder and neck.

Electricity flashed through her. She almost came, almost went over the edge. If he'd bent her over and pushed his cock into her right then she would have, but he didn't and desperately she regrouped, pulled her response back. She didn't want to come the way she had before, without him even inside her. She wanted him as desperate as she was, as hungry, as on fire and blind to everything except the sensation of being together.

She jerked away and fell back on the bed, her gaze angry and defiant and daring. Take me if you can, big guy.

He could.

THE FIRE IN her would scorch him alive. He knew it, and relished the burning. She challenged him, she pushed him, she dared him. She absorbed him on a level he'd never experienced before. Even her invitation was like beckoning him to a fight—and a fight was something he'd never backed down from. They might never settle this between them using words, but they would, by God, settle it in bed.

He crawled onto the bed, grasping her knees and pushing them apart. He paused a moment to look down at her crotch, dark pink and soft and wet, the sight setting him on fire. He slid between her legs and pulled her to him. He didn't stretch out on her—that was something he intended to relish when he didn't feel on the knife-edge of both tension and orgasm—but sat back on his haunches with her hips in his hands and her ass on his thighs. The expression on her face was so belligerent he wouldn't have been surprised if she took a swing at him. Nothing she dared would surprise him, yet on another level she was always surprising him, amusing him, interesting him.

He leaned forward a bit, gripped his cock in one hand and brought the thick head of it to her body, rubbed it back and forth, nuzzling her with it until he felt the soft give of her body as she opened to him, then he pushed forward and inside. He watched as the thick head of his penis slid inside her, stretching her around him. She sucked in a quick breath, stiffening a bit. He rubbed her belly, comforting, reassuring. He was big and she wasn't, but he wasn't about to hurt her by being too fast or too rough. He went slow, savoring every inch, burnt through and branded by a year of wanting exactly this, and now having it, having her.

She made a gasping sound, her body arching, her eyes closing. Watching her, he saw her nipples tighten and darken even more as he sank deep into her, pausing when he felt resistance, pulling back a little, then nudging ever deeper. Sharp pleasure arrowed up his spine, drawing his balls tight. Just the sight of his cock sinking deep into her, seeing the wet sheen on his skin when he drew back, was enough to send him dangerously close to climax and he willed himself to stillness, taking the time to look at her and memorize every detail of this first time.

She lay there completely exposed and penetrated, her head tilted back, eyes closed, fists knotted in the sheet beneath her. She felt fragile to him, small and slim, her skin soft. His hand would span her hip bones. Inside her, slick, wet muscles gripped him, clasped and relaxed on his cock, gripped again. Jesus, she could milk him dry, make him come with just that inner pulsing.

He pulled back, pushed in again, watching sensation ripple through her muscles.

Her.

The single word reverberated through his brain, shot power and heat and sensation all through his body. His balls tightened to the point of pain, his cock throbbed.

Her.

He stroked over the smoothness of her belly, up to tweak those tight little nipples, rub his palms over her breasts until they were harder and rounder, pushing into his touch. Jina's eyes were still closed, her neck arched, her lips parted as she reached for every sensation.

Shutting him out.

She was taking his body, but she was closing him out and taking only the sex, masturbating with his cock. She wasn't trying to touch him with her hands at all, wasn't reaching for him, wasn't gripping his thighs where they framed her hips.

Fuck if he'd let her.

Swiftly he changed position, letting his weight down on her, the movement sending him so deep she gave a small involuntary cry and her legs came up, clasping his hips as if she could control his penetration.

Her.

It had been her from the beginning—not just sex, not just interest or attraction or any of the other terms he was more comfortable with. This was a sea change, crossing a boundary into completely new territory without a map, GPS, or any other means of navigating. All he could do was what his instinct drove him to do . . . which was claim her.

He captured her head with both hands, sinking his fingers deep into her hair, and ravaged her mouth with a kiss so deep he lost part of himself. He lifted his head, snarled, "Look at me," and when her eyes flared wide, startled, he pushed in as deep as he could go, as deep as she could take him, and kissed her again. Angrily she bit at him and he laughed, kissed her again, fucking her mouth with his tongue as he fucked her body, wrenching a response from her and feeling her catch fire under him.

Her.

The knowledge slammed through him. Her. Only her. Forever her.

He pulled her legs high and took her as he'd wanted to take her for this past damned year, deep and hard, giving her everything he had and taking everything she had, pushing her into pleasure, blasting through the mental barrier she tried to keep between them, feeling her lose control and bite and claw as she came, riding her even harder through his own climax. Fucking her was like fighting a wildcat and he exulted in it.

Her.

His.

HE STAYED.

Jina lay limply, exhausted and devastated by the almost violent response he'd forced from her. She had almost done it, she had almost managed to reduce their coming together to nothing more than sex, but he hadn't allowed it and now, hollowed out and emptied yet again, she thought she might be glad. She'd thought this would never happen but now he was here with her, naked in her bed, and what they'd just done was more intense than she'd ever imagined. Levi made her *feel*. Even when she didn't want to, when her bruised emotions wanted nothing more than to hide, he read her and destroyed her barriers.

She expected him to leave—despite the scary presence of his

duffel—but he didn't. He got up and turned out the light, then got back into bed with her and pulled her tight against him. Having him there was a shock to her system; she wasn't used to sleeping with anyone, much less someone so big and hard and hot. He threw off heat like a furnace. She thought about making him leave . . . for about two seconds, which was when exhaustion swamped her. She melted against him, finding a comfortable resting place for her head in the curve of his shoulder, and went to sleep with his muscle-corded arms wrapped around her.

He woke her in the darkness a couple of hours later, his heavy weight on her, her body already lifting to his as if she recognized him even in her sleep. He stretched out a long arm and turned on the lamp, as if what was between them needed the light. The first time had been fierce and intense; this time was slower, hotter, and she gave up even the thought of keeping him at a distance. She couldn't, didn't want to. She felt richly feminine, strong enough to take him, to wring pleasure from him and also seize it for herself. She matched him, she fought him to a draw, climaxing twice before both of them were satiated and exhausted.

Yes! This was what she had wanted, to see him sweaty and almost unable to move, his eyes heavy-lidded with pleasure, a faint smile curving that hard mouth. She loved feeling him come inside her, loved the deep sounds he made, the way his powerful body flexed and shuddered. *She* brought him to that, put that expression on his face.

"We need to shower," she muttered when she had her breath back. She hadn't had a choice about going to sleep after the first time, but now she was acutely aware of how sticky she was. The realities of bareback sex were pretty great, but not neat.

He groaned, but didn't disagree. They showered together, slept, and he woke her again with her legs draped over his broad shoulders and his mouth on her, doing other things to her with his fingers that made her choke and cry out and come so hard her body bowed under his ministrations.

She'd thought: just one time, and she'd be done with him.

She was wrong.

Waking up with him was oddly more intimate than what they'd done together during the night. They had slept tangled together, with her more on top of him than not, and even when she'd rouse and think she should probably move to her own side of the bed, she hadn't. He made an excellent pillow and cover, all in one, giving off so much heat she didn't need covers despite the air-conditioning. She liked the feel of that big muscled body next to her, the roughness of his chest and legs, the calluses on his hands when he stroked her. There was nothing smooth or soft about Levi, but she had her own smoothness and softness, she didn't need more from him.

It was startling to realize how well they fit together, how evenly they matched.

Having him there while they prepared breakfast together was both strange and familiar, as if this might be the first time but it was also how things were supposed to be. The dichotomy kept her quiet; she didn't want to think about their situation or wonder about the future, she wanted to rest for a while and let things happen.

He let her mull; in that, he didn't push. In every other way, he was all over her. Even eating breakfast—he pulled her astride his lap, onto his erection, and held her there while they fed each other, rocking her just enough to keep him hard, keep him inside her. It was a whole new way of eating pancakes.

Though she wanted to keep that emotional distance, she couldn't stay on guard through the day that followed, or the night, or the next day. Levi showed no signs of wanting to go home. He texted the guys, he went for long runs—she joined him for one, though her feet got sore before the run ended and she had to stop—but he didn't go home. There were moments when she forgot, when the sheer joy of being with him burst through her dam of resentment. One was when she touched the PBJ tattoo on his bare shoulder and said, "Old girlfriend?"

He snorted, glancing at her over his shoulder with a wry gleam in his eyes. "Peanut butter and jelly. I was drunk."

Surprised, she had to laugh. "You're lying!"

"God's truth. I was drunk, and I was evidently hungry. I haven't been drunk since. I don't want to wake up with *ham sandwich* tattooed somewhere on my body."

His sense of humor unsettled her, though she'd seen flashes of it when he interacted with the other guys, but seldom with her. He would never be Mr. Fun and Games; his was the temperament of a hard-core soldier, normally wary, intense, dedicated. That he felt he could relax with her was—

She pushed the thought away. Being different with her indicated intimacy and connection beyond that of sex. She could handle sex with him. She couldn't handle anything else, not yet.

He was obviously giving her time to think, to come to terms with what had happened, and for some reason that annoyed her. She wanted to *forget*, not keep gnawing at details, not think about whatifs and maybes. She'd quit the team, and even though the decision had been what was best for her, forgiving herself for quitting would take a while, despite knowing deep inside that for her she'd hit a wall and leaving the team had been her only course.

She was brooding about it, on the second day, when he showed an acuteness of understanding that alarmed her. Baseball was on TV and he was watching it, an opened beer by his hand because somehow beer for him had come to share space in her refrigerator, when he said calmly, "Quitting is hard for you."

She flashed him an angry glance, and didn't take the bait. Probing at a sore tooth didn't make it feel better, and the subject was a very sore tooth for her.

"You're the prototypical middle child," he pointed out.

"Do *not* analyze me! I figured it out for myself years ago." She was squarely in the middle, nothing special about her at all. She was neither the oldest nor the youngest in anything; she had an older sister, and a younger one. She had an older brother, and a younger one. Every family slot with any built-in specialness had been taken by someone else. She had forged her place by sheer determination, never giving up, in constant competition with her brothers but not competing in any way with her sisters because she had the buffer of age between them. Ashley was several years older and they'd never been in the same age group until they were adults. Caleigh was several years younger, and ditto, though she was just now becoming adult enough for it to matter.

"I'm not analyzing, I don't have to. I'm just saying I get how tough it was for you."

Did he? Could he grasp how bone-deep wrenching it had been for her to come to that place where she knew she *had* to quit, that she couldn't keep on?

"It wasn't so I could have you." She glared at him, though he hadn't suggested anything like that.

"I know."

"It broke me." The words were wrenched out of her. "The desert broke me."

"You don't look broke. You look pissed."

Her scowl intensified, which she guessed verified his assessment. "I didn't want to be on the teams," she snapped. "I liked what I was doing, but I was assigned to the teams and once I was there, damned if I'd let you make me quit."

"Yeah, I wanted you to quit, from the minute I saw you. You know why." His face was impassive but his eyes glittered with heat, going over her from head to toe and making her feel as if he'd be on top of her if she made the slightest move.

She took the chance and gestured anyway, a wide wave that took in everything: her, the bedroom, for heaven's sake even the TV and the beer, because of the cozy intimacy.

"I didn't undermine you."

"I know," she grumbled. "I'd have hated you if you had. I wish you had."

"So you could hate me?"

"Would have worked out better that way."

Her statement worked in another way. He moved like lightning striking, snagging her with one arm and dragging her onto his lap. "I like the way things are working out now," he drawled, one eyebrow lifting.

"They aren't working out. We're having sex. That's all."

"For now." He paused. "Because I have trouble giving up, too."

After that threat—promise?—and not giving her time to mull it over, he dragged her along to the training site. She didn't want to go, because she couldn't work out with the team and that loss still ached. "I thought I'd be banned from there, now that I'm not on a team," she grumbled as she vaulted into his Vadermobile. *Vaulted.* Unbidden came the memory of the first time she'd ridden in his truck, and how much difficulty she'd had getting in, and despite herself she grinned.

"Nope. There are rules, but we aren't military. If anyone doesn't like it they can take it up with me."

That wasn't going to happen. Not many team members, tough as they were, wanted to take on Levi. They *would*, each and every one of them, but they wouldn't want to.

"Why are we going there?"

"I've been away for two days. I need to work out."

Annoyed, incredulous, she demanded, "What am I supposed to do, bounce up and down on the sidelines and *cheer?*"

He laughed. "I'd like to see that."

"Well, you aren't going to. Just give me the keys so I can leave when I get bored, which will be, oh, about three seconds after we get there."

"You won't be bored. The guys want to see you."

She wanted to see them, too. They'd been a huge part of her life for a year, to the point that she hadn't gone more than twenty-four hours without seeing them except for the two times she'd gone home to visit.

On the way, Levi tossed his phone into her lap. She gave it a questioning look, then turned the same look on him. It was his personal phone, not his work phone. "What?"

"Link our phones, so I can find you and you can find me."

"What the hell. That's kind of intimate, don't you think?"

He snorted out a laugh. "We're just getting started, babe. And that's 'babe' with a little 'b,' not a capital one." He paused. "I've always had a hard time thinking of you as Babe, instead of Jina."

And she'd thought of him as Levi, rather than Ace. She stared straight ahead, more struck by that than she wanted to be, undermined by the uneasy sensation that this thing between them was more than she'd anticipated. After a minute she silently linked their phones, then gave his back to him.

"What does this mean?" She shouldn't have asked. As soon as the words were out of her mouth she screwed up her face at her inability to keep her mouth shut.

He didn't let her off the hook. "Exactly what you're afraid it means."

Afraid? He thought she was afraid? She started to argue, then subsided into disgruntled silence, because he was right. He meant they were a couple, and couplehood implied all sorts of things she didn't know that she was emotionally ready for, because it was such an abrupt change from what they'd been before. On the other hand, if she unlinked her phone from his, he'd get the message.

She didn't unlink them.

She was still dealing with the idea that they were a *couple*, when they reached the training site. She started to open the door and jump down, and he said, "Wait."

"What?"

"Don't open the door."

She could see the other four guys walking toward them, and Levi's order made no sense. Even better—there was Voodoo! He was very thin, he was on crutches, but he was there. "Why? There's Voodoo! I want to—"

"Just wait a minute," he said impatiently. "I have my reasons."

"They had better be damn good, because I—"

He got out of the truck and slammed the door, cutting off her irate comment. He crossed in front of the truck, came around to her side . . . and opened the door for her.

Her mouth fell open. "What're you *doing?*" she whispered furiously.

"Making a statement."

When she showed no inclination to get out of the truck he reached inside, grasped her waist with both hands, and lifted her out. Then he closed the door and draped his heavy, muscled arm around her shoulders.

The five men approaching the truck skidded to a halt, three of them with their mouths open.

"What the hell?" Trapper said, and scrubbed his hand across his eyes as if he couldn't believe what he was seeing.

"She's not on the team now," Levi said bluntly. "And she's mine."

Silence.

Then Voodoo, leaning on his crutches, shrugged and grinned. "You're a braver man than I am."

Jelly found his voice and said indignantly, "You're not braver than me! I asked first—"

Levi shot a rigid forefinger at him. "Don't make me kill you."

Boom shoved a big shoulder into Jelly, nudging him a couple of feet. "You never had a chance, kid. Snake and I knew how it was from the beginning."

What? What? Jina gaped at them. "You did not! How could you?"

"We're both married," Snake said. "We have experience with insanity. You two couldn't even look at each other. Anyway—sorry you're not on the team, Babe, but welcome to the family, Jina."

TWENTY-FIVE

The plan had failed. Ace Butcher's team had been hit, but there were no fatalities. Drawing MacNamara in with the loss of one of his precious teams would have been so satisfying—destroying something important to him, the way he'd destroyed Dexter—but Joan Kingsley was, above all, a realist. She had to jettison that part of the plan, and move on to the most important part, baiting MacNamara into a trap and killing him.

Almost idly she wondered what her own odds of survival were, and estimated them as not very high. For one thing, Devan, who was working his own agenda, wasn't the most trustworthy of allies. She suspected that as soon as MacNamara was dead, she herself would be expendable to Devan. Fine. She felt the same way about him. Let the more skilled—or the most lucky—traitor win. He had skill sets she didn't, but she didn't much care.

Life was so bleak. She'd thought she could survive, for her son, for the possibility of a life afterward, but as time had ticked on she had become less and less interested. She wanted it over. One way or another, win or lose—just over.

To up the ante, she rather thought Graeme Burger would have to be sacrificed. Nothing other than the banker's presence would move the pieces into place the way she wanted. And it was time.

"*WHAT?*" AXEL MACNAMARA'S face turned dark red. He surged to his feet, sending his chair violently backward to crash into the credenza. "Are you certain?" he barked. "We didn't have any intel—Fuck! Okay." He disconnected, immediately called his contact at the FBI. "Graeme Fucking Burger just got off a plane at Dulles, facial recognition picked him up. Get someone on him before he disappears the way he did last time. The name he flew under is George Bachman." The initials were the same, which came in handy in case there was any monogrammed luggage or key ring, anything like that.

He disconnected from that call and paced his office, his movements choppy and agitated. He was furious on several levels—first that Burger had somehow managed to get on a plane in South Africa without anyone being alerted, which meant he had a fake passport, which meant he not only had the connections to get a fake passport but that he needed one, then that he hadn't been noticed at whatever airport where he'd made his connection to Dulles. Now at least cameras would pick him up, but he'd had time to get to the taxi line and leave the airport, and tracking him would take time.

The last time Burger had been in D.C., he'd outsmarted the best and disappeared for four hours. Not long after that, Burger had been connected to the intel that had drawn Ace's team into an ambush, and cost him three operatives. Oh, they were all still alive, but Modell had left the team and MacNamara's only consolation was that she'd be way more useful training drone operators than she had been in the field, and Voodoo and Crutch would never be able to do field work again. He was in the process of finding places for them that could use their expertise.

His cell phone rang and he snatched it up, glancing at the unknown number on the screen. That in itself didn't mean anything, not in his world, and it wasn't as if he had to deal with spam calls. "Yeah?"

An accented voice said, "Mr. MacNamara, this is Graeme Burger. I believe you know who I am. I desire a meeting with you."

Forty seconds later, Mac left his office like his hair was on fire. Tradecraft wasn't his specialty but he knew enough not to go alone to any clandestine meeting, and he literally didn't have enough time to contact any of his teams for backup. The ones that weren't on missions were at the training site, almost thirty miles away. There were plenty of people in the building, but none—then he turned a corner and he saw Ace Butcher, big and dirty, talking to Modell, who was consulting with the R&D department about something she wanted on the drones; for the past week, since he'd reassigned her, she'd been driving them nuts with tweaks she insisted were needed.

"Ace! Come with me." That couldn't have worked out better, because he'd rather have Ace backing him up than a whole fleet of FBI agents. A lot of federal agents never fired their weapons except in practice; Ace Butcher had, and would again without hesitation. "You have a weapon with you?" he asked as he blew past.

Butcher wheeled and fell into step beside him. "I always have a weapon. Mac, slow down. What's going on?"

"That son of a bitch Graeme Burger got into the country on a fake passport and he just called, wanting a meeting with me."

Butcher put on the brakes, grabbing his arm and pulling him to a halt. Not many people got in Mac's way, but his team leaders were made of sterner stuff and had never minced words with him; Butcher was even less inclined than the others, in that way.

"Hold on. The odds are good this is another ambush."

Mac pulled his arm free. "That's why you're going with me."

"Fuck," Butcher said with quiet viciousness. "Where are we going?" He already had his phone out, sending a text to his team. Mac didn't even have to ask, because he knew the way they worked. The address Mac gave him was too close by; he and Mac would arrive way before the team could get there to provide backup. The D.C. police department possibly could, but they were civilian, and best kept out of things like this.

He headed toward his car, but Butcher said, "We'll use my truck, it'll take more damage if things go sideways."

There was truth in that, because the damn thing looked like a tank.

"This is a bad idea," Butcher said.

Mac knew it was; not planning was always a bad idea, as was not being in control of the meeting. But Graeme Burger had mentioned a name that Mac couldn't resist, because he'd been hunting for the son of a bitch for almost two years now. Devan Hubbert was the alias of the Russian operative who had infiltrated the GO-Team organization and was helping Joan Kingsley and her husband feed info to the Russians. He'd escaped, and no whiff of him had surfaced in those two years; Mac had assumed he'd gone back to Russia. Maybe he had, maybe he hadn't, but what Mac wanted more than anything was solid info on the son of a bitch.

Butcher's phone dinged and he looked at the incoming text. "My guys are on the way but they can't get there in time, unless we stop and wait for them."

"Can't do that. Burger said he'd wait fifteen minutes, no more."

"Cutting it close, given what D.C. traffic can do."

Mac didn't reply. Butcher then sent another text, forget about all the safety concerns about driving and texting at the same time.

"Who are you texting now?"

"Jina."

"Who?" Mac scowled. Shit was going down fast and Butcher was texting some girl?

"Jina Modell. Babe," he elaborated briefly, because Mac might not know their given names but he knew every damn one of their nicknames.

"Fuck's sake, why? Cut through there," he said abruptly, pointing, because the traffic in front of them looked as if it was snarling and a parking lot looked like the better option.

Butcher wheeled the truck one-handed, shot across the parking lot, avoided both a pedestrian and a car backing out of a lot, and two-wheeled it into the cross street.

"Because she's a trained team member," Butcher said. "She's close, can get there right behind us, and she's armed."

JINA DIDN'T BOTHER excusing herself, explaining, or anything else that would take even a second. Levi needed her and the situation sounded dire, because he'd told her to bring her weapon, which was easy because it was in her car. He had re-armed her almost immediately after arriving back in the States from the disastrous Syrian mission. She bolted from the building, her heart hammering. What was going on? Mac had come running out of nowhere, commandeered Levi, and they were gone. Now just minutes later Levi was shooting her an address and telling her to come armed, and be on high alert.

"This isn't my gig!" she yelled furiously when she was in the car and no one could hear her and think she was crazy. She had no idea where the stupid address was. Quickly she put the info into her traffic app, asking for turn-by-turn instructions. "Shit!"

She knew why he'd texted her. The rest of the team was at the training site, and couldn't get to this address as fast as he needed. GO-Teams didn't call the local cops, because the repercussions could be splashed all over public media and they were very much dark and off-the-books.

Okay. Okay. Whatever situation she was walking into, she could handle this. Levi wouldn't have texted her if she couldn't. He and the guys had trained her, she knew how to use her weapon—not as well as they could, but she was competent.

If this was some kind of stupid surprise party, for whatever mo-ron reason, she'd kill them all.

To her surprise, the address was a house in a not-very-good neigh-borhood. Levi's truck was parked at the curb, but neither he nor Mac were in sight. There were no other vehicles parked at the house, which might mean something and might mean nothing. She drove past, neither fast nor slow, and pulled her Corolla into the first open space she came to. There were bound to be some people around, in the other going-downhill houses, but she didn't see a single soul. The sticky, hard-to-breathe heat and humidity didn't lend itself to outside activities, but surely there should be a kid or two around? But maybe not. Maybe the neighborhood housed mostly elderly people, a formerly neat place going downhill as the residents aged and were no longer able to take care of their properties.

She got her weapon from the console and slipped it inside her waistband, pulled her shirt down over it; that was the best she could do. She looked around, then got out of the car and closed the door as quietly as she could.

The neighborhood even had a slightly decayed scent to it, a sign that it was dying. Once most of the driveways had been concrete, but now huge patches were missing and weeds were taking over. She moved quietly around the house beside the one where Levi was parked, darted a quick look around the corner, didn't see anyone. No one poked a head out and asked her what she was doing. Maybe this house was deserted; no, there was a coiled water pipe beside the mi-nuscule back porch, and a bedraggled potted plant, wilting in the heat.

She slipped across to the target house, planted her back against the wall, checked around her for anything that might trip her, then darted her head around the window frame to see what she could see.

Nothing. It was a small bedroom, empty.

Okay, that made sense. She was on the back corner of the house, where a bedroom would normally be. Disappointing, but logical.

She moved on around the back, where she found the same tiny porch like that at the neighboring house. There was no plant, no water hose, but other than that basically the same. A tattered screened door hung halfway open. Silently she stepped up on the porch and leaned over to look in the kitchen window. The kitchen too was empty, but through a short, cluttered hallway into what looked like the living room she thought she saw part of a foot.

Okay. Now she knew where they were. She didn't know what was going on, or what she should do, but at least she had located them.

A single shot from inside shattered her nerves. It was a silenced shot, which didn't mean the little "pew pew" sound Hollywood evidently thought a silenced shot sounded like, but in the real world meant it wasn't as loud as normal but it was still recognizable for what it was, at maybe a quarter of the sound.

Levi!

That was the only thought she had, just his name, but terror and dread laced through her because she knew what one shot could do. She heard shouting, and without thinking she twisted the doorknob of the kitchen door and it opened.

Shock that it had opened combined with urgency, and she slipped through the small opening, her sneakered feet silent on the cracked linoleum floor. She didn't remember pulling her weapon but it was in her hand, the solid weight of it reassuring.

She heard two voices, Mac's angry and snarling, a woman's sharp voice trying to ride over his, but she didn't hear Levi. As she crept forward she caught a smell, one she'd smelled before, that of blood and death, the stench of bowels and bladder that had let go.

Levi.

She felt as if her own blood had drained from her body, as if her soul shriveled to dust. Without Levi, there was nothing. If that was him whose death she smelled, then she had nothing, and whoever was on the other side of that doorway was going to die. Not hearing anyone else, she focused on the voices she *could* hear, and they were coming from the left of the doorway.

She moved. She didn't know if she was quiet or not, didn't care. She rolled around the doorway, weapon outstretched and ready, her finger on the trigger. A silver-haired woman turned a startled face toward her and flinched, but retained her grip on the weapon she had pointed at MacNamara, who was tied to a kitchen chair that had been placed in front of her.

Shocked recognition rocketed through her. *She knew that woman.* She was famous, particularly in D.C., a powerful congresswoman who had been on several powerful committees, but who had resigned from them after her husband's death a couple of years ago. Kingsley. Joan Kingsley. *What the hell!*

Then out of the corner of her eye she saw more people, and she darted a quick look to the side. Levi. *Levi!* He was alive, on his knees with his hands locked behind his head, but someone she didn't know stood off to the side, a big, cold-eyed man, standing far enough away that Levi couldn't lunge and reach him, and his Glock was trained on Levi.

On the floor against the right wall, a slightly portly man lay sprawled in the inhuman, ungainly sprawl of the dead, his face turned away, blood slowly pooling around his head. She didn't know who he was, and didn't care. He wasn't Levi.

Instinctively Jina knew Joan Kingsley was the linchpin of this situation, whatever was happening, and she kept her weapon aimed right between the congresswoman's eyes. "Put it down," she said evenly. "You and the big guy."

"I don't think so," Joan Kingsley said. The startled expression was gone from her face, and in its place was a chilled detachment, an emptiness.

"Shoot the bitch!" MacNamara snarled, rocking violently in the chair as if trying to turn it over.

He would, too, but his rabid personality could well trigger a round-robin of shots that would result in Levi's death, and Jina thought she'd shoot MacNamara herself before she let that happen.

"Shut up!" she bellowed, taking her gaze off Kingsley for a split second, just long enough to shoot him a lethal glance.

Adrenaline was burning through her veins but she felt chilled herself, lightning impressions and assessments flitting through her brain. They were in a nightmare situation, one with no good solution. MacNamara was bound to a chair, unable to move, with Kingsley's pistol aimed almost point blank at his head. Levi was on his knees, also under threat, and the cold-eyed man's weapon was rock steady.

Jina was frozen, locked in the standoff. She was one person, and had no Ninja training. She loved Levi. She didn't love MacNamara, didn't even like him. If she saved anyone it would be Levi, but she wasn't sure she could do that. Her marksmanship was average, there was no way she could pull the trigger, control the recoil, and aim again at Joan Kingsley in time to save MacNamara's life. But if she shot at Kingsley, then Levi—

She couldn't even think the thought.

"There's no solution," Joan Kingsley said, her gaze cold and distant. She had the look of a woman who had taken the last step and had nowhere else to go. She had reached some inner wall, and there was no negotiation in her, no give, no indecision. "You can't win. There are two of us, and one of you."

"I can take one of you," Jina said, not giving an inch.

Joan gave a little shrug. "You might. You might not. Either way, you lose. On the other hand, if you put your gun down, you have a chance at life. MacNamara doesn't, regardless. He's mine. But you—you and Butcher, there—you don't have to be involved."

What a load of horseshit, Jina thought with utter clarity. There was no way the bitch would willingly let any of them live.

Options: If she shot the man guarding Levi, the reflex could well jerk his finger, which was definitely on the trigger, and kill Levi. Same with MacNamara, if she shot Joan Kingsley. Even if she killed one, the other would kill her.

Maybe.

Jina reached deep. She'd been through team training, she'd been taught to look at each situation logically. Levi wasn't bound. Mac-Namara was. If she shot the man and Levi was wounded or killed, MacNamara was still tied to the chair, still helpless, and he'd be dead too. If she shot Joan Kingsley, though, there would be a split second lag time before the man behind Levi could act, and in that length of time Levi himself would be moving. MacNamara might well be dead, though, because Kingsley was holding the pistol butted against his skull. On the other hand, he might not. Kingsley's hand might or might not spasm. No way to know.

It was a chance. A slim one, but the only one.

She couldn't help it. She looked at Levi, agony in her eyes, just a quick glance but enough for her to read him, to see the fierce readiness, the thought he was all but compelling her to see.

Fire!

She risked his life.

She pulled the trigger.

Levi hurled himself back and to the side, the move catching the other guy by surprise because neither direction was exactly what he'd anticipated.

Joan Kingsley stumbled back a step, then went down on her knees. A look of massive shock spread over her face. Jina wasn't accurate enough to try for a head shot so she'd gone for the torso, but it was a hard hit, right through the sternum and heart. Kingsley was dead there on her knees, and the knowledge was in her eyes.

Her mouth twisted, and very deliberately she lifted the pistol she still held, aimed it at the back of MacNamara's head, and took the shot. Jina shot again, and again hit her target, but she was too late.

The shot jerked the other man's attention toward Kingsley, a mistake she saw him realize right away, but it was too late. Levi was on him, death on the attack, one steely arm lacing around the man's shoulders while the other gripped his chin. Panic flared in his eyes, one brief second, then Levi jerked the guy's chin and it was over. A pop, and it was over, a life extinguished with one movement.

Levi let the body drop, gave Jina a sharp assessing look, then strode to MacNamara where he lay in the overturned chair. Jina let her arm drop to her side and stood frozen. She didn't need to check. She'd seen the shot, knew it was over.

She felt numb. She leaned against the door jamb, then slowly sank to the floor. Four people were dead; she didn't know who the other men were, but Joan Kingsley was a member of the House of Representatives, and Axel MacNamara had run the GO-Teams with ruthless efficiency and savage loyalty. There wouldn't be ripples of effect from this; there would be tsunamis. Congress would go on, but the GO-Teams—Joan Kingsley might have killed them, too, when she'd killed Axel MacNamara.

Jina covered her eyes with her hand. She'd risked Levi's life. She'd analyzed the situation, and done what she had to do, what her intellect and training told her to do. Levi wasn't dead, but it was because of his training. She wasn't dead, either; the Syrian desert hadn't beaten her . . . because of her training.

She'd risked his life. She'd assessed the situation, and made the call.

Exactly as he had done.

She heard him approaching, then both hands closed around her and jerked her up. His expression was hard, still set in battle mode, but his assessing gaze raked down her to satisfy himself she was okay. He put both hands on her face and tilted it up, studied her, then he pressed a kiss to her forehead.

"I risked you," she said, her tone raw.

"It was your only call," he replied, and gently tugged her in close to rest against him.

IT WAS DIFFERENT.

With MacNamara dead, the hierarchy at the GO-Teams was in flux, but on a different level things continued as usual. Maybe the teams would be disbanded. The decision would be made by some unknown higher up, maybe even in the Oval Office, but they had no way of knowing. Until the orders came down otherwise, training continued, and missions continued.

Crutch and Voodoo returned to duty, but neither of them could rejoin the teams; their injuries had left them with impairments that, while they could lead normal lives, precluded them from the strenuous and specialized training and missions being on the GO-Teams required. Ace Butcher's team would rebuild, but with other recruits. They stayed close, though, because career-ending injuries weren't friendship ending. The bonds forged on the teams weren't so easily broken.

The miserably hot summer faded, and the cool pleasantness of fall began edging toward winter, the days getting shorter, the mornings colder. Jina concentrated on the drone program, and some days she managed to forget those awful few minutes, and what it felt like to pull a trigger and end another human being's life. Joan Kingsley's dying muscle spasm hadn't ended MacNamara's life, she had very deliberately shot him during her own last seconds of life, but Jina knew part of that was on her. If she'd taken the head shot—but she hadn't. She'd been afraid of missing. She'd made the decision to go for the torso, and though it had been a killing shot, it hadn't been one that caused immediate death. Because of that, Axel MacNamara was dead. Four people had died in that awful little house, and some nights she woke up to stare blindly into the darkness, wishing those memories would fade but knowing they wouldn't, because they were now branded on her psyche just like the run through the Syrian night.

Levi, being a man, didn't try to talk to her about her feelings, but he'd been through combat and firefights, he'd made pretty much the same call regarding her life that she'd made about his, so he knew, and accepted. Whatever he read on her face, occasionally he'd simply lift her onto his lap and hold her, offering her the solidity of his presence.

If he was at home instead of on a mission, he was mostly with her at her condo, though occasionally he'd spend a night at his place. More and more, though, having two places was seeming like a waste of money. Jina hadn't said anything about that to him, yet; they'd been together a few months, not long enough for her to completely get accustomed to the idea. Too much had happened, too fast, and for her own sake she needed to slow down and let things settle down. She'd killed a woman. Life couldn't pick up the way it had been before that.

The team was the team. They all got together to socialize the way they always had. Crutch and Voodoo almost always came, though Voodoo—of all people!—had somehow attracted a serious girlfriend and sometimes they had other plans. Two replacement team members, nicknamed Irish and Palooka, had joined the team. Jina liked them well enough, but she hadn't gone through events with them the way she had with the original group of guys; as far as they were concerned, she was Ace's girlfriend and a drone operator trainer. Her replacement with the drone was a lanky, laid-back guy named Kelvin Grant, but they called him Ichabod, and he was cool with that. Their group had grown, but nothing remained the same.

They were all at Snake's house; the two-year-old hellion was now a three-year-old hellion, and he showed no signs of slowing down, so if the whole group was together it was deemed safer to keep him at home. Ailani mentioned what she was cooking for Thanksgiving, and Jina froze.

"Thanksgiving?" she croaked.

Jelly hooted. "Yeah, you know, that day with all the turkey? Comes around once a year, always in November? We got together a while back and decided to call it Thanksgiving."

She threw a pickle at him, then guiltily looked around for the little hellion, because if he saw anyone throwing food he'd be doing it for the foreseeable future. He was running through the house with the rest of the kids, though, so she was safe. Jelly scooped up the pickle and ate it.

"I forgot about it," she moaned, and rubbed her forehead. "How on earth . . . never mind. I'll call Mom and make arrangements." Then she stopped and her eyes got big, and she turned toward Levi. "I . . . oh, wow. Uh-oh."

"Forgot to tell her about me, didn't you?" he asked, smirking.

"No! She knows I'm dating you."

"If by 'dating' you mean 'living together,' yeah." But he didn't look upset, just amused.

"You could have been dating me," Jelly pointed out for about the millionth time.

"No, I couldn't."

"You shouldn't hold that tattoo thing against me—hey!" Suddenly riveted, because evidently he hadn't thought of it before, Jelly turned to Levi. "She still won't tell us what that tattoo is. You've seen it, right? I mean, you have to have seen it, unless she was lying about getting one."

Levi took a bite of his burger, chewed. "I've seen it," he finally said.

All the original team members looked intensely interested, the newer members less so but still intrigued. Terisa and Ailani both looked at Jina, who smirked at the guys, leaned over, and whispered the answer to the women. They both laughed and did a pinkie swear not to tell.

"That's just wrong," Trapper complained, glaring at the women. "You were *our* teammate, Babe, not theirs. You should tell us. Ace! Spill the beans."

Levi slowly shook his head. "Sorry, guys. The secret is hers to tell. I guess the only way you'll ever find out will be if her wedding gown is cut low enough in the back for you to see it."

The room went totally silent. The only noise was the shrieks of the kids, running somewhere in the house.

Jina thought her mouth might be open. She pushed on her chin, just in case, but nope, chin didn't budge so mouth wasn't open. Her lips felt numb. Her whole body felt numb. He couldn't have said that . . . could he? And what did he mean? Was it just a throw-away comment about a wedding gown because he figured someday she'd get married, or . . . no, guys didn't make throwaway comments about wedding gowns. That wasn't in their DNA. Their throwaway comments were about munitions, or morons jumping out of planes, or . . . or—

"Wedding gown?" she asked weakly.

"Unless you want to elope, in which case I guess they'll never find out." He winked at her.

"I vote for the wedding gown," Crutch said.

"Hush!" Ailani said. "You don't get a vote!"

Jina couldn't say anything else. Levi stood up and held out his hand to her, and numbly she let him lead her outside. The night air was chilly, so chilly it felt good when he wrapped his arms around her and pulled her close. "That wasn't a proposal," he said against her hair.

She found her voice, relief and disappointment warring inside her. "It wasn't?" She loved him, she thought. She hadn't let herself think about marriage or commitment or anything like that, but she loved him. Bad things happened. Neither of them had died. Life went on. It was time. "Then you'd better get right on that."

"Got the ring in my pocket," he said, and lifted her off her feet while he hugged her tight.

HER WEDDING GOWN wasn't low enough in back for the guys to see her little grenade tattoo. Let them wonder for the rest of their lives. The grenade was only for Levi.

ABOUT THE AUTHOR

Linda Howard is the award-winning author of numerous *New York Times* bestsellers, including *Troublemaker, Up Close and Dangerous, Drop Dead Gorgeous, Cover of Night, Killing Time, To Die For, Kiss Me While I Sleep, Cry No More,* and *Dying to Please.* She lives in Alabama with her husband and two golden retrievers.

LOVE LINDA HOWARD? DON'T MISS
TROUBLEMAKER

A thrilling, fast-paced novel of romantic suspense from sensational *New York Times* and *USA Today* bestselling author Linda Howard.

For Morgan Yancy, an operative and team leader in a paramilitary group, nothing comes before his job. But when he's ambushed and almost killed, his supervisor is determined to find out who's after the members of his elite squad—and why. Due to worries that this unknown enemy will strike again, Morgan is sent to a remote location and told to lay low and stay vigilant. But between a tempting housemate he's determined to protect and a deadly threat waiting in the shadows, keeping under the radar is proving to be his most dangerous mission yet.

The part-time police chief of a small West Virginian mountain town, Isabeau "Bo" Maran finally has her life figured out. She's got friends, a dog, and a little money in the bank. Then Morgan Yancy shows up on her doorstep. Bo doesn't need a mysterious man in her life—especially a troublemaker as enticing and secretive as Morgan.

The harder they fight the intense heat between them, the closer Morgan and Bo become, even though she knows he's hiding from something. But discovering the truth could cost Bo more than she's willing to give. And when Morgan's cover is blown, it might just cost her life.

Available now!